Storm over Rhanna

CHRISTINE MARION FRASER was born in Glasgow just after the war. At the age of ten, she contracted a very rare disease which terminated her education and put her into a wheelchair where she has been ever since.

A keen reader and storyteller, with a vivid imagination, she first got the idea for the story of *Rhanna* while on holiday in the Hebrides. *Rhanna* was followed by *Rhanna at War*, *Children of Rhanna*, *Return to Rhanna*, and *Song of Rhanna*. *Storm over Rhanna* is the sixth in the increasingly popular series about the enchanting Hebridean island.

Christine Marion Fraser lives in Argyll with her husband and daughter.

Available in Fontana by the same author

FICTION

Rhanna
Rhanna at War
Children of Rhanna
Return to Rhanna
Song of Rhanna

King's Croft
King's Acre

NON-FICTION

Blue Above the Chimneys
Roses Round the Door

CHRISTINE MARION FRASER

Storm over Rhanna

FONTANA/COLLINS

First published by Fontana Paperbacks 1988

ISBN 000 617532-5

Made and printed in Great Britain by
William Collins Sons & Co. Ltd, Glasgow

For Rhanna fans, old and new,
this latest book, is dedicated to you.

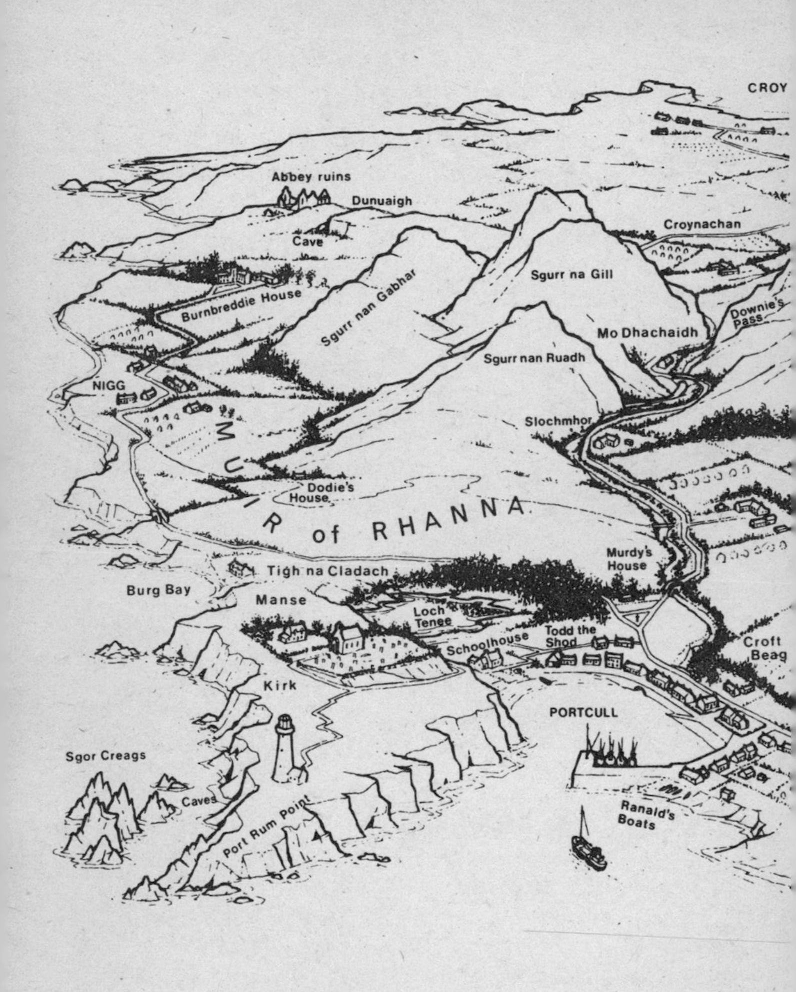
CROY
Abbey ruins
Dunuaigh
Croynachan
Cave
Sgurr na Gill
Burnbreddie House
Sgurr nan Gabhar
Downie's Pass
Mo Dhachaidh
Sgurr nan Ruadh
NIGG
Slochmhor
MUIR of RHANNA
Dodie's House
Murdy's House
Tigh na Cladach
Burg Bay
Manse
Loch Tenee
Todd the Shod
Schoolhouse
Croft Beag
Kirk
PORTCULL
Sgor Creags
Caves
Port Rum Point
Ranald's Boats

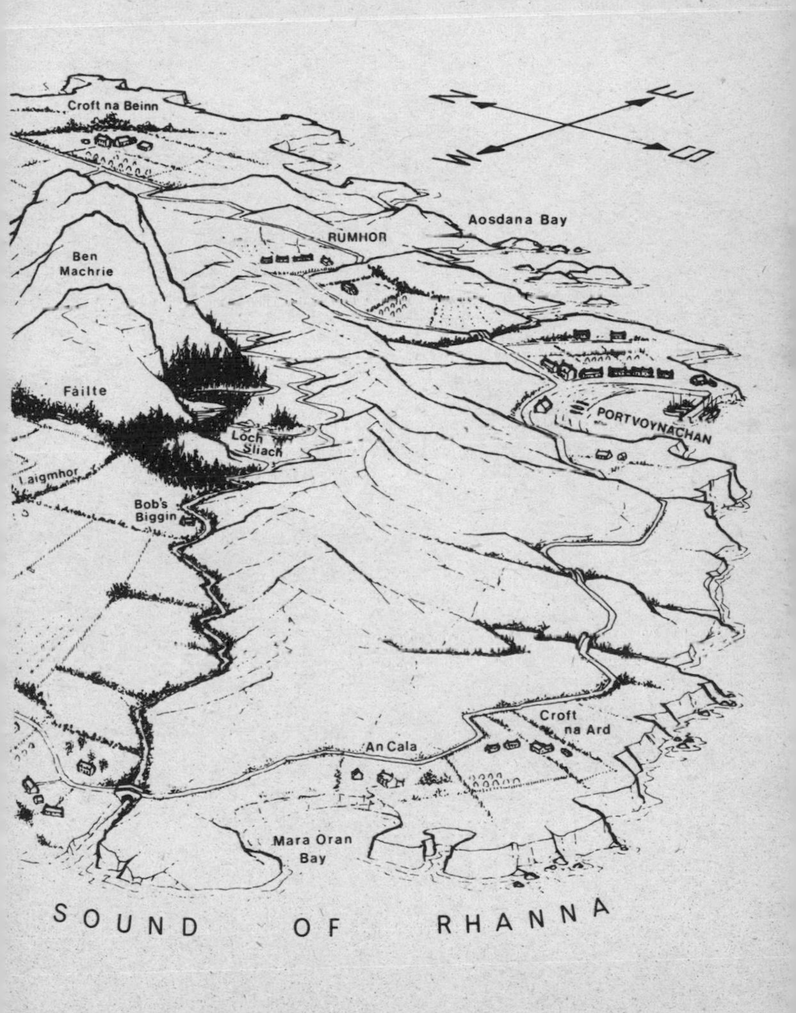
Croft na Beinn
N
E
W
S
Aosdana Bay
RUMHOR
Ben Machrie
Fàilte
Loch Sliach
PORTVOYNACHAN
Laigmhor
Bob's Biggin
Croft na Ard
An Cala
Mara Oran Bay
SOUND OF RHANNA

PART ONE

Christmas 1965

Chapter One

The Rev. Mark James arranged his long frame on the window seat of his study, lit his pipe and settled back to puff at it thoughtfully. His gaze roamed round the walls of his den, where hung some of his most treasured possessions. There were several lopsided child's drawings, gloriously uninhibited creations that never failed to bring a smile to his strong, dark face. Smiling birds with clumping big feet, climbing merrily up perpendicular trees with not a foothold in sight; squinty-eyed brides teetering on impossibly high-heeled shoes; ships with tall funnels rearing into garishly coloured skies. All executed by the hand of a little girl now dead, each picture as gay and exuberant as her life had been. On the dark, panelled wood above the fireplace hung a framed mosaic of exquisitely hued sea shells fashioned into delicate flower and leaf patterns. His wife, Margaret, had collected them on their honeymoon, and as soon as they got home she had made the picture and proudly hung it on the wall above their bed.

'It's not the most artistic effort but each time we look at it we'll remember the beginning of our life together.'

He could see her face now, her smiling mouth, her eyes shining as she looked at him for approval. His heart twisted. She was gone now from his life, both she and his daughter Sharon, taken from him in a car accident that had wiped out their lives as if they had never been. Only memories were left and sometimes he was afraid because in the secret recesses of his mind he couldn't visualize his wife and daughter as clearly as he wished.

Firelight flickered over the room, danced on the pictures, threw shadows over the faces of Sharon and Margaret looking out from their frames on the mantelpiece. His strong teeth bit into the stem of his pipe. Loneliness engulfed him. He knew a terrible longing for the happy sense of fulfilment that had once been his.

Mark had been minister on Rhanna for over four years now and he had found a great deal of contentment in his new life, though more and more of late there had been a restlessness in him. He had tried to ward it off by immersing himself deeper into his work, but he found difficulty keeping his mind on it.

The pages of his partially completed Sunday sermon were scattered about his desk – he couldn't concentrate and he was angry at himself for being so weak as to want...to want things that were, with each passing day, becoming more and more out of his reach...

Against his will his eyes were drawn to the window and he found himself gazing down towards Tigh na Cladach, Gaelic for the Shore House, a sturdy big place sitting on the machair above Burg Bay.

This was the home of Doctor Megan Jenkins. From his study window the minister could see all the comings and goings to and from the front door which was on the sheltered side of the house facing the Hillock. Just then the door opened and the last of the morning patients went sprachling away in the direction of Portcull, body bent against the wind howling up from the sea.

Mark James glimpsed Megan's slender figure before the door was firmly shut and the house seemed to huddle into itself, reflecting an air of almost secretive aloofness to the world. It was as if it had absorbed the elusive nature of its newest owner, for there was a great aura of reserve about the young woman doctor who had come to the island two summers ago to take over the practice from Lachlan McLachlan, the man who had tended the population nearly all of his professional life.

The minister's firm jaw tightened. From the beginning he had liked Megan Jenkins – no, something much more than that. The more he had come to know her the greater had grown in him a yearning that wouldn't be stilled. He recalled to mind how, after an initial slow start, their friendship had grown. In those early days he had done everything he could to make life easier for her in a strange place and in time they had become good neighbours, each day getting to know one another a little bit better. They had talked together, walked together, there had existed an easy rapport between them, they had discovered that they shared much in common, and then – foolishly – he had spoiled it all by letting her see that his feelings for her went far deeper than just friendship.

She had withdrawn from him then. 'Please, Mark,' she had told him, 'I'm not ready for anything of that sort – not yet – perhaps never. It might be better for both of us if we stopped seeing one another, that way neither of us will get hurt.'

From that day she had avoided him and he cursed himself for having spoiled what they had, a platonic relationship would have been better than this emptiness that was inside him whenever he thought of her.

He sighed deeply and stared at the house. The smoke from its chimneys was blowing hither and thither in a gale force wind that was whipping the Sound of Rhanna to fury, Atlantic rollers were thundering to shore, bedraggled bundles of seaweed had come up with the tide to drape themselves over the walls surrounding the garden at the back of the house. To the left of the bay the almighty cliffs of Burg reared up, menacing and sheer, broken by yawning black caverns into which the sea spumed only to gush with terrific force out of spout holes atop the cliffs. Vertical pinnacles of glistening black rock rose up out of the sea in front of the caves, treacherous reefs spread spiky fingers out from the bastion of Burg and on a wild day like this it was an awesome sight to watch the ocean heaving round the jagged crags, and to hear it thundering into the caves.

The minister could sit at his window for hours just watching the wonderful spectacle of a storm-lashed sea crashing over the skerries, but today he was in no mood to contemplate the wild grandeur before him. All his thoughts were centred on Megan, on how long it had been since he had had something resembling a conversation with her – and they were neighbours, dammit! The curse exploded inside his head. He couldn't help it, he couldn't! And yet he seemed to be the only one experiencing trouble getting through to her.

At first Megan had found it hard going getting to know the canny islanders and their ways, the male population in particular finding it difficult to confide their most intimate medical problems to a woman after the easy rapport they had shared with Lachlan. In the case of the womenfolk it had been easier, many of them declaring that at long last they could discuss their feminine complaints without fear of embarrassment. To quote Kate McKinnon of Portcull, 'There were times I would go to Lachlan wi' a bum problem and end up showing him a skelf in my finger.'

Yet, even though the women now found life easier as far as their personal troubles went, there were those among them who rejected the woman doctor merely because she was young, attractive, and as Behag Beag so succinctly put it, 'fancy free'.

People of Behag's generation simply did not trust a doctor who could attract young, healthy men to her surgery 'like flies to cow dung' and with nothing more serious wrong with them than 'hot breeks and an insatiable thirsting after passion'.

'She looks as though butter wouldny melt in her mouth,' sniffed Elspeth Morrison, whose years of allegiance to the McLachlan household had left her with the unshakeable opinion that the doctor had not yet been born to take Lachlan's place. 'But I know that sort only too well. Men and boys are no' safe wi' them and I for one wouldny like to see the kind o' things that go on behind closed doors.'

'Ach, blethers, you spiteful cailleach,' Kate McKinnon hooted, 'you would gie your left lug to see – ay – and maybe take part as well. You're nothing but a frustrated auld yowe since your Hector went and drowned himself wi' the drink.'

'My Hector respected me as a woman,' spluttered Elspeth in outrage, her bony, immobile face flushing crimson. 'He was never that sort o' man.'

'No?' taunted a delighted Kate. 'What way was it then that every time he came home from the sea your wash line just about broke itself wi' the weight o' the sheets hangin' on it – ay – and maybe a dozen pairs o' your breeks keepin' them company. Hector might no' have been much to look at but he had his passions like any man, and wi' him being away so often he was just burstin' to spend them on someone.'

'You're an evil-minded woman, Kate McKinnon, that you are,' gritted Elspeth through tight lips. 'Dinna judge everybody like yourself – it's no sheets and a bed for you. I've seen you and that Tam wi' my very own eyes, rolling in the heather – just like a couple o' heathens.'

'Ach well, I'm no' mindin' what anybody says about Doctor Megan,' declared Tina stoutly, her plump, good-natured face taking on a determined expression. 'My Eve works to the doctor and a nicer, kindlier body you couldny meet anywhere. Fine I know it myself too for she was that good to Matthew's mother when she near died wi' 'flu at the start o' winter. In every day she was and no' just a quick look either. On the bed she sat, homely as you like, cracking wi' Grannie Ann in the Gaelic and even accepting thon awful cough sweeties Granda John buys in Merry Mary's and keeps in his pooch beside his baccy. No, Doctor Megan's a good lassie and clever too. She has a way wi' the auld folk that's a fair treat to see and I for one will no' hear an ill word spoken against her.'

And that was the opinion of the majority of the islanders. Everybody had come to like and respect the new doctor. She had arrived on the island with a fair knowledge of the Gaelic language and had made it her business to nurture it so that now the old Gaels felt perfectly at ease in her company, while everyone else allowed their natural reserve to thaw bit by bit and even to address her as 'Doctor Megan' rather than the more formal 'Doctor Jenkins' as it had been in the beginning.

Only Mark James felt excluded from her life and yet he was her nearest neighbour, the man who had fetched and carried peat, water, and coal for her when she was so strange and new settling into the big old house by the sea.

The door of the study opened and Tina came in, her plump cheeks flushed from the heat of the stove, her fine hair hanging in untidy loops about her ears, for no matter how often she tied it into a bun it invariably escaped the carelessly applied kirby grips.

'You've put your feets up and are havin' a wee rest, I see,' she observed, gazing languidly at the untidy array of papers on the desk. 'A good thing too, you work far too hard as a rule and too much o' that is no good for anybody.'

Tina herself had her own methods for coping with work, her idea of cleaning the Manse floors being to slop a soapy mop around the kitchen to the accompaniment of a Gaelic air, sung untunefully but sweetly in her slow, throaty voice. When dusting or polishing she would trail a rag along a chosen route with her nose buried in a woman's magazine or one of the romantic novels she devoured so avidly, lips moving, eyes goggling as some sensual scene unfolded before her vision.

The minister had no complaints. Her presence in his home never intruded into his life, be he relaxing or working. Her easygoing attitude to almost everything she tackled suited him well, and she more than made up for her shortcomings by producing excellent meals for the Manse table. True the food was of the plain variety, unimaginative in the extreme but nevertheless tasty and palatable, and though never ready at the same time from one day to the next that never bothered him as he was a man who rebelled against set times and rules in his own home.

He and Tina suited one another. He would listen patiently to all her small domestic problems and in return she protected both him and his interests in her own quiet but oddly determined way.

Scliffing over to the window in a pair of down-at-heel boots she observed, 'There's my Eve coming from Doctor Megan's house. She'll have got through her chores early wi' her goin' to the Christmas bazaar in Portcull. I know fine she's meeting young Calum Gillies over there.' She smiled indulgently. 'She's an awful lass for the boys is our Eve. Mind you, she's nearly twenty-six now and it's high time she was thinkin' o' settling down but ach, it's natural for the young ones to have their fling first, and Eve has never caused me or Matthew a minute's worry in that respect for she knows how to look after herself. Auld Mirabelle who worked to Laigmhor aye used to warn me to keep my hand on my halfpenny and I just gave Eve the same advice.'

The minister's lips twitched. Tina was always coming away with some quaint observation or other and was perfectly frank in discussing the facts of life with him.

Her eyes roved gently back to Tigh na Cladach and she emitted a small, somewhat calculated sigh. 'It seems an awful waste – Doctor Megan down there on her own and you up here on yours and you such close neighbours too. You could save yourself a bittie money if you were both under the one roof, and though it would mean either myself or Eve losin' out on a job it would be worth it – ay it would.'

'But Tina,' objected Mark James, 'just think what the island would have to say about that.'

'Ach, I don't mean living in sin!' Her guileless eyes were round at the very idea. 'Oh no, never that and you a man o' God wi' your reputation to protect. I'm surprised at you, Mr James, for even thinkin' the thing. No, you and the doctor are both respected members o' the community and anything o' that nature would have to be done right and proper...' She let the words trail off and wandered to the fire to give it a desultory poke and place another lump of peat on the glowing embers. 'You see and keep warm now, you've no' been lookin' too good this whilie back – as if there was something worrying you and you canny be yourself for thinkin' about it. There's plenty peats in the pail in the scullery and while I'm mindin', your dinner's ready and keeping warm in the oven.'

Absent-mindedly she flicked her apron over a dusty patch on the mantelpiece before meandering to the door. 'I'll away home and get my own dinner and I'll be seeing you later at the bazaar. I've made a nice meat pie for your tea – all you have to do is heat it up.' She went into the hall, turning to add as an afterthought, 'There's enough in the ashet for two – it's no' easy filling a dish for just one.'

Mark James chuckled as he got up. 'Thank you, Tina, if I can't eat it all I'm sure Mutt and the cats will help me finish it. You go away now and get your own meal and don't be rushing over here too early in the morning.'

It was a palpable overstatement. The only time anyone had ever seen Tina rushing was to the wee hoosie after she had eaten too much spring rhubarb. There was no set time for her morning arrival at the Manse, that being determined by how early or how late she had seen her own family fed and catered for. She departed into the wild day leaving the minister to make his way through to the warm, roomy kitchen with its Welsh dresser, huge oaken sideboard, big shabby armchairs, and dark refectory table rung round with tapestry-covered chairs so threadbare it was difficult to make out the once rich patterns.

Mutt, a large, loose-limbed, floppy-eared cross between a spaniel and a labrador, stretched himself lazily before coming to greet his master, while three cats bestirred sleepily on top of the warm range to survey him with green, hopeful orbs as he removed his dinner from the oven.

Before drawing his chair into the table he poured milk into a large dish marked 'dog', and fetched a meaty bone for Mutt from the larder. It was very quiet in the room except for the busy lapping of the cats and the scrunching of Mutt's teeth. Blatterings of hail gusted against the window panes, the wind tore through the elms at the side of the house, making the branches creak and groan.

The violence of the day served to make the kitchen all the more cosy and Mark James looked about him as he ate. He loved the old Manse. It sat here, atop the Hillock, sturdy, aloof, almost arrogant in its seeming contempt of wind and storm. It was true that the roof could be doing with a good overhaul. Depending on wind direction it could leak quite badly, a fact borne out by the buckets placed at strategic points in the loft and one which made Tam McKinnon scratch his head in bemusement as he had no sooner fixed one section of slates before a new leak had sprung somewhere else. It could be a draughty house too, with wind sneaking through chinks in windows and doors and somehow finding its way round the draught screens placed about.

Yet, despite its inadequacies, it was a house of great dignity and reassuring comfort and Mark James had never felt anything but contentment from the day he moved in. In summer he found great solace tending to the walled-off garden surrounding the house, in winter he was quite happy reading by the fire in the evenings or having friends in for a strupak and a chat – yet, always there was the empty chair opposite him at the fire, the lonely table with himself sitting there eating rather self-consciously surrounded by all that bare table space, the unoccupied chairs facing the uncluttered table with what seemed to him a rather reproachful air.

'Will it always be like this? Will it?' In sudden anguish he spoke aloud to the empty room. Mutt stopped crunching to look up at him enquiringly, one ear comically alert, the other crumpled about his wrinkled muzzle. Getting up, he padded over to rest his soft nose on his master's knee and whine gently in sympathy. Mark pushed his long fingers into the animal's silky fur, fondled the ungainly ears, then abruptly he pushed his plate away, and rising from his chair he began to pace, up and down, up and down, pausing every so often to gaze morosely towards the window and the sea lying grey-bellied in the distance. The old floorboards squeaked, squeak, squeak. Mutt's sensitive ears twitched and he threw his master an indignant look. It was the time of day he looked forward to most – the dinner hour and the meaty bone, the anticipation of glorious freedom roaming machair and seashore with that big, beloved man figure walking along at his back, each of them delighting in the silent companionship of the other.

But today something was wrong. A sense of unrest pervaded the normally peaceful kitchen. Finally Mutt could bear it no longer. A worried whine rose up in his throat, he ran to the door to stare at it expectantly, his ridiculously floppy tail twitching in a signal of hope.

The minister stopped pacing and laughed. 'Alright, you daft Mutt, I've got the message. Come on then, we'll go down and see Megan for a wee while then you'll get your walk.'

Throwing on an ancient tweed jacket, he let himself out of the house, Mutt running along in front, busy nose close to the ground. The wind caught at the minister's tall figure, buffeted him so that it took all his strength to steer a straight course over the machair to the winding sheep path that ran down to Tigh na Cladach. Bending his dark head into the wind he tried to keep his thoughts calm. He was only paying Megan a visit, that was all –

and why not, for heaven's sake! That wasn't so unusual on an island where strupaks and ceilidhs were part of the everyday scene of things. A lot of people popped in and out of Tigh na Cladach – he had every right to do the same. He reached the gate and opened it resolutely. Mutt didn't follow. Instead he ran a little way forward before turning his melting brown gaze to the man at the gate.

'Go on, then,' grinned Mark, 'you play around for a while, I'll only be a few minutes, I promise.'

Megan was just finishing her meal when Mark James strode into the kitchen. At sight of him her cup clattered clumsily down onto the saucer, she half rose, a startled expression in her hazel eyes.

'Don't get up,' Mark James spoke calmly, 'I only popped in for a minute to ask if you might come over to the church bazaar with me this afternoon. I'm doing the book stall but I have plenty of helpers and could easily get away after a wee while...' He lowered his head and, looking as abashed as a small boy, went on quickly, 'I thought we could go for a walk – perhaps talk – it seems a long time since we exchanged two words together.'

His eyes were on her, smokey blue-grey eyes ringed round with dark navy. They were the most disconcerting pair of eyes she had ever encountered, with an expression in them that was so fathomless she felt herself drowning every time she looked into them. Down, down she was drawn, into dizzy depths without end...Her heart bumped inside her breast. She tore her gaze away from him and started to speak, too fast, 'Would you like some tea? I've had mine but there's plenty left in the pot...' Without waiting for an answer she began pouring, slopping some into the saucer – damn her shaking hands, his presence always did this to her and she wouldn't have it – she couldn't...

'Megan – Meggie, I didn't come for tea. I think it's time we talked – ' The use of his pet name for her was too much for her to bear. 'I'm sorry.' Getting up she almost ran to get her coat from the stand in the hall. 'I have to go out. I have several calls to make and then I must visit Shona McLachlan. Her baby's due at Christmas but I want her over in a mainland hospital before the winter storms really hit the island. She's healthy and strong but I can't take the risk of her having the baby here – '

'Megan!' Catching her wrist he spun her round to face him. She was very slender and quite tall but even so her head didn't quite reach his shoulders. His abrupt manoeuvre had caused a few strands of glossy brown hair to swing round and brush her cheek, a sudden rush of colour burned her pale skin, her thickly-lashed eyes had grown very wide and so bright with surprise they were a luminous shade of warm gold in the rosy flush of her face. Her breath caught in her throat as she stared up at him in a heady mixture of apprehension and expectancy.

Without another word he cupped her face in his hand and sought her mouth. It wasn't a gentle kiss. His lips were warm and hard, the bruising pressure of them taking her completely unawares. Abruptly he released her. She reeled away from him, blood pulsing, heart pounding. Gripping a chair back to steady herself she gulped in great breaths of air and glared at him through the thick curtain of hair that had fallen across her face. 'How dare you take such liberties?' she threw at him hoarsely. 'You a minister behaving no better than a heathen! You wear the wedding ring of your dead wife round your throat, yet you barge in here like some jungle animal with scant regard for the common laws of decency and respect for any woman, be they alive or dead. What would your wife think of her precious husband if she could see his behaviour now?'

It was cruel, deliberately and hurtfully cruel. She knew it and would have bitten back every word if she could. But it was too late. He had recoiled as every vicious barb fell upon his ears, yet his voice when he spoke was as steady as his unwavering gaze on her face. 'Margaret is always with me, wherever I go, whatever I do, yet she never stands in my way – just props me up a little bit now and then...'

Megan realized then that his voice wasn't so much steady as tight with hurt, so much so that he had difficulty getting the words to come out as he went on, 'She was a fair and compassionate woman and she would never have wished me to be as lonely – to be as alone as I am now.'

She couldn't bring herself to look into those searching dark orbs of his a moment longer. Yet she knew she had to send him out of her life. She must never allow herself to get to like him too much, her heart was still bruised and sore from the hurt of that other love which she still hadn't gotten over – and dear God! Here was this other man, this tall, dark man of God, so good to her since her arrival on Rhanna, so dear and kind, gentle and considerate... so warm and passionate and very, very powerful... She lowered her head, deliberately forced hardness into her voice, 'Then find yourself another woman, Mark James, it's as simple as that. Forget all about me, I – I'm not available.'

'You make it sound so cheap,' his voice was angry now. 'It isn't like that, Megan, and fine you know it! What's wrong between you and me anyway? We seemed to get along fine for a while and now you've grown so cold and hard I'm afraid to come near you. Is there someone else? Is that why you fled to a remote Hebridean island? To get away from whoever it was? Well, I tell you this, it hasn't worked. Whoever he is, he's as much on your mind as ever he was – perhaps more now that you're apart from one another.'

She turned away. She wasn't going to tell him about Steven Saunders. The trauma of that short, passionate affair was still very much with her, she felt the hurt of it would never leave her – and now this man, who so disturbed her senses – his very nearness threatened to shatter the fragile defensive shell she had built round her emotions...

'I'm sorry, Mark, I can't talk to you about it. It's too near and I'm not yet ready to open myself up to anyone, least of all you. I need time – oh God, don't push me. Who do you think you are anyway? Asking questions about my life. It's none of your business and never will be.'

His face tightened. A dark flush spread over his rugged features. His eyes seemed to reflect the grey stormclouds piling up over the great mountain of Sgurr nan Ruadh, which shouldered its sullen way into the sky beyond the shore house windows. 'I know who I am, Megan, I hope in time so too will you. You're not as hard as you try to make out. These are frail barriers you have built round your heart. One day I hope you will shake yourself free of them and will know again the joy of giving as well as taking.' He spread his hands in a gesture of appeal. 'At least – can we be friends? I feel so shut out from your life yet you seem to bend over backwards to please everyone else – or is that just an act you feel you have to put on to make your life on the island tolerable?'

'Go away, Mark.' She sounded remote, in full control of herself again. 'I don't need you or any other man lecturing me on my motives.' She glanced towards the window. 'Your dog is getting restless, stick with him, he'll not let you down, nor shall he desert you as a human companion might. Animals are a lot safer than humans, they give so much and demand so little in return. I'm getting one myself for Christmas. Fergus McKenzie's Sheil had pups a few weeks back, I'm collecting mine in a few days' time – she'll be all the company I'll need or want for a long time to come.'

He went, abruptly and quickly out into the stormy day, his strong face livid with hurt and anger. If he had turned back, if he had witnessed Megan sinking into a chair to put a trembling hand up to her eyes, and heard his name come out in a long drawn-out sigh, his heart might have filled with a hope that would have allowed him better to thole the dark days of despair that stretched before him like a grey road filled with shadows.

Chapter Two

Mo Dhachaidh was fragrant with the tantalizing smells of baking when Megan called in, and found Shona in the kitchen wrapping scones and cakes which she packed into a wicker basket sitting on the table. Ellie Dawn, an attractive, fair-haired child of three, was ensconced on the rug by the fire, contentedly eating a buttery scone, watched attentively by Woody the cat who was ready to pounce on any crumbs that came his way.

Shona looked up at Megan's entry, her face lighting to smiles. 'Oh, it's yourself, Megan.' She was one of the few who had, from the beginning, used the doctor's Christian name. 'Sit you down and I'll get us both a cuppy, though mind, I'll have to be quick with mine. I promised Mark weeks ago that I'd help out with the baking table at the bazaar, but kept putting it off with the result that I'm at the cow's tail as usual.'

Megan sat down on the old rocking chair that had once been Biddy's, the nurse who had tended the population of Rhanna for most of her life and who had never been forgotten by anyone. Her picture smiled out from Memory Corner, a rather crooked smile to be sure, for on the day it was taken her cat had chewed her denture and the effort of keeping the misshapen teeth in place and trying to smile at the same time had proved almost too much.

Memory Corner had been the idea of Helen, better known as Ellie, Shona's eldest daughter. It was nothing grand, just a small neuk on the broad, white window-ledge, scattered with photos of those who had been special in Shona's life, adorned by a vase of red holly berries nestling amongst glossy green foliage.

In pride of place was a picture of Ellie herself, a child whose sweet youth seemed to capture the very essence of summer itself. Her arms were full of buttercups, her radiant smile poured laughter into the room. She had been just thirteen when she died, and in the trauma of losing her Shona had nearly lost her reason and with it the precious things and people that had made her life the sweet thing it was. Now there was Ellie Dawn, the baby whose arrival had been like a miracle. Never never would she take the place of Shona's firstborn daughter. She was a delightful little human being in her own right and she had given her parents so much joy they both felt it could never be surpassed. But soon there was to be another, and Shona was brimming with so much happiness it seemed to spill over like sunshine and cast its light on everyone with whom she came in contact. Megan felt the warmth of it touching her. Ever since the interlude with Mark James she had been aware of a deep sense of misery tugging at her heart, but now, in the presence of Shona, with Ellie Dawn grinning at her and everyone in Memory Corner smiling out at her, she felt uplifted and suddenly very aware of her surroundings; the purple-black clouds scudding over the dour face of Sgurr na Gill beyond the window, the stooped figure of Dodie, the island eccentric, loping along the winding glen road towards the huddled white houses of Portcull lying in the distance, the indignant mutterings of the hungry hens gathering outside Mo Dhachaidh's walled garden, the rushing of the burn over the stones, the bleating of the sheep from the slopes of Ben Machrie... and on the rain-washed horizon, the barely discernable tall chimneys of the Manse poking into the clouds... Hastily she pulled her eyes away from the window, drew her attention back to Mo Dhachaidh's warmly bright kitchen.

Shona had noticed the doctor's interest in the window,

and going over she touched her daughter's photo with a tender finger. 'Did I ever tell you about her?' she asked softly, a little faraway smile hovering on her lips.

Megan shook her head. 'No, you didn't. I've heard, of course, how she died but –'

'No, no, not that,' interposed Shona, coming back to sit at the fire and gaze into it as if she was seeing pictures in the darting flames. 'I want to tell you how she lived. She was such a happy wee lass. When I think of her I always seem to see her smiling.'

She went on, talking in a quiet voice about Ellie, and as she talked Megan could almost hear the child's laughter chuckling out from every corner of the room. Shona's face was glowing. At almost forty-three she looked like a girl with her shining auburn hair rippling about her shoulders and her golden skin smooth and unlined. Although in her ninth month of pregnancy she was very fit for a woman so close to her time, but Megan had been quick to notice a weariness in the deep-blue eyes Shona had turned on her when she had first entered the room.

'When she died I thought I would too – I wanted to. I think I did everything I could to make myself ill,' Shona's voice was low, ashamed, 'I thought only of my own grief, of what my darling child's death had done to me. I was too selfish and full of my own misery to notice anybody else's – most of all Niall's. His heart was broken yet I turned away from him when most he needed me – ' she threw the doctor a sidelong glance – 'sometimes we do that when our hearts are sore and heavy. We tend to think we're the only ones to have suffered at the loss of a loved one. When Mark James came to try and talk some sense into me I ranted and raved at him for interfering, and when he told me he had not long lost his wife and daughter I could have curled up and died with my shame. But by confiding in me he helped me take the first steps towards life again. I'll never forget him for what he did for me. I like to think that in some small way

I helped him too, but deep down I know that's just wishful thinking. I have a very special affection for our minister, Megan. He's strong and good and considerate to everyone he meets yet I often think – how lonely he must get sometimes. Not just because he lost his family but because he has to shoulder so much responsibility. I suppose in a way a minister's job is much like a doctor's. Everybody rushes to tell you their ails but no one stops to think you might have your worries too – they forget ministers and doctors are human beings with the same troubles and sorrows as the rest of us.'

Megan's face was burning. As Shona talked she wondered wildly if Fergus McKenzie's daughter could see into her very soul, and she was the first to pull her eyes away from the other's keen assessment.

'I'm sorry,' Shona shook her head. 'I didn't mean the talk to turn in Mark's direction – it's just, well, I don't like to see him getting hurt but what's between you and him is really none of my business.'

A sharp retort sprung to Megan's lips but she controlled her anger and said in a tight voice, 'Shona, I didn't come here this afternoon just to drink tea and talk about the minister. It's you I want to talk about. You certainly look well enough and I know you say you feel fine but –'

'But at my age I should be sitting with my slippered feet up the lum contemplating my old age pension.' Shona laughed and threw the doctor a roguish look. 'It's what all the cailleachs are saying but I know you wouldn't want to come into that category, would you now? You're far too young for that – though on the other hand,' she eyed the other woman thoughtfully, 'you seem older somehow – och, I don't mean that in a cheeky way,' she added hastily, 'it's just, well, you do tend to take life a bittie too seriously – and if you don't mind me saying so, yourself with it.'

Megan's flush deepened. She liked Shona McLachlan. She was like her father, straight-forward and honest and often disconcertingly forthright. From the beginning she had felt at ease in the older woman's company. There were no barriers here. Shona treated her not so much as a doctor but as a friend. Megan liked that very much. God knew she needed someone like Shona in her life. She had many acquaintances on the island but somehow it seemed to stop there, and she often felt lonely and uncertain in the new life she had chosen for herself.

In the next few minutes she was to find out the reasons for that as Shona, taking her silence as a sign of disapproval, went rushing on, 'Ach, don't look like that, I aye did have too much to say for myself. If Father or Niall were here now they would be throwing me warning looks and Father in particular would be knitting his black brows and glaring at me.' She stared into her cup. 'If Mirabelle was here she would be reading the tea leaves. She's that bonny plump lady sitting beside Biddy in Memory Corner. You would have loved Mirabelle, we all did. She looked after us McKenzies for years and when I was a bairn at her knee she often took my cup from me and told me the most impossible but wonderful things that would happen to me when I grew up. She taught me how to read them too...' Reaching out, she seized Megan's cup and, peering into it, murmured sagely, 'Ay, there they are, the initials MJ interwoven round a big heart – but of course, these are your initials, Megan, yet, they could just as easily be those of Mark James.' She caught a glimpse of the doctor's crimson face and sighed. 'There I go again, but this time I'm no' going to apologize. I *did* think – we all thought – that you and the minister would get together and live happily ever after, but I can see it's no' going to be that easy – and, well, I have to say it, you only have yourself to blame. You've made good headway with the Rhanna folk, they all like, trust and respect you as their doctor but so far that's all you are to them. You need friends as well as patients but, for some reason, you haven't made them. No one can get through to you, and if Mark James doesn't stand a chance what hope is there for the rest of us?'

'You're wasting your time here, Shona,' Megan said dryly. 'You would have made a fine psychiatrist. And it isn't all my fault, you know. You islanders are a canny bunch and can be a regular clan when the mood takes you. I have tried, I tried very hard with Babbie Büttger but from the beginning I sensed a resentment in her because I dared to take Lachlan's place.'

'Ach, Babbie didn't mean any of it.' Shona smiled indulgently at the mention of her friend who was the district nurse on Rhanna. 'She didn't take kindly to you at first, not just to you but to the idea of a whole new way of working. She and Lachlan were a team for countless years, you have to take that into account. But she's over that now and only too willing to meet you halfway, yet she was saying only the other day you won't let her get near you, that it's a case of work and nothing more.'

Green sparks shone in the doctor's hazel eyes. 'Oh, so you and she have been discussing me, though perhaps talking might be a more apt word.'

'Ay, we've been talking.' Shona sighed, wishing now she hadn't let her tongue run away with her. 'It's natural for people to talk about one another and with you being so new here – well – your name is never far from everybody's lips.'

'Woody's got a big belly!' Ellie Dawn turned a rosy face from the fire and shrieked with glee. She was playing with the cat who had rolled on her side to allow the child's fingers to probe into her soft fur. Shona snatched her daughter from the rug and hid her giggles in the warm flesh of the little girl's neck. 'Nancy Taylor of Croft na Beinn was here this morning,' Shona explained to her visitor, 'and if you know Nancy and her mother, Kate McKinnon, then you'll understand where this wee rascal gets her vocabulary.' She rubbed her nose against

Ellie Dawn's and gazed into the child's golden-brown eyes. 'Woody is going to have babies soon – round about the time we're going to have ours, is that no' right, you wee whittrock?'

Ellie Dawn leaned forward to pat her mother's stomach with a chubby hand. 'Baby,' she stated with the utmost solemnity, 'in Muvver's belly.'

They made a charming picture, mother and daughter, the rich red tresses of the one against the pale gold of the other, the infant's small fingers innocently touching her mother's body where they would.

'You're right, of course, I should have made friends by now,' Megan spoke awkwardly. 'I suppose I've been so intent in getting my patients to accept me that I've overlooked too much else. Could I – would you mind if I started off with you, Shona?'

'Ach, I've aye been your friend, you were just too busy to notice, that's all.' Shona spoke easily, secretly relieved that the doctor hadn't taken offence at her. 'It's difficult in a small community – to keep up the professional side yet to know just when to let the barriers down a bit. But Lachlan managed the two very well and with a bittie experience so will you.'

'Lachlan again,' Megan smiled ruefully. 'A very difficult man to live up to. I wonder if I'll ever be half as good as he is,' she finished wistfully.

'Och, of course you will,' Shona reassured. 'When he came first to the island he had the sacred memory of Auld McLure to contend with. An old rascal was McLure, he flirted with the de'il at every turn yet the rogue was beloved by the old folks. According to gossip he wasny much of a doctor but had the knack of putting people at their ease and was just as much at home taking a dram by a crofter's fireside as he was downing brandy in the laird's mansion.'

Megan laughed. 'God rest the ancient McLures of the world – and talking about rest, you have an uncanny ability for taking the talk away from yourself. I don't know how on earth we got round to discussing Auld McLure but speaking as your doctor as well as your friend I want you over in Oban on the next boat, so start packing the things you'll need and I'll make the necessary arrangements.'

'Oban!' Shona was aghast. 'But I'm not due for another three weeks yet and I've no intention of wallowing in a maternity bed when both Ellie and Niall need me here, and besides –'

'Oban,' Megan spoke firmly. Besides what she had heard from the gossips' ready tongues, she was well enough acquainted with the McKenzies to know how stubborn they could be. 'The winter gales are starting in earnest now and I'm not taking any risks with you – ' she paused and rushed on – 'in your condition and at your age.'

'You're worse than Lachlan any day,' grumbled Shona, her brow furrowed in what Megan had privately christened 'the McKenzie scowl'. 'Forbye that you sound just like Elspeth Morrison. She's aghast at the idea of me ready to drop a bairn let alone still able to enjoy the lusts of the flesh, as she calls it.'

At that moment Niall's whistle sounded in the hallway and Sporran the spaniel, who often accompanied him on his veterinary rounds, bounded into the kitchen to pounce on Ellie Dawn and roll her over and over on the floor. Woody spat her disdain at the antics of the young dog and stalked away, both nose and tail high in the air, while from under a mound of russet fur Ellie Dawn yelled her delight at Sporran's boisterous intrusion onto the scene.

'I've fed the hens, they nearly flattened me when I got to the gate and I guessed there was a hen party going on in here.' Niall smiled at the visitor as he spoke, his brown eyes sweeping over her trim figure with frank appreciation, a twitch of laughter lifting his mouth on catching Shona's grim expression. Cheekily, keeping one eye on her, he reached out and helped himself to a scone from the basket, grinning in anticipation of the rebuke he knew would follow his action.

Shona rapped him smartly on the knuckles as she might have done a schoolboy and scolded, 'Your eyes were aye bigger than your belly. You might have got away with it at Slochmhor but I'm no' your mother and will no' stand for your nonsense.'

'Big belly, big belly,' Ellie Dawn chanted, coming over once more to stroke her mother's stomach and lay her little head on it as if it was a cushion.

'You see,' chuckled Niall, 'you're corrupting our bairn with your bad language and you've the cheek to talk about Nancy. And what a way to treat a husband whose only crime was to pop into his own home for a minute to see how his wee wife was faring.'

'Oh, I know fine you're keeping an anxious eye on me,' Shona spoke rather sharply. 'You're all doing it. Father's aye looking in on any flimsy excuse, no' to mention Babbie and Kirsteen, Fiona and Ruth, even Phebie though I can thole her better because she's the only one who doesn't make me feel like a decrepit cailleach ready to drop into my grave at any minute.' She picked up her basket and tossed her auburn head proudly. 'Now I'm away with this stuff before it gets mouldy with age like myself. Fetch your coat, Ellie, you and me will have a lovely walk together down to Portcull.'

'I'll give you a lift,' said Niall quickly. 'I'm going down that way myself.'

Shona glowered at him. 'No you're not. You said at dinner time you had to go to Portvoynachan this afternoon.'

'*I'll* give her a lift.' Megan's tone brooked no nonsense. 'I'm just off home and will drop you off on the way, Shona. It's a fair walk to the village and I've just told you, you'll have to take things easier from now on.' Turning her eyes away from Shona's furious face she spoke appealingly to Niall, 'I've just been telling your wife I want her over to Oban on the next boat. She's rebelling at the idea, so do you think you could try persuading her it's all for the best?'.

'Whoever tried persuading a McKenzie?' Niall laughed. 'Mirabelle used to say they were all as pigheaded as mules. But don't you worry, Doctor, my wife will be on that boat even if I have to carry her to the harbour myself and tie her up in the hold.'

Shona rushed after him as he strode out to the hall, catching up with him as he reached the front porch. 'Just who do you think you are, Niall McLachlan?' she demanded tearfully, rage almost choking her. 'You've no right to speak to me as if I was a daft bairn – and – and in front of Miss High-And-Mighty too.'

'I don't think – I know who I am,' he retorted, his own eyes flashing. 'I'm the husband of a beautiful, stubborn, bad-tempered woman who is too – too glaikit to see that we are all anxious about her because we love her very, very much.'

'Glaikit!' she stormed. 'Oh no, Niall McLachlan, that's been your stamp ever since I first clapped eyes on you in the Post Office when I was a bairn of five and you called me names and was the cause of Mirabelle yanking my breeks down to my ankles and skelping me on the bare bum...' All the fire went out of her suddenly as she saw the sparks of laughter starting in Niall's eyes. 'I'll never lose my McKenzie temper, will I? But it was only because you and Megan ganged up on me after I had seen you looking at her and lusting after her with your eyes.'

He gave a shout of merriment. 'Now you *do* sound like a cailleach – Elspeth in particular. As for admiring Megan, well, I wouldny be human if I didn't enjoy those nice legs she shows off to the world – but – I'll tell you a secret, Mrs McLachlan – ' he nuzzled her ear with his lips making her shiver – 'they aren't a patch on yours and never will be and the rest of you is just as lovely.' Tenderly he placed his hands on her stomach. 'Particularly now, with our bairn growing inside you. You're so soft and vulnerable-looking, with secrets in your eyes as if you know something the rest o' the world doesn't. You glow with an inner light, everything about you is bigger –' he smiled softly and his arms tightened round her, 'and I don't just mean physically. You radiate desire, warmth. I don't know how I've managed to keep my hands off you this whilie back.'

'It will be over soon.' She melted against him, brushing his mouth with hers. 'Then we'll be back to normal and you can do as you will with me. I'm a wanton woman, Niall McLachlan, and never could hold myself back with you.'

'And you will go to Oban as Megan wants?' he breathed into her ear.

'Ach, of course. I was going to say so anyway when you barged in and started pinching cakes. I want this baby to have the best possible start in life and would never do anything to jeopardize that.'

He glanced outside. Fat yellow-grey snow clouds were piling over the peaks of the hills, the air was brittle with cold. 'The wind's dropped,' he nodded, 'it will snow soon.' As he spoke the first wisping flurries whispered against the porch windows. 'You take care,' he told her, and giving her a final squeeze he went whistling out to the little Morris Minor that carried him on his rounds, leaving her to go back into the kitchen with a light step and the smiles back on her face.

At sight of her, Megan's heartfelt sigh of relief came out louder than she had intended and, giggling, Shona took Ellie's hand and led the way outside with Sporran dancing at their heels. Megan's car was an old but comfortable red Mini and into it they all crammed only to pile out five minutes later after countless abortive attempts to get it started. Megan tossed her hair back from her face and gave vent to a long drawn-out sigh of frustration. 'It's been playing up this good while back but I never had the time to get it fixed, and now the battery is flat as well as everything else.'

'Never mind,' consoled Shona, 'Angus McKinnon will soon get it going again. He's as good with engines as he is with house repairs.'

'But,' Megan eyed her doubtfully, 'I heard that Angus has a reputation for putting more holes in a roof than he fixes, and Grannie Ann was telling me only yesterday she caught him sleeping off a hangover in her hayshed when he should have been mending her chimney.'

'Ay, he is a bittie clumsy forbye being heart lazy,' Shona admitted with a twinkle, 'but he is the only motor mechanic this side o' the island. No one really specializes in cars, folk like Angus just tacked them on to his jack-of-all-trades business as the need arose. We'll likely see him at the bazaar. You can have a word with him there.'

'Shona McLachlan, you're going to get your own way after all! I wasn't going to the bazaar and I didn't want you walking to the village but now it looks as if we'll have to, doesn't it?'

'Ay, you're right there, Megan – and Niall just away in front o' us too.'

Shona's sorrowful tones were wasted on the doctor. The sparkle in her eyes made them very blue, her cheeks were glowing, her nose a bright cherry red in the freezing air whistling through Downie's Pass. An impatient Sporran was already bounding away ahead and Ellie Dawn was bouncing in her mother's arms, chivvying to be let down and away with the dog.

As they all walked along the winding glen road Megan found that she was thoroughly enjoying herself. Shona was in an abandoned mood. Despite her girth she skipped along, her hair a banner of flame against the grey sky, and her infectious enjoyment of the snow-harried day transferred itself to Megan so that she felt stimulated and alive as she hadn't been for a long time. Soon her own face was frost-stung to the colour of the holly berries nestling among the rowans on the lower slopes of the hills. The River Fallan rushed along, the burns frothed down the rocky slits of the corries, the snow whirled about them in sluggish eddies that melted on their faces and clung to their eyelashes.

'Oh, I love it when it snows!' Shona cried ecstatically. 'I hope it gets thicker and thicker so that we can play in it and give Ellie sledge rides.'

Megan didn't remind her of the forthcoming journey to the maternity hospital in Oban. Instead she followed Shona's example and seized Ellie Dawn's free hand so that the little girl swung between them, her shouts of joy mingling with Sporran's barks on the deserted road. At Slochmhor's gate they were joined by Phebie, bearing a basket similar to Shona's.

'I must get this jam and stuff down to the hall,' she greeted the trio, her plump face breaking into smiles as Ellie Dawn rushed to meet her. 'Lachy offered to take me in that daft motor o' his but I'd have frozen to death waiting till he got the damt engine started.' She eyed the doctor in some surprise. 'Forgive an auld wife for being nosy *and* impudent but it's the first time I've seen you walking this road, Megan. Have you adopted the island ways and taken complete leave o' your senses or has this wild lassie made you as daft as herself?'

Megan smiled. 'A mixture of both, I suppose, combined with a car as cantankerous as your own.'

'Och well,' Phebie said comfortably, falling into step beside them, 'it's nice to have a bittie company on a day like this. I'm past the age o' enjoying the experience of skiting and slithering about on my behind, so if I get into difficulties you two can hold me up on the way.'

In the high fields above Laigmhor, Fergus and old Bob, with the help of Davie McKinnon, were rounding up the sheep, bringing them to lower ground before the snow really settled on the land. The dogs were barking, running purposefully about, dark dots on the whitening hills.

'I see Sheil's working again,' observed Megan. 'The pups must be ready to leave her now. I can hardly wait to get mine home even though I know the wee devil will wreak havoc in the house. At least it will give my patients something to talk about and might keep their minds off me for a bit.'

She glanced meaningfully at Shona as she spoke. Shona shrugged her shoulders and smiled knowingly as she replied, 'Oh ay, a pup will certainly provide a talking point – to your face, that is – behind your back the gossips will just say you're getting to be an old maid before your time with naught but a dog to keep you company in the long winter evenings.'

Megan shot daggers at her tormentor and a fresh argument might have sprung up between the two had not Phebie drawn to a sudden halt. 'Wheesht you two, I'm hearing something funny back there. A noise like thunder. Can you hear it?'

They held their breath, listening. The hill peaks were covered in great fat rolls of yellow-grey cloud. They looked muffled, huddled into themselves in dour, silent secrecy. Shona frowned. 'It's as quiet as death up there on the hills. There's no thunder about, just a wheen of juicy plump snowclouds,' she chuckled, 'it's likely just the gurgling of my belly you're hearing. Whenever I drink tea these days it makes a terrible noise going down, as if everything inside was being squeezed by this huge bairn I'm carrying.'

They had only taken a few more paces when, with one accord, they all stopped, ears straining, eyes searching the rapidly whitening road behind them. Sure enough, far in the distance there came a sound like an echo of drums and in a short while a large dark mound hove into view, growing closer and more discernable with every passing second.

'It's only Croynachan's bull,' Phebie said in some relief. 'I wish Tom would see to these fences o' his, that damt cratur' breaks loose whenever the mood takes him. It's no' the first time he's roamed the island. We'd better try and stop him before he reaches the village.'

The bull came closer, great swirls of stoorie snow churning round his rushing legs. He was a Department bull, given the fanciful name of Venus by Tom Johnston who had acquired him in the spring of that year. He was a brown and white shorthorn, a magnificent creature, young, highly strung, full of vigour and lust, but as easily frightened as a kitten.

Shona retired to the roadside with Ellie, leaving the others to wave their arms in the air and try to head the bull into a nearby field. When he saw the womenfolk in his path he skidded to a halt, nostrils dilated, saliva trailing from his frothing mouth to billow in glistening streamers over his massive neck.

Sporran took over then. He had no fear of farm animals, having come across many while accompanying Niall on his rounds, and with more enthusiasm than expertise he somehow guided the bull towards the gate which Shona was pushing open. The wet ground was treacherous, covered as it was with new snow. Her feet slithered away from her and she fell heavily, all the breath knocked from her lungs.

Venus forgotten, Phebie and Megan rushed to help Shona upright. The child within her gave a tremendous jolt and seemed to turn right over, at the same moment pain seared through her.

Megan saw the sudden pallor on Shona's face. Annie's cottage was nearby and to this abode Shona was led, thankfully to sink into the nearest chair the moment they were inside. Nobody ever locked their doors on Rhanna, least of all Annie and Torquill Andrew whose frequent ceilidhs made their home a very popular rendezvous.

'I'll be fine when I've had a rest,' Shona tried to speak calmly but was unable to stop gasping when another pain seized her. 'You two get along, I'll wait here with Ellie and follow on when I catch my breath.'

'Indeed we will not,' Phebie spoke briskly. 'We'll all catch our breath and then go on to the hall together. It isn't far so we can all take our time.'

Outside the snow was falling thicker and faster; Venus lingered uneasily beside the still-open gate, Sporran lay watchfully outside the cottage; a growl like thunder sounded on the hill slopes. Shona placed her hands over her stomach as if to protect the life within. She didn't say anything but she knew that she was going into the first stages of labour.

Chapter Three

'By God, she's a cold one right enough, eh, Mr James?' Tam's nose was as brightly red as the scarf he wore tightly wrapped round his neck, but he sounded cheery enough as he fell into step beside Mark James on the way to the village hall.

'Indeed she is, Tam,' agreed the minister who knew well enough by now that the islanders bestowed genders on almost everything under the sun.

'Ay, she is angry the night.' Canty Tam leered in his vacant fashion at the foaming sea, as if hoping to see the Green Uisge Hags riding to shore atop the crashing waves. 'This is the sort o' night the Hags like best, the sea all a-thunder and the snow smothering the land in ghost blankets.'

'Ach, you're havering, man! I've been out in every kind o' sea and never yet seen a Uisge Hag.' Hector the Boat spat scornfully into the snow but even so his watery blue eyes were uneasy as he strained them landwards. 'Now, if you had told me the Snow Bochgans would come a-hauntin' us I maybe would believe you. They have a rare old time to themselves in this weather.'

'The Snow Bochgans?' Canty Tam's eyes slid abruptly from the sea to look in awe into the old fisherman's whiskery walnut face.

'Ay, you've surely heard o' them? They're ghostly pale hobgoblins who hide in caves in the hills, all dead and silent till the snow comes and wakes them up wi' a frozen kiss. Then they come fleein' and screechin' down the braes, slitherin' about and laughing.' Hector was warming to the tale he had made up on the spur of the moment, and was well rewarded by the dawning of a new kind of horrified delight on Canty Tam's face.

'I suppose we just might get a visit from them this afternoon?' Mark asked, keeping his face as serious as he could.

'Oh ay,' nodded Hector vigorously, 'sometimes they come on their own but I've heard tell there's a bloody great Ullabhiest lives up there in the caves wi' them,' Hector forgot to mind his language so carried away was he with his story, 'if it takes it into its head it flees along beside them, a huge de'il o' a beast wi' bloodshot een and six horns on its head that it uses to shove boulders and trees out o' its way...'

At that precise moment, Shona and the others appeared from Glen Fallan out of a curtain of snow that folded about their bodies and that of Croynachan's bull trotting along behind them in a rather spirited fashion.

The pipe fell from Hector's mouth, Canty Tam emitted a crazed screech and began scuttling towards the hall, yelling as he went, 'The Snow Bochgans are comin', the Snow Bochgans are comin'!'

Hector the Boat was frozen to the spot, hardly able to believe the evidence of his own eyes. 'I only made it up, it's no' true, it's no',' he muttered as if in prayer.

The minister and Tam said nothing. They saw at once that the womenfolk were in a state of distress and rushed to help.

'Thank God,' gasped Phebie, 'I thought we were never going to make it.'

Quickly they explained what had happened and without more ado the two men took hold of Shona, and supporting her between them made off for the hall.

There came shouts on the Glen Fallan road. Tom Johnston and his son came pelting along, closely followed by Fergus and Davie McKinnon. Confused by all the noise, the bull let out a bellow, kicked up his heels and with head down slewed off in the direction of the bay leaving everyone far behind.

Supporting Shona, Tam and the minister staggered up the hall steps only to be met with the stout resistance of the closed door.

Canty Tam had done his work well. Everyone was well used to his tales of witches and monsters, but no one had ever seen him in such a state before and some of his terror had transferred itself to the more superstitious islanders.

'*Something* must have scared the shat out o' him,' Todd the Shod stated rather fearfully and had then rushed to bolt the door.

When Megan and Phebie put their fists to the door and began banging on it, Canty Tam in a state of near hysteria screamed, ''Tis the Bochgans! They're here, I tell you! Clawin' and slaverin' at the door to get in and kill us!'

Molly McDonald pursed her lips at such utter nonsense and made her way over to look from a window. ''Tis no' the Bochgans, you silly man!' Tis the doctor and the minister and Shona McLachlan. Near dyin' they are by the look o' them.'

Todd the Shod put his face next to Molly's. 'It's the minister and the doctor right enough and poor wee Shona as white as the driven snow.' His eyes roamed into the distance and saw Venus heading for the shore with the men from the glen fast on its heels. 'God – it's thon bloody great bull o' Croynachan's – it must have chased the lassies.'

There was a shamefaced stampede to open the door. The women catapulted inside, Shona and Phebie to collapse on hastily fetched chairs, Megan, with Ellie in her arms, to lean against the waiting ones of Mark James. For a moment she was glad to melt into their steadying embrace, then, as she felt his arms tightening around her, she pulled herself away to look round dazedly. 'Is Shona alright? Bloody hell, that brute had to come along when it did! She's hardly fit to walk, let alone run!'

There was a surprised raising of a few eyebrows. The new doctor had never been so publicly flustered before and *never* had she been known to swear.

Elspeth, lips folded in disapproval, dug her elbow into Kate's side and intoned meaningfully, 'That's the true Doctor Megan coming out. She'll never have Lachlan's dignity, never.'

But no one had ears for Elspeth and her opinions just then. The excitement going on outside was much more tempting than the attractions inside the gaily decorated hall. Everyone rushed for vantage points at the windows, and it was quite a mêlée with children trying to worm their way in and the adults themselves behaving no better as they jostled and elbowed one another, Behag Beag even going to the length of perching herself on a chair the better to gain an uninterrupted view.

'Would you look at these legs,' hissed Captain Mac to Wullie McKinnon, 'I've seen better-shaped porridge spurtles and that's a fact.'

'It's no' her legs I'm seeing,' sniggered Wullie, 'it's her breeks. I aye kent she would wear them down to her knees but never did I dream they would be as red as a winter sunset.'

'Ay, ay, the cailleach is showin' her true colours right enough.' Captain Mac's face was redder than Behag's bloomers with suppressed mirth. 'Maybe we should carry her outside and wave her at the bull. We would all see red then and the big bugger would be that busy chasin' her it would maybe run itself to a standstill. Just look at it out there. If it doesny stop chargin' about soon, it will go right into the water and get drowned.'

'My, my, he's a spirited one that,' nodded Kate, elbowing Elspeth's sparse shoulders out of her line of vision. As mischevious a cratur' ever to set foot on the island forbye the fact he's all balls and no brains.'

'Kate McKinnon!' admonished Elspeth in disgust, while Jim Jim smirked and observed, 'Ach well, Kate, there's a few like him on the island and no' just four-legged cratur's either.'

'Ay, and you were maybe one o' them in your time,' answered Kate smartly. ''Tis a pity they canny castrate menfolk the way they do the beasts, we might all get a bittie peace then.'

'Ach, c'mon now, Kate,' Tam grinned slyly at his cronies. 'You wouldny want the like o' that to happen. You enjoyed your bit of fun as much as the rest o' us, no matter how you like to pretend otherwise.'

'Fun! I'll fun you, Tam McKinnon! I spent half my married life lying on my back birthing bairns because o' you and your fun.'

'Ay, and the other half just lying on your back.' Tam's whispered words were meant for the benefit of his cronies, who were showing suitable appreciation of his bold remarks in grins and nods. But to a man they stopped laughing when Elspeth turned round to glare at them so fiercely they all wilted away from her as, with a flounce of her severe grey head and using her elbows like battering rams, she dug her way out of the crowd to go and pour her belated sympathies into Phebie's ears.

'Fancy spendin' the night wi' that one,' growled Tam. 'She'd hack you to ribbons and come back later to lick up the pieces.'

'Ay, 'tis no wonder her Hector went and died on her,' grunted Todd, rubbing a big hand over his old appendix scar where Elspeth's bony appendages had dug in. 'If she had been my cailleach I'd have died too just for the sake o' a minute's peace.'

'Ach, she's no' that bad,' observed Captain Mac thoughtfully. 'She's a lonely body, and uses her tongue to cover up her feelings – I hear tell she's a good cook too,' he added obliquely.

'Ay, and maybe you've taken leave o' your senses,' hooted Tam derisively. 'What good would her cooking do to the likes o' you – unless you've just gone mad altogether and are thinkin' o' marryin' her? You've no' been like yourself at all since that Hanaay widow told you she wouldny marry you if you persisted in the idea o' livin' in a houseboat.'

'Look you, stop your blethering and get outside to help wi' that bull,' ordered Kate. 'If he goes in the water there will be no gettin' him out and Tom would have a fine job explainin' that away to the Department.'

Rather unwillingly the men abandoned the warmth of the hall and made their way out into the bitter day. Venus had worked himself into quite a state and had gone galloping along the bay to the treacherous finger of Port Rum Point, there to make his way over the tiny fringe of white sand that separated the rock from the swirling waters of the Atlantic Ocean.

'Get ropes!' yelled a frantic Tom. 'We'll have to try and head him off. If he tries to go any further he'll slip and I'll have lost him forever.'

There was a general scramble to fetch ropes and anything else that might be needed to haul the wayward Venus to safety. In a state of terror he was standing on the slippery rocks, bellowing his fright to the world, all the fire gone out of him as quickly as it had come.

'Ach my, would you look at the sowel.' Tina was standing at the door, her voice heavy with sympathy as she watched the attempted rescue of Venus. 'The poor cratur' must be sorry he ever broke free. He's no' really a bad bull, just young and full o' life.'

'He's sorry! I hope he drowns out there and if he doesn't he deserves to be shot!' the doctor rounded on the minister's housekeeper. 'You're a foolish woman, Tina. He's caused a great deal of trouble and all you can do is stand there and sing his praises!'

Tina recoiled, hurt and surprise showing in her soft brown eyes. Mark James left Shona's side and strode over to pull Tina gently away, not glancing once in Megan's direction. She stood where she was, dismayed and angry at herself. She hadn't yet recovered from the fright she had recently experienced, she was worried about Shona and the effect all this might have on her, and she had shown herself in a bad light in front of people she was only just beginning to win over. Now she felt herself back at the beginning and a great sigh escaped her as she wondered for the umpteenth time if she had done the right thing coming to this island. To make matters worse, twice in just one day she had incurred anger in a man whose good opinion she had come to need very much indeed – even if it wasn't very apparent to him that she needed him at all. If only he could keep his feelings on a more even level, how she would have enjoyed just talking to him, just being with him…

Fergus brushed past her at that moment, too anxious to find out how his daughter was faring to assist any further in the rescue of Venus.

'Shona, are you alright?' he demanded urgently, bending down to put his strong right arm round her shoulders. He had lost his other arm in a terrible accident near the Sgor Greags, but it had happened a long time ago and he was used to his disability now.

'Father,' Shona greeted him breathlessly, 'I don't think I'm going to be able to wait to get to that mainland hospital. I'm…' She let out an involuntary groan of pain that brought Megan hurrying over to order her to lie back and breathe deeply.

'No,' Shona forced herself to sit upright. 'I'll be fine in a wee minute. It might just be a stitch though I think it might be better if I went home.'

She bit her lip and turned very pale and without further argument lay back in the hard wooden chair.

A knot of people had gathered to watch the little drama with interest and Megan whispered to Phebie, 'Hardly the most private place for anyone to go into labour, we'll have to get her home as quickly as possible.'

Phebie, having been well fortified with hot tea from the kitchen urn, had recovered both her wits and her equilibrium, and she stared at the young doctor's worried face sympathetically. 'You really think she's started then?'

'Undoubtedly. All that exertion would put anyone into labour – pregnant or no. Oh, I've no doubt with her being a McKenzie she'll take it all in her stride but – will the rest of us?'

Phebie showed some surprise. 'Och, Megan, Lachy delivered hundreds of babies on the island in his day, it was the natural way o' things then.'

'Then – but not now. Far better a maternity hospital with all the proper facilitics.'

'Well, all I can say is, doctors these days are getting soft,' Phebie spoke quietly but firmly. 'A lot of the island women would far rather have their bairns at home instead o' having to trachle miles away over the water wi' hardly the sight o' a loved one to see them through the loneliness of being in a strange place wi' strange people. As for facilities, all you need is a bed and a cot and plenty o' loving care, the mother does the rest.'

'All very fine, Phebie, but what about complications? I believe Shona's own mother died having her and there must have been other like cases.'

'Complications can arise in hospital too,' Phebie sounded unusually stubborn, 'and despite all the modern facilities as you call them, mothers still die, babies too. It ought to be a matter o' choice. I wouldny have missed having my own two in the comforts o' my own home, not for all the tea in China, and I happen to know Shona feels exactly the same.'

'I see you're the old-fashioned type,' Megan's face had grown red, 'but we all have to move with the times, even an island like this one where everyone seems hellbent on clinging to the old ways whether they're good for them or not.' Her hazel eyes were snapping, her very ears red with chagrin. This just wasn't her day, everything and everyone seemed to be against her, even Phebie whose placid nature had always soothed and comforted her. Impatiently she clicked her tongue. 'All this talk is getting us nowhere and my damned car had to break down just when I need it most – sorry, I've cursed more today than in the whole of my time here – does anyone on the island have a vehicle that works? Could someone go and look for Niall? He ought to be here.'

'Todd has a car,' Fergus broke in brusquely. 'I'll go and ask him to fetch it round – Niall could be anywhere on Rhanna and will be held up with the snow.'

'Ach, the damty thing will never start,' Molly spoke with assurance. 'Todd last used it to take a tourist party over to Croy and that was away back in July. I doubt he has the battery out now for he's aye tinkering around wi' the blessed engine. He has a good horse and cart though,' she added, eyeing the doctor with some defiance. 'In the old days we would put a pregnant lass into a cart and take her over the roughest roads. It was a good way to get things moving and it was said that a lad born after a good jolting at a horse's backside took to the crofting life no bother.'

'Literally born to it,' said Phebie, hiding a wicked grin into her hanky.

Mark James, coming back from the kitchen where he had left Tina sipping tea, assessed the situation in one glance. 'I'll get along up to the Manse and bring my old Thunder. She'll grumble a bit, but then so does anything as old as she is.'

'Thunder? That isn't a horse – is it?' Megan sounded suspicious.

'Bless you no, lass,' laughed Molly as Mark James strode away. 'Thunder is the name o' the minister's old motor car. She makes a noise like the clapping o' the heavens when she is starting up and the name just suits her fine.'

The minister had paused at the door to murmur something into Kate's ear and, brisk and cool-headed in times of emergency, she led Isabel and Molly away to the nether regions of the hall. They were soon back, between them carrying a box of old curtains which in no time at all had been whipped round Shona to form a makeshift screen.

'Och, Kate, what would I do without you?' she sighed gratefully. 'You're aye on the spot when you're needed and seem to know just what to do.'

'Ach, think nothing o' it. I did the same for auld Biddy and Todd thon time they were both laid up in my house and neither wanting to bare their bums to the other – look you, laddie,' she rounded on Fergus, 'will you get out the road this minute and stop gawping at the lass as if she was maybe going to drop her bairn on top o' your toes?'

Fergus had been anxiously hovering at his daughter's side, hindering more than helping as the womenfolk bustled about. At Kate's blunt words he glowered darkly and, taking his pipe from his pocket, jammed it between his teeth, making no attempt to light it.

'Father,' Shona spoke warningly, 'will you stop looking like that? I've had babies before. Do something useful – like taking Ellie for a walk round the hall. Santa ought to be back soon so let her see the tree while she's waiting.'

'Eve's taken charge o' her.' He bit into his pipe, his restless gaze looking beyond the brightly-lit hall to the Sound of Rhanna lying black-bellied under distant grey clouds. The snow had stopped momentarily, as if held suspended by some giant breath, and in the lull darkness seemed to swoop down to embrace the island. The wind resumed its attack, keened in over the sea, whipped froth from waves that hurled themselves viciously against the slimy finger of Port Rum Point. Beyond the pocked face of that grim promontory the Sgor Creags rose up, like grey gloomy old men eternally meditating the wild Atlantic.

Against that backdrop of untamed grandeur the

massive Venus looked small and insignificant. The men swarmed round him, coaxing him to safer ground. But he had run himself into a state of exhaustion and offered no resistance when a rope was slotted through his nose ring and he was led gingerly over the slippery rocks. As docile as any gentle-eyed cow he ambled amiably along the village street, every now and then emitting a soft little grunt to indicate his total subjugation to the human animal.

'I see he's been rescued,' Canty Tam's disappointed breathy voice was warm in Fergus's ear. 'I was just after thinkin' the Uisge Hags would get him too. A Rhanna bull is no' near as good as a Rhanna man but he would have been better than nothing and would have kept them off us for a while.'

The scene outside was wiped out as great windblown gusts of fresh snow hurtled over the landscape, blattering against the window panes to melt and slither down. 'Ach, your head's too full o' nonsense, man,' growled Fergus, 'go and find something useful to do for a change. You never seem to do anything else but slink about looking for trouble.'

Canty Tam was not offended. He *knew* about Green Uisge Hags better than any other in these parts. They took boats and men and did terrible things to them way down there in the depths of the ocean. Folk hereabouts blamed storm and tide for such disasters but he knew the real and awful truth, and giving Fergus a pitying glance he shuffled off to find more amenable ears.

Fergus shivered, hating the sight of the white world, fighting to keep back memories of long ago when Helen, his first wife, had died on a blizzard-racked morning giving birth to Shona...

'Father,' Shona grabbed his hand and held it tight. 'I know fine you're worried about me, that you hate it every time a McKenzie woman has a baby on the island. But inside myself I wanted it this way – in fact you might almost say I willed it to happen. I won't have any more babies and my dearest wish is to have this one on Rhanna.'

He looked down on her earnest face and his black eyes grew tender. 'Ay, and you aye did get your own way. Niall's right when he calls you a red-haired witch. You go around casting your spells on people and events and somehow manage to turn them in your favour. It wouldny surprise me in the least if poor old Venus was part o' your plan. He seems to have done you a favour after all, even if he himself comes off worst in the end. Croynachan is talking of sending him back to the Department. If no' we might have Rhanna women dropping bairns out of trees and God knows where else.'

The men were drifting back into the hall to be fortified with tea from the ever-brewing urn. There was a general bustle while everyone belatedly resumed their positions at the various stalls and the children squabbled to gain the best places in the queue for 'Santa's Maritime Cave'. This was an innovation dreamed up by Captain Mac, who, with his flowing white beard and jolly bulbous nose, made a perfect if slightly inebriated Father Christmas.

Somewhat out of breath from his efforts to help with Venus, he settled himself graciously into the depths of an enormous clam shell which had been made from the remains of an ancient rowing boat, now painted white and liberally embellished with streamers of dried seaweed. Mermaids and dolphins cavorted on the walls of the cave which had been fashioned after the style of a tinker's tent and covered over with a fish-smelling, moth-eaten tarpaulin. Hidden in the corner, a red light glowed mysteriously, bathing Captain Mac in an enigmatic glow that further enhanced the colour of his Santa suit and turned his nose into a bright red beacon.

Hurriedly he swigged from the bottle that was hidden in his roomy pocket, smoothed down his luxuriant whiskers, and in a deep, resonant boom called, 'Enter the cave!' for the benefit of the first little visitor who was peeping round the door with huge, wondering, awe-filled eyes.

'The minister's coming back!'

Wullie McKinnon, at his mother's insistence, had been keeping watch at the door. Peering through the snow-spiked darkness he wished he had made himself scarce when the going was good. Still, it was for Shona, and he had always had a soft spot for the only daughter of McKenzie o' the Glen.

Wiping snowflakes from his lashes and an errant drip from his nose, he watched the lights of the minister's motor car wavering down the brae from the Manse. It was very quiet out here, with the snow muffling the sound of the sea and no noise of anything else to break the silence. Rasping his sleeve over his nose he put his face in at the door and yelled, 'Come on, lads, the minister's motor's no' working. He's freewheeling down the brae. Bring Angus, we'll need him to look at the engine.'

An unwilling Angus was ousted away from the tombola stall which he had haunted in the hope of winning a bottle of malt whisky.

'I'll open the wee envelope for you, son,' offered Tam affably, 'if you have the winning number I'll be sure to tell you, you can trust me.'

'Ay, to keep it for yourself,' grumbled Angus, unwillingly handing over his newly acquired ticket to his father before following his brother and a few other stalwarts out to where Thunder had just slithered to a halt.

The vehicle was ancient, rusty and unreliable, possibly owing to the fact that its owner only ever used it when the breezes of summer had given way to the gales of winter. At the men's approach, Mutt's big, shaggy, smiling face looked out of a window.

Angus guffawed with laughter. 'Look, lads, I doubt Mr James has allowed his dog to take over the driving. 'Tis no wonder the damty motor wouldny go right.'

Mark James smiled. 'No, Angus, I drive, Mutt only does the steering – and then only under strict supervision.'

The men roared with appreciative mirth, then as one swarmed round the vehicle to instruct, encourage and torment Angus who had lifted the creaking bonnet to peer knowingly at the engine in the uncertain light of a storm lantern held aloft by Mark James.

Chapter Four

'For heaven's sake, doesn't anything on this island work?'

The words of frustration were torn from Megan who was waiting with Fergus at the door, helplessly watching the activity round the minister's motor car, shivering in the bite of the wind tearing through her rather flimsy clothing. 'And just listen to them arguing and laughing as if it was some sort of picnic. Don't they ever take anything seriously?'

Fergus sucked on his pipe, his own impatience making him inwardly curse the good-natured banter of the men, yet his inbuilt loyalty to his kinsmen forbidding him to utter one word of agreement to a stranger. For that was how he thought of Megan and if he had felt like talking at all he would have told her that if she wanted to make any sort of agreeable life for herself on the island she would have to stop criticizing and learn to take the islanders as she found them. Too many strangers came to these parts and tried to impose their opinions on the natural inhabitants, and when they were ignored they were wont to wonder why and imagine themselves hard done by.

He, more than anyone, had found it difficult to get to know the new doctor, let alone like her, and he knew she felt exactly the same way about him.

'You'll no' burrow your way into that black-hearted McKenzie,' Behag had warned sourly, 'he's as dour and thrawn as Malcolm his father before him, ay, and just as unlikeable. I should know too, I've kent him all my days yet never kent the black-eyed cratur' at all, if you get my meaning, Doctor.'

Fergus wished with all his heart that Lachlan was still the island doctor, that it was he instead of this young female standing beside him now, the high heels of her fashionable shoes beating an annoying tattoo on the steps as she paced back and forwards. Taking the pipe from his mouth, he was about to snarl at her to be still when Kate came hurrying out, her face full of concern when she addressed Megan, 'I'm thinkin' we had better try and get the lass along to my house. Her pains are getting worse by the minute. I've had many a bairn in my own bed in my day and it's just a step or two along the road. She could be quick wi' this one and if that Tam gets wind o' it he'll be raffling it along wi' the Christmas cake, for he's that daft wi' the drink he couldny tell the difference.'

If the situation had been less serious Megan would have seen the funny side, as it was she did laugh outright, but only with sheer relief for at that moment a great cheer from the men coincided with the glad sound of an engine bursting into life.

In minutes Shona was being helped outside and into the vehicle. Squeezed in beside her were the doctor and Fergus with Ellie on his knee, in the front the minister sat behind the wheel, Phebie was in the passenger seat with Mutt cooried beside her, watched jealously by Sporran who it had been decided should remain behind with Kate. The little spaniel was not in the least pleased with the arrangement and glowered long and hard at the usurper as if to say, 'So this is my thanks for all my efforts this afternoon, this big mutt gets all the attention while I have to stay behind and *walk*.'

'Och, let him in,' decided Shona, 'he was a dear brave wee soul today and if it hadn't been for him we could all have been trampled to death.'

So a triumphant Sporran was hoisted into the back, the grin on his face widening when, at the last moment, an uninvited Elspeth squashed herself in beside an audibly protesting Mutt.

'Since you are going my way, Minister,' said Elspeth by way of explanation, removing Mutt's ear from her mouth and settling her sparse frame into the seat with determination. 'Besides, I'm thinkin' I'd like to be there when the doctor hears his son is about to bring a new McLachlan into the world.'

Two sets of eyes sparked with annoyance at her thoughtless remarks, Megan's because Elspeth still insisted on calling Lachlan 'the doctor' and Shona's because Elspeth always managed to rile her with insinuations that Niall had done himself no favours in marrying a McKenzie, and that any achievements within the family must be placed very firmly at his door. She was about to warm the old woman's ears with a few choice remarks of her own when a glance at her father's face stilled her tongue. He looked as if he would like to kill the 'auld yowe' as he called her, and Shona put a warning finger to her lips and snuggled against him to bury her face into the comforting warmth of his neck.

Thunder jolted, jumped forward, settled down as Mark James held the gear in place. Another cheer sounded from outside, the men's faces slipped away like moons in the night.

'Good luck, Shona lass!' Tam called cheerfully. 'We'll wet the bairn's head the minute we hear it's arrived.'

'Hmph,' snorted Elspeth, 'the rogue has already drowned it forbye any sorrows he might have floatin' about in that empty head o' his. Him and his sons are good for nothing but drinking and hiding when there's work to be done.'

'Angus got this temperamental machine of mine to start,' the minister pointed out grimly as he strained to see through the small semi-circle made by the sluggish wiper. 'He and the others might appear to make light of things but somehow, in the end, they get them moving and I for one thank God for their like.'

Elspeth merely grunted while Megan, remembering her own hasty words of condemnation, blushed red in the darkness. Mark's eyes caught hers in the mirror and she lowered her head, utterly dismayed by the turn of events. If only her own car hadn't broken down none of this would have happened. She wouldn't be here now, in Mark's rattling old motor, with the seat springs hurting her thighs and draughts whistling round her neck. The scuffed leather upholstery was permeated with the rather pleasing scent of his pipe smoke. It made her very aware of him, the great strength of his presence, the little homely and humorous habits that had made him stick a notice on the windscreen, proclaiming, 'This vehicle somtimes runs on petrol but mostly on luck and the occasional prayer.'

She studied the powerful shoulders hunched over the wheel, the shape of his dark head – the top of it just missing the roof by inches. A smile touched her lips. He was so different from Steven in every way – if only, if only...

A silence descended over everyone. Not even Phebie seemed able to offer any of her usual cheerful chatter. Little Ellie was cooried into Fergus, sleepily sucking her thumb, the tiny cloth rabbit from Santa's sack held tight to her breast.

Shona wanted to hold her small daughter, to stroke her hair and tell her that everything was alright, but the vehicle's interior was so claustrophobic and cramped that in just a few minutes her stomach seemed to have attained enormous proportions. She felt as if she was swelling up, bursting out with pain, drowning in rivers of perspiration that poured down her face. And then came the nausea, thrusting upwards in waves that made her swallow and gasp out, 'Where are we now, Father?'

Fergus cleared a circle of steam from the window and peered out. The snow whirled, driven by a moaning wind that shrieked through Downie's Pass, obliterating familiar landmarks, all but blotting out the lights of

Laigmhor wavering faintly up ahead. Thunder's single wiper had been getting slower and slower as gradually it clogged up, now the little motor whirred uselessly, allowing the blade finally to become pinned against the bonnet.

'Damn!' The minister's curse came from under his breath yet even so Elspeth glared at him with downright disapproval. He caught the look and grinned faintly. The old lady could always be trusted to rise to the bait, no matter how grim the circumstances.

'We're at Laigmhor,' Fergus rapped out the words just as the machine slithered to a groaning halt. 'We'd better get Shona home.'

'Home.' The word fell sweetly on Shona's ears. Her father would always think of Laigmhor as her home and dearly though she loved Mo Dhachaidh she knew that the big old farmhouse would never completely relinquish its hold on her... But if she didn't go back to her own house that night, what about Niall waiting there, wondering what had happened to her..? Quickly she voiced her thoughts. The minister smiled at her reassuringly. 'I phoned from the Manse when I was up there getting Thunder,' he glanced briefly at Megan, 'I also took the liberty of phoning Babbie to tell her to stand by at Mo Dhachaidh.'

'You thought of everything,' Shona said dryly, angry because in all the trauma she hadn't thought of either Niall or Babbie.

'Not everything,' his tone was equally dry. 'I didn't know we wouldn't get as far as Mo Dhachaidh so, as there's no phone at Laigmhor, I'll get along there and let them know what's happening.'

'Stop off at Slochmhor and phone from there,' suggested Phebie, 'it will save you a hike and Lachy will be glad to hear what's going on. Don't let him come back here though, he's had his day o' trudging treacherous roads.'

'The snow's stopped for a minute,' Fergus reported as

he got out of the car. 'It will give us a chance to get home reasonably dry.'

Everyone struggled out, complaining of pins and needles, uttering exclamations of amazement at the amount of snow lying in the glen. The white world stretched, sparkling in the light of a half moon rising up over the sea. A movement near the house caught Shona's eye. The deer had come down from the hills and were helping themselves to the remainder of the hay Donald had scattered for the sheep. High in the heavens, directly above Laigmhor's chimneys, a great star glittered; light splashed from the house to lie in orange pools under the windows. Ellie Dawn was entranced by the snow and reached down chubby fingers to pluck handfuls and throw them high in the air.

Despite her pain, Shona experienced a euphoria such as she had not known since childhood. 'Oh, Father, it's so bonny,' she cried, 'and that star, surely it's a good omen. Everything is going to be fine. Come morning a new life will be born into this beautiful world.'

'Ay,' he agreed gruffly, putting his arm round her, 'you were aye a one for this sort o' weather but I canny thole it and neither can the sheep. I just hope we got them all safely down from the hill earlier.'

'Ach, you're a fake,' she giggled, 'I've seen you wi' my very own eyes romping like a bairn in the snow, and the sheep are fine or you would have had plenty to say about it before now.'

The dogs went bounding ahead, delighting in the freedom, silent and purposeful in their sniffings and leg-liftings. Phebie and Elspeth were hurrying as best they could along the snow-bound track, holding each other up as the way got rougher and the slope more slippery, keeping their vision trained on Fergus who was leading the way with the storm lantern held aloft.

The minister was making sure Thunder's doors were shut when Megan came struggling awkwardly back to retrieve her bag from the rear seat, the high heels of her shoes no use at all on the treacherous ground.

'Here, let me help you,' he put out his hand as she came back with her bag, 'you'll get nowhere fast in those shoes.'

Without a word she bent to remove her footwear and, clutching both them and her bag to her breast, began to scrunch along in her stocking soles.

A muscle tautened in his face. He fell into step beside her. 'Quite the stubborn little madam, aren't you? And bad-tempered into the bargain. Poor Tina didn't know what hit her back there. She thinks the world of you too – always ready to champion you if need be.'

Once again crimson flooded Megan's cheeks and she hated herself for being so out of control of her emotions. He always did this to her, made her feel like a silly, awkward schoolgirl without any sophistication whatsoever. 'I don't need anyone to champion me as you put it,' she spoke coolly to hide her feelings, 'but I'm sorry about Tina. I like her and will most certainly apologize next time I see her.'

She started to hurry away from him, her foot slipped and down she went. Instantly he was beside her, scooping her up as if she was weightless, his teeth flashing at her look of complete outrage. Her angry face was very close to his, the silken wash of her glossy brown hair cascaded over his hands. Just for a moment she stayed perfectly still, gazing into his eyes, noting the firmness of his well-shaped mouth. Her heart began to beat too fast, an unbidden longing consumed her reason. His arms were warm and so very safe around her body and she recognized for the umpteenth time how powerfully attractive he was – attractive and dangerously persuasive. She cursed him, she cursed his magnetism, she cursed all men possessed with that fatally charismatic charm.

'Let go of me this minute!' she gritted, her fists coming up to beat uselessly against the hard wall of his chest. 'If you don't put me down I'll scream and scream till the whole of Rhanna comes running.'

'Oh, I'm sure they would find that a cakewalk in this weather.' His voice was perfectly calm and conversational, both facts inciting such anger in her that she began to writhe in his arms, to pull his hair, to dig her nails into his face till she felt skin breaking.

He was maddeningly cool. 'Stop behaving like a snarling little she-cat and for goodness' sake stay still or I'll drop you. It's Shona who's having the baby – remember. Only she has the excuse for tossing her body about in torment and it's high time you were up there seeing to her.'

With that he ran with her to the house, his long legs carrying him effortlessly through the snow. Megan glimpsed Elspeth's shocked countenance as they flashed past, and if she hadn't felt like crying she would have laughed her head off.

It was quite a party which staggered into Laigmhor's kitchen out of the bitter night.

Prior to the intrusion, Bob the Shepherd had been gazing restlessly up the lum, furiously puffing his pipe, Gaffer's head heavy on his knee, the dog's eyes peacefully closed though every so often, in common with his master, his attention had strayed to windows and doors as he listened for some sound to come out of the blizzard.

Kirsteen had been sitting on the seat opposite Bob, darning a pair of Fergus's socks, Tuffer's purrs reverberating on her knee. Every so often she had got up to open the door and look outside, straining her eyes for a sign of life in the white, empty wastes outwith the farmhouse.

Both she and Bob had been on edge ever since the latter had come limping in with a twisted ankle to say that Fergus and Davie had gone off in pursuit of Croynachan's bull and that he, Bob, had tried to follow them only to fall down heavily in the snow. 'I had a fancy I saw Shona and some other womenfolk on the road,' he reported gloomily, 'wi' that bugger Venus hot on their heels but the snow was getting heavier and I couldny right make head nor tail o' anything much.'

After that he had remained in the kitchen to await his tea while Kirsteen administered to his ankle. The table was set ready for the evening meal, the clocks ticked, peat sparks exploded in the lum. All was drowsing and peaceful in the interlude of waiting for the master of the house to come home. At the sound of voices Kirsteen jumped up, tense, waiting, and then the door burst open, shattering the peace of the slumbering room.

Mutt preceded everyone, his big, ungainly sodden feet skiting him indoors faster than he had intended. Behind him came Sporran, eager for the welcome that always awaited him at the friendly old house. It was too much for Gaffer. He was up, growling deep in his throat, not in the least swayed by the friendly lop-sided grin splitting Mutt's hairy, happy face. The sheepdog crouched, ready to spring, deaf to his master's commands to 'come away and be still'.

Bob forgot all about his ankle and made a lunge at the dog. Down he went, in amongst a pile of dogs, cats, and trampling feet as the humans came through the door in ones and twos, brought up by Mark James with Megan in his arms. No one had time to look askance at that last amazing sight, not even Elspeth who was too taken up with her own discomforts to bother with those of anyone else.

For a few minutes there was complete pandemonium. The dogs barked, the cats hissed, Ellie screamed with glee at the entire novelty of the evening, Bob cursed, everyone else was speaking at once.

Dazedly Kirsteen pushed her hair back from her eyes and wondered if she could possibly escape to have a nervous breakdown somewhere private. But order quickly emerged. Mutt and Sporran were shoved unceremoniously into the parlour while Gaffer was relegated to the lesser comforts of the barn. There he was quickly bullied into a cold corner by Sheil who wasn't in the least swayed by the fact that the pups she had been nursing peacefully before the intrusion were the boisterous offspring of the big bossy Gaffer. With the departure of the animals the kitchen became quieter and facts big and small weren't slow to emerge. All the womenfolk noticed Megan's hectic colour, the over-bright eyes, the ragged marks of her fingernails on the minister's temples and upper cheeks, but only Elspeth stared openly enough to make an issue of it and only she shook her head in a rank disapproval that said more plainly than words, 'Fancy our very own minister bearing the ravages o' passion for all the world to see and at the hands o' the doctor too. Heathens, the pair o' them! No' fit to tend animals never mind human beings.'

She muttered her way over to the fire to stare at it as if she was glimpsing hell fire, while everyone congregated round Shona as Fergus helped her off with her coat.

'Set her down here,' directed Kirsteen, indicating her own recently vacated chair.

'I'm not a sack o' tatties, you know.' Shona attempted jollity though she was very glad to sink into the cosy chair. 'Mark,' she took and held his hand. 'You've already been a Godsend but Niall will be wondering what's happened, Babbie too.'

'I'm on my way.' The minister lifted the lantern from the windowledge and turned to the door, whispering to Megan in passing, 'Just tell them it was a wildcat we met on the way up or Elspeth will never let you live it down – me either for that.'

'You deserve all the gossip that's coming,' she hissed back furiously. 'Don't expect me to lie for you – after all, aren't you the very one who preaches honesty from a raised dais every Sunday of your life?'

He brushed past her quickly, but not before she saw in his eyes an anger that very nearly matched her own for intensity.

Kirsteen handed round tea which was gratefully

received by everyone with the exception of Fergus who went bounding away upstairs to light fires in those rooms he thought might be needed. Kirsteen and Phebie followed close on his heels and so too did Megan, after she had checked to make certain that her patient wouldn't need her for a while.

'Mercy on us all,' Elspeth sipped her tea and stretched her booted feet to the fire's blaze, 'I needed that cuppy more than anything else. This is one experience I'll no' forget in a hurry. At my age I'm no' able to take the excitement o' a motor car journey over these treacherous roads.'

'Ach, you could hae stayed in your own house in Portcull and left the space in the motor for folk who needed it,' growled Bob, adding sarcastically, 'I am sure Phebie and Lachlan dinna need you to hold their hand every minute o' the day and night.'

'I prefer to bide at Slochmhor,' Elspeth imparted haughtily. 'Doctor and Mrs McLachlan are used to me doing for them and I am sure I don't mind the sacrifice if it means making certain they get all the attention they have become used to all these years.'

'Sacrifice!' snorted Bob. 'Looking to Lachlan and Phebie is no sacrifice to you and fine you know it. You make money out o' your house lettin' it out to visitors and are only too happy to bide at Slochmhor for your own convenience.'

He winced as Elspeth's stout footwear came in contact with his tender ankle. He and the old woman had been at loggerheads every since he had won a small fortune on the football pools, an event which had made him suddenly popular with the spinsters and widows of the island. Elspeth had been one of those who had tried to ingratiate herself into his affections with offerings of home baking and cooking and she had been among the first to be decanted from his doorstep in no uncertain manner. Since then, her attitude towards him had been distinctly offtaking which had made him avoid her at every turn. Now here she was, stuck beside him, her frost-purpled nose rapidly thawing to a bright red, the stiff little hairs on her upper lip positively bristling with self-pity, her thick tweed skirt visibly steaming as the fire's heat dried the damp out of it.

Shat coloured, that skirt, Bob decided to himself, shat coloured and shat smelling, like a yowe's fleece after a good soaking. 'Take your big feet off the hearth, woman,' he ordered sharply. 'Can you no' see my ankle's gone soft on me and needin' all the space it can get?'

Elspeth's lips folded, ''Tis more than your ankle's gone soft, 'tis your head forbye. A fine time to be mumpin' and moanin' about your own self when other folk have more than their own troubles to contend with. Where am I to sleep the night, I'd like to know? All I want is my own bed at Slochmhor and instead I'm stuck here wi' a bodach as selfish as Satan himself.'

Bob groaned. He was in for a night of it. He would never make it up to his biggin in this weather with this ankle – and his tea would be late in coming too, if ever. He glanced at Shona stretched out on her chair, little Ellie cooried sleepily beside her, and his heart melted.

'Och, Shona, my lassie,' he soothed in his lilting voice, 'wheesht now, you'll be fine in no time at all – ' he paused, the full import of the situation coming home to him. A baby would be born at Laigmhor that night and through the mists of memory he saw Mirabelle heating water on the range, billows of steam rising, Mirabelle plodding upstairs to take 'Bakin' sody' to Biddy who had had heartburn from too much rushing. And then the baby – this young woman with the bonny red hair falling over her face and her blue eyes brilliant with pain.

Struggling up, he went over to place an awkward arm round her shoulders. 'That bull o' Croynachan's brought this on, eh? I dinna ken much about women and bairns but I knew you wereny due for a whilie yet.'

'Ay, Venus is enough to make anyone have a bairn.'

Shona gripped the edge of the seat and shut her eyes. All she wanted was a cool bed and respite from prying eyes – Elspeth's eyes were always prying – and more than anything else just then she wanted Niall to come through the door.

'That buggering crazed brute,' Bob spat his anger into the fire, a sly grin touching his mouth as Elspeth scuttled hastily out of the way. 'Croynachan will need to give it back to the Department o' Agriculture. It's a fine beast, but just a bittie too frisky to be biding among civilized cratur's like ourselves.'

'Is that what you call yourself?' Elspeth turned a sarcastic face. 'The Vikings themselves had more common decency than some I could name hereabouts.'

Bob's faded blue eyes could still blaze fire when he was severely riled. They blazed now, so effectively Elspeth noticeably wilted under their glare. 'Ay,' he hurled, 'and they maybe just conveniently forgot it when they were plundering other folk's lands and ravishing the women – no' that you would have been in any danger o' that if you had been alive then, though mind – ' thoughtfully, he eyed Elspeth's wizened countenance – 'it wouldny surprise me if maybe you did go as far back as that. Wi' a face like that on you, you look as though you might have lived forever.'

'Will you two stop bickering like a couple o' bairns and do something useful wi' your time?' Fergus blazed as he came back to help Shona upstairs. 'We're putting you in your old room,' he told her as they ascended slowly upwards. 'I thought you would feel at home there. The bed has been moved out of the alcove to give more space all round.'

Shona sighed. Here was the little haven where she had spent her childhood, so full of happy memories the very walls seemed to have absorbed the laughter. For a moment she stood on the threshold, gazing round her with affection. *Her* room, the sunshine room, with its soft yellow curtains and gold-coloured carpet and its sense of happiness pervading every corner.

Without a murmur she allowed Kirsteen and Megan to undress her and help her into bed. Gratefully she slid between the cool sheets and closed her eyes. 'Oh, Kirsteen, this is bliss,' she murmured, 'I never thought I was going to make it, especially downstairs just now with Bob and Elspeth snarling at one another. How on earth are you going to manage having us all here?'

'Och, I'm used to folk arriving at the most unexpected times.' Kirsteen tried to sound lighthearted even while she tried to guide her seething mind into some semblance of order. Mentally she was working out how she was going to feed everyone, but Phebie soon solved that problem by appearing upstairs to announce she had made enough sandwiches to feed an army.

'I just grabbed cold mutton and eggs from the pantry and dolloped them in between layers of bread,' she said cheerfully. 'I'll bide wi' Shona for a while – you had better go down and see to your guests,' she added with a wicked twinkle.

Doors banged from the nether regions of the house, accompanied by deep male voices. 'It sounds as if more have arrived,' Kirsteen said with a groan, stepping back quickly as Niall came bounding in, bringing with him the cold sharp scent of frost. Going straight to the bed he took his wife in his arms and kissed the tip of her nose. '*Mo cridhe*,' he said into her hair. 'It looks as though we'll have our baby on Rhanna after all – thanks to that damned bull o' Croynachan's.'

'Och, Niall, it was meant to happen this way. I'm no' mad – I'm glad.'

Slower footsteps sounded on the stairs and Lachlan cáme into the room, his brown eyes smiling at sight of Shona. 'Just like old times, eh, *mo ghaoil*? I think you must have planned this. I wouldny be surprised if you told me there was some sort o' conspiracy between you and Croynachan.'

'Lachy McLachlan!' Phebie tried to sound severe. 'I

told the minister no' to let you come here the night. Look at you, frozen to the bone and too much o' a bodach to go tramping snowbound roads at the dead o' night.'

'I'll bodach you!' he protested indignantly. 'And you must be a cailleach if you thought I was going to sit alone at home contemplating my old age with all this excitement going on here.'

Babbie arrived, hat slightly squint on her thatch of red hair, green eyes sparkling with mischief as she threw herself down on a chair to fan herself with her hat. Oh, oft times had auld Biddy done the self-same thing and everyone in the room looked at the young nurse with affection, thinking to themselves how easily she had slipped into Biddy's place, both in manner and dedication.

'Stop gawping the lot of you,' she laughed. 'I know fine you're thinking that Biddy did this, that, the other, and I'm following in her footsteps. Well, I tell you now, I'll never work till I'm a cailleach ready to drop into my grave with my fingers raw to the bone. I'm far too fond o' my comforts for that so you get out that bed this minute, Shona McLachlan, and administer to *me* for a change. I've tramped for miles in hostile country thinking betimes – ' Biddy again, she laughed – 'I would never see Anton again, and after all that I had to tramp all the way back again with one distraught husband and one excited grandfather hauling me along in their hurry to get here – no' to mention a minister with legs on him made for stepping over hills in one giant stride.'

Megan glanced at all the appreciate smiles around her and wished – oh how she wished – she had Babbie's ease of manner and quick repartee. Just then a valiantly suppressed groan escaped Shona and Babbie was on her feet at once, a cool efficient little nurse, shooing everyone out, herding them to the door as if they were sheep.

'And don't come back unless it's necessary.' Megan

sounded too harsh and gave a rueful little smile when Niall turned and threw her a look of deep reproach.

In minutes the room was empty except for Lachlan hovering at the door to say a few last reassuring words to the woman in the bed.

'Lachlan,' Megan's voice stayed him, 'I didn't mean you of course – there's hours yet to go but when the time comes, perhaps you'd like to be here.'

But he shook his head. 'No, Megan, I'm retired now remember, and so feeble my wife thinks I should be tucked up by ten every night with a good book – a good book, mark you, perhaps she's of the opinion a bad book might be too much for my poor old heart.'

'Lachy!' Phebie's voice came indignantly from the passageway, and with a wink he went out to be seized by his wife and smacked hard on the bottom. 'You know fine you'd love to be there when the bairn comes,' she accused softly, 'that's the only reason you sprachled along that snowy road tonight.'

'Oh no,' his protest was too quick, 'I'd best get home once I've warmed my ancient bones with a cuppy.'

'Well I canny go and leave Kirsteen with all this mob to contend with,' Phebie spoke firmly. 'You're here now so you'll just bide where you are and make yourself useful.'

Babbie came to join them, closing the door behind her. 'Phebie's right,' she stated, picking up the conversation, 'for one thing we'll need a referee to control Bob and Elspeth, and both Niall and Fergus are going to need nursing through this night. They've started pacing already, I can hear them in the hall. Forbye all that,' she placed a persuasive hand on his arm, 'I would like you here, it will be like old times again – I've missed working with you and don't care who knows it.'

'Well, I do,' he sounded unusually stern though he kept his voice low. 'Megan's a good doctor, Babbie, and I had hoped you would have gotten into your stride with her by now.'

'Och, I have,' she spoke apologetically, 'but – oh hell! Why pretend? It hasny been easy, there are barriers there yet. She's shy and strange here still and just won't let herself unwind. Besides all that, I know she's a bittie nervous about Shona. She wanted her over on the mainland and now this has happened – I can feel her tension.'

'Och, alright,' Lachlan relented so willingly it brought smiles from the two women. 'But I warn you now, I won't go near that room again unless she asks me and that's final. Now I'm going down for a cuppy before Elspeth squeezes the pot dry.'

Shona tossed restlessly, hot and pain-racked and very, very glad that Kirsteen had thoughtfully tied her hair back with a blue ribbon she had found in the dresser drawer. That little blue ribbon had brought the memories rushing back, made all the stronger by the sight of Mirabelle's homemade rag dolls smiling down at her from the mantlepiece. The feeling of things past was very strong in the peaceful room, with the fire blazing cheerfully up the lum and the polished wood floor reflecting the orange flames. She could almost hear Mirabelle plodding upstairs with the jug of hot water to fill the rose-patterned china bowl on the dressing table, could almost feel the patient old hands tying the ribbons into her hair...

Overwhelmed suddenly, she felt the slow, helpless tears pricking her lids. 'I wish Mirabelle was here,' she choked miserably, 'auld Biddy too. Oh God, I loved them both and now they're gone and suddenly I feel very lonely – yet I haven't cried for either of them for years.'

Megan turned a hot face from the fireplace where she had been standing gazing quietly into the flames. She had heard the whisperings outside the door – and wished she hadn't. Those impassioned words of Babbie's had been low but distinct enough... Heaven help her! Would she ever fit in here? It might be better if she went away – back to the world she knew – but not back to Steven

Saunders, that handsome, charming creature who had said he loved her but had turned away from her when real beauty and perfection came along. He would be angry at her leaving him, he was the sort of man who always took the initiative in this sort of thing. If she hadn't come to this faraway island he would have come after her – and she couldn't take any more hurt, not yet... 'You really loved Mirabelle, didn't you?' she forced herself back to reality.

'Ay, I did that, she was the only mother I knew really, my own died having me – here, in this very house. It's strange, I've had three babies but never one born in this dear old house I love so much.'

'Three? But I thought...'

'I know. This afternoon I told you about my first little girl but I never told you about my son. I was only sixteen – and unmarried. It caused quite a scandal at the time but I didn't care. He was Niall's baby but he was away fighting in the war and knew nothing about it. By the time he came home it was all over. The little boy was stillborn – as perfect a mite as I ever saw – fair and bonny and as dead as last summer's roses.' She bit her lip and closed her eyes as a fresh contraction seized her. When it was over she opened her eyes to see Megan standing over her, a deep, sad uncertainty stamped across her young, attractive face.

'Don't be afraid, Megan,' she said softly. 'This baby is going to be fine, it's far too much o' a fighter to be anything else.' She frowned. 'Something bothers you all the time, doesn't it? You're lonely, lonely and afraid, that's what ails you and you'll never be happy till you get it out o' your system. At first I thought you were in control of all your emotions, people tend to think that about doctors. Ach, it's a shame when you think about it because underneath you're just as fragile and vulnerable as the rest o' us.'

Megan's face had turned white. There was something about this house, this room, this young woman with the wonderful blue eyes whose mother had died giving her life and who once knew someone called Mirabelle...

Suddenly Megan was very comforted by the fact that Lachlan was downstairs, calm and level-headed, and very much attuned to the McKenzies whom he had known all his days on Rhanna and who didn't overwhelm him as they tended to do her. She moved to the door. 'I'll bring you up a cup of tea. It seems to work miracles on the island.'

'I'd like a cuppy better.' Shona's dimples showed. 'It tastes far better than just an ordinary old cup of tea.'

'Right, one cuppy coming up – and I'll send Niall up with it. You've hours to go yet and I'm sure he's driving them all crazy downstairs with his pacing about.'

Chapter Five

It was snowing again. The wind had once more risen to blizzard force and went roaring round the house like an enraged lion. It banged on the door of the byre making the cattle moan uneasily in their stalls; the timbers of the stable shook till Myrtle, the big Clydesdale, snickered with fright and the dogs in the barn next door whined warningly and flattened their ears as if facing a tangible enemy.

Fergus and Mark James, storm lanterns held aloft, moved about checking the beasts, making sure everything was well and truly tied down before they departed back to the house in amicable companionship, smoking their respective pipes and saying little because that was the way both men liked to be when there was nothing to be said and a waste of breath saying it.

Fergus had always liked and respected the minister, and though he was no churchgoer he occasionally went along just to hear the other man's deep, soothing voice recounting sermons that for once made a lot of sense, they were so plain spoken.

At the kitchen door Fergus paused, his rugged face somewhat embarrassed when he said, 'I was lonely once, and in my lone, self-centred world I was convinced there was no other way o' life for me. But I was wrong, there was someone who was willing to share my life, to thole me as I was without trying to change me. The odds are in your favour, Mark, you're no self-centred pessimist and things will come alright for you in the end.'

It was a long speech for a man normally so thrifty with

words. Mark was taken aback. Through lacy curtains of snow he stared at Fergus, was about to enlarge on the subject but thought better of it on realizing that the other man had just made a statement, not an opening to a conversation. 'I'll come in for a wee while, then I'll get along home.' He stamped his feet to rid his boots of snow, turned and said briefly, 'Thanks, Fergus – for saying what you did. I'll remember it.'

They understood one another, there was no need for further words. Together they went into the house and back into the parlour where Fergus had lit the fire.

It had been a long time since the room had been used, and though the dry peats burned ferociously the air was still musty, the corners cold. Draughts moved the curtains, flurries of wind gusted down the lum, inciting sparks to crackle and race over the burning turf.

Old Bob stirred from a restless nap to prod the fire with the poker in an effort to keep the bitter cold of the night from seeping into his bones. He wished he was back in the cosy warmth of the kitchen but all the menfolk had come in here to escape the bustle of women in the other room, and Bob didn't fancy being in there 'among a cackle o' skirts'.

Phebie and Kirsteen had spent the last few hours making tea, heating water, and putting Ellie Dawn to bed, an event which had in itself proved a full-time occupation as she was so excited about the coming baby she simply wouldn't settle down to sleep. In the end Elspeth went upstairs with her and fell asleep exhausted beside the little girl, her bony arms lovingly clasped round a teddy bear. Ellie was fascinated by the sight, so overcome with the novelty of it all that she soon cooried down beside the old woman and sang herself to sleep.

Kirsteen, coming down to report the incident to Phebie, found that lady snoring in the ingle, her mouth falling open in her rosy face, her little contented snores tickling Tuffer's ears. Babbie, in a quest for coffee for herself and Megan, popped her head round the door and burst into chuckles at sight of Phebie. Flopping down in a corner of the ingle, she stretched her weary limbs and shook her head when Kirsteen enquired if there was any progress upstairs.

'No, the wee bugger is saving itself for better weather. It could be a few hours yet. Phebie's doing the wise thing. You ought to get to your own bed, Kirsteen, you've done all you can down here. There's so much steam in the room you could charge folk to come in and have a Turkish bath.'

But Kirsteen shook her head. 'No, I doubt if I could sleep. I'll just sit here with you for a while and have a quiet blether. I'm certainly not going into the parlour, Fergus only stopped in his pacing to go out with Mark to check on the beasts, and from what I can gather Niall and Lachlan are at it too. All three of them are driving old Bob loopy.'

They sat companionably together in the ingle, talking quietly, though Babbie remained alert for the least sign that would tell her she was needed upstairs.

No such state of peace existed in the parlour. Niall, Fergus, and Lachlan all paced together, keeping to their separate paths as if a set of invisible lines had been painted on the floor and was apparent only to them.

'All we need is a set o' traffic lights in here,' Bob muttered under his breath, 'tellin' them when to go and when to stop. 'Tis enough to make the head o' any sober man go round in circles.'

But Bob was far from sober. All the men had swallowed a few stiff drams and Bob's eyes closed drowsily. The only thing to do in a situation like this was to shut it out of sight and, with the drams warming his blood and weighting down his eyelids, he found that an easy enough matter – just as long as you ignored the squeaking of the loose floorboards lying on Niall's route and listened instead to the reassuring crackle of sparks flying up the lum.

*

Bob woke from a long nap and gazed round stiffly, as if hoping that he might have slept the night away and was expecting to find everything back to normal.

Seeing the three men padding the floorboards in exactly the same fashion as before, he shook his grey head in disgust and got creakily to his feet to go to the window and pull back the curtains. The clouds were thinning, drifting apart, once more exposing the cold face of the moon riding high above Sgurr na Gill. The world beyond the window was not the same one that had greeted him the previous morning. The wind had piled the snow into drifts that humped themselves over walls and hedges; little groups of trees were silvery-black etchings in the virginal fields; moon shadows lay everywhere; silver glints on the hills were icy burns tumbling down through the corries; huddled grey blobs that were sheep were cooried in the lee of walls and trees and might just have been boulders on the landscape but for an occasional movement here and there.

It was bonny. Old Bob drank in the beauty of it for a long time, though when he finally let fall the curtain his weather report was a gruff one. 'She's about blown herself out. Come morning the sun will be shining.'

'Might as well get some proper sleep, Bob,' advised Lachlan, 'it's the womenfolk who are holding the fort tonight.'

'Na,' Bob took one look at the restlessly prowling menfolk and rejected Lachlan's suggestion fiercely. 'Thankin' you kindly, Doctor Lachlan, but I think I'd be best off wi' the cats in the kitchen. I hear tell the wildest one o' them all has fallen asleep wi' the bairn upstairs so I'll be safe enough wi' Phebie and Kirsteen for a whilie.' Grumbling under his breath he limped through to the kitchen to find Kirsteen and Phebie asleep together in the ingle and a bedraggled Elspeth crouched over the fire sipping tea.

'That bairn,' she greeted him, 'she kicks worse than did my Hector wi' a bellyful o' drink. I'm black and blue all over and will be sore for a week – but ach, she's such a bonny, good wee thing and I was the only body wi' the knack o' getting her off to sleep.'

'Is there a droppy tea in the pot?' Bob asked cautiously, eying Elspeth's gloomy face with trepidation and wondering if he would be better off back in the parlour away from her 'viper's tongue'.

But a small glow burned inside Elspeth that night. Her 'cough bottle' reposed empty in her pocket, its contents having found their way into the numerous cuppies she had disposed of in the course of the last few hours. To Bob's surprise she answered his query affably enough and seemed actually pleased to have his company. 'Ay, that there is. Sit you down here by me and I'll pour you a cuppy.'

A strong brew warming his rheumy hands, Bob leaned forward and whispered confidingly, 'Between you and me, I couldny take any more o' that three in the parlour. Paddin' about like caged lions they are, all crashin' into one another every time one forgets the line he's supposed to be in. 'Tis as well the minister went home, he has a habit o' starin' up the lum as if he was glimpsing heaven.'

Elspeth raised her eyes to the ceiling. 'That he is – *her*,' she stated rather vaguely. 'The mannie is besotted by her – and him a man o' God whose thoughts should be as pure as the driven snow out there. She's a temptress that one, eyes on her as soft as a cow one minute and the next glintin' like a Jezebel at the very sniff o' a man.'

'Ach, but the minister's a lonely man, Elspeth, and the doctor a lonely young woman. You canny deny there's naught worse than loneliness in a man or a woman.'

Elspeth dropped her eyes, an action which caused little pockets of dry flesh to sag down over her cheekbones in wrinkled folds. 'Ay, you're right there but her loneliness is her own doing for she will no' let anybody near enough her heart to ease its soreness. Oh ay, that's what it is right enough. Doctor Megan didny just come to Rhanna for the good o' her health...' she lowered her voice to a ragged hiss, 'she came to escape a *man* – I saw it wi' my very own eyes.'

'How could you see it?' Bob sounded scornful.

'Well, you know how that Rachel Jodl moves in all thon fancy circles that are never out the gossip columns? Rachel sends the magazines to Ruth McKenzie seeing how she's interested in seedy literature like that. Well, I was in one day wi' a message for Lorn from his father and I saw one o' they magazines lying on a wee table innocent as you like. I thought it would do no harm to have a wee keek at it so I told Ruth I would like to look at the pictures and she gave it to me to take home.' Elspeth's eyes gleamed. 'There inside was an article about a man called Steven Saunders – a rich young playboy was how he was described, wi' his people owning a yacht building firm on the south coast. There was a picture o' the lad wi' a fancy woman hangin' on his arm. A right wee floosie she was too, wi' more than half her bosoms peepin' out her frock, but a title to her name nonetheless. The article said she was just one o' a string since his break-up wi' Megan Jenkins, a young doctor who had fled the scene more than a year since wi' her whereabouts unknown.'

'And will you be after spreadin' this over the island?' Bob asked peremptorily.

'Ach no, indeed I will not. I was never a one to spread gossip o' that nature as fine you know yourself,' she ignored Bob's derisive grunt and went on, 'it will all come out in the end anyway, things like that aye do, but the news will no' come from me. Though she is no' all she seems I have often felt sorry for the lass, for as you said yourself she is a lonely cratur'.' A calculated coyness crept into her voice as her garrulous mood swept her on, 'Ay Bob, I know fine what it is like. I've been lonely myself betimes since Hector's passing and have often wished the companionship o' a good man – nothing more than that,' she added hastily and primly, 'friendship, that is all.'

Bob's faded blue eyes blinked. For a moment he looked ready to up and run to the comparative safety of the male-dominated parlour, but suddenly a twinkle lit his face. 'I've felt that way myself since that wily bugger Joe went and married himself to Grace.' He sighed heavily. 'Ay, many's the night I'm cold up there in my biggin thinkin' o' Grace and Joe cosy and happy together in their house by the harbour, and wi' Captain Mac biding there now I see my changes o' Grace growing less and less.'

Elspeth's eyes gleamed. 'I know, I know! The disgrace o' it. I aye liked Captain Mac for he has manners on him even though he has spent most o' his life at sea, but never never did I think he would be as brazen as to move in wi' Grace and Joe, and the old man past caring about what goes on under his own roof. Mind, the bodach landed a good catch in Grace. She looks after him that well I doubt he might live for another hundred years yet – if the Lord spares him of course.'

'Ay, he might at that.' Bob settled himself back in his seat to delve one gnarled hand into the depths of his waistcoat pocket. From it he withdrew a very fancy hip flask, made of silver and leather with a little silver screw top attached by a chain. 'Will you hae a dram wi' me, Elspeth? I ken fine you are no' the sort o' woman to imbibe but this has been a strange sort o' night. I'm sure you will agree that a wee snifter will put us both on our feets.'

Solemnly Elspeth held out her cup. 'Just a wee tate,' she intoned graciously. 'As you say, I'm no' one to tipple in the normal way o' things but these past hours have been anything but normal.'

Bob was almost ashamed of himself as he uncorked the flask and poured a measure of spirits into Elspeth's cup – almost but not quite! It would do no harm to lead the woman on a bit. The besom deserved to have the wind knocked out her sails and, by God! He was going to enjoy doing it. For too long now her viper's tongue had spat its poison at him and for once he was going to get the chance of biting back!

At past two in the morning a baby's cry shattered the stillness of the house. A powerful cry it was too for such a tiny bairn, certainly loud enough to penetrate the thick old walls of the house and filter downstairs.

In the kitchen Elspeth and Bob stirred unwillingly from a companionable slumber, Kirsteen and Phebie sat bolt upright to rub sleep from their eyes and stare at one another in dawning delight.

'I slept, after all I slept!' wailed Kirsteen guiltily.

'Shame on you,' chuckled Phebie, 'and you a step-grandmother again. The bairn will never forgive you.'

In the parlour the men stirred on the couch where they had collapsed exhausted some time before, and looked at one another.

'It's here.' Niall's haggard face was disbelieving.

'Ay, it sound like it.' Fergus lifted his face upwards, listening.

'I'm a grandfather again.' Lachlan's weary brown eyes suddenly lit.

'So am I.' Fergus spoke a trifle shakily, his deep laugh springing to his throat.

'And I'm a father again.' Niall stared at the other two. Pandemonium broke out, they all began laughing and slapping one another.

'You have a son! And Shona's fine!' Babbie's joyous shout reverberated from the banisters. Everyone ran into the hall to gaze upwards at her triumphant face, Elspeth's spindly legs just as swift as younger ones, Bob's twisted ankle forgotten in the excitement of the moment.

'A McLachlan son.' Elspeth was so overcome with the

emotion of the moment she grabbed Bob and kissed him soundly on the lips. He recoiled, shock on his seamed countenance, then he remembered and the gleam returned to his eyes.

'Woman, woman! I never kent you possessed such passions!' he cried, advancing on her.

With a shriek she was off, scurrying back to the kitchen to shut the door soundly in his face. Banging on it, he shouted, 'Let me in, you daft cailleach. I only want to be alone wi' you for a whilie! Surely there's no harm in that?'

'Go you away, Bob Paterson, we're both far too old for such nonsense!' Elspeth's words were warning but a softness had crept into the querulous tones.

'If your idea is to play wi' her, you'd better no' take it too far, Bob,' laughed Phebie, 'she might just take you seriously.'

'A cat can play wi' a mouse,' answered Bob enigmatically, but retired from the door just the same as if he had decided that there was safety in numbers after all.

Niall was too dazed to take in much of anything, and could only shake his head in wonderment when his father grabbed hold of him and said, 'A son, Niall.' There was a glint of tears in Lachlan's brown eyes. 'I never thought I'd live to see the day.'

Niall could only nod, too filled with emotion to be able to express what was in his heart. Phebie hugged them both. 'Just wait till Fiona hears this. It's what she was praying for, a lad to keep on the McLachlan line.'

Megan came out to join Babbie at the banisters and said a few quick words in her ear. Both women looked very serious suddenly and when Niall shouted, 'Can I come up now?' Megan shook her head and said, 'Not yet, Niall, I want to see Lachlan for a moment.'

Everyone looked at everyone else as Lachlan left them to make his way upstairs.

*

'I don't believe it,' Megan drew a hand across her forehead. 'I just don't believe it – ' she stared at Babbie. 'How could I have missed it?'

'It happens,' Babbie ran a hand through her red curls and went over to the bed to smooth Shona's hair back from her brow.

'Where's Niall?' Shona spoke urgently, sweat breaking on her as fangs of pain gnawed at her.

'He's downstairs waiting to see his son, don't worry, everything's going to be fine.'

'I thought it was over,' Shona's knuckles were white on the bed rails, 'what's wrong, Babbie? I have a right to know what's happening.'

Babbie sat down heavily on the bed, her freckles vivid in the translucent pallor of her tired face. 'Weesht, Shona,' she soothed. 'Lachlan is just coming. You mustny fret, just stay calm and you'll be fine.'

'Oh, it's fine for you to talk, Babbie Cameron – I mean Büttger. You've never had a baby, you don't know what it's like!'

Babbie forced a grin. 'That's the Shona I know best – fiery tempered, fighting like a hell cat.'

Tears sprung to the other's eyes. 'Och, I'm sorry, Babbie, I don't know what I'm saying – it's just – I'm afraid.'

'I know.' Babbie kept her eyes on the door, willing Lachlan to come through it quickly.

Gently Lachlan smoothed the hair from Shona's brow and said in a strange, bubbly sort of voice, 'Shona, *mo ghaoil*, in my day I've been shocked, surprised, delighted at some o' the things my patients sprung on me. I truly believed these days were done with but you've proved me wrong, lass, the McKenzies have done it again.'

'Lachlan! What on earth are you havering about?' Shona cried. 'Done what? What's wrong with me?'

'Nothing, lass, everything's right.' He was jubilant, his

eyes snapping merrily in his thin, sensitive face. 'You're going to have another baby, that's what – the wee devil should arrive anytime now.'

'Twins!' Shona sat bolt upright. 'But how could I be? I know I was bigger this time than with any o' the others – but twins!'

'Oh, it can happen more times than you would believe and they have a habit of running in your particular family. Megan missed it because it was probably lying in a position that made it difficult to detect...'

With a wild whoop Shona was kissing him, kissing Babbie, totally incoherent with amazed joy. Megan stood a little way apart, watching the scene, her face hollow with weariness and something else – an anxiety that she couldn't hide, not even when Lachlan came up and took her hands. 'She's all yours again, Megan, it won't be long now. I'll save a good big dram for you when it's over with.'

'Oh, Lachlan,' she burst out in a miserable whisper, 'I feel such an inadequate fool – how could I have missed it? I should have known but I didn't – I didn't.'

'Megan, come out here for a minute.' He led her out to the passageway and made her face him. 'Now just you listen to me, my girl. This can happen to the best o' us, believe me. There's a dozen reasons for twins to go undetected, especially in a woman who's had several bairns. Whatever you do, don't blame yourself.'

He shook her a little and smiled, that slow, warm smile that had soothed so many of his patients. 'You get back in there with pride in your heart and no more nonsense concerning your so-called inabilities.'

She gave a watery sniff and smiled back. 'Alright, but only if you come with me. Oh, come on now, you're longing to, I know – and,' the smile deepened, 'just think how exciting it is – now knowing if it's another boy or a girl.'

He gave a shout of laughter. 'You're on – and I bet five pounds it will be another boy.'

'I say a girl.'

'Right then, Doctor Megan, let's get in and find out. But first, spare me a wee minute. Both Niall and Fergus are going daft down there thinking the worst. I want to see their faces when I break the news.'

Chapter Six

The atmosphere in the kitchen was even more electric than it had been in the parlour some hours before. Fergus and Niall, tension oozing from them, were back to their pacing while Kirsteen and Phebie, in an effort to fill the anxiety-laden time, were seated together at the fire, darning and knitting respectively.

Elspeth had fallen asleep, her boisterous grunts and snores filling the silent room and making Fergus more irritable than ever.

Bob was frankly drunk, a state he had decided was the only sensible one to be in with everyone at such fever pitch.

'Fergus,' Kirsteen sighed and looked up, 'couldn't you sit down for a wee while? You're wearing out the rug and you'll get holes in your socks again. At least put on your slippers. Why you have to pad about in your stocking soles is beyond me. Ruth gave you a lovely pair of slippers last Christmas and you've never even had the good manners to try them on yet.'

For answer he went to the door for the umpteenth time that night and looked out. The storm had long abated, the morning sky was awash with moon and stars that bathed the virginal landscape in a blue, ethereal light. Moving outside he stood for a long time, breathing deeply, remembering the last time twins had been born at Laigmhor.

Fluffy white clouds were piled on top of Sgurr nan Ruadh with silver edges to them and strange shapes like ghost faces in the moonlight.

'A fluffy cloud morning.' The voice of Lewis, his dead son, seemed to sigh on the breeze blowing down from the hills...

'Fergus McKenzie! Put these on this minute or you'll catch your death.' Kirsteen was beside him, stooping down to push his sodden feet into slippers. Pulling her up, he held her close to nuzzle his lips into her hair. 'I was thinking o' Lewis, remembering how it was when he and Lorn ran and played here as tiny bairns. I mind o' a time just like this, the new snow soft on the ground, Lewis out with his sledge, forgetting Lorn in the excitement o' the moment – '

'Oh yes, I remember that time too.' Kirsteen put her fingers to her mouth and stared into the distance as if seeing the scene unfolding before her vision. 'Lewis was halfway down the slope when he looked back and saw Lorn watching him from the fence. He was off that sledge so fast he almost broke his neck and then he came running back up the brae to grab Lorn and help him down to the sledge – but,' she glanced up at him, tears in her eyes, 'it was such a small thing yet – you remembered.'

'It's the little things I remember most, *mo cridhe*,' his voice was husky, 'about our children – about our lives together in this house.'

'And now it begins all over again.'

'Ay, and I wish to God this night would end...' He stiffened. From somewhere above, a thread of sound penetrated into the dreaming morning. 'Kirsteen, did you hear that? Was it a baby – or a cat?'

There was movement within, an instant awakening that brought the whole house to life. Niall came rushing out to whirl Kirsteen round and kiss her, the next instant, in his excitement forgetting himself completely and kissing Fergus also.

Both men erupted into gales of laughter that released the raw tensions of the night. They shook hands, kissed Kirsteen all over again and, tripping each other up, they all rushed back inside to demand, 'What is it? Does anyone know yet?'

Bob reeled to his feet, held his glass high and hiccuped. ''Tis a baby! Unless o' course it's pups! May God bless her and all who sail in her.'

'Bob Paterson, you're drunk.' Elspeth spoke thickly for she was as drunk as he and looked almost attractive, with her grey hair falling in disarray over her face and a flush on her cheekbones lending sparkle to her eyes. 'You've got holes in your shocks,' she observed in slurred tones, 'and your feets are non to clean either. 'Tis high time you had a good woman to see to you, ay just.'

'And will it be yourself having that priv – that priv – that honour?' Bob slurred, pulling her against him to rub his whiskery chin against her thin cheek.

'Bob Paterson! You're a God-forshaken barbarian, that you are!' The admonishment strangled in her throat, she landed back in the rocking chair with a thump and a hiccup, her black clad legs zooming high in the air as the chair shot backwards on its rockers.

'Ay, ay, they're white I see,' chortled Bob, his inebriated state daring him to hook one horny thumbnail into her knicker elastic and let it go with a decided ping.

Her outraged yells went unheeded. There were feet on the stairs, swift feet that forgot to be tired in their hurry to reach the kitchen. Babbie stood in the doorway, green eyes lit, red hair a rumple of colour in the lamplight. 'Guess – everybody guess what it is,' she imparted breathlessly.

'Oh, Babbie, don't,' pleaded Kirsteen.

'I'll carry you outside and roll you in the snow,' threatened Niall grimly.

'I'm all yours,' she grinned mischievously, then, as he descended on her, 'och, alright, spoilsport. It's a girl, a beautiful little girl, all red and wrinkly and bald but decidedly beautiful for all that. Now – don't all rush me at once, men first, preferably fathers – they're more experienced.'

'You're immoral, Babbie Büttger, always was and always will be.' Niall folded her in his arms and pressed a kiss on her mouth. 'And you're the finest wee nurse this island could have – Biddy would be right proud o' you.' He turned away quickly. 'A girl.' He spoke the words aloud for his own benefit and no one tried to stop him when he went quickly outside to savour a few richly deserved moments of solitude.

Megan placed a new little bundle in Shona's arms. 'There you are, Shona, your daughter, and you've earned every inch of her.'

Shona lay back exhausted, every fibre in her body craving for rest so that she was almost too weary to lift her hand to the little head that cooried in warm to her breast. But her eyes were very bright when she looked over at Lachlan standing by the fireplace. 'Lachlan, look at her. Yesterday I never knew she existed, today she's here, warm and real.'

'I know, lassie, quite a surprise for you – for us all – a special gift from God.'

'Ay, a gift, that's what she is – and now, can I have her big brother to hold just for a whilie? I want to stare at them both till I fall asleep.'

Megan went through to the room once shared by Lorn and Lewis. From the old family cradle that had rocked generations of McKenzie babies she lifted the little boy and bore him back to his mother who kissed the small fair head.

'I feel as if my son and my daughter have somehow been given back to Niall and me – ' Shona looked up. 'I just know it's a bonny morning, all clean and sparkling under the stars.'

Lachlan blew out the lamp and opened the curtains before he and Megan went quietly out of the room.

Shona lay back. The sky outside the window sparkled with pinpoints of light. 'Thank you, God,' she said simply and closed her eyes, her babies snug and warm in her arms.

Outside the door Megan smiled at Lachlan. 'You owe me five pounds, Doctor Lachlan.'

He linked his arm in hers. 'I owe you much, much more, Doctor Megan. You let me share that wonderful moment back there and I'm indebted to you for that.'

'Well, it isn't every night a man gets to become a grandfather twice over – I still can hardly believe it.'

'Me neither – but I soon will when the womenfolk start skirling in my lugs and the talk is nothing but babies from now till next Christmas!'

'This is for you.' It was morning and Fergus, coming in from the barn with a tiny black and white bundle in his arms, looked haggard in the searching wintry sun streaming in through the kitchen window. 'She's the one you wanted and you might as well have her now. She's a quiet wee thing and the rest are giving her a hard time o' it.'

Megan took the trembling little dog to her bosom and kissed the tip of the black, button nose. 'She's adorable. I love her already and I don't know how I can ever thank you, Mr McKenzie.'

His dark brows knitted. 'The name is Fergus, only strangers get called mister around here – and Megan,' roughly he took her hand, gripping it so hard that she winced, 'you're a fine doctor and I thank you for everything you did for my daughter last night.'

Megan was so stunned she could say nothing and went quickly to the door to hide her discomfiture.

'A big speech from a very silent man.' Kirsteen smiled as she caught up with the doctor and walked her to the gate. 'From this day forward you can do nothing wrong in the eyes of McKenzie o' the Glen.'

'But – I only delivered babies,' Megan replied in bewilderment, 'I've brought dozens into the world.'

'Ah – but these were Shona's babies, there lies the difference,' nodded Kirsteen wisely. 'Fergus loves all his children but Shona is his only daughter and she has always been very special to him. When Helen, his first wife, died, he had no interest in anything for a long time, not even his own daughter. When he finally came to realize how much she meant to him he became terrified of harm coming to her.'

'I see,' Megan nuzzled the pup's downy ears. 'Thank God everything went well, then. I dread to think how he would have reacted otherwise.'

'When Helen died he blamed Lachlan for it,' Kirsteen explained quietly. 'For years they didn't speak. It was only after Fergus lost his arm that things became right between them. I'm only telling you all this because what happened here last night will spark off a lot of old memories amongst the older ones who will take a delight in recounting them to you.'

Megan took a deep breath and lifted her face to the hills. It was a beautiful morning. The island sparkled in an excess of sunshine that threw long shadows over the fields and turned the winter bracken a deep bronze shade. Since dawn the villagers had been out with shovels clearing snow from Downie's Pass to allow traffic through. It had been the sound of voices that had awakened Laigmhor from a few hours of hastily snatched sleep. Phebie, Lachlan, and Elspeth had all departed after breakfast, soon after that Anton had come for Babbie in his tractor.

Megan longed to tumble into her own bed and give herself up to the luxury of complete relaxation but morning surgery started in an hour and she had been wondering how she would ever get through it. But now, with the cold hill air filling her lungs and the island shimmering under the sun, she felt wide awake and wonderfully alive. Perhaps it was because Fergus McKenzie had thanked her so sincerely and called her Megan, and that somehow his very acceptance of her made her feel suddenly welcome on the island. She didn't know, but she felt good and whole within herself for the first time in months and the smile she turned on Kirsteen held a great deal of vitality. 'Thank you for telling me the things you did. I'll get along now.'

'Are you sure you won't let Fergus run you home in the tractor?'

Megan laughed. 'No, Anton already offered but I want to walk. It's such a bonny morning.'

'And your Welsh is becoming more Scottish with every passing day. Och well, you had better go – at least you'll get along quicker wearing the proper footwear.'

Megan looked down at her feet which were enclosed in a pair of Kirsteen's own stout Wellingtons. 'I'll have to get a pair. I keep forgetting I'm no longer in the city and must stop wearing those flimsy high heels of mine.'

'Oh no,' Kirsteen pretended horror, 'the cailleachs would have nothing to talk about then. Behag positively bristles with self-righteous condemnation whenever she hears your heels tapping along. You wouldn't want to spoil her little pleasures – would you now?'

'Perish the thought, she would die altogether if the entire population of Rhanna became so perfect she would have nothing left to excercise her tongue on.' With a cheery wave she walked away down the track and onto the road. The dark head of Mark James appeared out of what looked like a gigantic snowball but which was in fact his motor car smothered in a drift. 'I don't think I'll be able to dig her out yet.' His grin was less than rueful as he unwound his long legs from the driver's seat and got out, Mutt close on his heels.

'Legs were invented before wheels,' Megan imparted airily, surprised at how gladly her heart welcomed the sight of him.

'Ay, and bare feet before shoes,' he replied smartly, a glance down at her feet bringing a cheeky grin to his face. 'I see you've found sense at last – though mind, they do nothing for your legs.'

'You impudent bugger,' she smiled back at him, noting the little laughter crinkles at his eyes, the way those eyes shone in his rugged face yet were so fathomless she could easily have lost herself in their smoky depths.

'Will you let me walk with you?' His request was irrelevant, he was already falling into step beside her.

'Only if you say you're sorry about last night. You made a fool of me in front of everyone. Elspeth nearly had apoplexy.'

'I know,' he choked mirthfully. 'It was a joy to see her face and I'm not going to apologize for any of it. I loved every minute of holding you in my arms and wish I could do it more often.'

'Mark,' she said warningly.

'Alright. If it makes you happy I'll say "sorry" even though it's a bittie self centred of you not to even dream of returning the compliment. I still get the feeling I was attacked last night by a wildcat. Kirsteen was so sorry for me she bathed my wounds and even put antiseptic on them in case they started to fester.'

Her eyes were drawn guiltily to the trails of ragged scratches down one side of his forehead. 'It was rather drastic of me,' she conceded unwillingly, 'but at the time I didn't care what I was doing and would again if I had to – though I am sorry I marked you so badly.'

'A real heartfelt apology,' he chuckled, 'my cat could have done better but has never had the need since her claws aren't nearly as dangerous as yours.' He glanced at the pup. 'I see you've acquired your new companion. Have you given her a name yet?'

'I thought perhaps Muff, she's so soft and warm.'

'Muff – it sounds a bit daft.'

'So does Mutt, but it suits him – he is daft.'

He looked at her. She was laughing. For the first time since coming to Rhanna she was really laughing, her hazel eyes shining with amber lights, her cheeks aglow, her hair a warm coppery brown against the backdrop of white.

'What happened, Meggie?' he said quietly. 'Last night you were tired and angry, today you're alive and happy.'

'I don't know, Mark. Everything just seems better, more wonderful – the new babies, the puppy, Fergus calling me Megan and thanking me, the beauty of the morning. You and me, not fighting each other anymore but just being natural. I feel as I used to feel before... Och well, I think I'm finding myself again and it's a very nice feeling, Mark.'

'Morning, Minister – Doctor.' Behag was at the door of the Post Office, brushing snow from the doorway with a moth-eaten besom, her palsied head seeming to nod its full approval of the young couple on the road though her knowing beady eycs instantly nullified the illusion.

'And to you, Miss Beag,' came the polite chorus.

'I see you've been in the wars, Minister,' Behag peered into Mark's face. 'I only ever saw these once afore on a man's face.' She folded her lips meaningfully. 'Thon time Ruth McKenzie nearly scratched Lorn's eyes out his head. A terrible thing just, a Christian lass behaving like a heathen, but then she had good reason to do as she did wi' him carrying on behind her back. Sinful it was, ay sinful, though he got his comeuppance for that piece o' nonsense and serve him right too.'

'Yes indeed, Miss Beag,' agreed the minister before he and Megan made good their escape, hiding their giggles behind their hands as they knew full well that the post mistress's eagle eyes watched their progress along the village street.

'I told you we'd never live it down,' Megan hissed at him.

'Ach, forget Behag, her and her like can talk their heads off and never know the truth of what happened. It's between you and me and I really think we ought to call a truce and be friends again. Can we?'

'Yes, I think we can, as long as it's out in the open like this where we can be seen.'

It was enough for Mark James. He was very happy as he walked with Megan into Portcull where the chimneys smoked peacefully in the bright winter sunshine.

'What will we call them?' Shona wondered, glancing from one new baby to the other, her eyes very blue in the sweet pallor of her face, the sense of awe which had flooded her being since the moment of wakening from a deep, refreshing sleep, growing more intense as the full enormity of last night's happenings came home to her.

Niall shrugged, equally bemused by the turn of events. 'I don't know. I canny take in the fact that we've got two new babies let alone dream up names for them.'

Her eyes glinted with mischief. 'How about something really fancy? Like the names these Hollywood film stars bestow on themselves. Gail and Storm – they arrived in a blizzard so what could be more appropriate?'

'You dare!' he exploded in a burst of laughter. 'Can you imagine it! Storm McLachlan! Father would never forgive us and Mother would have a fit!'

Ellie came toddling through to climb in beside her mother and coorie down comfortably, her little hands gently stroking the heads of her new brother and sister.

'Santa brought them,' she decided, abandoning her mother's teachings in favour of a more romantic delivery.

'That's it!' Niall cried, lifting up his little girl and whirling her round the room. 'They're Christmas babies so we'll give them Christmas names – simple names, like Joy –'

'And Joseph,' Shona finished triumphantly. 'They have a ring to them, Joy and Joseph.'

'Joseph Niall McLachlan,' he decided.

'And Joy Shona McLachlan.' She held out her arms. 'Come on, into bed the lot of you, the whole McLachlan family.'

'Five of us now,' he said in fresh wonderment.

'Ay, we're a complete family again.' She looked at him. The years rolled back, engulfed them both with memories, evoked a tear, a silent sharing of grief for a little boy lost, a darling daughter taken in the morning of life. Their hands touched, love pulled them back to sweet reality, the void was closed, wounds healed. They smiled at one another in fulfilment and peace.

'We'll have a ceilidh,' he vowed, 'the finest Christmas celebration ever.'

'With Santa,' nodded Ellie.

'Ay, with Santa.'

'And a sack.'

'A sack too.'

Ellie clapped her hands. 'Filled with babies!' she screeched and fell about laughing at the very idea of such a ridiculous thing.

Chapter Seven

'Fancy, two o' them – at her age. I'll say that for her, she never did things by halves.' Behag, having closed the Post Office for half an hour to 'go her messages', stamped the snow from her boots, plunked her shopping bag on the counter of Merry Mary's shop, and settled back for a good chinwag. Since her retiral, Behag had a lot more time on her hands and often harked back to her days as the Portcull post mistress as she liked to refer to herself. Occasionally though, Totie and her husband Dugald took time off from both the Post Office and the little corner grocery shop still known to everyone as Merry Mary's. It was then that the two retired ladies came into their own once more and though Behag wouldn't admit as much, she liked nothing better than to get back behind the counter of the Post Office, there to observe and comment on all aspects of village and island life. She was in full fettle that morning, having rearranged Totie's cubby holes and drawers to her own liking and taking the opportunity to show everyone that the Post Office premises had never been the same since she had signed them over to Totie's more relaxed regime.

'I have cleaned, polished and dusted,' she informed Merry Mary with a self-satisfied toss of her scrawny head. 'If you ask me the place has never been touched since the last time I took a broom to it. I have never seen so many spider's webs in the corners and, of course, the floor has never tasted a lick o' polish for months.'

'Well, I canny say the same for this place,' Merry

Mary was determined to be fair. 'It is that clean you could eat your dinner off the counter though mind, I have no time for the way Doug allows boxes to pile up in the back shoppie. I was aye proud o' how neat I kept it myself and could just lay my hands on whatever I was looking for – now, what were you blethering about when you came in my door just now?'

Despite the condition of the roads, the news of Shona's babies hadn't taken long to filter over the island and, since the shore roads were comparatively clear, the usual small knots of humanity had gathered in favourite meeting places where gossip could be dispensed with comfortably if not always companionably.

'Ach, about Shona McKenzie's confinement of course,' Behag imparted with asperity. 'You're surely no' telling me you haveny heard about it.'

'Of course, the bull had a lot to do wi' it.' Kate buried her cherry red nose into her hanky, emerging to add, 'And the bugger gave me the cold forbye. All thon draughts from the hall door opening and me having to crawl home late wi' snow up to my een.'

'The bull never gave her twins!' exploded a round-eyed Mairi. 'I think 'tis only fair Niall should get the credit for that.'

'Ach, Mairi,' reproved Kate irritably. 'Have you nothing at all between your lugs but stale air? That bull o' Croynachan's was the cause of all the trouble. It wouldny surprise me in the least if Tom decided to send the bugger back to the Department.'

'Och no, he'll no' be doing that.' Nancy came breezing in, brushing snow from the manly trousers she had worn for the journey down to the village in her husband's tractor. 'One o' the roadmen brought a message to Croynachan from Laigmhor this very mornin'. I saw it when I looked in to see was Mamie needin' any messages from the village.'

'Oh ay, and what was it after saying?' asked a curious chorus.

'Wouldn't you like to be knowing?' beamed Nancy, her dimples deepening as she recalled to mind Shona's note which read: *Give Venus a second chance. By some miracle I've had two babies instead of one and it was all Niall could do to persuade me not to call one of them Aphrodite.* 'You wouldny understand it anyways,' Nancy went on rather loftily, 'Tom had to explain it to me, him being a keen reader o' thon highbrow books. It was something to do wi' Greek mythology and names wi' fertile meanings.'

'Ay, it would be,' Behag sniffed darkly. 'Shona McKenzie was aye a one for things like that. There will be no living wi' her now she's the mother o' twins.'

'Ach well, they run in the family,' Nancy said comfortably, her round, attractive face softening as she went on, 'and is it no' beautiful just? Her having a wee lad and a lass? I mind fine the time she lost her first wee boy and then when our own Ellie died I near died myself wi' the pain. She was such a bonny, bright girl – aye singing and happy to be alive.'

'Ay, right enough.' Behag's jowls relaxed as she recalled the times Shona's daughter had brightened the Post Office. 'She was a dear good wee thing and surely the nicest cratur' ever to come out the McKenzie family.'

'She was a McLachlan,' Barra reminded her sister-in-law. 'As much Niall's daughter as Shona's.'

'She came out a McKenzie woman.' Behag glowered into Barra's pleasant plump face, her mood not improved when Robbie sprang to his wife's defence by nodding and smiling in complete agreement. 'Oh ay, a McLachlan right enough.' Merry Mary emerged from behind a pile of shopping bags on the counter. 'Just as the two new babes are McLachlans and will be proud o' it someday. And here – ' she threw some battered-looking oranges into the nearest bag ' – is it no' lovely just? A son to carry on the McLachlan name. My, my, our own Lachlan will be a proud and happy man this day and I for one think we should all have a wee dram to celebrate wi' him.'

'Amen to that.' Tam rubbed his hands briskly when Merry Mary produced a bottle of whisky from under the counter and went through to the back shop to look for glasses.

'You canny take strong drink in these premises.' Behag spoke in a shocked hiss as Merry Mary came back bearing glasses and a bottle of sherry for less hardened palates.

'Oh can we no' just?' Robbie gleefully told his sister. 'But seein' you don't approve, Behag, you can aye go home and hae a quiet sup from that wee bottle you used to keep hidden in the salt girnel.'

Behag's scraggy jowls tautened as a titter ran through the assembly. Never never would Robbie have dared to speak to her like that in the old days when he and she shared the family house! It was the influence of that Barra. She had been too long in the city for her own or anyone else's good, bringing her wild, uncivilized ways to a God-fearing island like Rhanna, and casting her influence over a weak man like Robbie... Behag licked her dry lips as whisky and sherry flowed into glasses – a wee tate would do no harm on a cold day like this... She was about to accept a glass graciously for the sake of welcoming the McLachlan twins into the world when Holy Smoke sidled in beside her and beamed his dry, insincere approval all over her.

'You are a fine upright woman, Miss Beag, and are quite right no' to allow one drop o' the de'il's brew to touch your lips.'

Behag was furious. Holy Smoke, real name Sandy McKnight, was a small, bedraggled bachelor with mournful features much like Behag's own, including drooping 'bloodhound' eyes and layers of sagging flesh about his neck. From his shiny bald head there sprouted a few pathetic sandy hairs, the same colour as the sparse straggling moustache which strived vainly to disguise a perpetually downcast mouth. His expression was as dour as his nature though it underwent a metamorphosis whenever money was discussed, mentioned, or produced, especially over the counter of the tiny butcher's shop he had recently opened in Portcull. A crofthouse and a sizeable croft had gone with the cramped, wooden premises that had once been a saddler's, and when Holy Smoke wasn't in his shop he was out there in his fields seeing to his beasts and his poultry, too tight-fisted to hire a man to do it for him.

His attendance at kirk was faithful and pious as were his denouncements of the evils of tobacco and spirits, though from the day Todd the Shod spied him smoking a pipe behind a rock on the seashore his opinions were as much worth as the nickname Todd had immediately bestowed on him.

Ever since his arrival, and for some obscure reason known only to him, he had attached himself firmly to Behag, and the dour old post mistress, perhaps seeing her own personality reflected in his, shuddered every time he opened his mouth. Her dislike of him was fiercely intense, an emotion that deepened with each passing day, for no matter how spiteful her tongue, how cutting her manner, it was like water off a duck's back for all the good it did her. Her feelings were further strengthened by all the teasings and jibes his advances brought raining down upon her palsied, disapproving head, so that Behag positively shrunk into her already shrunken frame every time Holy Smoke was near enough to breathe the same air as herself.

Now her pinched nostrils dilated, she threw him a look that would have shrivelled a worm and in a high-pitched, defiant voice she intoned, 'I'll be having a dram wi' the rest o' you, if you would be so good, Mary. After all, it's no' every day twins are born on the island.'

The sniggers and elbow nudging died away, Merry Mary scratched her ginger head in bemusement. 'Will it be sherry, Behag?'

'No, it will be whisky, Mary.' Behag's head fairly

shook with the occasion of the moment. 'A good stiff one at that. 'Tis a cold day and I will no' be going back outside wi' frozen blood.'

'Miss Beag,' Holy Smoke spoke reprovingly, 'I canny rightly believe this. Are you feeling unwell? You're no' being like yourself and that's a fact.'

'I am well enough,' Behag's voice shook. Grabbing the glass from Merry Mary she raised it high and cried, 'Health to the new McLachlan bairns,' and downed the contents in one gulp.

There was a short stunned silence during which Holy Smoke seemed about to have apoplexy, the rest stared in wonder at Behag, particularly Robbie whose round, blue, unblinking gaze seemed stamped upon his countenance forever. During his bachelor years his sister's narrow outlook and strict adherence to all things she considered proper had caused him to suffer a life of unrelieved hell. 'She's human,' he breathed in Barra's ear, 'after all, she's human.'

'Behag,' with reverence Tam removed his cap, 'you are a man among women and I take my hat off to you.'

'Ay, you have a seasoned throat on you, Behag, and no mistake,' Barra looked askance at her sister-in-law. 'In all my days in the city I only ever saw one woman do that and it was in one o' the roughest houses I've ever been in.'

Behag inclined her head, an action which lent her the appearance of a lop-sided bloodhound with her eye bags tilted floppily and the lobe of one big rubbery ear escaping her headscarf to brush against her narrow shoulders. 'Maybe you were lookin' in a mirror at the time, Barra,' she suggested acidly, grinning quite good-humouredly when Barra went off into one of her infectious laughing fits, plonking herself down on a sack of tatties to throw up her hands, open her mouth and give her lungs full throttle.

Everyone, bar Holy Smoke, joined in her mirth and it was with tears streaming down her face that Barra raised hcr glass to toast the new McLachan bairns.

'The McLachlan bairns.' The toast was echoed all around. 'And God bless our very own Mr James for getting Shona safely home,' added Kate. 'If it hadny been for him she might have had her babies in the village hall or at best in my house.'

The doorbell jangled to admit Dodie, more unkempt-looking than ever, a week's stubble darkening his spotty chin, ungloved hands blue with the cold, pale sad eyes watery and sunken, the biggest drip anyone had ever seen dangling from a nose nipped raw by the keen air. All his life Dodie's big feet had carried him swiftly and effortlessly over all sorts of terrain, now his worn Wellingtons scliffed the floorboards as he dragged himself over to the counter and requested in a courteous whisper, 'Half an ounce o' baccy, Mary, and it's sorry I am just the money is all in halfpennies.'

The first instinct of everyone there was to move away from the old eccentric's vicinity. He had never been particular about personal hygiene, considering it only necessary to bathe for such grand occasions as weddings or funerals, and to resort to the less drastic measures of feet steeping for other island events. Everyone, while accepting him as he was, could never quite reconcile themselves to his smell, though only by innuendo had anyone ever indicated that he fell short of the norm, for he was as easily hurt as a child and it was a pitiful sight indeed to see the tears pouring down his guileless weather-beaten face and one which was to be avoided if at all possible.

'One good thing about Dodie,' Grandma Ann had often said, 'he couldny smell any worse if he tried and a cut onion is as good as any antiseptic I know to dispel thon awful guff you get from his feets, especially when he is moving afore the wind. 'Tis a habit o' mine to carry a wee bittie onion in my pouch just in case Dodie stops me for a blether at any time. Granda John says I'm the only woman he knows who smells perpetually o' onion scent but far better that than be gassed to death.'

But Grandma Ann was wrong about two things. Dodie could smell worse, a condition easily achieved by simply ignoring the existence of soap and water, and the pungent odour of onion juice did *not* cancel out every other smell, Merry Mary discovered that when she rushed to cut two onions and place them near a heap of papers on the counter. Dodie's overpowering aroma gushed forth, triggering off a spate of coughings. Hastily the men lit pipes, billows of smoke clogged the atmosphere, making everyone cough afresh and Holy Smoke to glower and eye the door as if calculating how quickly he could get outside and have a fly smoke himself.

Merry Mary scrunched her finger tips over the small pile of coppers on her counter, keeping her nose as close as possible to the cut onions. The money was a penny short. Glancing up she saw Dodie's thin face, the cheeks hollowed to unhealthy dents beneath the lacklustre eyes. Concern flooded her kindly features. Removing her own lacy hanky from her sleeve she thrust it at him, bade him blow his nose, then going to the tobacco tin she axed off a good ounce which she wrapped quickly in newspaper.

'Will you be having a dram wi' us, Dodie?' she enquired softly. 'You will maybe have heard that Shona McLachlan had twin babies last night and we are all taking the chance to celebrate their arrival on the island.'

'Shona wi' twins?' A flash of interest flitted over Dodie's woebegone face.

'Ay, that's right. No doubt you'll be going along to Laigmhor to see them for yourself – though mind you'll have to be careful. From what I hear they're just tiny wee cratur's and canny be doing wi' too much germs about them the now.'

Dodie failed to take the hint. 'Ay, Shona will have to keep them away from all thon sick animals Niall keeps in his wee hospital, these is no' healthy and fine I know it myself too. I got belly ache once from clappin' an ill doggie, though Lachlan blamed it on a lump o' venison I had lyin' in my larder for a whilie.'

'You will have a dram, Dodie?' Tam, swallowing hard, threw an encouraging arm round the old man's bent shoulders. 'It will help to keep the cold from your bones.'

'Na, na,' Dodie backed away, 'I'd best get home for my dinner.'

'Come and have it wi' me and Wullie,' invited soft-hearted Mairi, 'there's plenty in the pot for everybody and a nice wee treacle pudding for after.'

But Dodie was not in a sociable mood. ''Tis kind you are, Mairi,' he intoned mournfully, 'but you see – ' his dreamy grey-green eyes filled with tears, his large adam's apple bobbed frantically above a greasy scarf ' – I haveny been able to eat much o' anything since Ealasaid went and died on me.' Into brimming eyes went horny knuckles to scrub desperately. 'I miss my bonny cow, more than anything in this world I miss her! I canny sleep and I canny eat and – and these smelly onions o' yours are makin' my eyes cry, Merry Mary!'

He was sobbing, great heartrending sobs that shook his gaunt frame and made everyone there eye one another in head-shaking sympathy.

Shamefaced, Merry Mary scooped the offending onions from the counter and threw them into the bin. Without a word she went into the back shop to reappear with a hastily wrapped parcel which she pushed towards Dodie. 'Take this home wi' you, I have enough and plenty left for my own table and what is in there is just the thing for a body wi' a delicate appetite.'

'You are makin' my teeths water, Mary,' Kate peered curiously at the innocent-looking parcel. 'Will you be letting us in on the secret with you?'

'Ach, it's just meat,' Merry Mary said carelessly, not about to tell Kate of all people that Erchy the Post had been indulging in a spot of salmon poaching and had been good enough to share the spoils with her accompanied by strict warnings not to divulge their origins to another living soul.

''Tis good you are, Merry Mary.' Dodie scooped up his packages and backed to the door.

'Dodie, Dodie!' Tam pulled a pair of thick woollen gloves from his pocket. 'Be putting these in the nearest dustbin on your way home. I have a dozen pairs lying in a drawer and know fine Mairi has knitted me another dozen for Christmas. These have a hole in them and are no use to me now.'

Dodie took the gloves, his horny fingers rasping over the warm wool with real affection. 'The nearest dustbin, Tam,' he nodded and went out, tripping over Merry Mary's cat in his hurry to be away and try the gloves on for size.

'I'll dustbin you, my lad,' Kate whirled round on her husband the minute the doorbell stopped jangling. 'I made these for you wi' my very own hands just last month and the only pairs o' anything you have lyin' in your drawers are dirty socks full o' holes as big as your head.'

'Ach, he wouldny take them any other way,' Tam returned placidly. 'The bodach looked that cold I would have taken the very suit off my back if I thought he would accept it from me. Yon cratur' is dyin' on his feets and will never be himself again till by some miracle he is able to afford another cow.'

There were murmurs of sympathy. 'Ay, he's no' been the same Dodie since Ealasaid went and fell over the cliff last summer,' nodded Mairi. 'In calf she was too and that heavy her feets just slipped on the grass.'

'We'll all have to pray for him,' Holy Smoke suggested primly. 'The Lord is our strength and salvation.'

'We might ask the minister to say a wee word on Dodie's behalf next Sabbath,' Mairi took up the proposal eagerly. 'I'm sure Mr James wouldny mind.'

'Ay, he is a good man is Mr James,' agreed Merry Mary, picking up the conversation where it had left off before Dodie's arrival on the scene, 'he's aye there when he's needed yet often he himself must feel the need o' a sympathetic ear. 'Tis just a pity he and Doctor Megan never got themselves together as we all hoped. He's such a bonny, fine man but too shy for his own good when it comes to affairs o' the heart.'

'No' as shy as we all think!' The door opened to admit a puffing Elspeth, boots caked with dirty snow which she stamped on Merry Mary's hair rug before coming in to sit herself down on the sack of potatoes still warm from Barra's recent possession.

There had been no real need for Elspeth to come down to Portcull. Phebie's larder was well enough stocked and would have lasted a few days yet, but Elspeth had voiced a desire to replenish the flour bin and off she had sprachled over the snowy glen road, rejecting an offer from Archie Taylor to squash in beside Nancy in their tractor.

'We've been toastin' the new babies.' Merry Mary leaned her elbows on the counter and addressed the newcomer. 'Will you take a dram yourself?'

Elspeth opened her mouth to refuse. Her head was still thick from last night's indulgences but surely 'a hair o' the dog' would do no harm and would help to chase the cold from her bones. 'Just a wee nip,' she condescended primly, 'to damp the heads o' the wee mites and to tell the truth, I'm needing something to buck me up. I'm fair exhausted after being up all night and could fine have put my head down this morning till I saw the empty flour bin.' She gave a martyred sigh. 'Phebie has grown that used to me seeing to everything she just lets the wee things slip her mind till it's near too late to do anything about them.'

'And last night?' Kate ignored the old housekeeper's complaints. 'When did the first bairn arrive and was it the girl or the boy?'

All eyes latched on Elspeth with interest. Here was a first-hand account of the latest happenings and one and all stretched their ears in order not to miss a word that was said.

'And the minister?' Behag had not forgotten. As soon as Elspeth finished speaking, the 'Portcull post mistress' pounced. 'You were saying something about him when you came through Mary's door.'

'Oh ay, the minister.' Elspeth pursed her lips; and launched into a highly exaggerated account of the things she had witnessed 'wi' her very eyes'.

'Here yes, I saw his face for myself when himself and the doctor passed by the Post Office a wee whilie back,' Behag supplemented eagerly. 'When I made some innocent remark about the scratches both o' them went off down the road laughing as if it was some sort o' marvellous joke.'

'Well, it was no joke, I've never seen such marks on a man,' Elspeth shuddered dramatically. 'The skin was all bloody and torn where she had clawed him in some sort o' fit o' passion –'

'No' even on yourself when Hector had finished wi' you?' Kate couldn't resist asking.

But for once Elspeth failed to rise to the bait, so enraptured was she with the richness of her story. 'I tell you, the pair o' them were outside for ages, no' even the cold of last night raw enough to cool them down. Then he comes runnin' in, all heated and wild-eyed, Doctor Megan in his arms, her hair hangin' about her like a gypsy woman and her face afire wi' something I will not demean myself to name –'

'Even though you yourself seem to know all about it?' It wasn't Kate this time, it was Barra, her eyes glittering with anger. 'I don't suppose it might have occurred to you that the whole thing was entirely innocent and very easily explained.'

'Ay, Barra's right.' Several voices spoke up. 'You were only seeing one side o' it, Elspeth.'

Elspeth looked disdainfully down her nose. 'None o' you know what you are talking about but I do. I have certain facts in my possession about the new doctor, damning facts they are too but I will be fair and give her the benefit o' the doubt and just wait and see how she turns out. And don't bother to ask what these facts are. I will bide my time for I am no' the sort o' woman who likes to see another in trouble.'

'Ach, havers!' said Barra forcibly. 'You've aye had it in for the minister and the doctor. Simply because neither conform to your old-fashioned ideas about how such people ought to behave.'

'Anyways, it was what we all wanted – to see the two o' them maybe getting together,' Tam put in eagerly.

Elspeth glowered at them all, but particularly at Robbie's attractive little wife with her soft waving grey hair framing her smooth features. 'Just because you knew the minister in Glasgow, Barra, doesny give you any right to judge. You only knew the man in the pulpit, no' the flesh and blood cratur' I saw last night. I am just like the rest o' you,' she went on solicitously, 'I wanted to see the minister and the lady doctor getting themselves together – but no' like that, flaunting their lusts about for all the world to see. She's a harlot is Doctor Megan, and he is that besotted by her he would do anything to own her.' She looked round at all the intent faces. 'And anything is what he will do before he is very much older. You mark my words and see if I'm wrong – and if I am, I'll crawl on my hands and knees to kirk and beg the Lord's forgiveness.'

PART TWO

Spring 1966

Chapter Eight

It had been a severe winter with hurricane force winds storming over the island and leaving a trail of havoc in their wake. The old elms surrounding the kirkyard and the Manse had withstood years of cruel battering but that winter proved too much for one. On a fierce night in January its gnarled trunk had come crashing down to plummet straight through the south gable of the Manse, shattering the roof and allowing rainwater to pour unchecked into the living and kitchen quarters.

It had been quite a sight that, the upper trunk of the twisted elm lodged in the roof timbers, its black branches springing free to groan eerily in the torturous elements. People had come from all over the island to stand, stare, and sympathize while Tam and a dozen other men laboured to saw the trunk in half and remove it bit by bit from the roof.

After that had come the repairs to the structure itself and for a time part of the house was out of bounds while the work went on.

Tina had been in quite a state over the catastrophe, more flustered than anyone had ever seen her.

'That bugger,' she moaned, referring to the tree as if it was imbued with human powers and had planned the whole episode, 'it has ruined my kitchen and made a right mess o' the minister's study. I could *kill* it, that I could!'

'Well, at least no one got hurt in the accident,' Matthew pointed out, 'no' even the animals.'

'But it's the inconvenience to Mr James!' wailed Tina

who, easygoing and languid as she was, had taken the minister's welfare very much to heart and disliked seeing him put about in any way. Gallantly she rose to the occasion, bringing hot meals from her own kitchen to set upon the refectory table which fortunately had suffered no damage, and had been moved with everything else to a little back room with a fine view of the hills and a good 'drawing' fire.

It had been quite an upheaval, moving the goods and chattels of man and beast to the new quarters, and by the time everything was in place the small room was very cluttered.

'You couldny swing a cat in here,' Tina declared, eyeing the heaps of fur draped round the fire with unusual belligerence. 'These cratur's take up all the space, Mr James.' She sighed heavily, for many's the time she had tripped over one of those self-same cratur's whilst ambling about the kitchen with her nose in a book. 'You will either have to move them out or move yourself into that wee cubby hole across the hall. You just canny eat and work in here as well, and you canny move your desk into the parlour for you need that room for visitors.'

Tina had few rules in life but 'the parlour for visitors' was one that had been inherent in her from birth, a code of practice no amount of inconvenience would ever change.

'Don't worry so much, Tina,' Mark told her patiently. 'The cubby hole will do as a temporary study and it won't be for long, Tam is getting the repairs done slowly but surely.'

'Slowly more than surely, Mr James,' she returned with mild sarcasm, 'Tam McKinnon wouldny hurry if it was Buckingham Palace itself wi' a tree in the roof and I never could abide a body wi' no respect for their betters. If it was me I would have had you back in your own study long ago and myself back in my own kitchen.'

The minister hid a smile. Tina was as sublimely

unaware of her own shortcomings as she was the hands of the clock, two facts he found easy to overlook since her presence in his house had the same effect on him as a walk by the sea on a balmy summer's evening.

Tina's worries and the minister's inconvenience were solved from a most unexpected quarter when Megan appeared in the Manse one bright morning to say with an offhand air, 'Eve has been telling me of your difficulties here. There are plenty of rooms at Tigh na Cladach, one of them just perfect for you at the back of the house with a view of the sea. You could work away in there undisturbed, it's well away from the waiting room and surgery.'

Mark was so taken aback that she had gone out again before he had time to make any sort of comment, though Tina, hovering nearby with a feather duster in her hand, made enough for them both.

'Well, well now, there's a thing, a very fine thing indeed. You will be taking her up on the offer, Mr James, that you will, then I will no' have to be worrying about you anymore.' She nodded lazily, the movement sending flyaway loops of hair cascading about her face together with a dozen kirby grips. 'I aye said she was a good lassie, and though she has her wee tempers her heart's in the right place.'

Affectionately the minister ruffled her baby-fine hair. 'Big words, Tina, but I know fine you've never forgiven her for lashing out at you that day of the bazaar.'

'Ach, she had a demon in her at the time, Mr James, and still has for all she tries to hide it. It tears her heart, one way and the next and she'll no' get rid o' it till her eyes are opened to the truth that's starin' her in the face.'

The profundity of her words took his breath away. For a moment he was tempted to tell her she had been reading too many books, but one look at her serious face stilled his tongue. 'What truth?' he contented himself with asking.

'Och, Mr James,' she chided gently, 'you're as blind as

she herself and I'm no' going to waste my breath explaining. Just know this, she'll go after it for a whilie and think she's found it only to discover she's chasin' rainbows without substance. There is no pot o' gold at the end o' rainbows, Mr James,' she assured softly. 'The gold is where we can feel it and see the beauty wi' our half-blind eyes.'

'Tina,' he shook his head. 'You speak in riddles – and you're also one of the greatest romantics I've ever met.'

She laughed then, her dimples denting her smooth cheeks, 'Ach, it was a poem Ruth McKenzie wrote in one o' they wimmen's magazines, but the rest is mine – from me myself.'

'Ay, it sounds more like Ruth than Tina,' he grinned. 'Talking about Ruth, her first novel is to be published in the spring, I believe.'

'Ay, that it is,' Tina bubbled with enthusiasm, 'I can hardly wait to get my hands on it for Ruth was after telling Shona a wee bittie about it and Shona was after telling me. Ach my, it's that sad I had a wee greet to myself, I enjoyed it that much. 'Tis all about love and great passionate dramas – ' she caught his laughing eyes. 'Och, there I go, blethering on and me wi' half a day's work yet to be done – you've kept me back wi' all your nonsense,' she giggled, 'but it can all just wait till tomorrow now that you've decided to move your books and papers down to Tigh na Cladach.'

'Tina, I haven't decided anything yet!' he protested, but it was to the generous proportions of her receding back. She was already away 'sorting' his things to take to the doctor's house.

There followed some of the happiest times he was ever to know for many a long day. Oh true enough, he disciplined himself to writing his sermons and visiting his flock in the daytime, but when the early darkness of winter afternoons gathered in there came that precious hour of the day he was to remember and treasure in all the black times that lay ahead.

With the drapes pulled over the windows, he and Megan, Eve and Tina, would gather round the sitting-room fire to drink tea and eat the fluffy scones Eve and Tina took turn about baking. It was the easiest thing in the world to be greedy about these tempting titbits. Thick with creamy butter or oozing with homemade bramble jelly, they evoked memories of childhood summers when all the world was blue and busy with grazing cows and brown berry pickers whose laughter drifted over the green meadows. The fire blazed, the clocks ticked, animals snored serenely, Eve and Tina talked in soft voices about the island, the sea, men and boats, both mother and daughter occasionally breaking into song in their lilting, pleasant, out-of-key voices, which didn't matter anyway because the songs were in the Gaelic and the music of that language is kind to less than perfect voices.

To Mark James they were the finest ceilidhs he had ever known, with the sea lapping the winter dark outside and the fire-shadowed room wrapping them round in a shell of warmth. All time was forgotten, all enmity melted away, hurt and bitterness belonged to the past, nothing that was unpleasant intruded into the chintzy room. When Eve and Tina departed into the night it was just Mark and Megan, the house dark and quiet around them, the firelight playing on the soft gleam of her hair, dancing over the sweet planes of her face, caressing the chaste contours of her slender body.

They hardly spoke, hardly looked at one another, they were just there together, Mutt and Muff draped about their feet, all warm, all safe from wind and storm. Never once did he touch her. He knew that if he did so he would break that spell of enchantment so precariously won. The man in him rebelled, longed to break out and enfold her, but his better sense warned him to be patient.

All too soon reality intruded, the hands of the clock swung relentlessly round to the hour of evening surgery. Firelight was violated by paraffin lamps, flaring up, flooding out, but better that than the harsh glare of electric light. Megan had a generator but only used it when necessity called, particularly in the surgery.

He always left before the first patient arrived.

'I don't want them talking,' she told him rather defensively. 'You know what they're like.'

'Ay, I know and I understand.'

But he didn't and all he could hope for was a day when she would cease to care what others thought and concentrate instead on him.

He dreaded the day when work on the Manse would be finished, and he would have to go back to his lonely rooms with just his hopes to carry him through from one day to the next.

But come the day did and with it came Tam, right pleased with himself as he presented himself in the little back room to stretch his feet to the fire and take his time over the strupak Tina brought him.

'She's as good as new, that she is.' Tam's referral to the roof was a fond one, though he had spent the last few weeks cursing the same structure upside down. 'It was a bugger o' a job mind – ' he grinned apologetically, more for his own lapse than for the minister's benefit, for Kate had warned him to watch his tongue while working about the Manse.

'But Kate,' Tam had protested, 'you allow your own to run riot in front o' Mr James. I heard you wi' my very own ears last Sabbath.'

'Ach, that wasny swearin',' she had returned indignantly, 'I just told him the kirk had more draughts than a tink wi' holes in his breeks and the mannie agreed wi' me for he laughed in that nice way he has.'

'Ay well, as I was sayin', it was a terrible job just,' Tam continued with an apologetic cough. 'Every time we got a good section fixed the wind came in the night and blew her all down again but the bu… the slates are all back on now and she is tighter than a drum, better than she ever was and will no' collapse again – except of course if another tree comes crashing in on top o' her,' he ended with a mirthful screech.

'A balm to my troubled breast,' Mark laughed.

'You were sayin', Mr James?' Tam enquired politely.

'You're an optimist with a pessimistic tongue, Tam, in other words you have a way of saying the wrong things in the best possible way and I'm delighted to be watertight again, thanks to you and the others.'

'Ach well, there is nothing to beat your own roof – though mind – ' Tam winked heavily, 'you did no' too bad for yourself while you were waiting. That's *one* house will no' blow away in a hurry even though her very feets are near steepin' in the ocean. I should know for it was me put her to rights when Burnbreddie the Younger took over the estate. James Balfour, his father, just let everything fall about his ears and old Andy Devlin, who used to bide in Tigh na Cladach, was just as bad. He hadny even the gumption to set hammer to nail when bits o' the house were blowin' about his lugs and it's thanks to young Burnbreddie the house wasny razed to the ground years ago.'

Settling back in his seat he shoved a hacked thumbnail under the rim of his cap. 'You never kent the old laird, did you, son? He was well afore your time, a rascal if ever there was one, as sinful as the de'il himself wi' an eye in his head for big buxom wimmen and wee servant lassies alike…'

Tam rambled on. Mark James was a practised listener. Outside the rain blattered, the wind whistled mournfully. No matter, his roof was on again, he was watertight – and no more those wonderful hours spent with Megan in the big old house so close to the sea, 'her very feets were near steepin' in the ocean'.

*

The carts were down on Mara Oran Bay, loading up with gleaming orange seaweed tossed up by the last high tide. Crofters and farmers from all airts had congregated at the bay to reap the bounty of the sea. It was a long time since anyone had seen such thick banks of seaweed on the normally clean sands and one and all hastened to take advantage of it, for nothing was finer dug into the tattie ground. This was the best time, before the spring work got underway and spade had yet to be put to the soil.

It was a warm, balmy day in the middle of March, the calmest day the island had seen since the onset of winter. The Sound of Rhanna was a deep blue under an azure sky; tiny far-flung islands were misted and unreal, and if one didn't know they existed they might have been mistaken for delicate lilac clouds merging into the white cumulus on the horizon. Odd boat-shaped objects stood out on the skerries, and could have been an extension of the grey rocks but for occasional barkings and plaintive moanings that identified them as seals; seabirds mewed and muttered among the rock pools as they probed for molluscs; on the machair above the bay early lambs frolicked, glad of the warmth beating down on their tiny bodies after the soakings they had endured since birth.

No one said much about the weather.

'Better to talk about it in whispers,' advised Hector the Boat, 'else we might bring the wrath o' the ocean down about our lugs.'

'Ach, it's no' the ocean that hears,' Canty Tam was scornful, 'tis the Uisge Hags who cock their lugs for the foolish talk o' silly men.'

'Ay, and you're about the silliest to be born,' Jim Jim spoke from his place on a hollowed-out rock just made for the convenience of men like him, too old to work but never too old to enjoy watching others doing it.

'Well, only this very mornin' my mother was after sayin' that the Hags are no' finished wi' us yet,' Canty Tam persisted smugly. 'She says the worst storm has yet to come and with it will come strife and trouble that will affect many a man, woman, and child on Rhanna.'

'Ach, yon mother o' yours is a witch herself.' Fingal McLeod paused in his labours and came limping over to join the little group by the rocks. 'I've heard tell she brews all sorts o' evil potions in thon big black pot she has, and feeds them to the towrists for good sillar.'

''Tis no' evil potions,' scorned Canty Tam, 'and you're the one who's daft if you dinna ken that. She makes tablet and toffee that melts in your mouth. The towrists are just linin' up at our door to have a taste.'

'Ay, and it sticks to your teeths and rots them.' Ranald pulled a rueful face as he poked a tarry finger into his mouth. 'Between her tablet and Barra's cakes my teeths are in a fine state and will have to be sorted next time thon dentist mannie comes to Rhanna.'

'And when's that?' Jim Jim clicked his teeth experimentally and winced. 'My own are needin' replaced for every time I chew my meat a wee sharp corner cuts my gums.'

'Ach, it will be your second set o' baby teeths comin' through,' guffawed Ranald. 'Isabel was after saying you are comin' into your second childhood wi' all the daft things you get up to these days. Anyways, the dentist will no' be here till summer so you'll just have to thole your teeths till then.'

'I doubt it will no' be soon enough for poor auld Dodie.' Captain Mac tapped his pipe on a rock and made himself comfortable beside Jim Jim. 'These rotten brown molars o' his are giving him gyp this whilie back. His face is all swollen wi' the pain o' them.'

All eyes turned on Dodie working away silently beside the tall, fair figure of Anton Büttger who gave the old eccentric employment whenever he could.

'It's no' toothache that's Dodie's problem,' Jim Jim shook his head wisely. ''Tis heartache. He's no' been the same man since he lost Ealasaid, and seems to greet all the time. I've seen him wanderin' the moors, crying on her as if she was still alive, the tears pourin' down his face as he goes along.'

'Ay, it was a tragedy for a poor, simple cratur' like Dodie,' agreed Fingal sadly. 'It will be a whilie before he can afford another. Yon cow was his bread and butter.'

'Ay, and he was hoping to get an even better calf out her when Croynachan's bull came to the island,' nodded Jim Jim. 'For all he's supposed to be soft, Dodie has aye had his ambitions. There was a time he dreamed o' having a whole herd o' beasts to call his own.'

Captain Mac ran his fingers through his luxuriant beard, his keen eyes fastened on Dodie's bent figure humping seaweed into a cart. 'Ay, he'll no' get that now. I doubt his days o' dreaming are done with for he's getting on in years and will soon no' be able to do manual labour. Ach, 'tis sad, sad indeed, he's a changed man altogether these days. You know the way he was? Never letting any event go by his notice, aye makin' and takin' a wee gift to somebody or other, yet when wee Shona McLachlan had her twins last Christmas there was nary a sign nor smell o' Dodie. She was that disappointed she mentioned it to me, for Dodie was aye about her place wi' his painted stones and wee presents o' one sort or another.'

''Tis one storm he'll no' weather in a hurry,' said Jim Jim. 'He's come through a lot in his day, but Ealasaid was his life and without her he's just a poor lost cratur' without hope.'

'Talkin' o' storms,' Captain Mac's experienced eye was fixed on the horizon where a band of slate-grey cloud had swallowed up the distant islands, 'I doubt this bugger is right after all. There's another brewin' over yonder. She'll be here by nightfall or my name isny Isaac MacIntosh.'

Canty Tam smirked. 'Ay, trouble is comin' right enough, I can feel it in my bones. My mother is aye right, she was hearin' storms afore she was born and arrived in one in a wee blackhouse over by the cliffs of Burg.'

'Ach, it was her own winds she was hearin' for the wife is full o' them,' Captain Mac threw over his shoulder as he clambered from the rocks to resume his neglected tasks.

As predicted, the storm came that night, preceded by a sullen early darkness. Mark James, his lamps yet unlit, wandered into his study and over to the window to watch the strange, yellow half-light gradually being swallowed into rolling black clouds that had hung threateningly over the sea since mid-afternoon.

The little houses of Portcull sat round the bay, white pearls against the black hills, sturdy edifices that had withstood wind and tempest for the past hundred years and more. One by one lights flickered in the windows like amber eyes blinking open, till gradually a bright semi-circular necklace ringed the throat of the bay and brought an illusion of warmth to the blackening night.

Beyond the bay the sea heaved, restlessly chafing against the land, the oncoming waves showing white bellies as they rolled and broke.

Mark settled himself into his favourite window seat to light his pipe, and to allow his gaze to wander down to Tigh na Cladach sitting so close to the waves that no one had ever needed to gather seaweed to fertilize its garden. It was tossed in naturally and if the tide was really high it draped itself everywhere, even over windowsills and once, it was said, actually to hang from the roof gutters in tattered banners. It was a wonder the house itself had stood the test of time but there it remained, as proud a structure as any house could be in that position, its garden walls taking the full brunt of the batterings so that they had to be repaired regularly though only when all fear of storm was safely past. Tam McKinnon was too wise in the ways of weather to risk anything undermining his efforts. He had warned Megan not to plant a single seed in her garden for weeks yet but she was an incomer and knew best, that was what everyone said when they saw her out there in her Wellingtons, lovingly tending the pale spikes of daffodils and tulips she had planted last autumn.

'A miracle those Wellingtons,' was the general opinion. 'But you'll no' catch her in them out o' her garden. She wears thon fancy shoes o' hers everywhere – even to the wee hoosie before her plumbing went in.'

'The boots were Kirsteen McKenzie's doing,' Elspeth pointed out knowingly. 'She converted the doctor thon time o' the awful snow when Niall's twins were born – though mind, 'tis gey strange now that I come to think on it. She had her shoes clasped to her breast that time the minister came leapin' in wi' her in his arms. At the time I thought they were havin' high jinks to themselves but maybe it was *him* converted her, though 'tis about the only thing he's wanted to change for he seems to like her fine wi' the rest o' her fancies intact. Oh ay, I saw him sneakin' away from her house in the middle o' the night thon time his own house was injured.'

The minister smiled dourly to himself when these little snippets reached his ears. So much for Megan's wish not to get herself talked about. No matter what time he had taken his departure from her house, the talk would just have been the same; 'the middle o' the night' obviously implying any hour between darkness and dawn.

He sighed a little to himself in the warm darkness of his peaceful study. The faces of Margaret and Sharon looked down at him from the mantlepiece. 'My darling girls,' he murmured, 'if only you were here beside me. How different my life then.' Mutt came padding through to rest his muzzle on his master's knee. 'Perhaps things will change soon, eh, Mutt? Spring is just around the corner, everything will be better when the sun shines and the land grows green again.'

Far beyond the cliffs of Burg a tiny light flickered on a crazed sea. Things were about to change for Mark James, but in a way he could not have foreseen that wild night in mid-March, 1966.

*

Out on the Sound of Rhanna the forty-foot cruising yacht known as the *Mermaid* plunged into one trough after another, her gleaming white hull disappearing for long seconds at a time only to rise up once more, like some fabulous bird whose wings had gone out of control.

The two young men in her fought to lower the wind-whipped sails that were threatening to capsize the boat. They had made the journey from the south coast of England in a series of hops. The weather had been fine when they set out from Tobermory that morning, but they were far from land when the storm warning came over on the radio.

'We'd best make for the nearest anchorage,' the dark-haired man advised. He was the son of a wealthy sail maker, a responsible enough sort in his way but always ready to embark on any adventure that chanced along. He had become renowned for his revolutionary sail designs, and had come on this trip to find out how his latest ideas would work on the *Mermaid*.

'We're as near Rhanna as anywhere else.' The second young man set his jaw in the stubborn lines his friend knew so well. 'Might as well go on. She'll make it alright. Dad and I have had her out on worse seas than this.'

He was the only son of a highly successful boat builder. All his life he had been indulged and spoiled. Tall, fair, utterly charming when it suited him, people had always run after him. Women fell at his feet, men liked him because he was generous and completely without fear of any kind. In other words he was a daredevil, his conceit leading him to believe that he was master of any situation. He had always laughed at life, had taken what he wanted from it without fear of the consequences. Wherever he went he won friends, made enemies, enjoyed himself to the full without having to work for it.

His father trusted him with nothing except boats. He was a wizard with them, loved every exciting, blood-stirring moment he spent out on the sea with the wind in his hair and the waves scudding beneath him. This trip was partly to do with taking the *Mermaid* on open-water trials, partly to do with a matter that had tormented his arrogant heart for more months than he cared to remember.

'She'll get us there,' he repeated in answer to his friend's arguments. 'Don't be so bloody gutless, old boy. We've weathered worse.'

One and a half nautical miles from Rhanna's seaboard, the *Mermaid* sailed into a maelstrom. Here the tide race met, here the mighty forces of the oceans roared and fumed in savage torment.

The *Mermaid* bobbed like a cork in the crazy mêlée, completely beyond the control of human hands. Beneath the black waves sharp fangs of hidden reefs crunched into the yacht's bow. She groaned, tilted. The mast collapsed, complete with sail and rigging, the halyards fouled the engine prop as they went over the side.

A scream rose above the snarl of the storm. The young sail designer scrambled over the slippery deck, his left arm hanging uselessly, broken by the weight of his own body when he had crashed down heavily on top of one of the hatches.

But he wasn't aware of any pain. He was too shocked at the sight of his friend lying in a crumpled heap on the slopping timbers, torn and bloody and unnaturally twisted. His body had taken the full force of the mast as it toppled over, thudding into bone, flesh and muscle before coming to rest, half in, half out of the water. The scream had been at the sight of the mast coming towards him. He wasn't making any sound now. He was unconscious...

Chapter Nine

'The phone's ringing, Righ.' Hugh McKinnon lifted his eyes above the rim of his newspaper to look expectantly at his uncle seated opposite.

Righ nan Dul, slippered feet stretched to the fire, lowered his own paper to gaze in some exasperation at his big, strapping nephew. Righ had been the Keeper of the Rhanna Light for many years, but since the lighthouse had become automated his job now consisted of checking and maintenance, an important enough position in its way but all rather boring to a man who had led such an active life. But he wasn't getting any younger and was glad enough to pass uneventful hours in his tiny cottage perched close to the lighthouse, his position as the island's coastguard providing him with occasional bursts of excitement that were more than enough to lend a bit of spice to his peaceful existence.

When his fisherman nephew had come to live with him he had found it strange sharing his lonely home, but in time he grew used to it and even to be glad of the company despite the fact that the lad was so lacking in initiative he might easily have walked off the edge of a cliff if directed to do so.

'Answer it then, son,' sighed Righ patiently. 'You know I have a bad leg and canny leap out my chair every time the damty tellyphone jingles. I canny bide the thing and would never have had it on my own account.'

Hugh uncoiled his rangy body from his chair, his big, solid, stockinged feet making the floorboards groan as he strode heavily into the tiny, cold hallway to lift the phone gingerly and say in a scared, breathy whisper, 'Ay?'

A booming voice sounded metalically over the line. Hugh held the instrument away from his ear, an offended expression on his weathered, youthful face. From a safe distance he heard the speaker out before turning his face back into the kitchen to say in his slow drawl, ''Tis for you, Uncle Righ, something about a Mayday call, the man said.'

'You mean you let him go on all that time thinkin' you were me!' Righ snorted in annoyance, heaving himself out of his chair to limp out to the hall.

'Ay, 'tis me, Righ McKinnon,' he explained, remembering to give his proper name and not the more familiar title that had been bestowed on him from his first day at the lighthouse.

'Then who the hell? Oh, never mind. This is Anderson speaking from the coastguard station at Oban.' He went on to explain that he had just received a distress call from a yacht called the *Mermaid* which had run into trouble roughly one and half nautical miles off Rhanna with one of the two man crew badly injured. 'I've asked the Barra lifeboat to stand by,' the voice went on, 'and will also alert any shipping in the area though I doubt the existence of any in these seas. Anyway, Righ, get your lads together and see what you can do – mad buggers, out on a pleasure trip on a night like this...'

Righ laid the 'phone gently back on its cradle, as if it might rise up and bite him at any moment. 'Hugh, get along to the coastguard hut and sound the siren!' he yelled.

'Now, Uncle? I haveny finished readin' my paper yet.'

'Ay, now – and be quick about it. A yacht's in trouble off Rhanna. The coastguard at Oban has alerted the Barra lot but we'll no' be needin' them if we're smart off our mark.'

So saying he hobbled out to the porch to don waterproofs and Wellingtons and to grab the storm lanterns, one of which he pushed into Hugh's hands as he rushed past, coatless and hatless.

'Stupid bugger!' cursed Righ. 'His mother must have dropped him on his head when he was a bairn!'

But despite his lack of application Hugh was supremely agile, and in a matter of minutes the siren was wailing into the night, alerting the Rhanna lifeboat crew and frightening the life out of everyone living in the near vicinity, not least Ranald whose cottage was right next to the coastguard's hut, and who leapt out of his door to see what was happening, braces looped about his thighs, hair standing on end.

Straining his eyes into the rain-lashed night he made out the soaked figure of Hugh dashing out of the hut. 'What's happening, Hugh?' he yelled.

'A ship in trouble,' Hugh's voice floated faintly back, 'the Barra lifeboat's comin' and all shipping in the Sound has been alerted.'

Ranald scratched his head. Shipping? On a night like this? Still, something was afoot – something big by the sound of it. Ranald's eyes gleamed and his imagination, fed on the many adventure novels he read with such enthusiasm, ran away with him. Maybe it was a cargo vessel run aground on the reefs, its hold packed to the gun'ales with gold bullion... His mind ran riot, carried him back to those wild, romantic days of smugglers and pirates, even while the parsimonious streak in him saw to it that he never got completely carried away. He cast his vision along the length of Portcull.

Scurrying figures were strung out along the length of the road, ousted from comforts and pleasures by the insistent moan of the siren. Ranald rushed inside to don outer garments, then rushed back outside to warn those outwith earshot of the siren of 'the shipwreck off the coast of Rhanna'.

Neither Megan in the shore house nor Mark James in the

Manse heard the thin wail coming from the coastguard's hut. All Megan heard was the continuous roar of the sea, while the only sounds heard by Mark were the rushing of the wind in the trees, the flaying of tortured branches, the ominous creaking made by twisted, aged trunks. It was high and exposed up there atop the Hillock, though the Manse itself sat in a walled-off hollow guarded by the doubtful protection of a little woodland.

Mark stirred restlessly at his study fire while Tina bustled about, piling fresh peats in the grate, puffing a little as she did so for it went against her nature to pay any sort of attention to the hands of the clock. But she was in a hurry that evening, and turning a rather flustered face from the fireplace she told the minister, 'Matthew is going to visit Old Joe the night so I said I would see he had an early tea. Yours is in the oven. See and take it while it's nice and hot. Och my,' she blew away some errant strands of hair, 'I canny be doing wi' all this racing about, but as soon as I've seen to Matthew I have to fly along to Grandma Ann's and Granda John's house. 'Tis the old man's birthday and I said I would help out wi' the wee ceilidh they're having for him. The old folks like a wee bit o' fuss on their birthdays and who can blame them? 'Tis funny right enough,' she giggled girlishly, 'people past the age o' seventy seem to enjoy nothing better than boasting about their advancing years, while folk o' my age just pray to God that everyone will forget they were ever born at all – if you see my meaning, Mr James?' With that she was off, rushing into her coat, muttering to herself all the while. 'Tis no' natural, no' natural, we were never made for all this hurry,' was her parting shot.

The door closed on her. The house was silent once more – except for the groaning of the trees outside the window.

Mark wondered how long his new section of roof would last in this storm while down below, in the cosy living room of Tigh na Cladach, Megan listened to the boom of the waves and thought that this time the sea would surely come in on top of her. She wished that Mark would visit, she was ready for him now and recalled to mind those happy times they had shared when the Manse roof was being repaired. They had been relaxed in one another's company, had found so much to talk about, or had simply been quiet together, listening to music, sitting back at ease in the peaceful room hearing the sough of the sea, aware of one another but not in an awkward way.

Steven Saunders belonged more and more to the past, Mark ever more to the reality of the present – yes, she was ready for him, but she knew he wouldn't come to her. She had rebuffed him too much, had wantonly hurt him so that he was wary of visiting her unless specifically invited.

She would wait for awhile. If he didn't come to her she would go to him – but first she would have a bath, it might help her relax.

The two people whom destiny might have brought together that night, remained sublimely ignorant to the activity brought about by a cry for help which was to destroy any chances of happiness that might have been theirs – if only...

Grant McKenzie and Matthew, Grieve of Laigmhor, had been visiting Old Joe when the siren sounded. Both men were firm favourites of the grand old rogue of the sea. He had known them since 'before they were born' and into their respective ears had fed his stories of mermaids and water witches for as long as they could remember.

Old Joe had married 'Aunt Grace' Donaldson when he was one hundred and four years old and in 'the prime of his life' according to him, and he had enjoyed almost a year of married bliss in her cosy little harbour house with its views of the sea and all the busy comings and goings of the harbour.

But his health had failed that winter. Although still rosy of cheek and as placidly cheerful as ever he had grown slower, more tired altogether, taking more and more to napping in his chair by the fire, pipe clenched in his gnarled, weather-beaten fist, his white head sunk onto his sark. But never did he give in enough to take to his bed. 'The day I do that will be the end o' me,' he told the pink-faced, kindly little woman known to everyone as Aunt Grace.

'Well, Joe, you canny live forever,' she told him, gazing at his ruddy old face with fond eyes. But she wished he would. Everyone wished that. He was a legend, was Old Joe. To generations of children he had been uncle, father, grandfather. As the years rolled on and he never seemed to change, everyone was of the opinion that he was as immortal as the stories he told in his lilting Highland voice. He wasn't, of course. He was just an old man who had been for so long part of island life, it appeared an impossibility that he could ever depart from it. Now the old enemy had caught up, subtle changes had taken place in him. His sea-green eyes were more deeply sunk so that his white brows bushed down over them; hollows robbed his fine old face of its roundness; his purple-veined hands shook when he supped food; numerous other deficiencies made him angry at being unable to command hitherto easily controlled faculties.

No one had ever seen Joe angry before. He had never been an irritable man but one of even temperament. True he had been irascible at times, but that was when his advancing years had forced him to give up his house and go to live with Kate McKinnon, whose dominion over him he had not relished one bit.

His new anger was only for himself, a luxury he only indulged in the privacy of his own home and then only in short bursts. Hardly a day went by without someone popping in for a crack and a cuppy. As a result the kettle was never off the boil though Aunt Grace seldom complained. It was those visitors who kept her darling old sea dog going – as long as his mind was on the affairs of others it was off himself.

Anyway, Captain Mac had been a good help to her since coming to stay that winter. Since the death of his wife his had been a nomadic existence, travelling about the Hebrides, staying with relatives for short spells before he was off again to his sister's croft on Hanaay. He was never happier than when on the sea or close enough to it to watch its many moods.

'Betimes I'm thinkin' the bodach believes the ocean would cease running if he wasny there to spy on it,' Mac's sister Nellie confided in Grace, but Grace understood men like Captain Mac. She was married to one, wasn't she? And she enjoyed the company of Captain Mac and 'to hell wi' the gossipmongers.'

For the gossips had talked when Aunt Grace opened her doors to the retired seafarer with his happy-go-lucky nature and as much fables in his head as Old Joe himself.

It was a disgrace, folks said, Aunt Grace and Captain Mac under the same roof, for had he not been in the running when Dugald's sister had come from Coll to settle herself on Rhanna? And now that Joe was growing more feeble with every passing day, God alone knew what tricks the pair were getting up to.

'She's an able wee body is Grace,' a dissaproving Kate told everyone. 'And Mac is a lusty old chiel wi' more than a keen eye for the women and Grace in particular.'

'Ach well, 'tis hardly a den o' iniquity,' Tam put it reasonably. 'Grace is no' likely to get herself pregnant at her age, is she now? Both herself and Mac are far too fond o' Joe to do anything that might upset him – forbye that, Grace is promised to Bob Paterson when the time comes and Mac has his eye on other pickings.'

'If you're thinkin' o' that Hanaay widow you can think again, my lad. She has no time now for the bodach and his silly ideas o' living in a houseboat. I hear tell she's got herself another man wi' normal thoughts in his head.'

''Tis no' the Hanaay wife I'm thinkin' about.' Tam grinned secretively and refused to enlarge on the subject, much to Kate's chagrin.

'Ach, you're havering as usual,' she snorted, 'and it makes no difference to my opinions on the matter. That two are just bidin' their time till my dear innocent Joe goes to meet his Maker and no one can tell me otherwise.'

'Your dear old Joe!' Tam spluttered. 'You gave the poor old bugger a dog's life when he was under your thumb. Worried away at the cratur' like he was an old bone wi' the plague. I mind once I found him in his room greetin'. Ay, that bonny, brave old man greetin' like a baby because you had cut his hair for the third time in a month and made him change his drawers twice in one week. He told me he was beginning to feel like a monk paying penance for all the sins he never committed.'

'Tam McKinnon!' Kate's lusty screech had made her husband back away in trepidation. 'I *worshipped* that bodach and tended the old bugger hand and foot. He was a wreck before I took and cared for him and that's the thanks I get. A monk, eh? Paying penance for sins he didny commit – well, you're just about to pay yours for all the lyin' and cheatin' you *did* commit! Off wi' your vest and drawers this minute, my lad, and while we're about it fetch the shears from the scullery till I crop your hair!'

If Joe had heard all that he would have felt very sorry for Tam and laughed at the rest – he could afford to laugh now he was out from under Kate's well-meant but overpowering rule. As for the talk about Grace and Captain Mac – that was the biggest laugh of all. From the day they had wed Grace was devoted to himself, and if later on she thought to take either Mac or Bob to her kindly bosom, well, all power to her elbow. She had given him more happiness these last months than he had known in a lifetime, and if her capacity for loving reached out to embrace others he would be glad in the knowing that she wouldn't spend the remainder of her life alone and lonely.

So Old Joe was happy as things stood. He worshipped Grace, enjoyed the agreeable companionship of Captain Mac, and he looked forward to the visits of all those bairns who had shared their eager youth with him and now came to entertain him with their talk of family and home.

Yet, betimes it was strange, mused the old man, hearing these boys talk about their children when only yesterday they were bairns themselves, no more than knee high, eyes big with wonder, cheeks bulging with the boilings he kept in a jar for them to enjoy as they listened in eager silence to the tales he had to tell. Good stories they were too. Forbye entertaining children he had been one of the best seanachaidhs on Rhanna, keeping everyone spellbound at winter firesides when gales battered the land, and it was safe and good to be indoors where all the witches and Hags were contained within the bounds of his fertile imagination. That one about the one-eyed Hag of the Minch – God, it was good that. The warty caillich had been one of his favourites – now, had the eye been on the right or the left side of her face? Or had it been in the middle? He chuckled and lay back in his chair, his green eyes very faraway under their straggling canopy of white...

'Did you say somthing, Joe?' Matthew looked at the old man and his eyes filled with tenderness as he wondered if such a frail body would see another summer on Rhanna.

Joe stirred, came back to reality with an effort. 'I was wandering, lad,' he explained softly, openly admitting for the first time that his concentration wasn't as it had been.

'You're tired, my man.' Aunt Grace put a pan of milk to heat on the fire. 'You'll sup your cocoa and then get off to bed.'

Grant got to his feet, his strapping youthful figure

suddenly filling the small room. 'Ay, it's time I was going anyway. Fiona likes me home in time to see Ian to bed.'

His apologetic grin successfully hid his thoughts. 'Come home early, Grant,' his wife had told him as they kissed at the door. 'There's a storm brewing and I love it when Ian's in bed and it's just you and me together on the sofa. It's so cosy with the wind howling and shrieking outside.'

'Havers, woman,' Old Joe told his wife stubbornly, and hae a sup afore you go?' he glanced enquiringly from Matthew to Grant.
dram than that bairn's food you have there in the pan.'

Captain Mac looked at Grace, she nodded, and he went over to the sideboard for the whisky. 'You'll stay and hae a sup afore you go?' he glanced enquiringly from Matthew to Grant.

'Och well,' Grant folded himself back into his chair. 'Fiona and the baby will keep for a whilie yet.'

Matthew grinned, 'Ay, and Tina will be over at Granny Ann's the night. Granda John is having a birthday. There will be a wee ceilidh waitin' for me there so it will do no harm to get warmed up a bittie first.'

Old Joe shivered suddenly. An oddly oppressive feeling of doom enveloped him, a sensing that something terrible was about to happen to someone there – in the room. He had experienced such things before, way back in his younger days when men were lost at sea never to return to their islands. It was just the storm, he convinced himself...

'You're cold, Joe,' Grace was there, happing his knees in a tartan rug. 'A wee tot will be just the thing to heat you up.'

'Ach, just someone walkin' over my grave,' the old man made light of it, 'but I'm no' for dyin' yet, no' when there's good whisky waitin' to be supped.'

Captain Mac was not a whisky man. Into his own glass he poured a large measure of rum, then seated himself down to plunge the poker into the red hot cinders in the grate.

Everyone waited. It was a familiar ritual, one peculiar to Mac. The poker was withdrawn, its red-hot tip immersed in the rum, inciting the liquid to hiss and sizzle and release the fragrance of burning rum into the room.

Captain Mac took the glass in his big brown hands and settled himself back with a contented sigh. It was his favourite time; his pipe; his rum; his stockinged feet planted squarely on the hearth; Joe in his chair; Grace in hers; the company of friends, well kent, well loved. Raising his glass he cried, 'Slàinte! Here's to us, wha's like us!'

'Damt few and they're a' deid.' Joe had been waiting for his cue.

'Not all,' Mac spoke softly. 'There is one among us very much alive and kicking.' Affectionately he regarded the old man in the chair opposite, the lamplight shining in his thick thatch of white hair, gilding the lush beard with silver. 'God, man,' Captain Mac shook his head and pulled thoughtfully on his own luxuriant whiskers, 'I'm seventy years old myself yet I mind you telling me your tales when *I* was a bairn. The love I had for the sea was nurtured in me by you and to my mind you're worth your weight in gold. To you I raise my glass. A toast to your abiding strength. To Joe!'

'To Joe!' Everyone toasted, everyone drank. Aunt Grace sipping daintily from her glass, heedless of a large tear that rolled and splashed down into it.

'And now.' Captain Mac took Joe's pipe, plugged it with a fill of baccy, did likewise to his own, folded his feet comfortably and looked around. ''Tis a night for the best seanachaidh in all Rhanna to tell us a tale or two.'

'Ach yes.' Aunt Grace beheld her husband's shining face and gave her willing consent.

'Ay, that would be grand.' Grant relinquished his vision of himself and Fiona cuddled together on the couch. There was plenty of time for them to indulge their passions – Old Joe's time was running out, let him savour what was left. 'I'll pretend I'm a boy again wi' all the mysteries o' the world lying at Joe's door waiting to be revealed.'

Matthew settled himself more comfortably on his cushion, drew up his knees and stared into his glass. In it he seemed to see Tina's bonny, placid face, the youthful ones of his children, those of his parents. His father was seventy-eight now, his birthday ceilidh would be in full swing with all his cronies popping in for a blether and a dram. Matthew smiled. A new pipe nestled in his pocket for Granda John, as he was known to everyone. Grandma Ann was forever complaining that the old one spewed more foul-smelling reek than a lum on fire...

'I am thinkin' o' a wonderful day in summer,' Old Joe had began his tale, 'when all the sea was calm and blue and faraway islands were like dazzling gems way off on the horizon. Me and my mates were aboard a fishing vessel trawling for herring in the Sea o' The Hebrides...'

The lilting old voice was like a song, musical, soothing. Outside the wind rose to gale force but inside Aunt Grace's little harbour house it was summer – an illusion brought about by one old man whose gift of storytelling had been granted to him long before the cradle...

After Tina had departed into the night, Mark went through to the kitchen to take his meal from the oven and set it on the table. He tried to feel appreciative of the warm fire, the peace, the delicious steak and kidney pie steaming provocatively on his plate. But it was no use. After just a few forkfuls he pushed the food away half-eaten and rose from his chair to pace about the house, watched anxiously by Mutt who had been hoping for some tasty titbits from his master's plate before the cats polished off the lot. The Manse cats were ruthless opportunists. Whenever they thought they could get away with it they ganged up on the big, floppy, good-natured dog to wrest from him his own particular place at the fire; the most comfortable chair; the tastiest scraps from the table.

No matter how much he worried or fretted the cats seemed somehow to win, and it looked as if they were going to come up trumps again tonight. From the corner of one golden-brown eye Mutt could see them, sneaking up on the dining chairs to paw the plates towards them with an expertise born of long practice. Tub, a huge shaggy white cat, was the leader. Whatever she did Tib and Tab just followed suit. At this present moment they were all licking the plate containing the soup dregs, from that they progressed to the dish containing the remains of the mouthwatering meat pie...

Mutt could stand it no longer. His jaws drooled profusely, a worried whine rose up in his throat. But it was all to no avail. The master of the house was in one of his deeply thoughtful moods. A great sigh shuddered out of Mutt's dejected frame and he retired to the kitchen fire, there to sink his nose in his paws and reflect on just how unfair life was to an honest-natured dog who had never, and to his own cost, stolen anything from any table – except maybe in the daft, long-ago days of puppyhood when he hadn't known any better.

Mark, for once oblivious to small domestic upheavals among his animals, paused in the hall, frowning. Something about this night was making him uneasy and it had nothing to do with the gale blowing outside. He was used by now to such adverse weather conditions. They were part and parcel of island life and he had long ago learned to cope with them. No, it was something else, a feeling that all was not quite right out there in the wild, blustery darkness.

Striding through to his study, he went straight to the window to pull back the curtains and peer outside. His instincts had been right. There were lights out there, not the familiar lights of the village but a moving mass of them, bobbing and winking all along the road to the harbour.

Without a moment's hesitation he ran to the hall stand to don his heavy tweed jacket and grab a torch from the window ledge. Mutt came out of the kitchen to watch him, reproach in every taut muscle.

Mark laughed. 'Ach, alright, lad, you can have it. But not a word to Tina, you know how she fusses about my meals.'

Mutt sighed again. Surely, surely, his master knew him better than that. Had he never taken note of the fact that his dog never took things from the table? Or were all human beings too wrapped up in their own affairs to bother with those of their animals?

With drooping tail Mutt slunk sadly back to the kitchen where his nose told him that every last scrap had been scoffed from the plates – and worse, in his short absence those devilish cats had taken over his very own special cushion with the lovely loose cover wherein all sorts of small doggy treasures could be hidden from feline eyes. Tub and Tib were sprawled over one side of it, Tab plunk in the middle, all contendedly washing their whiskers and licking gravy from their lips, their green gleaming orbs watching him with self-satisfied triumph.

It was too much. Mustering as much dignity as he could into his floppy, clumsy limbs, Mutt padded over to his master's chair and jumped up to bury his nose in his tail in an effort to try and forget all about the injustices of life in the safe and happy realms of sleep.

Once outside the house, Mark James ran to the gate atop the Hillock which was a quick way down to the village and one he used most often in preference to the more conventional route along the driveway.

'*He breeah*!'

The minister almost jumped out of his skin. To have the Gaelic for 'it is fine' thrown at him out of the pitch blackness of that drear demented night was nerve shattering to say the least. Frantically he swung his torch in the direction of the voice. The small circle of light found and stayed on the woebegone countenance of Dodie, who appeared to have just come out of the kirkyard. The sight of his stooped and flapping black figure did nothing to soothe the minister's nerves.

'Dodie!' he exclaimed. 'What on earth are you doing up here on a night like this?'

The old eccentric shuffled his huge feet in embarrassment. 'Will you promise no' to be telling a soul if I whisper a wee secret to you?' he babbled excitedly.

'No, of course not, but I'll never hear if you whisper. Just talk in your normal voice for I can vouch that there's no' another living soul up here to eavesdrop on you.'

Dodie drew a sodden sleeve over his nose. 'Well, I put a wee stone in a corner o' the kirkyard in memory o' my Ealasaid. No' another body knows about it but myself and yourself too, now that I've told you, Mr James,' he finished in respectful tones for he had taken to the young minister from the beginning and always felt at ease in his company.

'Ealasaid you say!' Mark had to shout to make himself heard above the howl of the wind.

'Wheesht, wheesht!' Dodie warned in panic, glancing over his bony shoulder as if expecting the entire village to have ringed itself round the Hillock 'to spy on him'.

'Ay, ay, you remember my bonny cow? She fell over the cliff last summer and I miss her that much I thought to put up a wee stone for her so that I can come up here and speak to her the way I used to when she was alive –' The tears were spilling, stemmed only by the old man's fiercely scrubbing, frozen hands.

'Come on, man,' Mark put a kindly hand under Dodie's sharply defined elbow realizing as he did so that there was so little meat on the old eccentric's bones they seemed to stick out of his shabby layers of clothing at every angle. He had grown frail these last months and the minister suspected that he had pined himself into a state of near starvation. 'I'll take you back to the

Manse,' he explained as he guided the stumbling, clumsy footsteps back up the brae. 'You can have a bite to eat there and a good heat at the fire.'

Dodie made no protest but allowed himself to be led inside to the kitchen, there to be greeted rapturously by Mutt who adored the smelly old man, not just because he always carried a titbit in his tattered pocket whenever he had to pass the Manse, but also because he was the one human being in all the land who seemed really to understand animals and everything they tried so hard to convey.

Quickly the minister made a pot of tea and heated some soup from the big pot Tina had prepared that morning. He left Dodie seated cosily by the fire, dunking bread into his soup, Mutt's muzzle rested adoringly on one jutting kneebone, Tub, Tib and Tab draped respectively on the chair back, the chair arm, across Dodie's bent but amenable shoulder.

Mark knew that when he got back Dodie would be gone, leaving only his aroma and his dirty dishes behind, and as he hurried down the brae he vowed that something would have to be done to ensure that the old man's lonely cottage up in the hills wouldn't become his tomb, for if he went on the way he was doing he would most certainly starve himself to death altogether.

Mark walked along briskly, body bent into the wind, eyes closed to slits to protect them from the blatters of icy rain hurling over the land. Guided by the mass of storm lanterns he arrived breathless at the harbour. The doors of the big boatshed were open wide, inside a crowd of men were working at the winch before knocking away the chocks that helped keep the Rhanna lifeboat in place.

''Tis yourself, Mr James.' Ranald held up his lantern to scrutinize the minister's face. 'A terrible thing just, eh?'

'What's terrible, Ranald?'

'A boat in trouble out beyond the Sgor Creags – a big boat I'm thinkin' too. Maybe a cargo vessel or such like.'

Mark was well used to Ranald and his fantasies, but the very mention of the treacherous rocks out there by Port Rum Point brought a shiver to his spine. He had heard so many stories about their dangers. Fergus of the Glen had lost his arm in a terrible accident many years ago while trying to rescue his brother Alick from the sea; that same brother and Rachel Jodl's father had died on those self same rocks when a fishing boat had run aground.

Mark went into the shed to help the men. The twenty-foot diesel-powered boat was starting to move down the slipway that would plunge her straight into the water. At the last moment the minister saw Grant McKenzie's face, beside him that of Matthew, Tina's husband.

'Grant! Matthew! Good luck, I'll pray for you! I'll pray for you all!'

The boat hit the water with a mighty splash. The crowd on shore held their lanterns aloft and cheered. Mark dug his hands in his pockets. Beside him old Jim Jim shook his head and remarked, 'That bugger Canty Tam was right after all – if you will excuse the language, Mr James. This very afternoon he predicted the worst storm of all was yet to come – and she's here, Mr James, she's here! He'll get wind o' this in a whilie and will be over to see will the men be bringing back dead bodies from out the ocean.'

Mark blinked rainwater from his eyes and stared out beyond the black waters of the harbour. 'God go with you,' he prayed silently – and wondered why his thoughts were only for the men in the lifeboat and not for those in the stricken vessel out there beyond the reefs.

Chapter Ten

The lifeboat left the comparative calm of the harbour to meet with the full fury of the Atlantic Ocean. Captain Mac was at the wheel, his big capable brown hands planted firmly on its wooden rim, his keen blue eyes screwed to slits in his bewhiskered face as he strained his vision into the black night. The rotating wiper whirred valiantly round, sloshing rivers of water off the window, but even so the business of steering the boat through the savage night was a nerve-wracking one and only a man of Captain Mac's experience could have tackled it so calmly, standing there as he was, nonchalantly humming a Gaelic lullaby under his breath.

'Are you trying to send us all to sleep!' Grant roared into his large, hairy, puckered ears.

Captain Mac drew his sleeve across his nose and yelled back, 'I was just thinkin' o' my mither and how she used to sing to Nellie and me when we were bairns and feart to go to sleep for the bogles who haunted the night!'

'You're not feart now, surely?' Grant yelled above the scream of the wind.

'I'm aye feart o' a sea like this! She's a force no' to be reckoned with and a bittie respect never did any harm – besides,' he chuckled, 'if I sing loud enough I might just succeed in frightening the warts off Canty Tam's water witches. We have enough to contend wi' wi'out them fleeing about us trying to steal our breeks!'

The little boat bucked and tossed as she came round the headland of Port Rum Point to meet a crazed sea torn apart by ferocious waves. A roar of thunder ripped the heavens apart, almost deafening the crew of the lifeboat. Close on the heels of the thunder a streak of lightening gashed into the Atlantic, imbuing the crashing waves with a strange blue-white light.

'The wheel, Grant, take the wheel!' ordered Captain Mac. 'Make a good fight at that bitch out there or she'll have the boat and all o' us before this night is over.'

Grant planked his strong hands on the wheel and Captain Mac stumbled away out of the wheelhouse onto the crazily tilting deck. A wall of water twenty feet high reared above the snout of the boat, then collapsed to pour itself over the deck in a frothy tide that swept Captain Mac off his feet. His ribcage made a thudding sound as it came in contact with the rails to which he clung for dear life, all the breath squeezed from his lungs. Gasping for air he peered through sheets of salty rain which ran down over his bushy brows, half-blinding him.

'Can any o' you see the flares?' he yelled when he had sufficiently recovered his breath.

'Ay, ay, over there, Captain,' Matthew pointed. Bright explosions of arching light lit the sky some distance away but no one had any time to try and determine their position. The Sgor Creags rose up suddenly, like glistening black fangs out of the jaws of some hellish sea creature.

Captain Mac half slithered, half ran back to the wheelhouse to wrest the wheel from Grant and work with it like a man demented. 'The Lord be blessed, we're no' going to make it,' he muttered under his breath, his bloodshot eyes wide and staring as in fascinated horror he watched the glistening pinnacles looming ever closer.

'Look, Captain, I can see the yacht,' Hugh yelled in high excitement.

'Never mind the damty yacht,' panted Captain Mac. ''Tis us I'm trying to save the now!'

'It *is* the yacht!' Righ confirmed, glad that his nephew had got something right for once. 'She must have escaped the whirlpool and drifted wi' the tide. Just in time too for she's on the turn again if I'm no' mistaken.'

Sweat was on Captain Mac's brow with the effort of fighting the wheel. 'Man, man, you're right!' he cried joyfully. 'She is on the turn! If I wasny so busily occupied I would kiss ye, that I would!' His heart was beating swiftly with fear and excitement. Fiercely he ground the wheel round and could have wept for joy as he experienced a sharp lift to the sea. The rocks were receding, the boat was in open water, bucking swiftly towards the *Mermaid*.

The men on deck sent up a cheer. 'We've done it!' We've done it!' Hugh's yell was full of triumph.

'We've no' done anything yet!' Righ barked at his nephew. 'And you'll no' do another thing till you put on your lifejacket! Why are you no' wearing it, you dunderhead?'

'I – I forgot,' stammered Hugh.

'Forgot nothing! No one told you so you didny bother. Get one out the locker this minute before I drown you wi' my own bare hands.'

But Hugh had no time to make a move for just then an enormous wave took and lifted the boat, tilting her so that the crew slithered about the deck. There was a terrific thump as the bow crashed down into the trough, rode up out of it and almost collided with the port bow of the *Mermaid*. There were shouts and orders and Hugh, utterly respectful and obedient of his uncle in the normal way of things, stood undecided...

'Here, take mine,' a voice spoke behind him, 'I'll work better without it.'

'No, no, I canny,' protested Hugh, 'Uncle Righ said...'

A bundle of soggy material was thrust into his face, smothering his words, and with cold, fumbling fingers he fixed the lifejacket in position.

A line had been thrown to the yacht but it fell back uselessly. One man stood on deck, frantically waving and shouting. Righ grabbed the hailer and began asking questions. The wind tossed the metallic sounds over the waves. The man bobbed down to return a minute later with a small hailer.

'My arm's broken. Can't seem to catch the bloody rope!'

'Bugger it!' cursed Torquill Andrew, mopping salt water from his eyes. 'We'll have to try and get closer.'

Lurching to the house he spoke to Mac who set his lips grimly and ordered, 'Get back out there, man, I'll do my best but canny promise any miracles.'

The lifeboat inched nearer the stricken vessel till it seemed as if the two would collide as they tossed like driftwood in the ferocious swell of the ocean.

'I can get over the gap!' Hugh, anxious to redeem favour in his uncle's eyes, extracted himself from the rest of the crew and rushed forward just as the man aboard the *Mermaid* successfully caught and secured a rope.

'Hugh, come back, you young bugger!' roared Righ, scuttling towards his nephew who was scrambling over the rails.

Hugh heard nothing above the roar of wind and waves. Below him the sea heaved, drenched him as he teetered on the edge of blackness. With his eye he calculated the distance that separated the two vessels. Bracing himself, he jumped – only to gasp in pain as something heavy grasped him from behind and pulled him backwards so that he hit the deck with a thump. In one terrific whoosh his breath left his body, his blood rushed in his ears but over and above all he was aware of horrified shouts, of boots pounding the deck.

'Christ Almighty! He's gone over, Matthew's gone over!' Torquill Andrew's voice was a high-pitched, disbelieving scream.

'Throw the belts! For God's sake throw the belts!' Graeme Donald's deep voice vibrated with shocked horror.

Lifebelts rained down into the narrow black channel

between the two hulls. A head bobbed momentarily amidst the freezing rush of waves, a white blob was upturned for a split second in time, one in which the heart of every watching man stopped beating for an instant. A hand punched up out of the water, scraped the blackness in a futile attempt to grab at one of the belts – then it and the pale, featureless blob disappeared and there was only the scream of the wind, the gushing of rain, the relentless snarl of the ocean wastes.

'Who was it? For God's sake who was it?' Hugh's fists beat the sopping deck. 'It canny be Uncle Righ, it canny – oh dear God! Did somebody say it was Matthew? It was my fault – mine.' He began sobbing in the darkest agony of his soul. The stench of his own vomit choked him. He was beyond caring. All he wanted in those dread uncertain moments was to curl up into himself and die.

'I'm going in! I must get him, I must!' It was Grant McKenzie, a demented Grant, near hysterical in his anguish. He plunged forward, ready to meet all the brutal, elemental forces nature had thrown at them that night. It took every pair of hands to keep the young man from pitching headlong into a watery grave and as the lifeboat turned and headed back to harbour with the *Mermaid* in tow, he sank to the deck, broad shoulders hunched, his dark head in his hands, sobbing as helplessly as a babe who has lost its way in a dark night.

'She's coming back – the lifeboat's coming back!' The crowd had waited patiently on the shore, some taking shelter in the boathouse, the less able drifting back to the comforts of hearth and home, the majority huddling together to talk in quiet voices about the latest excitement to hit the island.

At the sound of Ranald's lusty shout everyone surged forward, lanterns held aloft, blinking rain from their eyes as they peered into the darkness.

Mark James stood a little way apart, hands deep in his pockets, sodden collars pulled up about his ears, trying to concentrate on things close to hand; the river of rainwater pouring down the channel of Ranald's sou'wester; the rustle of oilskins; the familiar bowl of his pipe clenched tightly in one pocketed hand – he wondered why the palms of his hands were so icily clammy; why his jaw muscles were so tensely clenched; why he was trying so hard not to let his mind focus on what was happening out there beyond the harbour. The lifeboat was closer now – into safe waters – the gleaming white hull of the yacht she was towing showing up starkly in the black harbour basin…

Quite suddenly all his thoughts were outward now, and the sense of unease he had felt during all the time of waiting spewed out in trembling anticipation of what was to come.

He ran with the rest to the pier to reach out and grab the ropes and help secure them to the bollards. Although Mark was with the crowd he felt himself to be apart from it, unspoken questions fluttering on his lips. He sensed rather than saw the grief of the lifeboat crew, and when eventually he looked at them he beheld the grey ghost of death sitting heavily on each pair of weary shoulders. And then he noticed something else, a sight he thought he would never see: Grant McKenzie weeping – that handsome, brawny, carefree young McKenzie crying like a baby into his salt-encrusted hands, his footsteps stumbling, allowing himself to be helped from the boat and led away without uttering one word of protest.

'My mither was right,' Canty Tam's thin, piping voice rose up from the crowd. 'She foretold the worst storm of all would bring disaster. The Uisge Hags have taken a Rhanna man – why else would Grant McKenzie be greetin' like a bairn – '

The cheerfully gloating words died in his throat. Captain Mac had him by the collars and was shaking him like a dog, for once in his life losing control of his temper.

'Mac, Mac, stop it!' The minister plunged into the crowd to pull Captain Mac away and lead him to the comparative quiet at the back of Ranald's boatshed. 'What is it, Mac? What in God's name is it?'

Mark had meant to sound gentle but instead his voice came out harsh and uneven. He looked into the old man's face – he *was* old now, old and haggard and utterly done, even his very whiskers seeming to droop with the rest of him as he stood there, bereft of speech, bereft of the very blithe spirit that had carried him so happily over the ocean of his life.

'Mac.' The minister searched the strong, weathered face, gazed into eyes that were black pools of misery. 'What is it?' he repeated, gently this time, his compassion for the other man overriding the sense of doom that lay heavy in his heart.

For answer the old sea captain searched some inner pocket to withdraw a large, grubby square which he held shakily to his eyes. 'Mr James,' he said huskily, 'if you'll be excusin' me...'

Burying his face into the hanky he blew his nose loudly and swayed suddenly on his feet. Mark took his arm and led him over to a pile of ropes coiled on top of some fish boxes. There the old man sank down, leaned his back against the wall and gave way to silent, uncontrolled weeping.

'I'm sorry, I'm sorry, Mr James,' he sobbed brokenly, 'I canny believe what's happened. It's too sore, too sore to take in – I loved that lad, he was a son o' the soil and should never have joined the lifeboat team. He didny know enough about the sea. I mind fine when he took over from Hamish Cameron yon time he drowned out there beyond the Point. He never thought he was good enough to be Grieve o' Laigmhor but the men loved him for he was a fit man for the job, none fitter.'

Something cold and cruel gripped the heart of Mark

James, squeezing, squeezing till he felt faint from the lack of breath. 'Mac,' he got out at last, 'you're surely not telling me that something serious has happened to – to Matthew?'

Captain Mac took a deep shuddering breath. 'As serious as it will ever be – he's dead, Mr James, drowned in that hellish sea out there – and the awful thing is he died stopping another lad from risking his life. Just went right over the side o' the boat and into the water. Young Grant McKenzie has taken it bad, he thought the world o' Matthew who aye had time to spare for him when he was a bairn growing up at Laigmhor.'

He went on to explain everything that had happened, ending, 'Some will blame young Hugh for no' putting on his own lifejacket but it was an accident, minister, everything happened too fast for it to be anybody's fault – except maybe those two foolhardy buggers who got into difficulties in the first place. Folks do it all the time, think they can beat the ocean. The like o' them have no respect for her power and this is the result. Ach, poor Tina, and her waiting for her man to show up at Granda John's birthday ceilidh. Matthew had a present for the old man. He gave it to me to keep for him seeing I was in the wheelhouse and might hae a better chance o' keeping it dry. 'Tis terrible just, I've never felt so bad about anything for many a long day.'

The full implications of Mac's news hit Mark like a blow over the heart. 'Mac,' he whispered, 'how can I tell them what's happened? Where can I find the strength?'

'Where you've aye found it before, son,' was Mac's simple reply.

'I'm only a man, Mac, with the same frailties as other men!'

It was a cry from the heart. He wanted to shout out that he couldn't always find his strength in God, that sometimes he felt so overburdened with human weaknesses he had to get down on his knees and pray for the Lord to give him more faith than he had. Instead he braced his shoulders and threw his arm round the older man. 'I'm sorry I said that, Mac, of course I'll give Tina and her family all the comfort I can but first I must see you home safe and dry.'

But Mac stayed him, his tear-stained face filled with understanding. 'I ken fine it canny aye be easy to carry the burdens o' other men but you were well chosen for the job, son. You're human, you see, no' some being apart, shoutin' thunder frae the pulpit then creepin' home to commit your wee sins in private. Na, na, you're one o' us, laddie, we can talk to you man to man and that is why every man, woman, and child on this island loves you like a brother.'

Mark took a deep breath. 'Thanks, Mac, I needed to hear that. No matter what happens, how difficult it's going to be, I'll remember your words and bless you for them.'

'Ach well, I don't suppose any o' us give you much thanks for all the good you bring into our lives. I'm no' much o' a kirkgoer myself but betimes I've heard you preaching and have come away frae kirk a much wiser man than when I went in. Tina will no' hear a word against you. Thon time your roof caved in she near drove Matthew daft wi' worrying about you and of course he just laughed in that nice way he had and tried to make her see the best side o' a bad job.'

He drew another shuddering breath. 'To think we were all sitting in Old Joe's house just a wee whilie ago, cracking and laughing and listening to the old man's stories. I think Joe saw something like this coming, for before we left the house he said a very strange thing. "Go easy the night, lads," he warned. "There's danger afoot and none o' you must let each other out o' your sight." We couldny stick to his advice of course and now this has happened. I just canny believe it, son, I canny.'

The hanky was to the fore again and Mark put his hand under Captain Mac's elbow to help him to his feet. Turning the corner of the shed they were in time to see a flying figure rushing down to the pier to plunge in amongst the crowd like a tormented thing.

'Dear God, it's Eve!' Mark rushed forward and caught the girl by the arm. 'Eve, come over here, I must talk to you.'

Eve had always been a calm, sweet-tempered girl with big, languorous blue eyes and a gentle, fair beauty that sat about her like a serene mantle. Matthew had adored her and had always declared that she was the most precious Christmas gift he had ever known in his life, for she had been born on the eve of Christmas twenty-six years ago and had taken her name from that memorable day.

She had never given her parents a moment's worry, was easy to live with for she laughed a lot and never allowed her temper to get the better of her – if indeed she had a temper at all. All the family were like that, Donald her elder brother even more than any of them with his quiet, shy smile, and his thoughtful manner. It was therefore all the more disconcerting to see Eve as she was now, wild-eyed, dishevelled, her sweet, young face contorted with fear. 'Is it true, Mr James?' she threw at him abruptly. 'I met Fingal – he told me there had been an accident – my father...?'

'Ay, Eve, God help me it's true.'

'Where is he? Where's my father? I want to take him home...' She was incoherent in her grief, her head turning this way and that, searching – looking for the man she would never see in her life again.

'Eve,' Mark took hold of her and tenderly stroked the bright gleam of her hair, 'Matthew – your father – went overboard into the water – the men couldn't save him – couldn't bring him back...'

She screamed then, the despairing tortured cries of a daughter bereft suddenly of a beloved father. It was a sound Mark was never to forget for the rest of his days and he was almost glad to be released of the burden of her agony when several womenfolk came rushing over to enfold the girl to them with murmurs of comfort and condolence.

A small band of villagers were coming along the pier, bearing a stretcher in which reposed the inert figure of a man. Beside him walked a stranger with a bloody gash on his face and one arm tied up hastily by the cuff of his jacket.

He paused when he reached the group of women with Eve in their midst. Somebody had obviously told him who she was as his words to her proved. 'I'm sorry, I'm so sorry this had to happen.'

There was no trace of accent in his voice. It was cultured, polite – slightly arrogant.

From the onlookers there arose a murmur of resentment.

'Ay, and so you damned well should be!' It was old Jim Jim, spitting his disgust to the ground, grinding it in with a stout boot as if he would like to do the same to the strangers who had come to Rhanna from out of the storm. 'Foolhardy buggers, out in a yacht in this weather, playing yourselves – at the expense o' others.'

The man shrugged. 'This is no time or place to try and explain. My friend is badly hurt and needs a doctor immediately so can we get moving for Christ's sake?'

'We're taking the chiel straight up to Doctor Megan's,' Torquill explained to the minister, his strong mouth curling in disdain at the stranger's impatient cheek. 'Maybe you would get along there, Mr James, and warn her we're coming.'

'Of course.' Mark was about to hurry away when he remembered Eve, and paused for an undecided moment.

'We'll take her home, Mr James.' Seeing his dilemma Barra spoke up. 'The doctor will want you, more than any other body, to tell her what's happened for it will be quite a shock to her havin' strangers trampin' in her door at this ungodly hour.'

'Thanks, Barra, I'll be along to see Tina as soon as I can.' He rushed away, glad of some action, glad too that the rain had diminished in volume though a bullying wind still tore at his clothes as he ran to Tigh na Cladach and pounded on the door.

Megan was attired in her dressing gown and had obviously just bathed. The scent of roses wafted out to him bringing some sense of beauty to bear on that nightmare hour of storm and death.

'Mark! What on earth –?' Her first thought was that he had come to see her after all – and she was about to tell him laughingly that the same idea had been on her own mind and he had disturbed her just as she was about to get dressed, when she noticed his dishevelled state, the sodden appearance of his clothes. 'Mark, you're soaked, what's happening?'

Taking her hands he quickly explained. She stared at him. 'A yacht in trouble – on a night like this? I never heard a thing – I was having a bath. All I heard was the roar of the sea.'

'I know, I heard nothing either, just saw lanterns on the shore – Megan, the men will be here shortly. Can you put on some lights?'

'Oh, of course.' She was bewildered, trying to collect her thoughts. 'Come in, Mark, I've kept you at the door. You must have a drink before you catch cold. The whisky is on the table in the living room.'

'No, no thanks, Megan,' he said hastily and she gave a funny little laugh. 'You always refuse a drink from me, it isn't poisoned, I can assure you. Och, don't look like that, it was a joke – help me with the lights. The generator was playing up earlier, I hope it can take the strain – '

Together they rushed around, switching on lights in the hall, the surgery. Only the living room remained bathed in a rosy ambience and in this room they collided. His hands brushed her breasts, he was painfully aware of her nakedness beneath the robe.

'Megan – Meggie.' He held her close and kissed her briefly on the mouth. She was warm and soft, the fragrance of her drying hair tantalized his senses, her skin was satin smooth against his cheek. 'Don't be angry,' he said huskily, 'I just wanted to touch something lovely after the sorrows of this night – you see, there's more – Matthew was drowned saving one of the lifeboat crew from going over. I can't believe it, I don't want to face Tina – she's a very special person to me. I had to hold you – to feel your strength touching me.'

'Oh, Mark,' she breathed, 'I'm so sorry, so very, very sorry.' Pulling his dark head down to her breasts she kissed the damp tendrils at his nape and held him close for a few brief, wonderful moments, stroking his hair, murmuring soothing words. He heard her heart beating, felt the warm, sensual fullness of her breasts lying under his cheek – but it was only a fleeting moment of joy. In seconds she was gone from him, rushing to dress just as the men came through the hall with the stretcher.

'In here.' Mark led the way into the living room. The stretcher was placed on the floor, the man in it moved slightly, groaned.

He was pale to the lips, bloody, bruised, and badly cut about the forehead but none of these could quite obliterate his youthful features and firm, clean-cut jaw. The soft lamplight shone on his crisp, fair curls, cast delicate shadows over his finely honed features.

'It's alright, old man, you're safe, or rather you will be if we can rustle up some action here.' The dark young man spoke impatiently and spun round on his heel. 'Where's the doctor?' he demanded.

'Here.' Megan snapped on the overhead light and came forward into the room. She had changed hastily into a loose-fitting cream Aran pullover and a pair of close-fitting blue jeans that showed her long legs and well-shaped bottom to startling advantage. Her damp hair was mussed attractively around her clean, shining face which was rosily flushed from all her rushing about. She looked small and very young in those moments, Mark thought, certainly nothing like a fully qualified doctor facing the daunting task of putting together the injured man who looked nearer to death than life under the telling glare of the bright ceiling lamp.

Respectfully the men moved to make way for her, their sopping boots leaving wet trails all over the pale beige carpet.

'He's all yours, Doctor Megan,' growled Graeme Donald. 'We've done our bit.'

No one was prepared for her reaction as she stood looking down at the man on the stretcher. She recoiled, seemed to shrink into herself, her hazel eyes darkened to disbelieving black pools in her suddenly white face.

'What's wrong, lass?' Torquill Andrew spoke kindly. 'Do you know the man?'

'Oh, she knows him alright.' It was the other man, a smile flashing in his good-looking, arrogant face. 'She was the reason he came here and why I got myself roped in for the trip. He couldn't give you up, Doctor Megan – ' his gaze swept briefly and impudently over her slender figure – 'now I can see the reason why. Daniel Smylie Smith,' he stuck out his one good hand towards her, but ignoring it she dropped down on her knees to examine the patient with trembling hands just as Babbie came flying breathlessly in.

'I came as soon as I got the message,' she imparted, pulling off her hat and showering everyone with raindrops in the process. She was like a breath of fresh air in the oddly tense stillness of the room.

'Babbie.' Megan rose to her feet. 'Thank goodness you've come, I'm going to need all the help I can get here tonight.'

It was the most unrestrained welcome Babbie had ever received from the new doctor, and though she was somewhat taken aback she laughed and said cheerily, 'Well, it's nice to feel needed.' She turned to the men. 'Come on, lads, it's muscle we need at the moment. Take the man through to the surgery before he melts on the carpet – and it's far too nice a carpet to get stains all over it. The sooner we repair him, the sooner he'll get home to wherever he came from.'

It was obvious she had heard all about the *Mermaid*'s foolhardy attempt to reach Rhanna during the storm – and probably she had also heard about Matthew. Behind the smile her green eyes flashed dangerously, her generous, laughing mouth was set just a little too firmly.

'Do I get some attention too?' Daniel Smylie Smith grinned at her teasingly and indicated his injured arm.

The smile disappeared. She eyed him coldly. 'Ay, you too, though being the hero you are you'll have to wait your turn – oh, by the way,' the smile was back, a shade oversweet, 'I hope you have a strong stomach, Mr Smellie. We're going to need your help in surgery – you'll come in useful for boiling water and the like.'

'The name is pronounced Smylie.' Daniel's pale grey eyes were icy.

'No matter how you dress up a name like that it's Smellie in these parts and aye will be,' Babbie returned pertly.

The men tittered appreciatively, their wide grins and agreeing nods forbidding further argument from the irate young man. Babbie had won and he knew it. To make an issue of it in front of these dour, silent islanders would only be to invite further ridicule.

Graeme and the others hoisted up the stretcher. The little procession moved through to the surgery. Mark James left the house quietly and without saying goodbye. He wasn't needed there anymore, Steven Saunders had come back to Megan. His name had never been spoken but there was no need for a formal identification, it had been there in her eyes when she had stood looking down at him, telling Mark that the hopes she had for so long kept buried in her heart had been realized that night. Ay, the storm had wreaked its havoc alright – robbing the island of one of its finest men, in his place throwing back a stranger who was of little import to anyone – except for one young woman whose life had just been starting to fall into place and who now saw it crumbling into fresh pieces around her.

Chapter Eleven

'I knew it, I knew it, I knew it!'

Elspeth Morrison scuttled into the butcher's shop, bristling with importance, her face as animated as anyone had ever seen it, her customary air of calculated reserve failing her so completely she forgot for once to be dignified, and banged the door so hard behind her a string of sausages slid off their hook to land in the sawdust beneath.

'Ach, Mistress Morrison!' wailed Holy Smoke, rushing round the counter to pick up the dusty sausages and run with them to the back shop, there to swill them round and round in a wooden tub filled with water.

'Can you no' be more careful, woman?' he admonished, emerging through to the front shop to replace the gleaming wet links on their hook, as he did so giving them an affectionate pat for all the world as if they were 'alive and kicking', a habit of his where his produce was concerned and one that brought forth scowls and mutters from the more fastidious housewives.

'Indeed I meant no harm, Mr McKnight.' Elspeth, the most fastidious of all, forgot to be appalled at the rude handling of the sausages. 'It is just, I am no' knowing where I am after all the tragedies o' last night. Poor, poor Matthew. He was a good man just and the Lord will punish those pleasure seekers who were the means o' bringing about his untimely departure. I am after hearing too that Hugh McKinnon was so upset about Matthew he has left the island and will no' likely come back. Of course, a poor simple cratur' like him should never have been wi' the lifeboat team for it is a fact he has no brains at all in his head and would forget to rise out his bed in the morning if nobody told him to do it. But forbye Hugh, I kent fine trouble was coming to Rhanna though I never said a thing to anyone. I just knew it would happen sooner or later.'

'So you are after shouting when you came through the door,' Barra commented dryly, eyeing the housekeeper's flushed face. Never had she seen the parched countenance so alive, and obviously neither had the rest of the shop for all eyes were turned on this most reliable harbinger of news, the business of shopping forgotten in the anticipation of the moment.

'A pound o' stewing steak,' Barra's pleasant voice was sharp. Turning her back on everyone, she addressed herself firmly to Holy Smoke whose dewlaps were still drooping after the incident with his precious sausages. 'And be quick about it, Mr McKnight. I have other things to do wi' my time even if no one else has and I *don't* want to hear gossip at a dreadful time like this.'

'Ay, ay, right away, Barra.' Holy Smoke hacked off a lump of red meat, weighed it, removed a tiny piece no bigger than a thumbnail, and threw the remainder into a piece of paper to wrap it up dexterously.

'You'll want to hear this, Barra,' Elspeth persisted tightly, twin spots of crimson boiling high on each cheekbone.

'A pound o' link sausages, Mr McKnight,' Barra almost shouted, ignoring the impatient mutterings of those who were urging Elspeth to divulge her news. 'And don't be giving me the ones you picked off the floor – clean ones or nothing.'

'But, Barra, these is all I've had time to make this morning!' cried Holy Smoke, aghast at the very idea of losing a sale. 'There is no' a thing wrong wi' them. You saw me taking them through and washing them wi' your very own eyes.'

'By God, that sounds terrible just, washing your sausages in your customer's eyes,' choked Kate. 'And Barra's right, it's no' hygienic pickin' links off the floor and swilling them round in dirty water...'

'My water is *clean*!' Holy Smoke strove to keep calm. 'I drew it from my own well just after dawn this morning.'

'Ay, and maybe washed your socks in it first,' dimpled Kate. 'And here – ' she peered at his hands, 'what's that brown stuff round your fingernails, Sandy?' Gleefully she looked round at all the laughing faces and asked, 'Now, it canny be nicotine, can it? Our Sandy neither drinks nor smokes.'

'No, no, it canny be nicotine,' came the delighted chorus.

'Then what else is brown and clings round the fingernails to such a degree?' Kate could hardly speak for laughing. 'Can anybody here tell me that and yet keep the subject clean?'

The shop forgot all about Elspeth in the joy of teasing Holy Smoke about his nails till Elspeth finally exploded altogether. Losing all vestiges of dignity she took a magazine from her bag, waved it vigorously in the air and shouted, 'Will you all listen to me for a minute! The yacht that was rescued last night belongs to no other than Doctor Megan's fancy man! It was him and some other highfalutin' playboy who was the cause o' Matthew drownin' in that boiling sea last night!'

The effect of her words left even Elspeth momentarily stunned. All laughter abruptly ceased. A pin could have been heard drop in the deathly silence that suddenly pervaded Holy Smoke's premises.

'And how do you come to know all this, Mistress Morrison?' asked the butcher with deference, his 'Sunday best mantle' of acquired gentility falling over him like a cloak though he simply could not keep a note of pure curiosity from creeping into the carefully-worded question.

Elspeth was nonplussed by the totally undivided attention she had craved and which was now so abruptly hers.

'Graeme Donald told me the man's name, that is why I know,' she stammered in some confusion.

'Ay, but who told you the rest?' probed Kate relentlessly. 'You are no' makin' yourself as plain as usual, Elspeth.'

The old woman's lips tightened. She was herself again, throwing back her severe grey head to impart grimly, 'I was after reading all about Doctor Megan and her fancy man in one o' they sleazy magazines Ruth McKenzie gets from Rachel Jodl.' Raising one scrawny arm she triumphantly waved the magazine in the air like a flag. ''Tis all in here, every word. Steven Saunders is the mannie's name, the spoilt son o' rich parents who own boatyards in the south o' England. He was in the gossip columns wi' a half-naked young woman hanging on his arm, just one o' a string he took to amuse himself with after he broke up wi' Doctor Megan. There was some talk o' marriage between him and her and some scandal about them living together in sin before his ring was on her finger – though mind, that was only hinted at for these journalist chiels will twist anything to make a bittie news.' She tried to make the concession sound sympathetic but no one was listening anyway. The damage had been done and everyone jostled everyone else in their efforts to get at the magazine and read its contents for themselves.

'By here, she's right enough.' Kate was reading avidly, her large elbows ably warding off grabbing hands. 'Doctor Megan's name is here in black and white and it says she just disappeared out o' the lad's life wi'out so much as a goodbye kiss or a note to say where she was going.'

'Of course I'm right, I wouldny lie about a thing like that.' Elspeth folded her hands across her sparse stomach and nodded self-righteously. 'I aye kent there was something about the new doctor that wasny just right. She didny come here just for the good o' her soul or to admire the scenery – oh no – she likely came to escape the gossip connected wi' her shameful affair and thought to hide herself on this good, clean-livin' island o' ours. Of course, me being the Christian woman I am, I would never have breathed a word o' my findings to another living soul but after what happened to poor Matthew I just had to tell someone.'

'Ay, about a dozen someones,' nodded Barra, her pink face growing pinker by the minute. 'And you mean to stand there and tell us you've known all this for quite some whilie and never opened your mouth to anyone – you of all people, Elspeth? Have you been ill and none o' us knowing a thing about it?'

Elspeth appeared dazed at this pointed airing of her own enormous self-restraint on the subject, though the look she threw Barra would have frozen the Dead Sea. 'I have no' been ill, Barra McLean,' she imparted haughtily, 'I just saw no point in raking up Doctor Megan's past for I kent well enough it would rear its ugly head sooner or later and I have been proved right. There was only one person I told and that was Bob Paterson for I knew well enough he wouldny tell anyone.'

'No, he wouldny,' Aunt Grace nodded her silvery head in placid agreement. 'Bob is a gentleman just and was never one to indulge in idle gossip.'

As if on cue the door opened to admit Bob himself, his faded blue eyes more watery than usual. He had taken the news of Matthew's death badly, having worked with him since he was a boy fresh out of school. Without glancing at anyone he went up to the counter, slapped down a few coins and gave a curt order for 'a quarter pound o' wee beefies.'

Holy Smoke weighed out the minute portion of minced beef. 'Could you no' just order a half pound and be done wi' it?' he grumbled. 'You could save yourself a journey down to the shop if you were a bittie more generous wi' your sillar and you a rich man from all I'm hearing.'

''Tis no' for me, 'tis for my cat,' grunted Bob sourly. 'I wouldny insult my own belly wi' your wee beefies for I know fine you put in more fat than meat then cover it wi' blood to make it look good.'

Ignoring the butcher's indignant denials he turned his seamed brown countenance on Aunt Grace. ''Tis yourself, Grace,' he acknowledged in a breathy whisper. 'How are you the day?'

'Ach, I'm right enough, Bob, but Joe's no' so good this whilie back.'

'No, I was hearing,' Bob nodded courteously, 'but he's had a good innings and canny expect to linger forever. Tell him I will be along to see him whenever I get a minute to spare from the lambing.'

'That I will, Bob.' Coyly, Grace lowered her eyes. 'I'll have some o' your favourite wee cakes all ready baked for you – that's if the bodach doesny get wind o' them first. He might no' be well but he aye was fond o' his meat and never could resist my wee fairy cakes.'

The shop listened avidly to these exchanges between the silvery-haired woman and the gnarled shepherd for it was a well-known fact that Bob was promised to Grace as soon as Old Joe had departed the scene.

'Off wi' the old and on wi' the new,' Kate had commented when the old folks' plans became common knowledge. 'Though if Grace finds anything new in that bodach o' a shepherd I'll be the first to congratulate her for discovering a miracle.'

'I thought Joe's teeths were too loose to be able to chew these sticky wee things you bake,' Kate piped up innocently, her chagrin never diminishing at Old Joe's offensive remarks about her own attempts at baking. 'He was after telling me only last week that his teeths are more often steeping in a glass o' water than they are in his head.'

'Ay, you're maybe right enough there, Kate,'

answered Grace with equal sweetness, 'but my wee cakes just melt in the mouth and have no need o' teeths to get them over. My good man just loves everything I make for him and has never had the need o' his teeths since the day he came into my home.'

'Ay, ay, you've looked after the bodach right well,' agreed Molly, enjoying the discomfiture of the forceful Kate who had all too often in the past made derogatory remarks regarding Molly's culinary efforts.

'But surely the bodach needs red meat,' persisted Kate, somewhat red about the ears with a displeasure that was further heightened when she realized she had played right into Holy Smoke's grasping hands.

'You are a wise woman, Mistress McKinnon.' His stained teeth flashed momentarily under the straggle of ginger hairs on his upper lip. 'No matter how old, a man was never the worse for a good dinner o' real meat in his belly.'

'Ach well,' Aunt Grace smiled benignly round, 'if my Joe has his way he'll be eating a good plate o' best steak afore he goes and dies on me. The dentist mannie will be here this coming summer and Joe's dearest wish is to have a new set o' teeths fitted for his funeral – and a right bonny bodach he will look too in his white goonie and his new teeths flashin' a smile at everyone who comes to pay their last respects.'

The shop was aghast at Aunt Grace's seeming hardness of heart.

'His mouth will be closed surely,' Barra said faintly, the whole question of dirty link sausages forgotten in all the talk of the moment, 'wi' a Bible screwed tight under his chin to keep it from sagging.'

'Ay,' put in Isabel, 'everything is closed in a body that's dead, Grace, surely you must know that.'

'Ach, you are all behind the times,' Aunt Grace admonished gently, her eyes growing dreamy as she went on, 'Joe and myself have talked about it and planned it all. My dear Old Joe will be the first mannie on this island to be smilin' at his friends on his deathbed – if the Lord spares him of course,' she added quickly and rather fearfully, for no matter the circumstances it was a belief of the old folks that unless they called on the Lord to spare them for any event – even that of dying, they might bring all sorts of unimagined disasters to fall on them.

A babble of questions arose at her words but holding up her hand she warded them off, sweetly but firmly. ''Tis no use you asking me anything for I'm no' telling. It's a secret between Joe and me so you'll just have to wait and see for yourselves.'

'Well, I doubt Doctor Megan would like to be knowing the trick o' these things,' Isabel said thoughtfully, 'unless of course she'll be too busy wi' this playboy chiel you were readin' about, Elspeth, to bother her head wi' very much else.'

Bob turned a furious face on Slochmhor's housekeeper. 'So, you wereny for tellin' anybody the things you told me? Keepin' it to yourself, eh? Well, I might have kent you couldny keep that gossipin' mouth shut – and here's me thinking you were maybe a changed woman wi' more in your head than venomous talk.'

'Bob, Bob!' wailed Elspeth, grabbing onto his sleeve and holding on grimly. 'I kept it to myself all these months and after what happened last night it would have come out anyway.'

'Na, na, it wouldny.' He spat his rage into the sawdust of the butcher's shop, making Holy Smoke cringe and rush for a broom. 'It's in the past and would have stayed there but for you digging it up like a rotten old bone. Have you no decency, woman! Terrible things happened on this island last night and all you can do is bray your gossip to the world, like an auld nag wi' the shiver o' death in its bones and naught else to do but make a noise –'

Spinning round on his heel he glared his fury on the shamefaced womenfolk. 'And you listened! Matthew lies yonder in some watery grave and as usual you came cackling and clucking from your homes to pry and listen and fill your empty heads wi' dirt! You should be ashamed o' yourselves – the lot o' you!'

Shaking Elspeth's hand from his arm he stalked out, anger in every rheumy bone, forgetting all about his 'wee beefies' in his haste to escape the shop.

Aunt Grace buried her eyes in her hanky. 'Oh, he's right, he's right! I've never seen Bob so upset before. He's aye been a good, quiet, brave mannie, God-fearin' and strict, and harsh speakin' betimes but a straighter, more honest soul you couldny meet – and now he'll be thinkin' the worst o' me.' She dabbed her wet eyes, beside herself with dismay.

'He loved Matthew.' Barra's simple statement spoke volumes. Lifting her parcel of meat, she paid for it and left the premises without another word.

The rest looked guiltily at one another. 'She's right,' Kate was very subdued, 'he did love Matthew, we all did but Bob worked beside him and knew him better than anybody wi' the exception o' his own family.'

'Tina is over at Granda John and Granny Ann's house,' Isabel said softly. 'I saw her walkin' over there this morning, her poor face all swollen wi' greetin'. I'll just get along over and see will they eat a wee bite o' dinner wi' me and Jim Jim.'

Kate nodded. 'And I'll see will the minister maybe want a bittie help in the kitchen. He'll no' have Tina to see to him for a good whilie to come.'

'It would have come out, it would. There was no call for Bob to speak so harshly to a woman o' my standing.' Elspeth, white-faced and shaken though she was, still managed to have the last word. But no one was listening, everyone's attention and sympathies had been transferred to the plight of Tina and her family, and it was a very crestfallen Elspeth who made her lone way along Glen Fallan to Slochmhor, her empty message bag testimony to her distraught state of mind. Only the treacherous magazine lay in the time-worn folds of the generous bag, and with a little cry of self-loathing she snatched up the offending publication to toss it viciously into the rushing waters of the River Fallan. The shiny pages opened out as if in a last burst of satisfied mockery before whirling away on their journey to the open sea.

One by one everyone vacated the butcher's premises. In minutes the shop was empty. Holy Smoke was left staring into thin air; from their hook the untouched string of sausages leered at him fatly, the pile of unsold black puddings mocked him from their marble slab. 'Forgive me, Lord,' he said flatly, and going through to his back shop, from there to a fair-sized wooden hut, he sat himself down on an upturned fish box and drew greedily on a freshly lit cigarette.

Bob wasn't the only person to be angry at Elspeth. When Ruth heard that her name was being bandied about in connection with the infamous magazine, she was outraged.

'The spiteful old bitch,' she fumed at Lorn. 'I never gave her that magazine – she took it when my back was turned and no' until now did I know what happened to it!'

'Och well, it's typical o' Elspeth,' Lorn tried to placate his enraged young wife. 'No one will believe you gave it to her so don't get upset.'

'No, but they will believe what it says about Doctor Megan!' cried Ruth, her violet eyes black with emotion. 'And she in turn will get to hear that I was supposed to have given Elspeth the magazine. I never even knew what was in it! When Rachel sends them I just skim through the pages for they're no' really my type o' thing. No, Lorn, it's too much. I'm going to see that old witch this very minute and tell her just what I think!'

'Ruthie, Ruthie.' He caught hold of her and kissed the tip of her freckled nose, his black eyes snapping with enjoyment for she was never more desirable than when she was angry. 'Don't demean yourself by running off to fight with an old woman whose only pleasure is in taking it away from others. She would like nothing more than to think she's riled you. No, your best defence is to keep a dignified silence. After all, you're something o' a celebrity on Rhanna and will be even more so next week when you go to Glasgow to launch your first novel. You're quite a special young lady, Ruthie, and must hold up your head wi' pride at all costs.'

'Do you really mean that, Lorn?' Her rage was evaporating quickly in the soothing circle of his arms.

'Ay, every word. You just canny allow yourself to go around behaving like a wee fishwife. People here look up to you and you mustny let them or yourself down. I love these flashes o' spirit you have but only when they're for my benefit – besides,' his arms tightened round her, 'I can think o' better ways to rid you o' your energy.'

'Is that so?' Her voice was soft in his ear.

'Ay, that's so.' His mouth was warm against hers and she forgot all about Elspeth with the pleasures to be found in loving this passionate young McKenzie who seldom took no for an answer.

Steven Saunders struggled to lift himself out of a pit of blackness, only to wish that he could return to that empty void of dreamless sleep as waves of pain throbbed through him, intensifying with every conscious second till he felt he must have broken every bone in his body when the mast came crashing down on top of him. He had thought then that he would never waken again from that nightmare time of storm and pain, and panic seized him as he wondered: was he still out there in that pulverizing sea with the scream of the wind all around him and the freezing rain battering his body unmercifully? It was dark, still dark, yet there was warmth, deep and penetrating, the heat of his pain gnawing into his head, radiating out to muscle, bone, sinew. But there was a light out there, somewhere beyond the storm, a blood-red light that wavered in front of his vision in heartbeats of time. And there was sound too, the sound of the sea – it *was* still there – black, terrifying – but no, this sea was breaking gently to shore – lapping, peaceful, and above it all was the sound of the birds – a thrush? A blackbird? No, it couldn't be.

He tried to open his eyes to look. Pain shot through his head, he groaned and cried out, 'Dan? Danny? Are you there?'

His throat was parched, the words came out in a croak. Swallowing hard he tried again, 'Dan – are you there? Are you alright?'

A cool little hand sent delicious tremors of calm through the raw nerves of his forehead. 'I'm here, Nurse Babbie Büttger. Lie still and don't try to move.'

Slowly, as if afraid something might snap, he opened his eyes. The red curtain dissipated gradually, in its place came pale light and pink flowers, splashes of golden sunshine, myriad pinpricks of dancing rainbow hues; up in some canopied corner there were flashes of blue and white, mere sensations of place and time – and silhouetted against them all was an attractive blob surrounded by a russet cloud, for all the world like the colour of autumn bracken on a Scottish hillside.

'I thought I was in a garden,' his lips were cracked, his tongue bone-dry, the words came trembling out, 'in Scotland.'

Something pink moved inside the blob. 'Oh, you're in Scotland alright, by some stroke o' the gods and the guts o' the Rhanna lifeboat team.'

The voice should have been pleasantly warm but harsh chords spoiled the musical tones.

'Rhanna, so we made it after all.' His vision was clearing rapidly. The voice now had a face, a freckled, attractive face with a wide, generous mouth and unusually beautiful green eyes that were watchful, patient – and something else he didn't want to acknowledge, as coolly they assessed his face.

He struggled to place his unruly thoughts into some semblance of order. Questions tumbled to his lips but before he could speak she countered each one, as if she knew exactly what was coming – but of course she would, she was a nurse –

'Your friend is fine, as a matter of fact he's downstairs now having his dinner.' Wolfing his dinner more like, she thought dryly, never had she seen anyone eat with such rude enjoyment. 'Nothing wrong with him but a broken arm. You wereny so lucky. When the men fished you out o' the storm you were almost dead – ' That sounded too harsh. She pulled herself up. 'You had severe concussion, one broken leg, a broken wrist, multiple bruises and lacerations over your entire body – otherwise you're in the best o' health and will live. You've been here three days now. What's left o' your boat was towed into harbour, the rest was smashed to pieces on the reefs. One or two bits have come in wi' the tide and will no doubt be keeping a few home fires burning – we collect flotsam on Rhanna, it's quite an occupation when the tide is out.'

'No matter, I'm insured – or rather, my father is. The *Mermaid* is his boat.'

'Ay, money can replace some things,' Babbie murmured grimly.

'You're angry, I sensed it from the minute I woke. Why? Have I done something wrong?'

Babbie studied him. She could see why Megan had lost her heart so completely over him. Despite the bruises and bandages his good looks were very apparent. He was long-limbed and powerfully shouldered with an even tan on his smooth skin that suggested long holidays in exotic places. A rumple of fair hair spilled thick and fine below the head bandages; his regular features were clean cut, the deeply cleft chin strong and determined – but the brilliant blue eyes were too closely set, the shapely mouth a shade on the cruel side. Above all he was possessed of a charm that was completely disarming. In amongst the purpled weals, the torn skin, the bloody marks, his white teeth were flashing, asserting his charm in no uncertain manner. Have I done something wrong? he had asked, puzzled, hurt, as if a foreign word had crossed his tongue, one that had never applied to any aspect of his life.

'Oh, come on, Nurse.' He was recovering his wits, his blue gaze chiding her along with his teasing nuance of tongue. 'Don't look like that, as if I was the big bad wolf in person. I'm glad to be here, I'm grateful to you and to everybody who saved my life. I compliment you on your efficiency in telling me so exactly everything I wanted to know, but you're behaving far from sympathetically to a sick man. I'm in pain, I'm thirsty, but above all I'm puzzled as to why you seem to dislike me.'

'I'll get you something to drink.' Babbie moved away from the bed, angry at herself for discovering that it would be the easiest thing in the world to succumb to that easy charm of his. 'As for the pain, the doctor will have to see you before I can give you anything.'

'The doctor.' He lifted his head from the pillow only to fall back with a groan. 'That was the one thing you didn't tell me, efficient Nurse-I-Forget-Your-Name. Who it was that patched me up, whose house I'm in...'

Footsteps sounded on the stairs. Eve came in, a pale Eve, quiet, withdrawn, big eyes dazed with the shock of knowing that her beloved father would never again return home, that his grave was the watery bed of the ocean which might or might not give up his body, according to its whim. She had insisted on carrying on working at Tigh na Cladach. 'I canny bear to stay at home, Doctor,' she had confided, 'Granny Ann and Granda John have grown old suddenly and Mother – well, I've never seen her so sad in all my days o' living wi' her. It's as if someone has taken and shaken all the peace out o' her and all that's left is a woman who stares at the world as if seeing its harshness for the first time. My father was her life, they were both calm and easygoing together, made for one another, they aye said that. Donald has taken time off from Laigmhor and is there to see to all the wee jobs about the place. I want to keep myself busy doing what I'm used to doing – I canny thole it any other way.'

She stood in the doorway, one hand on the knob, her curtain of fair hair falling over her face for she barely looked up when she said, 'Will you be coming down now, Babbie? I've kept your dinner warm in the oven. The doctor has waited to take hers with you.'

Glancing up she saw the wakeful man in the bed, coloured and went out again, her steps light on the stairs.

'Who was that little beauty?' Steven Saunders asked in his deep, cultured voice.

Babbie swung round to face him and it was then he noticed that her eyes weren't merely green but were speckled with amber dots that seemed illuminated from behind with a strange intense light. 'Her name is Eve,' she explained in a tightly controlled voice, 'and her family is one o' the nicest on Rhanna. Tina, the mother, works to the Manse, Eve to the doctor, Donald, the son, to Laigmhor. Matthew, the father, was Grieve there until three days ago – he doesn't work there any longer, his body lies yonder in the Sound of Rhanna. He was one o' the lifeboat crew called out on one o' the worst storms ever to hit this island. Matthew was a farmer, not a seaman, but crofter or fisherman, they're all willing to help save lives – even if it means losing their own.'

Babbie delivered all this in a toneless monologue, glad to get it all out, eager to relieve her heart of its bitterness. It wasn't fair, it wasn't professional. Steven Saunders was a patient. Both he and his friend were young, adventurous, and so bloody irresponsible she could gladly have taken the two of them and banged their idiotic heads together! And to hell with etiquette!

She was a human being first, a nurse second and her hands itched to slap that shocked, handsome face staring at her from the bed.

'It's my red head,' she threw the ridiculous explanation at him, 'but I'm grateful to it, it lets me get things off my chest instead o' bottling them all up to explode at a time when it's no earthly use to me or anyone else.'

With that she flounced out, bumping full tilt into Megan on her way up the stairs.

'Babbie,' Megan spread her hands in appeal, 'please stay with me. I – I need some support. You remember what I told you about me and Steve.'

Babbie paused. She remembered alright. Just a few nights ago, after Steven Saunders had been cleaned, stitched, bandaged, and tucked in bed, Megan had sat with Babbie in the kitchen drinking tea and pouring out her heart. She had been shaking, suffering from reaction. Babbie had made her drink brandy, had finally calmed her down enough to send her to bed before going home, exhausted, to her own. Crawling in beside Anton she had wished that she had normal working hours like everyone else. The responsibility of caring for other people at all hours of the day and night seemed a heavy one in those quiet, lonely hours of morning. But then Anton's stirring arms had gone round her and he had kissed her sleepily, reminding her what it had been like all these years ago, loving him, parting with him, waiting for him to come back to fill the empty, aching spaces in her heart. She had determined then to be as sympathetic to Megan as she could, and now she placed a firm hand over that of the younger woman. 'Megan, I know just how you feel, believe me, but it's you he wants, you he's asking for. He didn't come all this way, half drowned, half dead, to have some strange nurse chaperone his big scene with you. He's waiting for you so for heaven's sake be a big girl and go to him.'

Megan took a deep breath, nodded, and climbed slowly upwards, as if she was glimpsing heaven through the open doorway of the little spare room facing out to the sea.

In the dimness of the hallway, Babbie glimpsed Daniel Smylie Smith. His animated back was to her, one hand nonchalantly placed on the wall above his head, the other, the plastered one, lightly resting on Eve's small, supporting shoulder. Eve saw Babbie watching and guiltily hurried away. Daniel turned and smiled, that slow, easy smile of his that held just a hint of defiance. He had been here only three days and already he had beguiled everyone he had met. He was an easy young man to like, with his dark good looks and charmingly persuasive tongue. Those first flashes of arrogance had been born of fear, pain, and a certain defensiveness at finding himself in a strongly resentful situation. He was aware that the manner of his and Steven's arrival had caused a lot of pain and distress, and without actually appearing to pour oil on troubled waters he had very effectively done so just by going out and mixing with the islanders, by making himself helpful and agreeable to Tina and her family, and doing everything he could for them in their troubled time. Already he was quite at home with the fisherfolk of the harbour and even Ranald, that sly, likeable money grubber with an ever open eye for chance, had willingly, eagerly, and without mention of any kind of gain, allowed the *Mermaid* to be winched up into his boat shed so that work could start on it whenever circumstances allowed.

As for Eve, she hung on every word that issued from Daniel's lips, seemed always to be hanging round him watching him with those big, sad eyes of hers. Now the pair looked to be on the verge of something more than just friendship, and Babbie sighed. Surely not that as well as everything else. Eve was terribly vulnerable just now, and this dark young stranger's manly shoulders must seem a very tempting support indeed... Babbie brushed past Daniel and sought out Eve who was in the kitchen extracting a savoury dish from the oven and setting it down at Babbie's place at table.

Babbie sat down and drew in her chair to apply herself to her food as if there was nothing else at all on her mind. 'Eve,' she said with a deliberately absent-minded air, 'please don't think I'm interfering but it really might be best if you stayed away from Tigh na Cladach for a whilie. Your mother could surely be doing with your help at home – your grandparents too.'

Eve raised overbright eyes, a dark flush stained her fair skin. 'No, Babbie, you know fine there's neighbours popping in on them every hour o' the day but they'll no' be doing that here. There's been a lot o' talk about Doctor Megan and I canny just stand back and let her cope wi' all this on her own. She just hasny the time to be cooking and cleaning and pays me well to do it for her. But it's no' the money, it's me, whenever I sit still I think o' my father and all I do is cry. At least here I can be useful and anyway, I canny bide all the gossip that's going about the now. Father would be angry if he heard it and would certainly never have put the blame for what happened on these two men. It was an accident, Babbie, even Mother says so and you yourself have no cause to be banging yourself about, glowering at Dan the way you do. He's been very kind to me and I enjoy talking to him.'

Babbie ran a hand through her bouncy red curls, her smile unrepentant when she commented, 'So, it's Dan now, is it? Next thing you'll be telling me he's grown a halo and sprouted wings – och, alright,' laughing, she held up her hands, 'sarcasm is the lowest form of wit, I know, and I'm sorry but only for getting at you. Daniel Smellie Smythe is quite well able to take care o' himself and I won't be afraid to tell him so to his face.'

'Babbie,' Eve's face was more crimson than ever, 'don't pronounce his name like that. It's insulting and he doesny like it.'

Babbie stopped eating to look up, the picture of perfect innocence. 'What? Oh you mean Smythe. But I'm sure that's how he pronounced it. Smith would be far too plain for the likes o' him.'

Eve had to smile, but at the door she turned: 'Doctor Megan has asked me to stay here for a whilie to stop any gossip. I'm away home now to tell Mother and to get my things – so put that in your pipe and smoke it!'

Such was the welter of emotions in Megan's heart as she stood looking down at Steven that she was unable to sort out any one thought in those first trauma-laden moments, and could only say in an oddly remote little voice, 'So, you're awake at last. How do you feel?'

His eyes devoured her face. 'How do I feel? We haven't seen one another for nearly two years and you speak to me as if I was some sort of stranger. Oh Megs, my darling Megs, don't you know how much I've missed you? How often during our time apart I've asked myself why you left me – how you could bear to break away from me after what we meant to one another? Why did you leave me, Megs? Why did you run away and leave me with a broken heart?'

'Oh Steve,' her voice broke, 'you know the answer to that.'

'Megs,' his voice was warm, gently chiding, 'those others meant nothing. It was always you, only you. From the start you were special to me, darling, surely you knew that? If you say I still mean something to you I'll promise never to look at another girl again. Say you love me, sweetheart, tell me that I haven't come all this way for nothing. Tell me you've forgiven me for the others – if you don't, I won't be able to bear it.'

But it was something more, something much more than that which had made her take the drastic step of fleeing from him. He must know what it was. Behind all the charm, the sensual good looks, there must be another Steve, one who knew how badly he had hurt her...

'Steve,' she began hesitantly, 'I'm still the same

woman as before, nothing miraculous has happened to me during my time away from you. I'm not perfect and never will be – '

'Megs,' he pulled her down beside him. His mouth against her ear was a mere sensation of touch yet the contact was enough to make her shiver with a pleasure that was very nearly pain.

'Steve, I've missed you so terribly.' She spoke the words on a tremble of tears. 'Yet I wish to God you hadn't come back to open up all the old hurts.'

'Darling,' his lips moved over her face, 'there won't be any more hurts, only love and pleasure, and happiness.'

Quite suddenly, and without warning of any kind, Mark strode into her mind, strong, purposeful, yet his dark sensitive face full of a sadness which smote her to the quick. 'Oh, Mark,' she murmured the name on a half sob. 'There *will* be hurts, there will.'

Steven frowned. 'Have you been falling in love with someone else, Megs?'

'Yes,' she whispered, 'I think I was...'

'Then I came back to you just in time, didn't I?'

His mouth was about the only part of him that hadn't been bruised in some way, but it was all she needed just then. It was like a magnet, full, tantalizing, with that odd, cruel little half smile of his quirking the corners. She melted her own against it and knew again that wondrous thrill that had been missing for so long from her life. He allowed her to play with him for a little while before his lips quickened, hardened. Somehow his one good, unbandaged hand was on her breasts. She drew in her breath, the world spun away, and she was lost – lost as she had longed to be, yet had never wanted to be again – at least not with Steven Saunders.

Chapter Twelve

The sea never did give up Matthew's body. Every morning Tina went down to the lonely shores of Burg, sometimes accompanied by Eve or Donald, more often to wander in solitary seclusion, eyes sore with weeping, heart heavy with grief. The winds of the ocean swept over her, harsh at first, but as the days of spring progressed they became softer, laden with the promise of kinder weather to come.

But nothing could take away the bleakness in Tina's heart. She thought of her man, of how it had been with him, of how well they had loved in their own carefree, uncomplicated way.

He had been a good man, quiet, unassuming, hard working, never born to make a great mark in life but making it just the same in his own small world, in the lives of his wife and family.

'You were my man,' Tina whispered to the murmuring heartbeat of the ocean. 'I loved you and now I've lost you and I haveny even the privilege o' seeing your bonny body laid to its proper rest.'

Looking back along the shore she could see the doctor's house, chimneys puffing with busy smoke, garden awash with golden daffodils. Everyone had been wrong. Doctor Megan hadn't been wasting her time. As the earth warmed so her garden bloomed, first with drifts of snowdrops spilling about everywhere, then with brilliantly-hued crocuses bursting ebulliently over the gladed knoll to the side of the house. After them had come the daffodils, bullied by the cold winds of March, growing richer and thicker as a gentle heat came into a sun that not only drew forth the daffodils but also the first tiny, shy wild flowers growing low on the machair.

Every other day Eve came home bearing sprays of daffodils and early narcissi, and when Tina asked after the crew of the stricken yacht the answer was always the same. 'Oh, they're getting stronger all the time but it will be a whilie before Mr Smith gets his plaster off and even longer for Mr Saunders.'

Tina knew her daughter. The more evasive she was about 'Mr Smith' the more serious were her feelings for him. Men had always been attracted to Eve. With her happy-go-lucky nature, her fair good looks and comely figure, she had been twisting men and boys round her little finger since the age of fourteen. Those she had liked a lot had been constant companions for several months, affairs of the heart she had hugged to herself, as if by discussing them she was giving away some of the magic; the rest had been more pastimes, young men to go walking and dancing with, nothing more. Calum Gillies had been her latest companion but now his name was rarely mentioned, and Tina shivered and wondered how her bonny daughter would cope with a man as worldly-wise as Daniel Smylie Smith while her sore heart was in such desperate need of comfort.

Quite often Tina glimpsed her daughter walking hand in hand with Daniel, their heads close together, their footsteps measured and slow in the twists of golden sand over yonder in the secluded coves of Burg Bay.

One day Mark James sought out Tina as she wandered the seashore. She saw him coming a long way off, his tall, loose-limbed figure slower than she ever remembered, the steps of him unsure on the rutted sheep path twisting among the marram, his dark head bowed as if he wasn't taking in much of the things around him.

Tina's caring heart wept more for him then than it did for herself. More than anybody else she knew that this was a time of great trial for her beloved minister. Doctor

Megan's demon was hard at work, closing her eyes to everything but the reality of Steven Saunders under her roof. She was too blinded by enchantment to either see or care what she was doing to Mark James, and Tina sighed heavily while she wondered where it would all lead in the end. People would get hurt, nothing was surer, Doctor Megan, the minister – her very own Eve...

The smile the minister threw as he drew nearer couldn't disguise the unhappiness in his eyes. 'Tina.' His hands came out to take hers. Warm hands they were, warm and strong. She felt his goodness flowing into her.

'Ay, Mr James?'

'Matthew – will not come back.'

'I know that, the sea has him and will hold on to him.'

'And – you accept that, Tina?'

'I accept it – but – I'll never forgive the damty bugger for keeping my man when I want him home here on Rhanna, in a place I can be visiting him wi' a wee bunch o' wild primroses or just a great big armful o' buttercups. He loved buttercups did Matthew and used to say that for a humble wee flower they gave the greatest show on earth when they bloomed in their thousands all over the machair – '

With a huge shuddering breath she laid her head on his shoulder and cried on it, her fine, fair hair descending in flyaway strands all over his jacket, a deluge of kirby grips raining down to catch in his lapels, one or two even landing in his pockets.

'Tina,' he said huskily, 'you're a good woman. I hate to see you like this, the Lord knows you didn't deserve any of it to happen.'

'And so are you,' she sobbed, searching frantically for a hanky, grabbing his proffered manly square to scrub with embarrassment at her eyes and blow her nose soundly, 'a good man. Och, Mr James, we're both just two souls lost the now and it was lovely just, the way you let me greet on your shoulder.'

'Tina.' Straightening, he placed his hands on her

shoulders and looked her straight in the eye. 'The time has come – you know that, don't you?'

'Ay, Mr James, I know,' she nodded, and one by one, as if playing for time, she plucked her kirby grips from the clinging, hairy tweed of his jacket.

The memorial service was held out in the open, on the wide white sands of Burg Bay, with a gentle sea lapping the shore and the haunting cry of the curlew winging over from some hidden, lonely place.

From all over Rhanna folk had come to pay their last respects to Matthew's memory, the wide stretches of Burg had never known so many people crowding its wild shores. They stood waiting, a solemn band that wound round the great curve of the bay, their feet churning the golden sands, their voices hushed so that the crying of seabirds, the bleating of sheep, took precedence over all.

A few less gregarious souls had chosen to wait seated on the pink gneiss rocks close to the sea, others stood in the lee of the cliffs where the Well o' Weeping foamed up from an underground cavern. Though there was little wind that day, little eddies of air swept in and around the vast caves and black columns of rock that surrounded the Well o' Weeping, causing a plaintive sighing wail to reverberate in the caverns and whistle eerily round the lichen-encrusted rock pinnacles.

Shona, standing nearby with Niall, shivered as the sounds invoked in her a memory of the strange, lost feeling she had experienced last time she had been near the Well o' Weeping. On that day she had stood atop the cliffs, watching a small boat sailing away up the Sound. In it had been Niall and Ellie, her eldest daughter, whom she had never seen again, and the unease in Shona had been born of some odd premonition wrought in her by the Well o' Weeping which legend said had been made by the tears of the widows who had come there to mourn husbands, sons, and brothers lost at sea.

Taking Niall's arm she pulled him away, over to where Kirsteen and Fergus were surrounded by their grandchildren; Ellie Dawn; the twins sound asleep in their pram, watched over by five-year-old Lorna, the eldest child of Lorn and Ruth.

'I was just thinking about the day I made Matthew Grieve of Laigmhor,' Fergus greeted his daughter and son-in-law, 'the lad was overwhelmed, he thought he wasny fit for the job – but by God! He turned out to be the best Grieve Laigmhor ever had after Hamish. He had a quiet authority about him that the men respected and a way with the animals that was a joy to see. I've been wondering who will I get to take his place.' He looked at Lorn. 'You will be running the farm one day soon, I'll leave it up to you.'

Lorn's dark gaze sought out Donald, standing tall and fair beside his family. 'He's the natural choice, Father, he's got the same qualities as his father and I know fine you've already picked him as the one.'

Fergus smiled sheepishly. 'You know me better than I know myself. Donald it is then, we'll let him know after this is over.'

Mark James arrived, going straight down to stand by Tina and put a kindly, supporting arm round her shoulders. 'Are you ready, lass?' he asked softly, his eyes dark with the solemnity of the occasion.

'Ay, Mr James, I'm ready.' Tina's face was white and strained, she had grown thinner these last terrible weeks but there was about her a gentle dignity and an air of wonder at the sight of so many people crowding the bay. Her man had indeed been well liked. If he was here he would have smiled, that slow, bemused smile of his and voiced his astonishment that folk had taken time off from spring tasks for *him*. But he *was* here. Tina could feel the peace of him in her weary soul, calming her, soothing away her pain.

She threw the minister one of her languorous lovely smiles. 'I'm fine, Mr James, really fine. Matthew's here,

I can sense him at my side the way he was in life. I can hear his voice, tellin' me wee stories about how he sorted things out. I aye kent he exaggerated a bittie but he was my man and I just let him have his way. In the end all his fancies came true enough, he died a brave man, Mr James, and I'm proud to be here the day, seeing all these good folks come to say goodbye to Matthew.' She glanced over her shoulder. ''Tis Granda John and Granny Ann I'm worried about. They're no' able to stand in the one place for any length o' time and they wondered if it would be out o' place for them to sit on the rocks beside us. They have brought cushions and bits o' blankets for their knees but don't like to bring them out in case it isny good manners.'

'Och, Tina,' Mark found himself smiling, 'of course it's alright. I'm sure the Lord Himself would agree to old folks having a bit of comfort at a time like this.'

The old couple was soon settled. Mark James held up his hand. A hush fell over the crowd, the ocean sighed, the memorial service to Matthew began.

The deep, clear voice of 'the man o' God' carried over the bay, over the sea. He spoke about Matthew's life, his honesty and integrity. 'Rhanna has lost one of its finest sons but none of us will ever forget him, we will remember how he lived and even more, we'll recall proudly to mind how he so bravely and selflessly died.'

Behind him, Grandma Ann sobbed quietly, Granda John reached out a rheumy old hand to take hers and squeeze it comfortingly; Donald swallowed and stared out to sea; Eve put her arm round her mother and hugged her close.

From the corner of his eye Mark saw Megan making her way down to the bay, accompanied by Daniel who was helping her along. They melted into the crowd yet Mark was as aware of her presence as if she stood at his elbow. His heart beat a little faster, he was conscious of it even as he glanced up at Tigh na Cladach and noticed something else, a face at one of the upper windows, the face of Steven Saunders, staring down, watching proceedings – Megan must have moved his bed to the window...

'Mr James,' Tina spoke at his side, 'are you alright?'

He realized that he had paused too long, all eyes were turned on him, waiting for him to carry on. But his throat was tinder-dry, his concentration gone. Raising his hand he signalled for prayer. He didn't look at the window again. The singing began, rising, swelling: *Rock Of Ages: O Love That Wilt Not Let Me Go.* The notes of each hymn, each psalm, rose up to merge with the murmur of the ocean, to meet with the vast blue dome overhead.

Then came a hush, timeless moments of waiting – and then it came, the plaintive music of the pipes, away up there on the clifftops of Burg. Torquill Andrew McGregor, gold medallist at the Highland Games, was playing the quiet lament, 'Fingal's Weeping', followed by 'Last Farewell To The Isles', a pipe tune composed by a Rhanna sailor of long ago, one who had left his island never to return except in his music which had been handed down through generations of islanders.

It was a moving and never-to-be-forgotten farewell to Matthew; Torquill's magnificent, big-muscled body was taut and proud up yonder on the skyline, his steps measured, his kilt flying in the breezes, the drones of his pipes silhouetted darkly against the azure sky. When finally he broke into the beautiful and well-loved tune 'Going Home', everyone joined in, one by one, their voices rising, falling, soaring to a crescendo of poignant, glorious sound that echoed round the bay and seemed to keep on echoing long after the last notes died away. Then the hankies were out, everyone wept openly.

Tina leaned against her daughter and sobbed, 'Ach, my bonny man, 'tis proud I am to be his wife. Was it no' beautiful just, Eve? Never will I forget it, no' till my very own dying day.'

Elspeth Morrison stood apart from everyone, weeping

sorely, her gaunt, stiff face pale and woebegone.

'My, my, Elspeth is taking it badly right enough,' Isabel commented to Jim Jim, 'I doubt she's no' got a stone for a heart after all.'

But Elspeth's tears were for herself as much as for Matthew. She had truly believed herself to be making more than a friend out of Bob the Shepherd, but since the episode in Holy Smoke's shop Bob had not deigned to look the road she was on. He was back in Aunt Grace's camp, standing beside her now, courteously holding her bag while she patted her genial pink and white face with a tiny lace square. She was wearing one of her favourite hats that day, a worn 'chanty-shaped felt' to use Old Joe's description, liberally decorated with bright red cherries which had slipped from their mooring and were dangling rakishly over one dainty pink ear, the stretched lobes of which were also emblazoned with more cheerful cherries.

Bob seemed bewitched by her and was most attentive to her needs, smiling indulgently every time she turned to wave to Old Joe who had been carefully brought along to the doctor's house to watch the service from one of the lower back windows.

Elspeth winced at the sight of Aunt Grace's bountiful contentment. Daft old harlot, she thought vindictively, a string o' men at her skirts and herself at an age when she should be picking a plot in the kirkyard for her own burial.

She caught Bob's eye and attempted a watery, ingratiating smile but the old shepherd pointedly ignored the overture and Elspeth buried her face in her hanky afresh, glad of the excuse Matthew's memorial service had given her to shed her tears of bitter loneliness without fear of curious comment.

Captain Mac, his bearing respectfully restrained, came over and placed one big heavy hand on the old housekeeper's thin shoulder. 'There, there, lass,' he comforted awkwardly, 'just you greet and don't be ashamed o' one single tear. I know how you feel, 'tis fine enough to grieve surrounded by friends but 'tis sore, sore indeed to weep on your own.'

Her head jerked up sharply at his intrusion, quick words sprang to her lips but then she noticed his eyes, swollen to brown chinks under their hairy white canopy, and his bulbous jolly nose, more swollen than ever from his own unashamed weeping.

'You are a brave and sensitive man, Isaac McIntosh,' she intoned, unable to keep a wobble from her voice, "tis a sore life indeed and of all the folk here only you had the gumption to offer me a kindly word.' Wiping her eyes with a flourish she stuffed her hanky into her bag. 'I have a wee bunch o' flowers I thought to put in the sea in Matthew's memory. Would you be so good as to accompany me down for I'm that shaky I doubt I'll never manage it on my own.'

Gallantly he crooked his arm and they went together to join the throng who were tossing wreaths and flowers into the clean, clear waters of Burg Bay. The blooms merged and mingled, tiny wild flowers, floral sprays, expensive wreaths, spreading out all along the curving petticoats of the sea which lapped and tossed, lapped and tossed, before the outgoing tide carried its bounty to some unknown shore far, far away from those of Rhanna.

'Come on, Tina,' Mark put his arm round a lingering Tina and led her away, passing Megan as they went. She was noticeably alone in the crowd. Her surgery was strangely empty these days and while the fact niggled at her a good deal it also left her with a lot of free time for Steven. One or two of the islanders had dared to go along to Lachlan's with their 'wee ails' but he was having none of it.

'Oh no you don't,' he told them grimly. 'I know fine what you are all about and I will no' condone such childish behaviour. Megan's your doctor now so just you get along there and let her deal with you.'

Mark and Megan had not come across one another since that fateful night of the storm. Now she looked at him for a long time, her hazel eyes rather guilty as they gazed into his smokey grey-blue orbs. She was the first to turn from him and she went hurrying away, back to Tigh na Cladach and Steven Saunders who watched from his window and smiled – a crooked little smile that was oddly self-satisfied.

Spring came to Rhanna with a suddenness that was as disconcerting as it was welcome. Every morning the sun rose up out of a calm sea into a honey-gold sky shot through with softest shadows of lilac; every evening it sank below the Sound of Rhanna, a great fiery ball whose afterglow turned the sea into a sheet of flame in which small fishing boats sailed homewards and elegant yachts looked like beautiful birds with gilded wings.

Groups of islanders walked in the gloaming, the old Gaels to strain practised eyes towards the horizon for weather signs; the young ones to look at one another, the blood hot in their veins, the light of passion gleaming in their eyes.

But the weather held, the Hebridean days stretched, grew brighter and more bountiful with each wondrous dawn. Skylarks sung endlessly from morning till night, their ecstatic voices echoing over sylvan fields, filling the great shaggy stretches of moorland with music and life. And the machair bloomed, shyly at first but soon covered with a myriad of tiny blossoms; clumps of primroses peeped from every sheltered cranny; great yellow moons rose up to bathe the island in that wonderful golden light so peculiar to the Hebrides.

And in the paradise that was Rhanna Steven Saunders's wounds healed, his shattered bones mended. Each day he grew stronger, more able to cope with his diminishing aches and pains, more able to cope altogether with the world he found himself in. It was so different a world from the fast-paced one he was used to, so different a people from the sophisticated set he had moved in all his life. There was no acting the part here, few pretended to anything they weren't feeling at any given time. They were down to earth, cannily aware of the world around them, completely natural, warm-hearted, friendly – and so earth-shatteringly blunt he had had the wind knocked out of his sails almost from the word go.

Babbie had disconcerted him completely with her straightforward manner and equally honest tongue.

'Are they all like you on the island?' he had asked once, his blue eyes sliding lazily over her pert little face with its sprinkling of freckles.

'No,' she had answered smartly, 'I'm one o' the milder varieties. Just wait till you meet old Sorcha and Behag – no' to mention Elspeth Morrison – oh, and Kate McKinnon of course. She's so natural she'll strip you naked with just a few well-chosen words and leave you wishing you had hide to protect you instead o' skin.'

He grinned. 'Perhaps I wouldn't mind being stripped naked by this Kate woman – if she is as attractive as you, Nurse Babbie Büttger.'

Babbie had skirled with laughter at that. 'You'll have to judge that for yourself – Kate is what you might call a robust woman with a tongue to match. Now – stop blethering and get into that chair or I'll never get this bed made. The sooner you can start moving under your own steam the better for I have more than enough to do without being at your beck and call twice a day.'

He had sighed heavily at her words, a frown marring his handsome face. 'Well, thank heavens for you, blunt tongue and all. If it hadn't been for you, and Eve, and Danny boy, I think I might have died of boredom these last hellish weeks. Megan only comes near me when it's completely necessary. After me coming all this way and almost killing myself in the process.'

'She didn't ask you to come,' Babbie flashed, eyes

ablaze, 'and it might be better for all concerned if you and Mr Smellie Smith were to pack your bags and leave just as soon as you're able to do so!'

'Why? Why the hell should I?' His chin jutted aggressively. 'Megan did enough packing for both of us when she walked out on me without as much as goodbye! I was devastated when she ran off and vowed she could rot in hell for all I cared. But it didn't work out like that, she haunted me every minute of the day and night until I couldn't stand it any longer and I'm damned if I'll go back without her! I've never chased after any woman but Megan's different.'

Babbie studied him. His eyes were an angry brilliant blue in his fine-featured face, the full, sensual mouth was twisted into determined lines. 'Oh ay, she's different alright, Mr Saunders. No doubt she's the only woman who's ever run out on you and the truth o' that must be a bitter pill to swallow for a man as self-centred and as spoilt as yourself.'

'Don't go too far, Nurse,' he had gritted warningly, glaring at her. She had stared him out, her green eyes glittering coldly, and he had been the first to turn away.

From that day he had known exactly where he stood with Babbie and could never be in a room with her without feeling that she knew just what was going on in his mind. He had fumed and fretted in the confining prison of the little room that had in the beginning soothed him with its old world charm and its view of the sea – and the thought of Megan in the same house, her room just two doors away from his.

But she hadn't come to him as often as he had expected.

'Please, Steve,' she pleaded, twisting her hands together and keeping her eyes averted as if he was a sight to be avoided at all costs. 'I can't be with you every minute of the day. I have other patients to attend to...'

'I'm not one of your bloody patients, Megan!' he clipped. 'And to hell with daytime – there's the nights.

We're alone here and we have all the time in the world.'

'We're not alone, there's Eve and Danny to think about.'

'Are you blind, Megan?' he questioned rudely. 'They're so wrapped up in each other we might as well not exist! Don't tell me you haven't noticed that?'

She ran a hand through her hair, her mind totally confused by everything that had happened lately. Since Steven's arrival she had been in a turmoil, and so completely taken up with her own thoughts and conflicting emotions that she had barely been aware of anyone, far less Eve who had been so quiet since her father's death she might not have been there. As for Danny, hc always seemed quite happy to spend as much time as possible out of doors and was very seldom an intrusive presence.

'I hadn't noticed,' she admitted frankly, 'I'll have to talk to them both – oh God, I wish I'd known. The irony of the whole thing is almost too much to bear. Poor Tina, she's had enough to worry her and now Eve as well – and everyone will say I've encouraged it.'

'Megan, what the hell's gotten into you?' he demanded. 'You stand there, worrying about other people when it's us you should be thinking about – ' his tone changed, he became the Steven she had known and loved so well. 'Have you forgotten what it was like between us? How you loved me and couldn't stay one second from my side?' His eyes were burning into hers. Her heart accelerated, the old familiar ache was back in her breast. All she wanted in those moments was the feel of his arms around her, his mouth on hers. She stepped back from him, steeled herself to withstand that treacherous sensuality of his.

'No, Steve, I haven't forgotten, I've never forgotten – but – '

'Is there someone else? Is that it? Some man you thought you were falling in love with before I came along again? Tell me, Megan, because if there is, I'll know to stop hoping that you and I might have a life together.'

Her eyes strayed to the window, to the Sound of Rhanna churning restlessly, its turmoil reflecting her own mixed emotions. 'I told you before, Steve, there might have been someone else – but you've come back, and dear God! I don't know where I am anymore – what to believe – '

She had fled from him then – out of the room, down the stairs and he had hardly seen her since, except in her professional rôle and nearly always accompanied by Babbie.

Everything changed after that. Eve went back home to her mother's house, Danny back to England to soothe a lot of ruffled feathers, particularly those of Mr Saunders who, as soon as he knew his son's life was in no danger, had been furious at everything and everyone and was demanding to know how soon the *Mermaid* would be seaworthy once more.

'These insurance jobs take time, Mr Saunders,' Danny, looking suitably downcast, spoke sympathetically. 'You know yourself that the *Mermaid's* been checked over and an estimate for the damage should come through any day now. When it does I'll see to everything personally, have no fear of that.'

Steven employed Eve to write letters home, epistles that were designed mainly to appeal to his mother's forgiving and indulgent nature. Back came the replies. Of course it hadn't been his fault, she would pacify Daddy, meanwhile he wasn't to worry about a thing. He must get better in his own time and come home when he was quite well. Daddy would have calmed down by then.

Meanwhile spring had come to the Hebrides, a glorious, golden spring that beat into Steven's strengthening body like an impelling rhapsody. Beyond his window a turquoise sea lapped the white sands of Burg Bay, islands rode ethereally on the horizon; far-flung lighthouses twinkled over midnight-blue seas; each new dawn was an incredible mixture of light and peace and vast skies opening to the wealth of the sun.

On one such morning he woke with an unbearable longing to be out there in the awakening world and just a few hours later came Babbie and Megan, armed with clippers which snipped through his plasters till he lay surrounded by powdery crumbs and bits of shell that had encased his limbs for six long, itch-tormented, air-starved weeks.

The scar on his leg was vividly purple against unnaturally white skin and was tacked together by a neat row of stitches sticking up out of the surrounding fair hairs. Sheer relief made him laugh aloud, his wide mouth was slightly crooked, his eyes crinkling in his disarmingly handsome face.

'You're a dab hand at the embroidery, Doctor – and if I sound like one of the islanders it's because I've grown so used to listening to Eve and Nursie here I'm bound to take some of it in.' He gazed directly into Megan's eyes. 'It's strange, I never knew the doctor Megs – just Megs the woman.'

She stepped back from the bed, dismayed to feel the colour flooding her face, to find herself staring entranced at that cruel, smiling mouth which had so often in the past transported her to unbelievable rapture...

'Compliment Babbie – she put them in, I, I –' She couldn't very well tell him that her hands had been shaking so much she couldn't for the life of her have threaded a needle, let alone sew up his leg.

'Ach, we both sewed you up between us – ' Babbie began, only to be interrupted by his shout of laughter.

'What a nice sandwich that would have made! Me in the middle of two voluptuous women. If only it had happened that way. I would have found plenty to keep me occupied during my convalescence.'

Babbie's mouth twitched as she picked up the scissors. 'Lie still while I snip the damt things out. Biddy – my predecessor – once said, "The Lord giveth and the Nurse taketh away" and if you don't stop wriggling I'll take things o' yours away you wouldny like to be without.'

'Hell,' he groaned and lay back, one arm crooked behind his head, 'what did I do to deserve you? God help your regular patients. At least I'll soon be rid of you.' He winced – these scissors were none too gentle. Bitch! Still, he admired her despite everything. If nothing else she was a good nurse – and probably a little spitfire in other fields despite that cool front – the stitches were out! He was free! He laughed again. An infectious laugh that made even Babbie smile.

He was impatient to be up, to be out of the bed that had for too long been a lonely prison. He struggled to stand, supported by two pairs of feminine shoulders. The effort brought sweat to his brow – but he was upright at last. The sun streamed through the window, beat warmly on his lightly-clad body, brought out the sweet clean fragrance of Megan's shining hair. Something in him stirred, awakened – his hand came round to crook her chin, he pressed his lips to hers.

'Don't mind me.' Babbie was almost as taken aback as Megan and felt foolish, standing there supporting a man who was kissing another woman.

'Oh, I haven't forgotten.' His head swung round, impudently and briefly he claimed her mouth and very neatly her small sharp teeth pierced his lower lip. He staggered, fell back onto the bed, drawing his fingers over the puncture, examining them for a sign of blood. It was there, a tiny drop, as red as the colour which diffused his face.

'Bloody little spitfire!' he spat. 'It was only fun. I felt so good – I wanted the whole world to share it!'

'The whole world can, except me.' Babbie knew she had over-reacted but even so she spoke evenly and unrepentantly and without another word left the room. Megan, her eyes too bright, made to go after her but his hand came out to catch hers. 'Megan, don't go! For God's sake, what have I done that's so bad?'

'Please Steve, let me go,' she half sobbed, her voice no more than a whisper.

'No, Megs, I'll never let you go again!'

He wasn't a sick man any longer, he was the Steve Saunders she remembered, strong, in control, of himself – of her – of everything that she had tried to pretend she had regained in all those long, weary months away from him.

She allowed herself to go to him, to curl down beside him like a small girl in desperate need of reassurance.

'Megs,' he murmured into her hair, 'I thought I had lost you – not just while we were apart but here, on Rhanna, where I could see you and feel your presence – yet not have you at all.'

His pyjama jacket was open right down to his navel showing his smooth, still-tanned skin, the furring of hairs on his chest, his gaze was on her, slightly mocking – and something else: passion, smouldering, setting the blue eyes of him on fire. They held her own for a long, breathless moment before they travelled over her face to her throat, lingering on the curving swell of her breasts. She was wearing only a light blouse and the smile in his eyes deepened when he saw the firm swelling of her nipples. The sunlight was on her hair, turning the silken brown wash of it to a golden chestnut. His eyes played with her, tormented her as they slid from the delicate arch of her throat, the fragile curve of her shoulders, then focused once more on her mouth: the pale rose of her lips; the white, even teeth which were biting on her lower lip to keep it from trembling. With delicate slowness he bent and kissed the warm hollow of her throat, teased and played with her mouth till she could stand it no longer and with a little helpless cry she captured his mouth before it could elude her. Over and over they kissed, swiftly, breathlessly, till she pulled away from him, as if in need of respite from the overwhelming desires that were engulfing her senses.

'I'd better go down,' she whispered against his throat,

'Babbie will be waiting, we always discuss our schedules round about now.'

'To hell with Babbie,' his voice was harsh with longing, 'we need this time together, Megs, there's so much of it to be made up.'

His body was hard beneath hers, hard and powerful in spite of his recent injuries. She could feel the thump of his heart against her cheek: how she had loved that wilful, impulsive heart: every precious beat had filled her with delight and wonder... She pressed her lips to the sound of it and quite without warning a vision of Mark James came to her once more: the smokey-blue eyes of him boring into her soul, as if he had known all along that this moment would come for her and he could have none of her as long as the obsession that was Steven Saunders imprisoned her heart.

'Oh, Mark,' she sobbed his name against Steven's chest and some separate part of her begged Mark's forgiveness even as she allowed herself to relax and give her mouth to Steven.

'Don't cry, Megs,' he wiped her tears away with a practised finger, 'I'm here, my darling, and we're going to make the most of every second we have together.'

Chapter Thirteen

The evening boat brought Daniel Smylie Smith back to Rhanna, well pleased with himself as work on the *Mermaid* could now get started, and he had spent the last few days in Oban arranging for the relevant parts to be shipped over on the same steamer as himself.

He was even more pleased when, on presenting himself at Tigh na Cladach, he discovered Steven to be up and about and sipping sherry in Megan's homely little sitting room.

'You look well on it, old son,' Daniel enthused, 'and you'll feel even better when I tell you that work can begin on the *Mermaid*. I'll arrange some local help and be on the spot to supervise and make sure the buggers get their fingers out. From what I've seen they're not too keen on hard work in these parts though no doubt the finished efforts will be alright. That old geezer, Ranald, seems more than keen to let us continue using his boat shed so all in all everything's worked out well.' He winked. 'Should all take a few weeks though, and I must admit this place has grown on me so I mean to make the most of my stay – as no doubt you will too.'

Steven, somewhat pale after his first day up and about, held up a protesting hand. 'Dan, old boy, slow down. I've just spent six weeks on the boards and am in no fit state for all this breezy talk. I'll be taking my time getting myself shipshape again and a whole summer mightn't be long enough to do it in. I've still to *see* this island, remember, and while I'm seeing the sights I want you to keep out of the way.'

It was his turn to wink. The young men smiled at one another in complete understanding.

Morning brought Eve, so overwhelmed to have Daniel back she rushed to the kitchen to sit at the table and nibble nervously at her fingernails while she stared tearfully and unseeingly into space. Megan had never known Eve to bite her nails before. She felt uneasy and wished Daniel hadn't come back, and without more ado she went to find him and tell him he couldn't possibly stay at Tigh na Cladach.

Just a few hours after Daniel's return the island knew about it. Tigh na Cladach was instantly labelled a 'house of sin', more so now that the two men in it were up and about and able to indulge in 'all sorts o' mischief'.

'I told you she's a Jezebel.' Elspeth was emphatic in her condemnation of the doctor and this time her cronies were inclined to agree with her as their nods and 'ay's' so amply implied. 'No' content wi' corruptin' herself she's inveigled Eve into her web as well – and after all the tragedies that's happened in that family too. Tina is beside herself wi' worry as well as grief, Eve was aye a lass for the lads but she was careful wi' herself. The Lord alone knows what trouble she'll get into wi' that cityfied young man. He's just brimful o' fancies and conceit.'

'Fancy having to go there and have our ails seen to by a doctor wi' soiled hands,' Old Sorcha snorted, her wig, which was a startling auburn shade, falling over one eye through all her energetic noddings. ''Tis no' decent, no' decent at all. I'm thinkin' maybe I'd rather die than be at the mercy o' a scarlet woman.'

'A scarlet woman indeed!' hooted Kate. 'Were you no' the very wifie to have *three* men bidin' under your roof at one time and none o' them husbands or brothers!'

'That was a different state o' affairs altogether, Kate McKinnon,' Sorcha replied with dignity. 'These were just innocent lodgers wi' nothing more wicked in their heads than their own state o' health and how much better they would be breathin' in the good, clean island air.'

'One was a keep fit fanatic,' reminded Isabel, 'wi' muscles on him as big as a house and strength enough in him to take on a dozen wimmen at a time. But of course, you were in no danger there, Sorcha, we canny very well compare the likes o' yourself wi' a bonny young woman like Doctor Megan.'

'See you and keep a respectful tongue in your head, Isabel McDonald!' warned Sorcha, with such an indignant toss of her head that her wig landed squarely in Kate's lap to lie there looking for all the world like a dejected stray cat.

The very next day Daniel booked himself into Kate McKinnon's good auspices for an indefinite period and one month's keep in advance. A delighted Kate immediately forgot all the things she had said about the young man, and set about making him feel most welcome in her house by giving him the best spare room with a view of the sea and even going to the lengths of putting a china jug and basin in the wee hoosie so that he could wash his hands when he had finished his ablutions.

Many of the houses on Rhanna were still without indoor plumbing and Kate cheerily voiced this fact to Daniel along with the hope that he wouldn't find it a great inconvenience (here she skirled with hearty laughter) after being used to 'the fancy modern ways o' the mainland.'

'Of course not, Mrs McKinnon,' he assured her with one of his wide lazy smiles, 'I find it all very refreshing and am looking forward to a long summer on Rhanna.'

Kate was completely bowled over by his winning ways and dark, good looks. 'Ach, call me Kate, everybody does, and I'll just call you Danny. It's easier than thon awful mouthful you cry yourself.' She threw him a sidelong glance. 'You're here for the summer then? I hope you'll no' find the time hangin' wearily on your hands for there's no' an awful lot here for folks who have been used to bright lights and busy places all their life.'

'Kate, you misjudge me. I hate cities. Boats are my life, they've run in our family for generations. That's one reason Steve and I are such good friends. We both love the same things. I'm a sail designer. Steve a boat builder. We were trying out some new sails on the *Mermaid* when we got caught in the storm,' he grinned engagingly, 'so don't worry about me and how I'll spend my time here. I'll have plenty and enough to do getting the yacht put to rights as well as sampling all the beauties of Rhanna.'

'Including those wi' two legs,' Kate fished bluntly.

'Oh yes, those as well, I would be a poor sort of chap if I had failed to notice the local attractions. I've never seen such lovely girls, so natural and easy to get on with.'

Kate was entranced. Later she voiced her feelings to Tam, 'He's a fine young man, that he is, and I take back everything I said about him. 'Tis no wonder Eve fell for him. She's a lucky lass to have the likes o' him take notice o' her.'

'You canny mean Mr Smellie!' Tam was frankly astounded. 'And you canny stand there and tell me he will be living here under our very own roof. The man is all mouth and I thought you o' all people would hae seen the truth o' that.'

'Ach, you're just jealous *and* blind,' Kate stressed forcibly. 'He's a grand lad and I'll like fine having him here so just you be mindin' your manners in front o' him, my lad. You will no' be taking off your jacket or loosening your shirt collars in the house and that goes for your braces too – and if I see one glimpse o' holey socks or dirty feets I'll take and throw you in the burn wi' my very own hands and that is no' a threat – 'tis a promise.'

Tam groaned and wished with all his heart that Mr Daniel Smylie Smith had never come back to Rhanna, while Kate bustled about, clearing the table and stoking the fire preparatory to making potato scones and mealy puddings, both delicacies for which she was renowned the length and breadth of the island.

The village was stunned when news of Kate's turnabout leaked out.

'The – the traitor! And the cheek o' her – after all her talk!' fumed Sorcha, clicking her teeth in agitation at the thought of one month's keep in advance. What was wrong with *her* house? she wondered furiously. It was only a short distance from Kate's own *and* she had in the plumbing. She could soon have had the bath cleared of coal and surely nobody would have minded the cloths of croudie cheese and the pats of butter she kept stored on the cool bathroom shelves. That Kate! Somehow she always managed to wangle things to her own advantage – and it wasny fair! It was simply no' fair! Sorcha was so incensed she turned up her hearing aid by mistake so that a loud whistling noise accompanied the chatter following her own remarks.

'Ach, 'tis only her mealy puddings the mannie is after!' Todd the Shod declared stoutly, wincing pointedly at Sorcha's hearing aid and moving out of her vicinity. 'Kate was aye sought after for her puddings and her homemade tattie scones.'

'Ay,' nodded Robbie, 'she might make rock cakes as hard as the Sgor Creags themselves but the towrists come back year after year to sample her breakfasts and that's about all for she canny very well get up to mischief wi' Tam bidin' in the same bed as herself.'

Fingal grinned lecherously, 'Och, use your head, man. Tam's that drunk half the time, he wouldny know the difference supposin' a dozen big chiels climbed into bed between himself and Kate.'

'You are right there, Fingal,' Sorcha took up the cudgels with a vengeance, 'Kate has aye been a very eventual sort o' woman. I've seen her at it too, dancin' and fleerin' wi' other men behind Tam's back and makin' no bones about her likin' for the physical side o' life either.'

'Essential,' corrected Molly, 'and turn your deaf aid down, Sorcha, you are makin' so much noise you are no' even hearin' what your own self is saying.'

Sorcha twiddled a knob and everyone was suddenly so deafened by the ensuing silence that all voices dropped an octave or two.

'I was saying,' Sorcha confided in a bass whisper, 'about Kate. You mind that time Rachel and Jon Jodl bought thon cottage over by Croft na Ard? Well, Kate was for taking a wee house-warming gift to give to Rachel and came to me to see would I like to come along too. When we got there, there was a very strange smell in the house, sort o' spicy and scented and curlin' round all the wee corners so you couldny help but sniff in the reek o' it. I've never smelt the likes in all my life so I asked Rachel, quiet like, and she told me it was incest. I was too shocked to utter a single word but when I looked there was Kate, swayin' about and actin' all queer as if the incest had got into her blood and she couldny help showin' her essentials to the world.'

'Ach, it would be incense!' Molly snorted derisively. 'Rachel has got some gey fancy ideas in her head wi' her being such a big name now and mixing among all thon long-haired musicians wi' all their acting and palaver. She goes about the house dressed in naught but a flowery kimona, wearing clasps in her hair and Jon starin' at her as if he could eat her, his eyes all glaikit and wet behind his specs. As for Kate swayin' and showin' her essentials, she will only have been caught up in thon provocative oriental music Rachel plays on her gramophone. You wouldny have heard a note wi' you being so deaf, Sorcha.'

'That might be so,' Sorcha sounded rather deflated, 'but it doesny alter the fact that Kate has aye had an eye open for chance, and if sillar's involved she's far worse than Ranald any day despite all her talk about the grasping ways o' others. She's encouraging that Smellie man to bide here on Rhanna for as long as he fancies, and by doing so she is condoning everything that has been going on and will go on going on under Doctor Megan's roof. Mr Saunders is up and about now from what I hear. There will be no holding him back and I for one will no' set foot in that house till the de'il takes his leave o' it.'

She glanced round, her lips folding in her plump, pleasant old face. 'Well?' she demanded expectantly.

Robbie shuffled sheepishly, knowing fine what Barra would have to say to him if she discovered he had been indulging in the idle chitchat which she found so distasteful. 'But, Sorcha,' he protested, 'we canny very well blacklist Doctor Megan's house. What about when we're ill and need her to see to us?'

'I'd rather die in my own bed than go into that house,' Sorcha declared stoutly.

'Or maybe go to old Annack Gow and see will she cure us wi' her herbs and other potions,' suggested Molly, her sensible nature strenuously rejecting Sorcha's drastic measures.

'Ay, Annack was aye a dab hand wi' her natural medicines.' Todd the Shod sounded immensely cheered for he had no intention of suffering unduly to please Sorcha or anyone else, also, since Annack was a great believer in the 'water of life' to cure anything from 'flu to rheumatics, the idea of her administering to him was not only appealing, it was imperative.

'Well, maybe none o' us will need either the doctor or Annack,' said Fingal as everyone began to disperse. 'The good weather is here now and I myself have never yet died when the sun is shining over the islands.'

Daniel's departure from Tigh na Cladach did little to still

the gossiping tongues, rather it caused them to wag more vigorously than ever.

'She's alone in there wi' her fancy man.' The shock waves of this realization reverberated from Portcull to Portvoynachan, from Croy to Nigg. 'There will be no stopping them now he's up on his feets, indeed nothing at all. The disgrace o' it is beyond belief.'

'Mr James will have to talk to them,' Holy Smoke was beside himself with pious indignation. 'If he canny make them mend their evil ways the Lord will smite them down wi' hellfire and they will smoulder in damnation ever after.'

'Ach no, the doctor doesny smoke,' Behag simply couldn't resist the ludicrous remark and was amply rewarded by the look of sheer guilt on the butcher's mournful features. ''Tis only liars who do awful things in secret and pretend to the world they are as pure as the driven snow.'

'Ay, like you wi' your innocent wee cough bottles hidin' in the salt girnel!' Holy Smoke bounced back in no mean manner. 'I will no' forget that day you swallocked raw spirits in a public place, Miss Beag, I had thought better of you.'

'At least I did it in a public place,' Behag's eyes glittered like red-streaked marbles, 'no' hidin' in some wee corner like a sly ferret.'

They went at it hammer and tongs. Behag was secretly delighted. At last! Holy Smoke was on her ground! She could better deal with this side of him than she could with his insincere, ingratiating ways and she enjoyed every minute of the ensuing verbal battle.

The talk concerning Megan was not long in reaching Babbie's ears. Her first instinct was to agree with it, her second to rebel at every last word being bandied about, for had not she, at her own choosing, deliberately and stubbornly placed herself in the self-same position as

Megan when she had nursed her husband-to-be all these years ago? She had insisted on spending her nights in the same room as him at the risk of her good name, and though other people had been in the house it all amounted to the same thing in the end.

'I'm going to have a talk with Megan,' she told Anton determinedly, 'she's maybe not even aware of the gossip going on behind her back.'

'*Liebling*,' he took her in his arms and nuzzled her lips, 'of course she's aware. You would have to be minus every one of your senses to be able to ignore it.' Quizzically, he regarded her. 'Has it ever struck you – she perhaps doesn't care what people think?'

Babbie flushed angrily and tossed her red head. 'Then she'll have to be made to care. The feelings of others are at stake besides her own!'

'Babbie,' tenderly he crooked a thumb under her chin and brought her attractive little face close to his own once more, 'have you forgotten what it's like – to be young and in love?'

'No, Anton Büttger, I have not, and that is why I must talk to Megan – she's in love with the wrong man and I must stop it before it's too late.'

'*Liebling*, perhaps it is already too late,' he suggested softly. 'They knew one another before, don't forget. She's had plenty of time to think things over and know if she still loves this man or not.'

'No, she hasn't made up her mind. That's what's been eating at her since she came here. I don't think any of us has seen the true Megan yet, the sort o' girl she was before she met this empty-headed charmer. She's forgotten how to enjoy her life, some women are like that. They are in love with the idea of romantic love and canny see the real thing when it's staring them in the face. I think Megan has enjoyed torturing herself over this man, but she's a grown woman and will have to face up to reality sometime – '

'Babbie, Babbie,' he chided laughingly, 'if I didn't

know better I'd say you've become more than just a little fond of our lady doctor.'

She stared at him, surprised. 'You're right, Anton. I have, I really didn't like her at all at first – now,' she spread her hands, her generous mouth curving into one of her radiant smiles, 'you aye see the truth o' things before I do – and while we're on the subject of truth, how dare you suggest that I'm too well past it to remember what it's like to be in love? I've never grown out of that particular state – and if you come upstairs with me this minute I'll prove it to you.'

'Even though we've only just got out of bed?'

She giggled, putting her arms around him and kissing the tiny fair hairs at the side of his ear. 'Daftie, it's mainly because o' that. I haven't made it yet and am far too lazy to suggest anything that might entail extra work!'

Slowly Babbie stirred her tea, looked thoughtfully at Megan, and cleared her throat. 'Have you a minute to spare? I want to have a talk with you.'

Carefully Megan lowered her cup onto her saucer and held up one protesting hand. 'I know what you're going to say, Babbie, and it was good of you to think enough of me to want to broach the subject. But – to hell with the gossips! I can take it. After all, it's not as if it's anything new, far from it. I've had myself talked about ever since I came here so I don't really have a great deal to lose.'

'Maybe *you* haven't – ' Babbie's quick temper flared and she knew she would have to control it or she could do more harm than good in the present situation. 'But what about Mark? I've never been much o' a churchgoer but I like and respect him and hate to see him getting hurt.' Her voice was so controlled it came out cool and rather flat. 'I, in common with many others, know only too well how much he cares for you, Megan. If you go on as you're doing he will have lost everything he's tried to gain these last months.'

'How can he lose what he's never won?' Megan's voice was low, she kept her head averted as if by doing so she could avoid the subject of Mark... Beyond the window the proud structure of the Manse loomed up – as if reminding her of what she had tried so desperately to forget since Steven's return to her life. Whichever way she turned Mark seemed to pop up. All the windows on this side of the house looked towards the hills; the Hillock; the kirk; the Manse. Pop! Pop! Wherever she looked the picture of a tall, commanding presence was there in her vision, compelling, persuasive, beseeching...

'Oh, damn the man!' she cried, facing Babbie now, her hazel eyes filled with misery. 'I never promised him anything! He was there, always just there, from the minute I arrived. I didn't want to notice him but he made me – and now Steve's back and I can't go on pretending to Mark any longer! Not that I ever did. I told him to go away, not to hope, not to bother me.'

'But all the time you didn't really mean that?' Babbie said softly.

'No, I didn't mean it. I was lonely, he was lonely, we found a certain solace in one another but it was a dangerous friendship. He was too serious, I couldn't handle it...'

'Really?' Babbie couldn't keep the sarcasm out of her voice.

'Yes, really, so take that knowing look off your face, Babbie.' She put her hand to her head in a confused gesture and said half to herself, 'I wish – oh God, how I wish – '

'That your precious Steven hadn't come back! Is that what you wish, Megan?'

A flush spread over Megan's face. 'You really should mind your own business, Babbie, you don't want to become an interfering busybody, I'm sure. We have enough of them with Elspeth and Behag around the place.'

Babbie pushed her cup away and stood up, unable to keep the temper from showing in her glittering green eyes. 'Like it or no you have your reputation to think about! You're the island doctor, an individual who deserves and needs the respect of a community like this and I'm going to see you have it – even if it means you never speak to me, other than in a professional capacity, for the rest o' your life!'

Megan stood up also, placing her hands on the table and leaning forward so that she was glaring into Babbie's angry face. 'If you dare to interfere in my private life you could very well find your words coming true...!'

Babbie didn't wait to hear more. Patting her hat briskly into place, she marched from the room.

'I mean it, Babbie!' Megan shouted, but it was to the stout timbers of the front door. Babbie was already halfway down the path, swinging her nurse's bag in such a nonchalant manner it made Megan more furious than ever.

'Trouble?' Steven came up behind her to slide his arms round her waist and nuzzle her ear with his tongue.

She shivered at the touch but moved away from him. 'Yes,' she said in a low voice, 'there seems to have been a lot of it since you came here, Steve, and I've – I've been thinking, it might really be better if you moved out of Tigh na Cladach and went somewhere else till you are ready to go home.'

'Like hell I will!' His face was livid, and grabbing her roughly by the arm he swung her round to face him. 'What's gotten into you, Megs? You do your best to avoid me at every turn and I'm damned if I'll have it! Don't you feel anything for me anymore?'

Wrenching herself away from him, she shook her head and said wearily, 'I don't know what I feel, Steve – except I'm very, very tired of your constant demands on my time and energy and of all the talk that's been going around since you and Daniel came to Rhanna so if you'll excuse me I – I have things to do.'

With that she left him, picking up her bag and letting herself out of the house, very aware that his blazing blue stare burned into her back as she walked as steadily as she could down the path to her car.

That very evening Babbie came back, coolly walking past Megan and Steve in the hallway and going straight upstairs. In her hands she carried two suitcases and these she took to the room recently vacated by Daniel. Laying them on the bed she calmly began to walk round the room, straightening an ornament here, twitching a curtain into place there, then, when she was quite satisfied that all was to her liking, she turned and made her way back downstairs, once more passing Megan and Steven, this time on their way up.

'Evening,' she nodded pleasantly, ignoring Steven's outraged look, Megan's angry white face, 'I won't be a moment. Just open the window a wee crack, Mr Saunders, Mr Smellie has certainly been living up to his name, the room will need to be aired for a week. Your new lady guest looks the particular sort, we must give her a good impression.'

In those terrible moments of rage, something truly astounding hit Megan. Babbie was behaving as only a true friend would behave, outrageously, daringly, fully believing that she was doing what she thought was best in the circumstances. Megan had always known that she was only tolerated by the island nurse. Babbie had been perfectly happy working with Lachlan, so contented that she had taken the coming of a new doctor very badly indeed. Between herself and Megan there had been an atmosphere, their work together had lacked spontaneity, talk had been stilted and mainly confined to medical matters – now Babbie was her friend, and in amongst her turmoil of mind there came a feeling of such gladness she found herself laughing and crying at the same time.

When Steven, his mouth twisted, demanded to know what she found so exquisitely funny, all she could gasp out was, 'She's my friend, Babbie's my friend.'

'Friend? Some friend! An interfering busybody more like. She deserves nothing better than to be banned from this house forever. She's ruined everything between us, Megan, and all you can do is stand there bursting your sides laughing.'

'Steve,' she collapsed onto the narrow single bed and reached for his hand, 'we'll still have plenty of time together and at least this might stop the gossip, you won't have to move out after all.'

He had no time to answer. Babbie was coming back upstairs, accompanied by a genteel-looking, silvery-haired lady with a sweetly sculptured face and a refined, though rather loud voice.

Introductions were made. Mrs Dolly Hosheit gazed round the room in approval then beamed fondly on Babbie, 'I'm so grateful to you for finding me this delightful place, my dear. My poor departed husband was an American and most of our married life was spent in that country. His greatest desire was to visit Scotland and tour the islands seeking his roots but unfortunately it wasn't to be. I'm his ambassador as it were, and I mean to go to all the places he used to speak about with such fondness. His Scottish blood was in his maternal side of the family – the Clearances you know, so long ago but one never lets go of such a turbulent and wonderful past – oh, the view! The view!' she shrieked, clasping her hands together. 'I just love listening to the sea, it lulls me to sleep and with me being *such* a light sleeper I'll be glad to waken and hear the waves outside my window – oh, and you did say the church wasn't far from here? I never miss Sunday worship if I can help it. My father was an English vicar, you know, and old habits die hard, yes indeed – ' she turned her smile on Megan, 'so, it's early to bed and early to rise – but you being a doctor will know all about that, poor dear.'

'Never mind, you shan't disturb me – I'm up with the lark every morning and I'm *so* looking forward to a real Scottish breakfast – porridge, new laid eggs, buttered bannocks and of course, black pudding. Emmit, my husband you know, used to talk and talk about all the things he would see, and hear, and eat, when he came to visit the Scottish islands – but I'm talking too much. It's just, I'm *so* excited by this marvellous island and this lovely old house – '

Steven had had enough. With a disgusted snort, he left the room. Babbie caught Megan's eye and fancied she saw a twinkle there. Leaving Mrs Dolly Hosheit to her raptures they moved out into the passageway, safely out of earshot.

'And just where did you find her, I'd like to know?' demanded Megan menacingly.

Babbie, displaying great interest in a spider's web stretched delicately in an overhead corner, said carelessly, 'Oh, she had come off the steamer only to find the hotel full and all the B&B signs covered over. I found her seated on her cases at the foot of the Hillock looking very tired and woebegone so I just popped her in my car and drove her here.'

'And if you hadn't found Mrs Dolly Hosheit, what would you have done?'

'I would have found some other poor soul – the island abounds with visitors looking for accommodation at this time of the year.'

'Babbie Büttger – I should despise you.'

'And do you?'

'No – in fact I think it's the funniest thing that's happened in this house for many a long day.'

Fresh laughter seized her. She collapsed against the banister, cupping her hands to her mouth in an effort to smother her mirth.

Mrs Dolly Hosheit was singing. The strains of 'The Skye Boat Song' floated with great exuberance out to the landing.

Babbie let out a huge snort, and sinking onto the top step she buried her head in her arms and laughed fit to burst.

PART THREE

Summer 1966

Chapter Fourteen

Ruth's novel had taken some time to filter through to the islands, and when it finally reached Rhanna it was greeted with a great deal of interest. The womenfolk sat into the 'wee sma' hours' devouring its contents, much to the disgust of the men who denounced the book as 'romantic nonsense' without having glanced at a single word. Yet these same men sneaked away to secluded places to read and enjoy, to laugh and to cry, as heartily as had their wives, sweethearts, and sisters.

All over Rhanna wee hoosies were commandeered for suspiciously long periods of time, and out would come the castor oil or the 'skitter cure' to send the menfolk running back to the wee hoosies, this time for longer periods and none of them spent in the pages of a book.

People passing by on the roads would wonder why a horse waited patiently in its cart shafts at the side of a field, little guessing that its master was in the near vicinity, his back to the sunny side of a dyke, his nose buried in the first novel of Ruth Naomi McKenzie of Failte.

Ruth walked tall, her limp forgotten, a euphoria in her that she knew would always remain now. It might fade a little, become pushed aside in the course of everyday living, but it would be forever a part of her life, there to boost her up when she felt low, lift her spirits whenever they flagged.

In a drawer in her bedroom reposed all the newspaper cuttings that had covered the launch of her book. She still couldn't believe any of that had happened, and from time to time she reminded herself by taking the articles out and reading them over and over till she knew almost every word by heart.

Lorn was so proud of her he bought her a little car of her own, and as soon as she was able to drive she felt herself to be on top of the world. In many ways she was still the Ruth everyone knew, quiet, reticent about her achievements, but the shy hesitancy was gone, in its place came a new confidence, she carried her golden head high, walked with a new spring in her step, smiled more and worried less.

'She'll be gettin' big-headed,' decided Behag vindictively, 'all thon palaver and fuss she had in Glasgow canny have been good for the lass.'

'Even though the palaver and fuss you had wi' thon tin medal o' yours was good for you,' pointed out Kate. 'At least we can all get the benefit o' Ruth and her writing while you're about the only one to get any sort o' queer pleasure gazing at yon medallion in its frame on the wall.'

'It is all a question o' taste,' Elspeth put in sourly, 'I myself have felt no benefit at all from reading Ruth's book. I might have known it would all be about lust wi' men and wimmen thirsting after each other's bodies.'

'Love,' corrected Barra firmly, 'Ruth's book is about love and I think it was beautiful just. There is a difference between love and lust, Elspeth. 'Tis just a pity you canny see it, if so you might be a more contented woman the day.'

'All things come to she who waits,' intoned Elspeth primly. 'In all my years o' marriage to Hector I never knew what love was like between a man and a woman, but there's time and enough yet and I have neither the time nor the inclination to stand here indulging in idle gossip. If you'll be excusin' me, I mustny keep Isaac waitin' any longer.'

Very erect and stiff, she walked away over to where Captain Mac was standing rather sheepishly by the War

Memorial. Gallantly he crooked his arm, she took it, throwing such a look of triumph over her shoulder that the knot of watching women gasped aloud at her 'brazen cheek'.

'The man's taken leave o' his senses,' snorted an aghast Behag, 'and wi' Elspeth Morrison of all people. I canny right believe my een.'

'Ach well, never mind,' consoled Kate wickedly, 'you'll aye hae Holy Smoke to slaver over and admire. There he is now, keekin' at you from between his black puddings. I doubt this hot weather is going for him too. Romance is in the air right enough, Behag, you had better keep a tight hold o' your breeks for if I'm a judge that mannie is planning to have them off you beforc this summer has had time to get started.'

'Kate McKinnon! Wash your mouth out wi' soap!' expostulated an outraged Behag. She scurried away, to the accompaniment of much mirth, only to be accosted by Totie Donaldson who was standing at the door of the Post Office, arms folded, a carefully controlled smile on her strong, handsome features as the sounds of merriment reached her ears.

'You are just the woman I wanted to see,' she greeted the crimson-faced ex-post mistrcss affably.

'Oh ay,' Behag said warily, looking over her shoulder as if she was expecting to see Holy Smoke bearing down on her.

'Doug and myself are going over to Oban for the weekend,' explained Totie, 'and I was wondering if you would mind looking after the Post Office. It would only be Saturday and Monday, we'll be back for Tuesday.'

Behag hummed and hawed for a few minutes, for never would she, by word or deed, allow Totie to see how much she enjoyed these little spells behind the counter of 'her premises'.

In the end she permitted herself a reluctant acceptance of Totie's proposal and hurried home to look out her 'business' overalls and her stoutest shoes, the last she claimed as being a necessary requisite in a job that required 'being on her feets all day' even though she changed them for slippers the minute she was safely behind the counter.

The next morning, complete with knitting bag, shopping bag, and purse, she arrived at the Post Office to settle herself in, after which she started prowling about, looking for dust, re-arranging forms, ink pads, and blotters. When all was placed to her liking, she sat back to await the first customer, knitting needles clacking busily, palsied head nodding back and forth, back and forth...

''Tis yourself, Miss Beag, I never thought you would be here but what a nice surprise, ay, a nice surprise indeed.'

Somehow Holy Smoke had crept in without Behag hearing a single thing. Not even the bells above the door had jangled out a warning and the old woman leapt off her stool like a scalded cat, her slippered feet landing with a soft thump on the floorboards, her head working so frantically her very teeth clattered noisily together.

'Mr McKnight!' She was recovering already though she screamed his name in a breathless protest. 'Just what do you mean by skulking in her like – like some sort o' deranged cat burglar? You scared me near to death wi' your creepin' and shufflin'!'

'Och, I'm right sorry, Miss Beag.' Holy Smoke looked sorry, his jowls sagged in uncontrolled layers over his collar, his dark, mournful eyes seemed suspiciously wet, as if the sight of Behag's fear was too much for him to bear. 'Are you alright?' he beseeched worriedly. 'You look pale, even your very teeths are shivering inside your head. Have you no' got your wee cough bottle with you? Maybe a swallock...'

Behag realized his concern was genuine and she snapped her lips shut on the stream of vitriol she was about to hurl into his large, purple ears. 'What is your business here, Mr McKnight?' she queried instead, her only intention being to get him off the premises as speedily as possible just in case her cronies arrived to tease and torment her with their insinuations.

The butcher shuffled. 'I was wondering, I came in to ask would it cost an awful lot to send a tellygram to Oban?'

Nervously he jingled the coppers in his pocket, as if the very feel of money could bolster him against the shock of having to part with it.

'It would be dear enough,' barked Behag, 'but you'll no' be minding surely? You must be making a fair deal o' sillar now that your shop is on its feets.'

He sighed heavily. ''Tis never easy running your own business, Miss Beag. I have been finding it hard going this whilie back. No one really likes me here and I am at a loss to know the reason why. Betimes I get so tired and depressed I could just give it all up and go back to being a simple crofter.'

She peered at him more closely. He certainly looked depressed, but then that was nothing unusual for him, all he ever did was moan about money – but he *was* tired-looking, she had to admit that, his eyes were sunk right into the back of his head, as if he had spent nights and nights without sleep.

'Ach well, it is the Sabbath tomorrow, you can rest then all you want.' There was a hint of uncustomary sympathy in her querulous tones. Holy Smoke picked on it immediately.

'Ay, you are right there, Miss Beag, indeed I will dwell on the Lord's mercy and sleep the good sleep of the righteous.'

'What was it you wanted me to put in the tellygram?' Behag's sympathy evaporated as quickly as it had come. Kirkgoer she might be, but she simply could not abide this man's whining religious quotations.

'Ay, the tellygram.' Behag waited, pencil poised ready. 'Well, it is to Mr Porteous at the slaughterhouse, just put, "Send no more meat, killing myself next week. Alexander McKnight".'

He paid up quickly, for that was the only way to make parting with money bearable, and sprachled out of the shop, the bells jangling noisily behind him, the draught from the shutting door raising a little cloud of dust from the mat. But Behag didn't notice. She was standing stock-still, staring after him, her rheumy fingers fluttering to her mouth.

'He canny mean it, the mannie canny mean it!' Her thoughts whirled frantically. Killing himself next week! What had driven him even to think of taking such a drastic step? He had mentioned being depressed, that nobody liked him and that he could give it all up – and never had she seen a cratur' so bone-weary as he looked – as if his depression had kept him from sleep for weeks...

The bells clanged again, a crowd of village youngsters came in clutching Saturday pocket money, followed by a group of tourists looking for postcards and stamps. Behag spent a busy day, one of the busiest she had ever known. Damt towrists! Rhanna was becoming far too popular – it was that Ruth and her sensual books, no' to mention Rachel Jodl and her music. The fact that she had a holiday home on the island had somehow leaked out. People were forever asking directions so that they could just ogle at the place, occupied or not, it didn't matter. For all they saw anyway, a bare crofthouse overlooking the sea – and soon they wouldn't even see that, Jon had left instructions for a wall to be built, trees and bushes to be planted...

It was no use! Behag simply could not enjoy her customary musings. Her mind was in a ferment, and for once she was glad when she could put the closed sign on the door and was free to pick up the 'phone without fear of being overheard.

She dialled the Manse. The minister's voice came over the line, slow and blessedly calm.

Despite her agitation she went through all her usual preamble. The 'phone did strange things to her way of thinking. When the instrument had first been installed she had placed G.P.O. notices everywhere on the walls, and these she followed to the letter whenever she had reason to clamp the earpiece against her long ears. To her the 'phone was not so much an inanimate object as some outlandish creature that had to be handled with all due care and respect – and not a little trepidation. So, though she knew perfectly well that it was Mark James speaking at the other end of the line, she had to go through the written rigmarole, step by step, black and white, gingerly clutching the instrument as if it might bite her at any moment.

'Hallo, hallo,' she whispered carefully, 'is that the minister speaking?'

The affirmative reply seemed to bring her great relief which came out in a long, drawn-out sigh. 'Mr James, 'tis me, Behag Beag,' she breathed the words so close to the mouthpiece he jerked his head away from the receiver at the other end, 'can I come over and see you right away, if it is no' too great an inconvenience? 'Tis a matter o' life and death.'

'Of course, Behag, I'll look out for you.' His voice gave no indication of his surprise at the content of her conversation, and he was there as promised, smoking his pipe at the Manse door, watching her scuttling along the road to the gate atop the Hillock. Tapping out his pipe, he went down the driveway to place his hand under her elbow and help her along. She was panting and puffing, more agitated than he had ever seen her.

'Catch your breath,' he directed kindly, though she was the last person he wanted to see that perfumed evening with lark song bursting in the sky and peat smoke hanging lazily in the air.

The old post mistress had always infuriated him with her dangerously vindictive tongue and petty insinuations. Often he could gladly have brained her if only to keep her quiet for a spell, but he was the minister, a being to be sought in times of need and he saw very plainly that she needed him now.

'Lean on me,' he instructed as her stout brogues caused her to stumble on a stone. From the corner of his eye he saw Megan and Steven walking away from Tigh na Cladach down to the wide white stretches of lonely Burg Bay.

Behag saw them also, but for once she was too taken up with her own worries to make comment. The heart of Mark James went with the slender young woman down to the calm turquoise shallows beyond the sands, the rest of him walked with an old woman, into the imprisoning shadows of the Manse, there to give Behag tea and listen while she poured her story into his ears. It was long and involved. How patiently his ear listened, how restlessly his being longed to break free from the shackles that bound it to duty...

'Are you quite sure of these things, Behag? Sandy was fine the last time I spoke to him.'

'As sure as daith,' Behag's tones were wounded, 'but look you – I have the tellygram here to prove it – the very words he dictated are written down in my very own hand. I just couldny sent it to Mr Porteous at Oban – no' till I showed it to you first.'

He studied the epistle, frowning, trying to read some sense into the long, spidery handwriting. 'Was Sandy in his shop today?' he hedged, unwilling to believe that a man so recently set up in business would want to throw it all up so hastily, especially a man like Sandy McKnight who must have sunk a good bit of capital into his shop and wouldn't rest till his investment had begun to show profit.

'I couldny see, I was in the Post Office all day and that busy I only had time for a cuppy and a sandwich in the back shop at dinnertime. Oh, but wait you, he couldny have been. Mamie Johnston came in complaining that she couldny get a bittie hough to make soup. At the time I wasny thinkin' straight and never even thought to ask about it – ' Behag paused, astounded at her own laxity.

'That certainly doesn't sound like Sandy, he has that shop open till the very last minute every day, on a Saturday in particular. It's all a bit of a mystery but I'm sure there's a simple enough explanation. Sandy has been working very hard lately, I've heard a lot of hammering and banging going on in that hut near the shop and he had those men over from the mainland doing some work, though what it is no one seems to have been able to find out.'

'Ay, you're right there, minister,' Behag forgot for a moment how concerned she was over the butcher's welfare and her eyes glinted disdainfully, 'Mr McKnight is aye doing things in a very secretive, and if you'll excuse me for sayin' so, an underhand manner. He was no' for tellin' anybody what he was getting up to in that hut o' his and must have paid the men no' to say anything either for they just acted as queer as himself when asked civil and innocent questions, though what he gave them to keep them quiet is anybody's guess for he'll no' part wi' a halfpenny unless he thinks he's gettin' a penny back in its place.'

'Och well, what he does to his property is his business, I suppose,' said Mark reasonably, 'but I'll get along there and see what I can do. You had best go home, you must be tired after such a worrying day.'

But Behag was having none of that. Into Thunder she climbed beside the minister and to the shop they went first. When they got no answer there they walked along the track to thump, bang, and shout at all the windows and doors of Holy Smoke's crofthouse, but it was as silent as the grave. Only the hens clucked about, pouncing on the woodlice stirred up by the visitors' feet.

'The Lord forgive me,' Behag wrung her hands in an agony of self-reproach. 'That poor, poor man! I was never kind to him, from the start I said things to him I should never, never have said and now he's at the end o' his tether and has maybe no' waited till next week to kill himself! May the good Lord forgive him for it is a sin and no mistake – but,' her currant-like eyes stared into the startled smoke-blue orbs of the minister, 'maybe it was me who drove him to it. He said he was depressed – that there wasny a soul on the island who had a kindly word for him and I was the worst – ay, I admit it!'

If it had been Todd the Shod standing there listening to such rantings he would have told her in no mean terms that she was enough to nag any man into his grave, and if Robbie hadn't escaped when he did he would most likely be dead and buried by now, but though Mark James thought as much, he was too well-disciplined to say so. Instead he led Behag back down the track to bundle her into Thunder and drive to Murdy's croft to ask if Holy Smoke had left instructions for the feeding of his hens.

'Ay indeed,' nodded Murdy cheerfully, 'he was in a queer mood and wouldny say where he was going or why – but of course, that is nothing new for a dour cratur' like himself.'

'But how could he go?' whispered Behag in dread. 'The steamer left early this morning and I saw him in the Post Office at nine o'clock.'

'Maybe he flew,' suggested Murdy with a grin, and disappeared inside when a voice beckoned him in for his tea.

Mark was just leading a very chastened Behag away when Murdy popped his head out of a window to shout, 'There is just one thing I thought was gey funny, he asked would I be good enough to put a wee notice in the Post Office window come Monday morning.'

'And what was it to say?' asked Behag in trembling anticipation.

'That he apologized to his customers for his shop being shut, and thanking everyone for all their past custom.'

'And why would he no' put such a notice up in his own window?' Behag asked through dry lips.

Murdy scratched his head. 'Ach well, I wasny right listening to his ramblings for he's like an old woman once he gets going but I think he said there was more o' a crowd queuing at the Post Office on a Monday morning and he didny want anybody to miss the message.'

'But why would he no' have given me the notice himself? I was in the Post Office all day and fine he knew it too for he was in there to see me this very mornin'.'

'Ach well, I think he's a bittie feart o' you, Behag,' smirked Murdy. 'He mentioned something about giving you a fright earlier and you near bit his head off wi' your rantings and ravings.'

'MURDY!'

Murdy banged his head on the sash in his hurry to answer the teatime battle cry but Behag didn't wait to listen to his muffled curses. She was away down the road, scurrying in front of the minister who, despite his long legs, had quite a job catching her up.

'Oh, Mr James, Mr James,' she sniffed in an excess of self-pity, 'what am I to do, I ask you? You heard Murdy, this is all my fault and I am going to the Post Office right now to 'phone the police and tell them Mr McKnight is missing – and – and maybe lying dead somewhere.' She twisted her hands together and began to cry, the tears running in little rivulets down the wrinkles on her cheeks.

'Oh, come now, Behag, I'm sure it isn't as bad as all that,' Mark James spoke a trifle wearily. Every minute spent in the old woman's company was stretching his nerves but he forced himself to stay calm, to speak soothingly and reassuringly. 'If it will help at all *I'll* 'phone the police and explain what's happened but meanwhile you get along home and get yourself a bite to eat. You look exhausted and I'm sure you must be needing your tea.'

'Ach, 'tis kind you are, Mr James, indeed, indeed.' Drawing out a large red flannel square she buried her face in its generous folds and blew her nose with gusto, then she reddened and hastily stuffed the piece of cloth back into her overall pocket, shocked at her own negligence in allowing a man – a minister at that – to cast his eyes upon a section of her very own, cast-off winter knickers. 'I'll do as you suggest, minister,' she conceded with a flustered nod of her palsied grey head. 'I am, as you so rightly say, weary to the bone and so sore on my feets all I want to do is sit down at my own fireside and have a wee quiet think to myself. I'll leave the matter in your good hands and will see you in kirk tomorrow where we will both pray that Mr McKnight hasny come to any harm.'

With that she was off, her sore 'feets' fairly sending up little clouds of stour on the dusty road, leaving the minister to get into Thunder, drive home, and make the promised call to the police at Oban. The desk sergeant took down all the relevant details and promised to send somebody over to investigate if Alexander McKnight didn't turn up in the next twenty-four hours.

Mutt was waiting at the study door, his brown eyes conveying to his master that it was high time he was taken for his evening walk, and so Mark walked with him, down towards the cliffs that overlooked Burg Bay. It was a perfect summer's evening, calm, warm, and tranquil. Gleefully Mutt dug into rabbit burrows, watered every tussock of grass along the way, before getting wind of Muff's scent which he followed intently, nose snuffled to the ground. Mark followed, lost in thought, a dark depression settling over him despite the beauty of the evening. When he finally caught up with his dog and stood looking down at the Well o' Weeping foaming away at the foot of the cliffs, he was poorly prepared for the sight of Megan and Steven sitting close together on the rocks. At that moment Megan glanced up and seeing Mark she half rose, her arm upraised in acknowledgement. Eagerly his own hand came up, but Steven had grabbed Megan and was pulling her back down beside him – Mark didn't wait to see more. His depression turned to something more, a despair and a longing that seemed to pluck the very heart from his body, leaving only an empty, aching void.

He turned away quickly, relieved that Mutt followed and didn't go diving down to the sands to pursue Muff's scent. The cuckoo was calling from the elms in the kirkyard, calling, calling, triumphantly and gladly, as if to say, 'I'm here, summer has really begun now, cuckoo, cuckoo.'

Something tore at Mark's senses, the realization that the most notorious harbinger of summer wrought no answering echo of gladness in his heart, and with dark head bowed he went on into the Manse to go straight to the parlour where he just sat staring at the bottle of whisky kept on top of the sideboard especially for visitors. For a very long time he stared at it, then roughly he uncorked the bottle and poured himself a good measure.

Yet he didn't touch it straightaway. With shaking hands he carried both the glass and the bottle through to the kitchen to set one on the mantleshelf, the other on the hearth, before seating himself by the fire and from that position looking with haunted eyes at the amber liquid reposing so innocently in the glass.

It has been many years since a single drop had passed his lips, yet there had been a dark and terrible time in his life when he hadn't been able to get through a single day without it. Margaret's coming into his life had cured him of the accursed habit. The climb out of the pit into which he had sunk had been a long and painful one. More than once he had slipped back into it but always she had been there with her love, her patient strength, and finally he had conquered it. After that he had achieved so many objectives, the greatest being his youthful ambition to become a minister. For him it had been a momentous achievement, and from there he had gone from strength to strength till he had believed himself the master of his own destiny – then Margaret had been taken from him, both she and Sharon wiped out as if they had never been. Devastated though he had been he had somehow kept going, sustained by the memories of Margaret's love through all the dark days, the endless nights following his loss. It had been a hard and bitter struggle during which he had fought a constant battle against the temptation of the bottle. But he had won, somehow he had won. Leaving the city to come to Rhanna had been the wisest decision he could have made. He had found a beautiful kind of peace on this lovely island and had thought his inner contentment would always last – but now it was gone, all gone, misery and loneliness were engulfing him once more. Seeing Megan with Steven had been the last straw and a pain like a knife twisted in his heart.

With a little sobbing cry he snatched up the glass and held on to it with two trembling hands. The raw liquor made him choke and gasp but after a few glasses he was beyond feeling anything. An anaesthetizing numbness washed over his mind, dulled his senses – Mutt whimpered at his knee, licked the beloved hand lying so inert and helpless over the side of the chair.

Mark stirred, made an attempt to lift his hand so that he could stroke that faithful golden head on his lap. But his limbs were weighted, held down by leaden muscles that refused to obey the weak signals from his brain. Funny that – a faint smile touched his slackening mouth, he was heavy all over yet he felt himself floating – floating... The glass slipped away from his nerveless fingers.. Mark James was asleep, there at his empty hearth, with his animals all around him and lark song pouring in through the open sash. It was only ten o'clock, they would sing for hours yet. It would never grow truly dark that short and wondrous Hebridean night.

It was the first night in many that Mark hadn't lain awake listening to the curlews and the larks. He needed to sleep, God knew, but not like this, a dew of perspiration on his brow, his sensitive mouth twisted as if the numbing effects of the whisky couldn't quite free him from the phantoms that flitted in his own private little hell.

Mutt never strayed from his master's side all through that strange, sad, lonely night. The cats came and went from the open window but the dog paid no heed. They were only cats after all, and while they loved the master of the house they weren't so attuned to his swings of mood. But Mutt knew, alright. He sensed the sadness in this beloved human and somehow he knew that things were going to get a lot worse before they started to get better – if they ever did...

The kirk was quieter than usual that sunlit Sabbath morning, and for that Mark James sent up a silent prayer of thanks. Behag had accosted him on his way down from the Manse, eager to know what the police had to say, twin spots of colour flaring on her gaunt cheekbones when he told her they would be arriving to investigate if Holy Smoke failed to turn up soon.

'Well, he hasny come back yet,' she said rather nervously, 'and there's no sign o' him coming up the brae to kirk – fancy that now, Mr James, he that hasny missed a kirk service since coming to Rhanna. There's something gey strange going on and though I dinna like the idea o' the police snooping around the place we will at least have done our Christian duty by bringing them here.'

She was in her place now, at the front of the kirk, sitting very upright, a self-righteous air about her that was no deterrent to the sly little innuendoes cast at her from those cronies who had got wind of her concern over Holy Smoke's whereabouts.

'He's maybe away posting the banns,' Kate had suggested with a snigger of pure enjoyment during the walk up the brae to kirk, 'wi' him being such a secretive mannie it's just the sort o' thing he would do so don't you be surprised, Behag, if he shows up complete wi' a wedding ring and his head burstin' wi' all sorts o' marriage plans.'

'You'll be very sorry you spoke in such poor taste, Mistress McKinnon, if the poor cratur' really has gone and done himself a mischief,' Behag had imparted with prim dignity and had thereafter ignored all the teasing comments she had to endure before reaching the safety of the kirk doors.

Shona was in her place in one of the front pews. Since the event of her twins she had rarely managed to get to kirk, but today Niall was looking after the whole family and now she sat gazing up at the pulpit where Mark James stood. He looked drawn and ill, the light from the windows fell on him, showing up the dark shadows on his pale face, a pallor that was emphasized by the blue-black richness of his thick cap of hair. His voice had always reverberated deeply and sweetly round the old kirk but today it lacked impact, he seemed unsure of what he was going to say next, and once he passed his hand over his head as if trying to soothe away some nagging, secret pain.

The congregation coughed and rustled, glanced at one another furtively and somehow knowingly.

'The man o' God is no' himself the day,' Jim Jim hissed at Isabel in Gaelic.

She poked him in the ribs. 'Wheest, you daft bodach, he is a human mannie first and foremost and must have his wee off days like the rest o' us.'

But Jim Jim was right. The man o' God was ill and Shona found herself paying more attention as to the reasons why than she did to the service, so that once or twice she remained seated when the rest of the congregation got up on its feet to sing the Lord's praises.

Mark James would always hold a very special place in Shona's heart. She had never forgotten how he had helped her in her time of terrible need, and had hoped that one day she would be able to repay him for all his kindness.

'He's such a dear man, isn't he?' Mrs Dolly Hosheit murmured in Shona's ear. 'I so love listening to that wonderful, sincere voice of his but today he seems a tiny bit off colour, wouldn't you say, my dear?'

Shona had of course heard how Babbie had taken Mrs Hosheit to Tigh na Cladach and she had smiled to herself at her friend's determination to save Doctor Megan's reputation. The pleasant and enthusiastic little Englishwoman had enjoyed every minute of her stay on Rhanna. She had visited ceilidhs, been invited into people's homes for cracks and strupaks, and had made herself altogether so agreeable to everyone that she had soon earned their affection and respect. She had been further delighted to find so many McKinnons on the island since her husband's family was of that line, but of them all she seemed to like Kate best and had struck up quite a friendship with her, much to old Sorcha's disgust.

'That Kate! That Kate!' she fumed. 'The island is full o' McKinnons but she is the one to get picked out as if there was a message written all over her saying, "Come and get me, I'm the genuine article". Oh ay, she aye lands on her feets and 'tis just no' fair for I am after hearin' she is cheatin' that poor wee Englishwoman out o' good sillar by *sellin'* her thon mealy puddings she makes – and here's me, bakin' and cookin' from the cradle and never so much as a farthing did I ever take for any o' it.'

'Ay, and it isny for the want o' tryin'', smirked Jim Jim and sprachled quickly away before Sorcha could deafen him with her whistling hearing aid.

'The minister was out late last night helping Behag Beag to find Mr McKnight,' Shona told the Englishwoman with a pleasant nod. 'And he was probably burning the midnight oil preparing his sermon for today.'

'That will explain his weary look,' nodded Mrs Hosheit. 'It is just a pity a fine man like that hasn't got a wife to look after him. He must get very lonely in that big house and I just wonder if he feeds himself properly.

I myself have never tasted such good food as since I came to Rhanna. Eve is such a marvellous cook and makes me all the things I like. Today however I have been invited round to Kate McKinnon's house for dinner. She is such a *fine* woman, so full of character and a very interesting person. I believe she has something to tell me about her roots and I'm very much looking forward to hearing all about it.'

When the service was over Shona sought out Mark James, laying her hand on his arm and saying persuasively, 'Come home and have some dinner at Mo Dhachaidh. You – seem troubled and shouldn't be so alone as you are now.'

He sighed, 'That sounds wonderful. Tina always leaves me something cold for my Sunday dinner and it would be nice, just for once, to eat at a family table.'

'Right,' she squeezed his arm sympathetically, 'come as soon as you can and bring Mutt with you. One more dog won't make much difference in a house full of animals and children.'

'Sounds just the tonic I need.' He smiled at her and her heart turned over for it was a smile which didn't reach his eyes, and when he turned to walk away from her there was a defeated little droop about his strong shoulders that was oddly disquieting.

Mrs Dolly Hosheit was thoroughly enjoying herself at Kate's house. Tam had been well warned to be on his best behaviour and though he squirmed uncomfortably in his stiff Sunday best, he was most mannerly and polite to the visitor and very attentive to all her little needs.

Daniel Smylie Smith was there at the table with the rest of them. Dolly already knew him by sight, and as they got talking over the meal she was enthralled to discover that his grandparents had been married by her father in his church in the very village in which she had been born and brought up.

'And fancy you being a McKinnon,' she beamed on Kate as if she had just discovered the fact.

'Ay, and as my maiden name was also McKinnon there wasny much to change when I wed my Tam – except maybe a few o' his wee habits.'

Tam wriggled and threw Kate a dirty look but the visitor didn't notice, she was talking about her husband who had come from the island of Mull.

'Mull?' interposed Kate. 'Well, well, there's a coincidence and no mistake, that is where my forebears came from.'

Dolly had grown quite red in the face with excitement. 'Really? Oh, but this is wonderful!' Her face fell, 'Emmit's people actually came from Ulva which was *so* devastated by the Clearances. With the islands being so close he was inclined just to refer to it as Mull.'

'Ach! This is just too much!' Kate pointedly ignored the dark looks cast at her by Tam. 'My people thought like your Emmit – they came from Ulva but it was easier just to call the whole area Mull when in conversation.'

After that there was no stopping either Kate or Dolly. They talked and talked till the latter lay back exhausted. 'What a wonderful time I've had here in your house, Kate. Not only do I find myself on common ground with this young man here, I also find that there is an undeniable possibility that you and my dear Emmit might have been blood kin. Oh, if only he was alive to hear all this for himself, how thrilled he would have been to meet you, Kate - and Tam too, of course. Before I leave the island you must tell me all about *your* ancestors and where they came from. I'm sure I'll discover even more of my dear husband's background.'

Finally she went, proudly bearing a huge parcel of Kate's homemade mealy puddings for which she had insisted on paying a ridiculously large sum of money.

'You went just a wee bittie too far that time, Kate,' Tam told his wife when at last they had the house to themselves. 'The wifie could have bought a Rolls-Royce wi' the money she paid for your puddings. I thought Ranald was bad but you're a hundred times worse.'

'Ach, Tam, she is a rich woman and is dying to spend some o' her sillar. She has already bought enough souvenirs to start a shop o' her own and she'll no' go wrong wi' my good home cooking.'

Tam sat back to regard his wife with a twinkle. 'Well, 'tis glad I am to have the house to myself for a whilie. You have been entertaining some very peculiar people here, Kate, the whole house reeks wi' the smell o' them.'

'You are talking nonsense, Tam,' Kate scolded with unusual primness. 'If Danny is no' steepin' himself in the ocean he is over at the doctor's house steepin' himself there. As for Dolly, she smelt that nice I commented on it and as generous as you like she gave me a wee bottle o' scent straight out o' her handbag.'

''Tis no' *them*, 'tis their names that reek. Just you try sayin' her name over and over, quick as you can. It sounds as if you are askin' a very rude sort o' question.'

Kate repeated the name and skirled with laughter, 'Ay, I see what you mean but trust you to think o' a thing like that. Rude name or no' she's a nice, friendly wee body and I like her fine.'

'Why were you after tellin' her you came from Ulva?' Tam probed, a frown on his honest, round face. 'If I'm mindin' right I met you on North Uist where you told me generations of your family went back into history.'

'Ach, it was what the wifie wanted to hear – and Ulva is only a stone's throw from Uist as the crow flies.'

'Ay, if you were maybe some kind o' giant who could hurl chukkies eighty miles over the ocean.'

'I have done no harm,' returned Kate with dignity. 'Dolly will go from this island thinkin' that she has found some o' her man's roots on Rhanna and she will be a happier wee woman still when she visits her next island and the next. You see, Tam,' she explained with a great show of calculated patience, 'the McKinnons are everywhere and Dolly is bound to find others wi' the same connections as myself for it is a fact o' life and one that you canny seem to get into that thick head o' yours – people believe what they want to believe and if they are the happier for doing so then who am I to deny them their simple wee pleasures?'

On Tuesday morning, four days after his 'disappearance', Holy Smoke stepped off a fishing boat at Portcull Harbour, looking mighty pleased with himself and genuinely surprised when he was immediately surrounded by a knot of villagers.

'For why have you come back?' asked Tam, casting a curious eye at the heavy-looking satchel the butcher was carrying.

'And why should I no'? I live here, remember.'

'Behag thought you were away to kill yourself. She's been driving us all daft since Saturday and has made the minister ill wi' her greetin' and worrying. The police have been here looking for you and broke into your crofthouse on Sunday night to see had you done yourself an injury, and they had to break into your shop too, to find out if you were maybe lyin' hanged somewhere...

Ranald delivered all this in a swift monologue which came to an abrupt halt when the butcher's yell of anguish rent the air.

'My shop! What for why did they do that? My freezer room! They maybe left the door open! Everything will be ruined!'

With that he was off, breaking into a demented run, half the village at his heels on the short journey to the butcher's shop. A great sigh of relief broke from Holy Smoke when he discovered everything to be in order but when his eye fell on a pile of packages lying at his door, he let out a fresh bellow of outrage.

'What's these?' he demanded, swivelling bulging eyes from the doorway to the surrounding array of faces.

'It will be your order of meat from Oban,' supplied Robbie. 'It came on last night's steamer as usual.'

'But, my tellygram! I got Miss Beag to send a tellygram from the Post Office first thing on Saturday morning, telling Mr Porteous to send no more meat. It will be ruined lying there in this heat and I will have to pay for it! I canny believe this! I just canny believe it!'

Everyone looked at everyone else. Behag had done it again! Somehow managed to get her wires crossed by misconstruing an important message. Once before, during the war, she had transmitted a misleading call for help with the result that the Commandoes had arrived on Rhanna to hunt down an imaginary invasion of German soldiers.

'Mr McKnight! 'Tis yourself! Thank the good Lord you are safe and well.' Behag puffed into the scene, red-faced and hot after her rush along the road from her cottage out of whose windows she had spied the commotion at the butcher's shop. If she had expected anything on her arrival there it certainly wasn't the stream of abuse hurled at her from Holy Smoke's rage-whitened lips.

'See you and keep a civil tongue in your head,' Behag warned shakily when she could at last get a word in, conscious as she spoke that several heads were nodding in sympathetic agreement with her words. It wasn't often that anything she said or did earned even the faintest approval and she took full advantage of it, puffing out her scrawny chest as she defended herself with the not inconsiderable might of her own tongue.

'But you never sent my tellygram!' wailed Holy Smoke. 'After me paying dear for it too and ending up wi' all this useless meat which will cost me a pretty penny also – and here's me thinkin' that at last I was going to make a little profit out o' my shop. As for killing myself, I would never dream o' doing such a sinful thing, and if you wereny such a silly woman you would have kent fine I wasny that sort o' man.' He paused to draw breath into his heated lungs, in his agitation also drawing from his pocket a battered packet of cigarettes, one of which he placed between his thin lips and lit with a shaking hand, much to the amusement of the throng who nudged one another and grinned their wicked grins.

'I never meant I was killing myself,' he repeated after a few inhalations of smoke, 'I meant I was killing my own beasts. I received a licencc to do so and I've been preparing myself for doing it for a long whilie now. I had the electricians over from the mainland wiring up my hut to make it into a proper freezer room, and for nights and nights I was in there myself, lining the walls and putting in fixtures till I near dropped wi' fatigue.' His mournful eyes beseeched the crowd, he spread his hands in appeal. 'I have worked hard to give this island a decent, hygienic butcher's shop, one where the womenfolk can come and know they are buying good, homegrown, fresh meat – and I come home to find this.'

He looked so forlorn standing therc, his cigarette dangling dejectedly from his mouth, his thin shoulders drooped, that the sympathies of the villagers were immediately transferred to him.

'Ay, you are a hard working cratur' and no mistake,' nodded Tam thoughtfully, 'but you rcally canny blame Behag here for thinkin' the way she did.' His magnanimity made the old lady sigh with relief. 'If it had been me I'm thinkin' I would have thought the same as herself, especially when you disappeared and nary a word about when you were coming back.'

'But I told Murdy to put a notice in the Post Office window saying I would be back the day!' Holy Smoke's voice was rising to a thin wail again. 'Is there no one on this island can take a simple message correctly?'

'I never thought to write it down,' Murdy spoke from the back of the gathering, 'I was busy at the time and just trusted to memory.' The admittance brought a look of shame to his nut-brown face, but when he spoke again his tones were defensive. 'It would have made no difference anyway, you just disappeared wi'out trace for you didny catch the steamer that morning and nobody saw you flying away,' he ended with an attempt at humour.

'Ach well, there is no mystery about how I got off the island on Saturday,' snorted the butcher derisively. 'I went away on a fishing boat after I had been to see Miss Beag. The fisherlads took me over to Oban far cheaper than that damt steamer has ever taken me. I had to get some spare parts for my generator for I canny have it breakin' down wi' me killing myself now. I just gave the lads the same as I gave the electricians to keep quiet about my wee secret, a few pounds o' my homemade links and black puddings and they were all well enough pleased at that.'

'Ay well, you'll maybe no' be in such a hurry to save sillar in future,' Tam warned as he began to walk away. 'My mither aye said, "Pay cheap, pay dear", and she was right too.'

Two policemen were coming along the road, heading straight for Holy Smoke's shop.

The crowd dispersed as if by magic to get on with their own belated work, leaving the butcher to explain himself and Behag to vacate the scene with alacrity since she had no wish to get herself 'mixed up wi' the law'.

But the incident never faded from anybody's minds, rather it grew in importance with the telling and became such a favourite tale at winter ceilidhs that those who had actually taken part in it were regarded with respect and not a little envy.

Certainly Behag was never allowed to forget her hand in the affair. Ever afterwards she had to endure the teasings of her cronies – and worse, when Holy Smoke had recovered from the financial blow to his pocket and had time to appreciate Behag's concern for his welfare, his ingratiating manner towards her grew till it got to the stage where whenever she saw him coming she would leave whatever she was doing and scuttle away to hide, be it to her own house or to that of a neighbour – for the doors on Rhanna were ever open to visitors, be it for a crack or a strupak, or simply to provide a refuge for beings like Behag when the world outside became too much of a burden.

Chapter Fifteen

Megan opened the door of Tigh na Cladach to find Mark standing there, not facing her but turned away looking towards the blue, heat-hazed peaks of Sgurr nan Ruadh. After a spell of cold, wet weather, the sun was out again, sparkling on the sea, shimmering on the sands. All over Rhanna the buttercups were out in their millions, turning the machair to plains of gold while in the meadows thousands of pure white daisies looked like snow from afar. In the less well-drained fields, marsh marigolds opened great yellow cups to the sun; bluebells purpled the woods; lapwing chicks ran with their mothers; seals basked on the rocks; calfs and lambs gambolled and played; larks trilled in the sky; the cuckoo called from wooded glens and high, hidden places.

Mark was wearing only a pair of light, fawn slacks and a pale blue shirt. Megan could see plainly where the white skin of his shoulders merged into the ruddy brown column of his neck and noted also how sweetly the thick dark hairs at his nape curled just a tiny bit outwards.

It seemed so long since he had stood near her like this that she wanted to reach out and touch him, as if to reassure herself that he was real and not just a tall, somehow unapproachable figure to be seen walking in the distance...

He spun round to face her just then and her hand, which had in fact been reaching out towards him, fluttered back swiftly to her side.

'Can you come quickly?' he asked before she could

speak. 'It's Dodie, the old man who lives on the hill track. I was cycling back from Nigg and found him lying unconscious at the edge of the moors about a quarter of a mile from his house, and carried him home.'

His voice was clipped and hard, so unlike the warm, deep, resonant one she remembered and something in her curled up and died for the want of that lovely voice she had known and loved, and for the ready, wide smile that had been so much a part of him.

He wasn't smiling now, his face was closed, tense-looking, his eyes dull and terribly void of that essential quality that had always been there, the love of life and all the riches it had to offer a man like him.

She looked at him more intently and her heart smote her to the quick. He was thin and ill-looking, with hollows in his cheeks and dark smudges under his eyes – and worse than these, a dreadful shadow seemed to enshroud him, wrapping him round in an invisible mantle of hopelessness...

'You – carried him?' She concentrated her mind on the reason he had come here.

'Ay, he isn't heavy, in fact there's nothing of him and I think that's where the trouble might lie. He's been starving himself. I put him to bed and cycled down here as quickly as I could.'

'I'll get my bag.' She disappeared inside but was soon back, Steven at her side, a handsome Steven, fully recovered, all the bruises healed, his hair shining like gold in the sun, his white teeth flashing in his suntanned face.

'So, you're the minister,' he greeted Mark. 'I've only ever seen you from a distance, I'm afraid I'm not much of a church goer. I hope you don't mind if I come along for the ride, it's a good opportunity to see a bit of the island – and besides, I mustn't let Megs out of my sight in case she disappears again. Oh, I'm Steven Saunders by the way though I expect you know that already. I seem to have earned a bit of notoriety since I came to the island.'

He stuck out his hand but Mark didn't take it, instead he began to walk away down the path, throwing over his shoulder, 'I'll leave my bike here and collect it later. If the two of you wouldn't mind, I think we had better hurry.'

They got into Megan's car, Steven settling himself beside her at the front, leaving Mark to climb into the back and somehow arrange his long limbs into the cramped space behind the front seats. On the drive through the village many hands were raised in friendly acknowledgement, but it was to Mark they waved; more and more lately Megan had found both herself and her house shunned, and while she told herself that she was enjoying the freedom, she knew it was just a pretence, that she longed for a return to the rapport she had only just been starting to enjoy with the islanders – before...

Her heart hardened. Let them run to old Annack Gow and her herbal cures, they would soon come back to her when they needed a real doctor. She kept her eyes on the road. Silence enshrouded the car's occupants, Mark sat hunched in the back, not saying a word, even Steven seemed lost in thought and only grunted when she spoke to him.

She was relieved when she at last stopped the car outside Dodie's cottage. It was very peaceful here, hens clucked amongst the heather, browsed lazily along the banks of the little burn chuckling over the stones. But inside Dodie's cottage was another story: ragged curtains at the tiny windows effectively shut out the sunlight, ashes spilled from the grate, dust lay thickly over the sparse furnishings – yet, in amongst all the neglect a small heap of lovingly painted stones on the cobwebby window ledge shone like jewels, each one painstakingly capturing the wild flowers of the moor, the birds of the seashore, all done by Dodie when he had had the will to fill his lonely hours with his own particular visions of art.

Since the death of his beloved Ealasaid, everyone who

had ever had time to spare for him had tried to help him in all sorts of practical ways but he had rejected all advances, more and more hiding himself away so that the familiar, loping figure that had for so long been part of Rhanna's landscape was rarely to be seen these days except on the quiet, solitary stretches of the Muir of Rhanna.

'Through here,' Mark led the way up a short passageway to a small, dim, airless room where thick curtains over the window closed out light and air. The room held only the barest necessities; a sagging iron bedstead; a dusty dresser in one dark corner; an antiquated bride's kist under the window; shelves made from fish boxes that looked ready to collapse at any moment.

On the bed lay Dodie, a rickle of bones and loose grey skin, huddled under a heap of assorted coverings, including a threadbare greatcoat and an ancient Macintosh. Megan took one appalled glance at the room and immediately rushed in to pull back the curtains, and called on the men to help her lift the lopsided sash. Fresh clean air swept in along with the sunlight upon whose beams clouds of dust swam and billowed.

'Will one of you help me get his clothes off?' She didn't look up as she spoke but it was Mark who helped her peel off the old man's garments, never once flinching as each successive greasy layer released a hotchpotch of repelling odours.

'Excuse me, I think I'll get a breath of air.' Steven rushed outside to lean against a wall and gulp in great lungfuls of scented hill air, leaving Mark and Megan to their grim task.

Dodie came round just as they reached his stale and repulsive undergarments, so worn they almost disintegrated in their hands. Dazed though he was, Dodie was quick to size up the situation. 'Here, you canny do that,' he babbled in utmost horror, a red stain diffusing the unhealthy pallor of his face. He shot upwards, stubby, calloused fingers grabbing blindly at the covers to pull them up and wind them round his skinny shoulders. He began to cry, great heartrending sobs that shook his entire body and made the rickety bed wheeze on its rusty springs.

'Dodie, Dodie, it's alright, it's alright.' Mark was beside him, enfolding the emaciated old man to his caring heart, watched by Megan who bit her lip to stop the tears springing to her eyes, so moved was she by the sight of that strong man holding Dodie to his breast as if he was a lost child; as lost indeed he was, so bewildered at finding himself naked in bed in the presence of a 'leddy' that he allowed Mark to hold him and comfort him in his terrible time of need.

'Listen, Dodie,' said Mark quietly, 'I found you today by the roadside. You're ill and need help and must let the doctor examine you.'

'Na, na, I canny,' wailed Dodie, burying his face further in Mark's shoulder, 'she's a leddy and never in the whole o' my life has a leddy been in my bedroom, never mind looked at my private body.'

'Not even your mother?' probed Mark gently.

'Ay well, maybe her,' Dodie conceded with a watery sniff. 'Though I canny mind a thing about it for she went and died on me when I was just a bairn. It was bad enough in the hospital thon time I was in wi' my nose. The nurses bathed me and I'll never, never forget the shame o' that. It wasny natural and I'll no' allow it to happen ever again.'

Mark patted the old man's bent shoulders. 'Wheesht, wheesht, man,' he soothed, 'I'm your friend and would never do anything to deliberately hurt you.'

An enormous sob shuddered out of Dodie's gaunt frame. 'Ach, I ken fine you wouldny.' His voice was weak suddenly as all the tension went out of him leaving him spent. ''Tis just that you brought the leddy doctor into my house and 'tis shamed I am just. If I had kent she was coming I would have cleaned the place up a bittie. It was different wi' Doctor Lachlan, he was here thon time I was smitted wi' Shelagh but I didny mind him so much, leddies are different, they aye smell nice and think everyone else should be the same but I was never one for that kind o' palaver myself.'

Above the old man's head of soft grey hair, Mark's lips twitched while Megan's hand went quickly to her mouth. 'I know that, Dodie,' Mark sympathized as solemnly as he could, 'but you liked it well enough when Mairi took you down to her house that time you were ill with your stomach. I heard all about how she gave you a nice bath and looked after you so well.'

'Ach, it wasny the bath I liked,' Dodie lay back on his slipless pillows, keeping his face well averted from Megan. ''Twas the nice dinners she gave me that I enjoyed – I like Mairi fine,' he enthused, forgetting his shyness at the thought of kindly-hearted Mairi, whose simple outlook on life singled her out as being the one female on the island he could really feel at ease with. Raising a shaky hand to scratch his head, he let out a horrified cry on discovering that his greasy cap was missing. In the diversion that followed Mark nodded at Megan who ran from the house into the brilliant June sunshine, where she found Steven and asked him if he would take the car down to the village and bring back Mairi McKinnon.

'Never mind Mairi-whoever-she-is.' Steven was not in the best of moods as Megan soon found out when he grabbed her arm and forced her in close to him. '*He* doesn't seem to like me very much, does he?' he asked, jerking his head towards the cottage. 'And I think I know the reason why. It was him, wasn't it? The man you thought you were in love with before I came back on the scene?'

'Och, for heaven's sake, Steve!' she cried. 'This is hardly the time or place for a postmortem. The old man in there is very ill and Mairi is the only person he wants just now. You'll find her house easily enough, it's the white cottage with the red windows next to Merry Mary's shop.'

'Alright, I'll go,' he growled sullenly, 'but later on I want some answers and I don't care how many sick old men have to wait while you and I have a little talk.'

The car whirled away in a cloud of dust, leaving Megan to sink back against the cottage wall and lean her head on the flaking plaster. She had to have a short breathing space, time to recover some of her senses before she went back inside that poor old man's room. She thought of how badly Steven had behaved during the entire episode, all he had been able to think about was himself, and she wondered how much more she could take of his petty jealousies.

Mark meanwhile had recovered Dodie's greasy cap from behind the bedstead where it had fallen, and once it was jammed firmly on his head Dodie seemed to regain some of his old equilibrium. 'I'm drouthy, Mr James,' he said, licking his dry lips, 'I wonder if you would get me a wee drink o' water from the pail in the porch.' Reaching under his pillows he withdrew a small engraved silver goblet.

'Be using this to fetch it in,' he instructed rather grandly. 'Liquid o' any sort has never tasted better than when supped from this bonny cup, it's that cool on my lips it is just like sooking a bittie ice from my own byre roof in winter.'

In some astonishment Mark took the goblet, and was about to ask where on earth Dodie had acquired such a fine piece when the old man held up his hand somewhat imperiously. 'Before you ask I'll be telling you, seeing you will no' be likely to tell anyone else. A tink gave it to me once in return for a few bit eggs and vegetables from my very own garden. I kent fine it was likely stolen and put it away thinkin' never to use it. I came across it just the other day and thought maybe it would help me to buy another cow like my bonny Ealasaid. It was that fine and cool lyin' there in my hands I decided to have a wee bit use o' it before asking would somebody maybe take it over to the mainland and sell it for me – the police will no' be lookin' for it now for it is nigh on twenty years since the tink gave it to me.'

His look of guilt smote Mark's soft heart to the quick. Taking the old man's horny hand, he squeezed it. 'Maybe you won't have to sell your cup, Dodie, just bide your time a bittie longer and who knows what might turn up.'

Steven had driven the car at such a pace that it wasn't long before Mairi appeared on the scene, complete with flasks of hot soup and tea which she made Dodie drink before successfully persuading him to allow her to wash him with the hot water she had somehow managed to heat over a few hastily stoked coals.

But even when she had got as far as washing his face and hands he was loathe to allow her to go further, putting up all sorts of verbal barriers in her path, the main obstacle being his inherent modesty and the fact that 'it jist wasny decent for a leddy to look at any part o' a man's private body.'

Sitting herself on the bed, Mairi swirled a soapy sponge over his bony shoulders and spoke to him in her soft, soothing voice. 'Do you mind that time the Huns were on Rhanna, Dodie? Ay, well that was the time Mistress Gray had a wee ceilidh for them and thon big Jerry – Zeitler I think he was – had managed to get dung all over his clothes and everything and Mistress Gray made him steep himself in the zinc tub, there in the scullery for everybody to see. I mind at the time thinkin' he would have that funny wee Hun sign everywhere and could only stand there gawpin' at him while he swore at me in German and turned an odd blue colour in the face...'

Dodie was so entranced listening to these revelations about someone else's 'private body' that he forgot to feel embarrassment at his own and before very long Mairi had him bathed, dressed in a pair of 'her own Wullie's pyjamas,' and smelling so strongly of talcum powder he sneezed mightily and demanded a cuppy to ease his tubes.

Then and only then was Doctor Megan allowed back into the room, her composed face giving no hint at the relief she felt on seeing a clean and shining Dodie, sitting up quite perkily against his pillows, one horny pinky crooked daintily as he lifted his cup to his lips, for he could put on the airs and graces when he liked, and he was determined to show the 'leddy doctor' he could display gentry mannerisms when the mood took him.

To her further relief he allowed her to examine him without too much fuss, and soon she was able to put her stethescope away and tell him that there was nothing wrong with him that a regular diet of good food wouldn't cure.

'I'll see to him,' Mairi offered in her calm, unflustered way. 'Wullie is working over at Nigg the now and passes by Dodie's house every morning in his cart. It will be no bother to me to clean and cook for an old man who asks little o' anybody. I would have done it long ago but the old rascal wouldny hear tell o' it. He's that thrawn betimes he deserves a good skelping but ach – he wouldny be Dodie if he was to allow us all to fuss and palaver over him though he let himself go too far this time, that he did.'

Megan laid a hand on her arm. 'Thank you, Mairi, for all your help here today. I don't know what we would have done without you, you're a good, good woman.'

Mairi looked at her with round eyes. 'Ach, doctor, I'm no' good at all. I have just done what anybody else on Rhanna would have done in the circumstances. It's the way o' things here, we all help one another in time o' need.' She smiled her oddly beautiful smile at the young woman. ''Tis just a pity you haveny found that out for yourself yet, we don't all go around gossipin' our heads off – though of course,' she added hastily, 'it fills the time when there's maybe a queue in the shops and everybody anxious to find out a wee bittie news about somebody else.'

With a pleasant nod she took herself off to the kitchen to clear away the things she had used to wash Dodie, leaving Megan to go outside to talk to an impatiently waiting Steven, and Mark to go through to the bedroom to talk to Dodie.

'You can have as many visitors as you like,' he smiled, 'and that includes myself, if you don't mind.'

'Ach no, I'll no' be mindin',' acquiesced Dodie graciously. 'Mairi will have all the wee bitties o' dust cleaned up by then and will maybe polish the fender if she knows visitors are comin'.'

'Something will have to be done about Dodie,' Megan told Mark when he finally emerged from the cottage.

'I know,' he said and that was all, turning away from her and striding over to the car without another word. Despite the heat of the sun she felt suddenly cold and was glad of Mairi's undemanding chatter on the otherwise silent journey down to Portcull.

Something was done about Dodie, several things in fact. A few days after Mark had found him lying unconscious by the wayside, he and Grant McKenzie walked together along the hill track, Grant chatting in his easy friendly way, small talk designed to keep the old man's mind off the letter he had received from the laird, requesting him to call in at Burnbreddie House at his earliest convenience.

A much recovered Dodie, still thin and pale to be sure but well fed and well rested after spending three days in bed, with Babbie, the doctor and Mark keeping a watchful eye on him and Mairi in regular attendance, was not anxious to reach the Big House and would have turned back but for Grant's persuasive hand under his arm. Dodie was glad of the companionship of this strong young McKenzie for he had been greatly alarmed to receive the epistle from the laird, and had spent an agonizing time of it imagining all sorts of dire meanings in the few words he had read over and over, in bed and out of it, sitting in the sun or by his lonely grate.

'I'm thinkin' maybe the laird is going to put me out my house,' he confided to Grant in a thin, frightened whisper. 'He's likely heard about me bein' ill – and forbye...' he gulped and looked at Grant through tear-filled eyes, 'I've been late wi' my rent this whilie back, I've no' been able to work wi' me no' feeling like myself since Ealasaid fell over the cliff and 'tis feart I am just in case I'll maybe get put into one o' they awful homes they have over on the mainland.'

Burying his face in his hands he began to weep, softly and helplessly, a fragility about his thin, humped shoulders that brought a lump to Grant's throat.

'Dodie, Dodie.' Throwing his arm about the old man he spoke gently and reassuringly. 'Nobody's going to send you anywhere you don't want to go, far less Burnbreddie. He's a decent sort and would never deliberately hurt anyone, especially someone like yourself who has always worked so willingly and so hard to the Balfours as a whole. He's probably just heard you've been ill and wants to see for himself how you are now, that's all.'

'He could have called to see me,' Dodie whispered wetly, adding with a touch of stubbornness, 'he wouldny have got his feets dirty, Mairi had the place that clean you could have eaten your dinner off the floor and that's more than can be said for that muckle place he bides in, even though that Peggy thinks it's the best kept house on Rhanna.'

They went on, Dodie's big, clumsy boots dragging, Grant trying to urge him on at a faster pace. It was a warm, sunless morning with a pearly mist swirling over the undulating stretches of moorland, but gradually it was drifting away, revealing the steep crags of Sgurr nan Gabhar and Sgurr na Gill shouldering their way out of their misty scarves.

A rustling and moaning came from somewhere close by, Dodie's voice tailed off in a rusty squeak, Grant's head jerked up. Out from a heather-covered knoll a young cow popped her head and mooed gently at them, her breath coming out in little puffs.

'Ach, is she no' bonny just?' Dodie forgot his fears, he seemed to soften and melt and went quivering towards the cow, speaking softly to her as he advanced till finally she allowed him to stroke her and pour words of love into her furry ears.

'She is just like my Ealasaid,' he blubbered the words wetly into the animal's neck, 'only younger wi' a different colour to her and maybe a bittie more meat to her bones.'

A tiny calf gambolled up, friskily kicking up its heels, heedless of Dodie, intent only on nuzzling its mother's flank before fastening its soft lips round one of her small teats. It was one of Venus's offspring, hundreds more were scattered over the island. Croynachan had had a busy and profitable time hiring out his bull. Now that summer was fully underway, the young shorthorn's services were much in demand. It was a long time since he had broken free, he needed his energies for better things and was very contented these days. No one was more glad than Croynachan that the animal had proved its worth, farmers and crofters alike were singing its praises and were delighted to have Venus in their fields serving their cows.

'She has a calf!' Dodie went daft altogether. 'My, my, would you look at it, 'tis beautiful just – like the one Ealasaid gave me three summers ago...' The tears were spouting, spilling over once more.

'Dodie, we must get along,' Grant hastened to say.

'Ach, I'm just coming.' Dodie's voice was husky, unwillingly he abandoned the peacefully grazing cow, the rapturously sucking calf, his footsteps faltering until Grant took his arm and made him hurry along.

As they neared Burnbreddie House Dodie came to an

abrupt halt, his face haggard with apprehension. 'It will be the cup,' he whispered in abject terror. 'It wasny me that took it though I aye kent in myself the tink stole it from Burnbreddie. Surely Mr James wouldny have told on me, he didny say eechie or ochie at the time or make me feel I had committed a sin.'

'Told what, Dodie? What cup are you talking about?'

'My bonny silver cup, the one given me by a tink years and years ago. I've never had the likes in all my life, just delft cups wi' cracks in them. Thon wee cup is like a miracle for it makes even water taste like wine and is also a fair treat filled wi' my very own rhubarb.' He threw Grant a sidelong, apologetic glance. 'I can eat it you see wi' my very own silver spoon, the neighbour o' the two I gave your mother when Lorn and Lewis were born as twins.'

A grin widened Grant's mouth. 'I know the ones you mean, she treasures them yet and all o' us, at one time or another, have wondered where she got them.'

Dodie fidgeted but said proudly enough, 'Your mother knows the truth o' that though it was a wee secret between her and me. I paid for them myself, out o' the money I got for doin' wee odd jobs to Burnbreddie. The third spoon is my very own secret, we all have them and this is one that will go wi' me to the kirkyard when my time comes.'

Grant gave a shout of laughter. 'No flies on you, Dodie! Silver cups and spoons; maybe a silver tea service for all I know! Will it ever end, I wonder?'

'Ach no, there is no silver tea service,' Dodie was shocked, 'just the spoon and the cup...' He stared at Grant with watery, haunted eyes. 'Maybe the police will be there waitin' to take me to jail! Why else would the laird send for me, he's never done the likes before – ' he dug in his feet. 'I'm no' goin', I'm just no' goin' and no' a soul can make me.'

'Oh ay you are,' Grant said gently. 'You're going because I'm here with you to see you through. I've never let you down yet, have I?'

'No, lad, you haveny.' Dodie gulped miserably and allowed the young man to take his hand and lead him along as if he was a lost child.

Chapter Sixteen

The laird was preparing to set out for his morning ride and was in the hall, pulling on his riding boots, when his wife Rena ushered Grant and Dodie through the door.

'Fine morning,' he greeted them pleasantly, giving his boots a final tug and wetting the tip of one finger to apply it to a minute speck of dirt on the otherwise immaculate leather.

The years had been kind to Scott Balfour, sixty past he was slim and fit-looking with a dark moustache and a big bushy beard disguising his overfull lips and receding chin. He was held in respect and liking on the island, for while he and his wife took occasional holidays abroad he had never been an absentee landlord but one who was content with his life on Rhanna and fair in his dealings with his tenants.

Every summer he held fêtes on the wide sweeping grasslands of the estate, and every Christmas without fail he threw open the doors of Burnbreddie House to give parties and balls to his tenants, annual events which were much anticipated and appreciated by young and old alike.

He made it his business to acquaint himself with the islanders and their problems, and just lately had been granted the earth-shattering privilege of being invited to partake of 'a wee taste' of Dodie's famous rhubarb, quite amiably allowing himself to be seated on a kitchen chair outside in the sun while Dodie went to fetch the treat, together with a 'wee polkie o' sugar' into which he was instructed to dip his stick of rhubarb. He had complied with obvious relish, flattered at being singled out for such an honour, displaying also a rare understanding of the ways of the more eccentric in his midst.

Straightening from his ministrations to his boots he smiled encouragingly at the visitors, but before anyone could make a move Dodie began to speak in a rush, in his excitement lapsing into Gaelic so rapid and confused that not even Grant could understand much of it.

'Dodie got your letter,' Grant explained when Dodie had talked himself to a tongue-twisted halt, 'he asked me to come along to – '

'Give him a bit of moral support.' Scott Balfour nodded understandingly and motioned towards a door near the stairs. 'In here.' He led the way into a tastefully furnished study. As they entered, the doors of a cuckoo clock on the mantlepiece flew open abruptly and out popped a gaily painted wooden bird frantically to proclaim the hour.

'I couldn't resist it when I spotted it in a shop in Austria,' Scott Balfour said with a laugh, 'Rena won't have it anywhere in the house so I'm stuck with it in here.'

Dodie was entranced by the clock, so much so he appeared to have forgotten his anxieties and just stared fascinated at the mantlepiece as if willing the closeted cuckoo to come flying out once more.

The laird looked at the old man and said pleasantly, 'I hear you've been ill, Dodie, and trust you're feeling better now. I wanted to pop along to visit but something or other kept cropping up so I sent a letter instead and here you are, still a bit pale-looking but on the road to recovery, I hope. Sit down, old man, you and I are going to have a good long chat about certain matters that have been on my mind for some time now.'

Dodie had torn his eyes away from the clock, they now raked the laird's face, fear-filled, completely void of their usual dreamy expression. 'You'll no' take my house away from me, will you, Mr Balfour? I'm fine and fit now wi' a good few wee jobs lined up for me. I'll pay the rent next week, maybe sooner, I have a few wee things I can sell, my own things, no' anything that's stolen, I wouldny want to go to jail, I'd die in jail! I dinna want to go to one o' they homes on the mainland either, I'll no' be a bother to anybody again, you can have your wee cup back, I only supped from it a few times and it's as good as new...' He began to babble, the words catching in his throat, all mixed up with dry, painful sobs that shook his bony shoulders.

'Dodie,' the laird was up, throwing his arm round the bent back, 'come on now, what's all this about jail? No one's going to send you away from here, I only want to talk to you, that's all. Sit down, sit down, old chap, take the weight off your feet. Grant, be a good chap and get him a whisky.' He indicated a drinks trolley set in a corner, all the while clapping Dodie on the back and uttering words of comfort. Taking the proffered drink, he set the glass to Dodie's lips and made him take a few sips before pushing him into a comfortable, leather-bound chair.

'Now you take it easy, old boy,' he instructed kindly, 'catch your breath, let yourself relax, you're all tensed up.'

Dodie was very glad to do as he was bid, and only when he was breathing evenly did the laird speak again. Placing his clasped hands under his whiskery chin, he regarded the old man thoughtfully.

'Now, listen to me, Dodie, and for heaven's sake try to keep calm. I'm not an ogre and would never do anything deliberately to hurt you, you surely know me well enough by now to realize that, don't you?'

'Ay, Mr Balfour,' whispered Dodie.

'Right, now that we've got that settled we'll get down to the reason I asked you to come here.' After that the laird didn't waste time. 'First a house. Mark – the minister – spoke to me some time ago about his concern for your welfare, old boy, and your taking ill the other day was the final crunch. He was worried about you living by yourself in that lonely cottage, out of reach of the village and no immediate neighbour to look in on you should you need help. But before all that I had decided you had become – well, not to put too fine a point on it, my dear chap – less independent than you used to be – age and all that, happens to us all. Both Mark and I decided a move nearer the village would be the best thing for you, I've been waiting for a suitable house to become available and now one has, Croft Beag...'

'But – I *like* my cottage!' Dodie wailed, utterly dismayed at this fresh turn of events. 'Och, Mr Balfour, say you'll no' put me out! I dinna want to go, I'm fine where I am wi' all my homely things about me and my wee hoosie wi' the fancy German pattern on the roof...'

'Dodie,' interposed the laird gently, 'the house I have in mind is a crofthouse with a piece of land attached, and though it's near the village it's not right in it. You can put your German sign where you like and will have plenty of privacy with only Mairi McKinnon and her family as your nearest neighbours.'

'Mairi? I fair like Mairi, she's no' like these other nosy cailleachs.' The threatening tears were suddenly arrested.

'Yes, Mairi, and I shall personally arrange with her to clean and cook for you, leaving you free to do all the things you love doing, like painting your stones...'

'And gardening,' put in Grant eagerly, 'Croft Beag has a fine bit o' cultivated ground and you aye said how much you would like a proper garden, Dodie.'

'A real garden,' Dodie's eyes were shining, not with tears but with a new-found enthusiasm, 'I'll be able to grow plenty rhubarb and sell it to the towrists in the summer – flowers too, these bonny wee orange trumpets and these others wi' the faces that smile all the time, even in the rain.'

'The place will be rent-free of course,' continued the

laird magnanimously, 'in return for all the hard work you have done for my family over the years – and a croft wouldn't be complete without a few hens and a cow grazing the field – and just think, Dodie, in the summer you wouldn't have to go tramping all over the island looking for her.'

He was well rewarded: Dodie was staring at him, speechless with joy, then he put his face in his big, calloused hands and began to cry, softly, brokenly, all the sadness and tension of the last long year spewing out in the tears that coursed freely down his face to squeeze themselves between his stubby fingers.

The other two men looked at one another, each of them experiencing a quiet, sweet happiness as they witnessed one old man's sorrows draining away in the tears he had bottled inside his lonely heart for so long.

'Just explain one thing to me, old boy,' said the laird, when Dodie was mopping his wet face with a sparkling white hanky that Mairi had thoughtfully tucked into his pocket earlier, 'what's all this about a stolen cup?'

Dodie explained breathlessly, ending, 'Maybe it wasny stolen from you, Mr Balfour, I never asked the tink where he got it but you had better have it anyway just in case.'

Scott Balfour grinned. 'You hang on to it, Dodie, I'll have a dram from it when I come to see that you're settling in at Croft Beag, we'll both have one.'

'Ach, you're a good man just, Mr Balfour, I'll never be able to thank you for all your kindness to me – and you'll no' forget what you said a wee while ago about a cow – will you now?'

'Dodie liked a cow he saw on the moor this morning.' A conspiratorial smile passed between the laird of Burnbreddie and the eldest son of McKenzie o' the Glen. 'She was a bonny young shorthorn complete with calf. I wasny sure if she was yours or Croynachan's.'

'She will be one of Croynachan's breeding beasts but I'm sure something can be arranged, I'll have a word with Tom as soon as I can.'

But Dodie would not be satisfied until the laird had seen the 'bonny beast' for himself, so into the estate Land-Rover they piled, after the laird had instructed old Angus the groom to take his horse back to the stables.

'But she's champing at the bit, Mr Balfour,' grumbled Angus, who hated change of routine.

'She isn't the only one,' replied the laird rather sourly, though he went willingly enough to where Dodie was waiting impatiently.

They found the cow easily enough, browsing among the sweet grasses at the edge of the moor where wild flowers grew in profusion and pollen dusted the mens' footwear as they swished along.

The cow looked up at their approach, a large white daisy sticking comically out of her pollen-covered lips from which a soft snort of warning issued forth, telling them not to get too close to her week-old calf who was peacefully asleep nearby.

Only Dodie advanced forward, his great clumsy feet as stealthy as a cat's, his tongue forming soothing Gaelic words.

'Does he always speak to the beasts in Gaelic?' the laird hissed in Grant's ear.

'Oh ay,' Grant took the question seriously, 'most o' the older folks do, it's the tongue the beasts know best. Tom himself likely does it – it's the native language o' both man and beast you see, Mr Balfour,' he explained with only the faintest hint of admonishment in his tone.

Dodie had reached the cow. As before she allowed him to pat and stroke her and finally entwine his arms round her hairy neck. Her green-coated tongue flicked out to lick his hand, releasing a sweet smell of clover; her enormously long, curly eyelashes tickled the coarse, weather-beaten skin of his face. His devotion and love were instant, tenderly sealed with a big, blubbery, smacking kiss placed plunk on the white star between the beast's ears. She didn't seem to mind any of it in the least, rather she gave every indication of enjoyment by rolling back her eyes along with her lips and uttering a soft little moo which was spoken directly into the hairy depths of Dodie's left lug. A great sigh shuddered out of him, his wet face was as content as it would ever be, and he knew that this was a rare day in his life, one that he would never, never forget.

'Ealasaid, my bonny Ealasaid, you've come back,' he said simply, and smiled.

Within a fortnight he was settled into his new home, Wullie McKinnon having driven up to Dodie's cottage to heave his meagre possessions into the back of the truck. The hens clucked in their crates among the jumble of furniture, Wullie started the engine, the truck began to rattle away on its journey down to Croft Beag, Gaelic for Little Croft, leaving behind the tiny cottage that had been Dodie's home for as long as he could remember. In days to come other people would live in it, for the laird had it in mind to gut it and make it suitable for visitors to rent in the summer months. Dodie took a last long lingering look at it, the peaceful glade, the purling burn, the wee hoosie shorn of its Swastika-patterned roof, his eyes beginning to swim. 'You've made sure you put my bonny sign in a safe place, Wullie?' he asked for the umpteenth time.

Wullie nodded, drawing his sleeve across his nose to rid it of its perpetual and famous drip. 'Ay, ay, 'tis down at Croft Beag along wi' the rest o' the stuff you salvaged from the Jerry plane so don't you worry about a thing. Mairi has been at the croft all morning getting it ready and will have a nice hot dinner waitin' for you.'

Mairi did indeed have a nice hot dinner waiting, but on arrival at Croft Beag Dodie was so astounded at the sight that met his eyes he was too excited to sit down and eat immediately. For the house was completely furnished from top to bottom, not new things by any means but good, solid, well-preserved furniture that had seen much service and would see much more before it was finished.

'The laird had it all brought down from Burnbreddie,' smiled Mairi, as she twitched a snow-white net curtain into place.

'And the clock! The bonny, talkin' clock!' Dodie was staring at the mantlepiece whereon reposed the cuckoo clock that had so captivated him.

'Ay, that too,' nodded Mairi, 'It was good o' the man right enough though I'm thinkin' he was maybe pleased to be rid o' it for it's fair deeved my own lugs all mornin' wi' its shoutin'.'

'I'll just unload these other things from the truck and put a match to them,' grinned Wullie, and went outside to begin heaving Dodie's goods and chattels into a large, ungainly pile.

But Dodie wasn't listening to anybody, he was over beside the clock, fondling its ornate carvings, waiting with bated breath for the hour to strike. When at last the cheeky little cuckoo shot vigorously against his nose, he clutched that appendage in his fingers and let out such a nasal screech of joy that Wullie stopped in his labours and was pecked on *his* nose by one of the hens who had managed to wriggle her head out between the spars of her crate.

After that there was no stopping Dodie. He pelted through the house like an express train, his boots squelching on the polished lino and wrinkling up the gaily coloured rugs that were scattered everywhere. He exclaimed over everything, touched, rubbed, familiarized himself with all the strange furniture, and when he was finished with that he galloped outside to stare with delight at his green acre and babble with pleasure at the sight of his 'bonny Hun sign' decorating the byre roof, having been nailed there by Wullie and Tam the day before.

'Everything is lovely just and will be even better when

Ealasaid and her bairn are safely home wi' me,' he enthused, as he came back inside to turn on taps and exclaim at the sight of fresh water gushing out. All his life he had carted pails of water from the burn, and he was so taken with the novelty of piped water he would have stayed at the sink for the rest of the morning turning the taps on and off had not Mairi pulled him away to lead him to the porch where she opened a door leading into a water closet.

'There is no bath,' she explained a trifle regretfully, for she was itching to deposit the old eccentric into one as soon as possible, 'but there is a fine big zinc tub hangin' on a nail here and at least you'll no' have to go out to a wee hoosie anymore.'

Dodie's relief at the lack of a properly plumbed bath was tremendous, and he wasn't too taken with the water closet either.

'I liked my wee hoosie fine,' he mourned, 'I had all thon airyplane levers in there wi' me and could play wi' them when I was waitin' for my rhubarb to work.'

'Ach, Dodie,' scolded Mairi, 'you didny think Wullie would throw these away surely? He has them safe and will fix them in here when he has the time and then you'll feel really at home.'

'Ach, 'tis good you are, Mairi,' he told her shyly. 'It will be fine havin' you for a neighbour, that it will, though I'll no' torment you for anything I wouldny like tormented for myself. It was private up there on the hill, you see,' he explained with dignity, 'and it will take me a whilie to get used to folk keekin' at me out o' their curtains...'

The cuckoo rushed out to proclaim the half-hour, enchanting Dodie afresh and leaving Mairi free to take the old man's belated dinner from the oven and set it on the table.

Scott Balfour was in the garden, helping Rena to tie up

some gigantic sunflowers, when Mark came cycling along the driveway. Seeing them in the walled-off garden at the side of the house, he dismounted and left his bike propped against the wall before going slowly through the ornate iron gate.

'Mark, how nice to see you, old boy,' greeted the laird. 'A bit hot for biking, I would have thought. Just let me finish here and I'll come and join you under the trees at the back. It's cool there and we can talk in comfort.'

Rena glanced at the visitor's hot face. 'I'll go and get you something cool to drink, unless – ' she turned back – 'you would like some iced whisky – or a long, cold glass of beer.'

'No, no, nothing like that,' Mark refused quickly.

'Oh, come on, Mark.' The laird finished tying the flowers and came forward to throw his arm round the other man's shoulder. 'I'm having one, just about time for a spot of the old mountain dew – it will help to revive you after the journey.'

'No!' Mark spoke too vehemently. 'No,' he repeated in a softer tone, 'a soft drink will be much more refreshing.'

Rena went off to the house, leaving her husband to lead the visitor to a huge oak tree around whose vast trunk had been built a circular bench which was shaded by the green, spreading canopy above.

It was very beautiful sitting there in the dappled shadows with the daisy-strewn grass smelling hot and sweet and the gladed woodlands rising behind, filled with birdsong and the chatter of red squirrels. In front of them, lush lawns sloped down to the sea where sandy coves and sheltered inlets abounded. The laird's motor cruiser could just be seen through the thick windbreak of rhododendrons, bobbing gently on its mooring in a calm little bay.

From the walled garden the scent of roses mingled with those of honeysuckle and sweet peas, and in the sylvan fields beyond, two gleaming chestnut mares browsed in the clover while in a small nearby paddock a tiny, shaggy donkey called Woolly stood near the fence, blinking sleepily in the sun, looking not in the least disposed to utter its ear-splitting brays which so attracted the children of Nigg that they often stopped on the road just to listen, and to wonder if it would be alright to go up to the big house and ask the laird if Woolly could come out to play. For out to play he did go whenever it was suitable, accompanied by the local youngsters who led him down to the sandy coves, where he paddled his hairy hooves in the water and gave the children bareback rides when he was in the mood to do so.

The delights of the place seemed to breathe life into Mark's soul. He allowed his heart to drink it in, to enjoy it while the sun shone and the birds sang – for already the days were shortening ever so subtly – before he knew it autumn would be here, with the first storms lashing those wondrously peaceful shores down there...

'You must come out in *Rena* with me sometime,' the laird had caught his visitor's wistful look and misinterpreted it. 'On a day like this there's nothing finer than a spin over the waves. I say, how about now? No time like the present, old man, and you look as though you could do with cooling down.'

'Thanks, Scott, but perhaps another time. I promised I would look in on Jack the Light and I've got some books I said I would hand in to old Meggie.'

'You work far too hard, Mark – ah, here's Rena with the drinks.' Jumping up, he took the tray from her hands and placed it on the bench.

'I'll leave this.' Smiling, Rena took a bottle of whisky from the generous depths of her gardening apron. 'I know my husband, after one he wants another and if Peggy sees him at the drinks cabinet she'll fold her lips into a thin line and later tell me, "The maister drinks too much. He leaves white rings on the sideboard I just canny seem to polish off and me wi' the rheumatics in my wrists."' She was an expert at mimicking the crotchety but utterly devoted kitchen maid, and went off to resume her gardening leaving the men laughing though, in Mark's case, it was mirth tinged with a terrible guilt.

'At least you don't commit your wee sins in private,' he murmured quietly.

'What was that, old man?'

'Oh, just something Captain Mac once said.'

'I know, he's always coming away with some quaint observation – are you sure you won't have a dram to keep me company?'

'Positive, you go ahead and enjoy it, I'm perfectly happy with this.' He sipped the long, ice-cold orange drink slowly, forcing his eyes away from the glass of whisky in Scott Balfour's hand. 'I only came over to thank you for all you did for Dodie,' he concentrated his mind on the old eccentric, 'he's absolutely thrilled with the croft and everything in the house and of course the cow and her calf. Old habits die hard though,' he smiled at the remembrance of his last visit to Croft Beag, 'I came upon him carrying his chamber pot out to his new rhubarb patch, and though he wasn't too pleased to be caught in the act he quite haughtily informed me he found the chamber more convenient than the water closet, since all the good of that went to waste in the sea.'

The laird chuckled. 'I've tasted that rhubarb. Damned good it was too if you can overlook its origins.'

'I was granted that honour as well, with Shona McLachlan, one warm day sitting out in the sun, complete with polks of sugar.'

The laird slapped his knee. 'I felt like a small boy again, dipping sticks of rhubarb into a paper bag. An old servant of ours made them just as Dodie does. Polky hats she called them – those were the days, eh, Mark?'

They reminisced, the laird growing quite sentimental as he talked about his boyhood. Mark was caught off-guard when suddenly the other man held up the whisky bottle and urged him to have one, 'to boyhood.'

The amber liquor glinted in the bottle. It was like a

magnet, hypnotizing him, capturing his whole attention so that his entire being seemed riveted to that deceptively innocent-looking liquid – his tongue came out to moisten his lips and from somewhere a voice spoke, out of his command, a perfectly calm voice saying, 'Och well, what's the harm – but just a wee one, mind.'

Half an hour later both he and the laird were in a most amiable and companionable frame of mind, with Scott Balfour speaking into his beard as he was wont to do whilst imbibing.

'I've seen him at it,' Peggy had voiced her disapproval to a few of her cronies. 'Kissin' and slaverin' into his very own whiskers and betimes lookin' mighty surprised when they didny kiss him back. He's that glaikit in drink he thinks anything that tickles must be a woman, though Mistress Balfour is far too sensible to let him paw her when he's in that state.'

'Ach, Peggy,' reproved old Meggie acidly, whilst praying that Burnbreddie's nosy maid would never discover her own tipple hidden under the crinoline skirt of a doll she kept on the mantlepiece, 'the man deserves his wee dram, for he's a good, kind soul and only takes a drop to be sociable.'

'That's as may be,' sniffed Peggy, 'but he's the laird after all and should show an example – even if it's only to these rough-speakin' crofters who visit him cap in hand and come away steppin' out as high as kings, brimful o' drink and cheek.'

But Scott Balfour paid little heed to Peggy's opinions. His own father had pickled himself in alcohol and his son had no intention of ending up like that. He simply enjoyed a dram in his own home and that's where it ended, and it was he who decided that enough was enough when he noticed Mark's reflexes were growing clumsy.

'Strange, old boy,' he mused, 'now that I come to think of it you've never once taken a dram from me –

hey, steady on, old son – '

He jumped up to go after the minister, who had risen to his feet and was making his unsteady way over the grass.

'I must go, Jack the Light – old Meggie – ' Mark tried to make his tongue obey the commands from his brain by speaking slowly and in monosyllables.

'I know, Mark, but wait and have some coffee first – '

'Must go.' Mark reached his bike, mounted and rode away, forgetting all about his promised visits to the old people of Nigg. The road twisted, turned, swooped downwards, upwards. His head spun, he concentrated grimly on the dusty grey ribbon in front, keeping his eyes strictly averted from the cliffs, the sea.

Something blurred his vision. Not that! Surely not that! He was a man. Men didn't cry. Oh God, he thought, how low have I sunk? Is this me? Really me? The Reverend Mark James crying? For what? For whom? Himself? Megan – ?

The road wavered, a grey-white blob suddenly rushed across his path, followed by a smaller, whiter blob – a ewe and her lamb... He swerved, his bike skidded from under him and he was falling down, down. His head thudded against a rock, and then there was only blackness – and no more pain...

'Mark, Mark, wake up. I know you can hear me, wake up.'

He groaned and moved slightly. His mouth was so dry his tongue stuck to the roof of it, his head throbbed with bands of red-hot pain. He tried to speak but couldn't – something icy-cold was suddenly there on his brow, soothing it, numbing the pain.

'You're alright, Mark, it's only me, lie still.'

Dazedly, he looked around him. He was home in his own bed and Babbie was somehow there, applying cold cloths to his forehead from a bowl of water beside the bed. Raising his head gently, she put a cup to his lips and he drank gratefully, gulping a little in his eagerness to get the fresh water down. It awoke his mouth, freed his tongue, allowing him to speak. 'Babbie, tell me, how did I get here?' he said urgently, taking her hand and holding on to it as if it was a lifeline.

She regarded him calmly. 'The laird brought you, he said something about following you to see that you didn't fall. You didn't go down far, only to a grassy ledge quite near the top. I was passing and somehow we got you up between us and into his Land-Rover.'

'There was no one else, Babbie? Please God no one else saw me!'

'No one else,' she smiled mischievously, 'only Scott Balfour and I know your guilty secret – '

'Guilty secret?'

'Ay, that he got you so legless you couldny even think straight, let alone ride a bike. Luckily you only gave your head an almighty bang so between it and your hangover you'll be in a fine state come morning.'

He lay back, relief flooding his soul. She suspected nothing, saw the whole episode as something of a joke. 'Babbie, you won't let on to anybody about this, will you?' He passed a shaking hand over his eyes, failing to notice the compassion that flooded into those hitherto laughing eyes of hers.

'No, Mark, of course I won't, what's there to tell anyway? Just a few drinks over the top, it's happened to me many's the time. We hold very responsible positions, you and I, and it's no crime to let our hair down now and then.'

Blindly, he sought her hand once more and squeezed it. 'Thank heaven for people like you, lass, you do so much good on this island.'

'Ach, no more than yourself! But we're both human with our own needs and desires – something I think you tend to forget.'

'I haven't forgotten, Babbie, that's my trouble, I'm so

wrapped up in myself I've been neglecting my work lately.'

'Havers! You're only one man, my lad, and canny do everything – man o' God or no'.'

She suddenly sounded like Behag and they both laughed.

'You'll have a bump on your forehead as big as a gull's egg before the day is over,' she warned him, 'and should think about taking a rest tomorrow. I'll go and see John Grey and ask him to take over the Sunday services for you. He's quite an obliging old soul in his dotage, though he might think it best to cancel the afternoon service at Portvoynachan.'

'I can't, Babbie, it's the McLachlan twins' christening tomorrow morning and I just can't let Shona and Niall down – oh Lord! I promised to go over to Mo Dhachaid this evening!'

He made to get out of bed but she pushed him back with a firm hand. 'Promises! Promises! You're full o' them, for this, that, and the other! Ease up, Mark, you're pushing yourself too hard. I'll see Shona and tell her you canny make it tonight though I don't suppose wild horses will keep you back from tomorrow's christening.'

He smiled. 'Neither wild horses nor Babbie Büttger.'

The door opened and Scott Balfour put an enquiring face round it. 'Thank the Lord you're awake, old man.' he tiptoed over to the bed, sober now, no longer 'kissin' and slaverin' into his very own beard' but perfectly lucid. 'I'm sorry I made you take that first dram, old son, you weren't used to it and it was my fault entirely you skidded over the cliff. When I saw you lying down there I thought you were dead – ' he straightened – 'say, you won't let on about this, will you, Mark? That old crone, Peggy, would never let me hear the end of it and Rena would make me do penance for a month.'

He held out his hand, Mark took it, laughing a little at the other man's hangdog expression.

A mournful whimper came from the hallway and the next second a shaggy, apologetic head wormed its way through the slightly open door to gaze with hopeful brown eyes in the direction of the bed.

'Mutt! Come on, boy, come on,' called Mark.

The dog rushed straight up onto the bed to wind his paws round his master's neck and to plant on it big, wet, adoring kisses. Mark fondled the dog's long, silky ears.

'I'll always have you, eh, Mutt lad, I'll always have you.'

The dog whined with pleasure, his warm body quivering. Mark didn't know why, but he wanted to cry suddenly and was glad he could hide his face into his dog's golden ruff. Life could be so hurtful but it could also be very sweet, and in those moments he tasted that sweetness and all because of the unquestioning love of one large, moist-eyed dog known as Mutt.

Chapter Seventeen

Mark never knew how he got through either the church service or the christening ceremony, but somehow he did, ignoring the questioning looks cast at the huge purple bruise on his forehead, the nudgings and the whisperings, concentrating instead on the twins, so beautiful in their long lacy robes, so trusting in their wide-eyed innocence.

'Joy Shona McLachlan and Joseph Nial McLachlan.' Their names rang from his lips, gladly, proudly. They both behaved like cherubs all through the ceremonials, the boy Joseph reaching out a chubby fist to grab a lock of Ruth, his godmother's, hair, the girl Joy gazing solemnly into Lorn, her godfather's, eyes, her chuckles of delight making everyone smile when he pulled a funny face at her.

They were big and bonny now, these babes, so different from the tiny mites Mark had seen on a pre-Christmas night just over six months ago. It seemed so close, yet so much had happened since then that it might have been aeons away. He caught Shona's eyes on him, those wondrous eyes that saw so much. She was very lovely standing there, the light glinting in her auburn hair, glancing off the warm flush of her cheek. She knew about him, he was sure of it, she saw things other people didn't – yet how could she know? It was his secret, his own guilty, dark secret...

At last it was over, the people were filing out into the porch, shaking his hand, one or two voicing sympathy regarding his bruises. Captain Mac winked. 'I've had one or two o' these myself – walkin' into doors that wereny there.' Knowingly, he tapped the side of his big, jolly nose and wandered outside.

Mark kept on shaking hands, automatically, nodding and smiling as he did so, wondering all the time what Captain Mac had meant, what he knew. It was just talk, innocent, mischievous, he was misconstruing everyday remarks, turning them, twisting them.

'Will we see you down at Laigmhor for the christening dinner?'

Shona was there, eyeing him, not pushing or forcing him in any way but just sounding friendly – kind.

'Ay, Shona,' he nodded, returning her smile, 'I'll be there, just give me time to change.'

'Mark, could you walk me home? I want to talk to you.'

It was Megan, pale-looking, her eyes gazing beseechingly into his. She had been in church for the christening, and though he had tried to keep his eyes averted from her he had been unable to do so. Every time he glanced in her direction he had found her gaze fixed on his face so intently he had felt that she was trying to convey some silent message to him.

He took her arm and led her away round the back of the kirk, out of sight of curious eyes.

They faced one another. She looked unhappy and tired, as if she hadn't slept much lately, the delicate skin round her eyes was slightly puffy, and he had the feeling that she had been crying recently.

Concern flooded his being, he forgot his own misery and knew only a longing to comfort her. 'Meggie, what is it? You don't seem very happy somehow.'

She caught her lower lip with her teeth. 'I'm not, Mark, things haven't been easy this while back. I've wanted so much to talk to you, to tell you things that have been on my mind but somehow you're always out of reach these days – at least, I get the feeling that you've been avoiding me ever since – since Steve came to Rhanna.'

'Avoiding you? Meggie, how can you say that? You're the one who's been out of reach. How could I interfere in the lives of two people who obviously have eyes only for each other? I know well enough that you're in love with him and certainly won't make a fool of myself by trying to come between you.'

'In love...? Oh, Mark, we must talk, straighten things out...'

They were walking slowly down the brae as they spoke, so absorbed in one another that they failed to see Steven coming unsteadily along the road from Tigh na Cladach. He was on them before either of them was aware of what was happening, grabbing Megan roughly by the arm, spinning her round so that she was forcibly held against him, her wrist twisted behind her back.

'So,' Steven growled harshly, 'this is what you get up to the minute my back's turned, flirting with your ex-lover boy and on a Sunday too for all the world to see! At least he might have had the decency to remove his robes before pawing you all over the place!'

He had been drinking, his face was flushed, his mouth slack and ugly. With a cruel laugh he tightened his grip on her arm, making her cry out in pain.

'Let her go,' Mark spoke evenly though he had to force himself to do so. 'I warn you, if you harm one hair of her head you'll have me to reckon with.'

'Is that so, holy man?' Steven's smile was menacing. 'I doubt very much if you've got the nerve to lift one goody, goody little finger, mustn't tarnish your reputation after all, what would your flock think of a minister who brawls on the Sabbath day!'

He gave an insane little giggle, and grabbing Megan by the neck he brought her face close to him, forcing bruising kisses on her mouth that made her cry out in pain.

It was the last straw for Mark. All his anger, longing, and frustration came spewing upwards together with the passions that he had tried in vain to suppress, robbing him of all those sensibilities that had for so long been his. Rushing forward, he pulled Steven off Megan and spun him round, his fist shooting out as he did so. Every shred of strength he possessed went into the blow so that his knuckles were like balls of steel.

Bone thudded into flesh, not just once but several times. Steven crumpled almost at once, his knees meeting the road with a sickening thump. He shook his head as if to clear it, his eyes dazed with pain and shock.

Mark wanted to hit him again and to keep on hitting him. White-hot fury churned inside of him, his curled fists itched for more. With a snarl of rage he plucked the young man from the road, held him by the collars at arm's length, and let fly at him again.

'Mark! sobbed Megan. 'That's enough, he's no match for you in his state, let him go.'

'You see,' slurred Steven, his mouth twisted and taunting despite the fact that it was badly swollen, 'it's me she loves, you bloody coward! Can't you get that through your thick skull? Go ahead and punch me to kingdom come, she'll only love me the more and despise you for hitting a man when he's down!'

His gaping mouth was just inches away, whisky fumes bathed Mark's face, he saw the blue eyes mocking him, and instead of feeling he was taking advantage of the other man he experienced a surge of such scorn that he began to shake Steven as if he was shaking a dog – only no dog that he had ever owned had taken such a severe beating.

Steven hung at the end of his fingers like some hideous scarecrow, hardly able to get breath, fear now flooding his dazed eyes. Mark's ears rang with the rattling of Steven's teeth, the ripping sound made by his clothing as it came to bits in his hands.

Several islanders had witnessed the fight from the beginning, others were running down the brae, black-clad figures converging on the road. Mark saw them as from a great distance, a devil seemed to have taken possession of him, taunting him, urging him on, allowing him to *enjoy* punishing this man who had hurt Megan, who had hurt *him*.

Megan was beside him, trying to pull him away, but he ignored her and took another swing at Steven's face.

'Enough,' panted the young man, 'for God's sake – enough. You think because of this you've won, don't you, but you're wrong – wrong! Be a man and let her go – you lost her a long time ago...'

Fresh rage seized Mark, his fists balled once more, found their mark with sickening accuracy.

'My, my, he's a bonny fighter,' Tam commented cheerfully.

'Ay, that he is,' agreed Todd the Shod, 'he's gettin' rid o' his anger at last. Every man needs to do that once in a while.'

'That Saunders mannie was hurting the doctor,' Granny Ann sucked noisily at a cough sweetie between words. 'I saw him wi' my very own een, pulling at her and twisting her arms. Mr James is no' fighting just for the sake o' it, he was goaded into it and no mistake.'

'That's as may be,' sniffed Elspeth in disgust, 'but fancy our very own minister behaving like a hooligan.'

'He is just behaving like a man.' It was Behag saying that, in a small voice to be sure but voicing an honest-to-goodness opinion for once in her life. She was more devoted than ever to 'the man o' God' since the incident of Holy Smoke's 'disappearance'. Mr James had been the essence of patience both during and after the event and she was going to give him her support now, no matter how much she disapproved of 'common brawling'.

'Behag is right, Elspeth,' Captain Mac took Elspeth's arm and gave it a fond squeeze. 'Why should he no' fight for what he feels is rightly his? None o' this would have happened if that fancy-talkin' mannie hadny come here. 'Tis my opinion our Mr James has just about had enough o' his kiddin' and swankin'.'

There were murmurs of agreement all round. Elspeth, feeling suddenly good and warm with Captain Mac's strong arm in hers, nodded. 'Ay, you could be right at that, Isaac, though 'tis a pity he didny take off his robes before letting fly at the chiel.'

'I canny rightly believe my ears,' Holy Smoke's rather high-pitched voice broke in, 'here you all are, on the Sabbath day, standing around watching our minister behaving like a heathen and soundin' as if you're enjoyin' it!'

'Ach, away and smoke your Woodbine, Sandy,' said a voice from the gallery, as it were. There were titters. The butcher subsided and said not another word on the subject.

Mark, his rage suddenly spent, released Steven who staggered back to land on the verge. He was handsome no more. Blood frothed from his nose, welled from his mouth, one eye was starting to close. Immediately Megan was on her knees beside him, staring horrified at his bloodied face. She looked up at Mark who had come rushing forward, her face pale, her eyes wild.

'You fool, Mark,' she threw at him. 'Have you any idea of what you've done? You've ruined everything, everything – and you a man of the cloth who should know better.'

A mist seemed to fall from Mark's eyes, allowing stark reality to rear up and hit him like a douche of ice water. 'Meggie,' he whispered, appalled at himself, 'I'm sorry, something came over me – I couldn't seem to help myself. I'm a man, Meggie, I just couldn't stand by and watch him hurting you.'

He threw out his hands in appeal, they were bruised and bloody, a great purple weal accompanied the bump on his forehead, both marks looking like alien obscenities above the pure white of his dog collar. He was no more the Mark James she had known than day was like night, and the knowledge of that pressed her down as if a leaden weight was on her shoulders, bowing them, forcing her head to droop wearily so that her hair hid her face.

Mark turned from her and went to lift Steven to his feet. The young man threw him off, his blue eyes glittering with dislike as he hissed, 'I could have you de-frocked for this. It's no more than you bloody well deserve.'

'You would be doing me a favour,' Mark returned, drained of everything that had motivated his actions a short while ago.

'The coward's way out, eh?' gritted Steven. 'No, I'll let you sweat it out till you're forced to do it on your own account and from the look of you, old man, I'd say that day isn't so very far off.'

Megan came to slip her shoulder under Steven's arm, for he was swaying on his feet and looked ready to collapse again at any moment. 'Help me get him home,' she appealed to no one in particular, and one or two of the men came forward to hoist Steven's weight onto their shoulders. The party moved slowly towards Portcull, leaving behind a terrible silence.

Mark stood alone, stunned, shaken by what he had done.

'Mark, come home with us, you're all in.' Shona was there, Niall at her side, supporting him with their words, their kindly concern. Brusquely he turned from them. 'I have to be alone, I'm sorry.'

He strode quickly away, skirting the knots of onlookers, clambering up the bank to cut across to the track leading to the gate atop the Hillock, his black robes flapping, making him look less of a man and more of a phantom. He disappeared into a dip, rose up again, receding into the distance, only his cloth lifting and falling, lifting and falling, till it could be seen no more.

The crowd dispersed, silently, rather sadly, its lack of comment adding to the sense of despondency that had followed their minister back to his lonely Manse up yonder on top of the brae.

*

Towards the middle of August the *Mermaid* set sail for home with three people aboard, her departure not nearly as spectacular as her arrival had been but interesting just the same as, with Ranald putting so many unexpected obstacles in the way at the last minute, it was a miracle she had managed to leave at all.

All through that long, hot summer, he had willingly given his services and the use of his shed to the young yachtsmen, appearing so eager to oblige that they had honestly taken him for a simple man with naught else in his head but the desire to please his fellow men. He had personally taken it upon himself to gather together a skilled workforce, so that every day, bar Sunday of course, his big boat shed had rung with the sounds of sweated labour accompanied by much banter and laughter, for no Hebridean worth his salt took any task all *that* seriously.

But busy hive of industry though the place had been there was something that could only be described as mystery in the air, an atmosphere that became noticeable whenever Daniel or Steven put in an appearance. Then, certain whisperings and sniggerings would all at once cease, and the ensuing time filled once more with determined hammerings and sawings.

But such things were of small import to the young strangers from the south, enough it was that Ranald did everything but touch his forelock whilst in their company, his cap respectfully held in his hands, his, 'Ay, Mr Smellie, I'll see to that,' or his, 'Ach no, Mr Saunders, 'tis no bother at all,' sufficing to keep them jubilant of spirit and easy of mind.

And so they remained, right up to the day the yacht was ready to go back into the water. Arriving at the shed, they found the double doors locked and barred with no sign of life anywhere until Ranald appeared from his cottage, an amiable enough expression on his face but an odd little gleam lighting his eyes.

'Well now, 'tis yourselves, lads,' he greeted the pair pleasantly, 'all ready for the road at last.'

'That's right, Ranald.' Daniel spoke a trifle impatiently as, now that the hour of departure was close, he was eager to be off while the forecast for the next few days was good. 'Unlock the doors and let us in, like a good chap.'

Ranald assumed a thoughtful air. 'Ach well, that I will do just as soon as we have settled on a fair figure for the use o' my shed and of course, wear and tear o' my equipment. The lads will be expectin' their money before you go and will want cash in hand seeing it's an awful trachle gettin' cheques cashed when you don't have the benefit o' a bank account. They will be lookin' for a wee bittie extra for the salvage work as so indeed will I, since I gave them a hand to fetch it in as well as the use o' my boats...'

'Salvage work!' Steven's howl of disbelief sent the gulls on the quayside flapping into the sky. 'What salvage work? There was no mention of that nor was there any talk of paying you for all these other things you mentioned!'

Ranald managed to look suitably humble. 'Ach well, Mr Saunders, it's no' nice to discuss things like these wi' visitors. We find it very embarrassing on the islands and know well enough it is only a matter o' honour that makes folks pay their debts wi' a good grace – '

'You're a bloody rogue, Ranald McTavish!' interposed Daniel, his face livid. 'You're either a damned clever actor or the biggest cheat that ever lived, for you gave no indication of any of this when you offered us the use of your premises.'

Ranald looked hurt. 'Mr Smellie, these is no' nice things you are saying, you should be ashamed o' yourself just. We might no' go swankin' about wi' our hands stretched out for sillar but we are no' the simple cratur's you seem to think, nor are we money grubbers either, just honest, hard-workin' lads who have to earn their bread and butter like anybody else. Of course, if you are too mean to pay up for a good job well done I will be forced to hold your boat as collateral till you are in a better frame o' mind – '

'Oh, for heaven's sake!' burst out Steven. 'Tell us how much you want and be done with it.'

'If you will just step into my cottage, I have the accounts prepared ready...'

'But I'm damned if you're getting salvage money,' growled Steven. 'There was nothing to salvage that I know of.'

Ranald, coming back outside with a sheaf of papers in his hand, stopped in his tracks. 'Mr Saunders! Me and the lads near drowned ourselves fishin' bits o' your boat from the sea – and if you don't believe me you can ask them yourselves for they will be here in a wee whilie to collect their wages. Where do you think we got all the bits and pieces to get the *Mermaid* back into her original condition?'

'From your junk heap?' suggested Daniel sarcastically.

Ranald cocked his head. 'Mr Smellie, that's no' in very good taste, and from a lad o' your upbringing too – '

'Never mind all that,' broke in Steven rudely, 'you'll get paid for everything else but no salvage money.'

'Och well, have it your own way, son,' Ranald spoke equably, 'no money, no boat, but I'm no' quite understanding your reluctance on the matter. Surely your insurance will cover all these sundries?'

'The sum has already been settled,' clipped Daniel.

'Ach, that's too bad, but neither o' you are short o' a bob or two and if you're wise you'll pay up – you see, lads,' he grinned at them good-humouredly, 'every extra hour the *Mermaid* spends in my shed will add to the final bill. I have lost out havin' her in there all these months through havin' to turn away a wheen o' business.

I wasny for tellin' you as I'm no' the sort o' man to rush a good job.'

'Show us your accounts,' ordered Steven brusquely, 'though I warn you now, if it's ready money you're after it will take a few days for it to come through.'

Ranald simply could not resist rubbing his hands together. 'I'm in no hurry, son, though of course it means I will lose more business wi' my shed out o' commission. I'm surprised mind, that modern young folks like yourselves could be so lax on such important matters. The weather might no' hold for one thing and for another it is an easy enough matter to pick up the tellyphone and ask for the money to be sent right away. Your parents will surely no' grudge a wee favour to a pair o' fine lads like yourselves.'

Steven's jaw tightened, Daniel's dark face was like a thundercloud and when he spoke it was through clenched teeth. 'I've travelled to all parts of the world but I think I can honestly say I've never yet met anyone as crafty as you are. You're wasting your time here, McTavish, you would make a fortune in the underworld and bankrupt everyone in the process.'

Snatching the accounts from Ranald's hand, he hurried away in the direction of the Post Office, Steven hot on his heels.

A few minutes later 'the workforce' arrived at Ranald's house to look questioningly into his sunburned countenance. He nodded and winked, a jubilant cheer went up and Ranald, once more rubbing his hands briskly together, bade them inside for 'a wee celebration dram.'

Glasses in hand, they arranged themselves at various vantage points near the windows so that they could comfortably watch Daniel and Steven 'rushin' around gettin' the money.'

It arrived by registered post the next day. Ranald received his share with many pleasurable nods and smiles, but before he turned away he tucked some notes into Steven's shirt pocket. 'There you are, son, you gave me three pounds too much and I wouldny like you to think I was the sort o' man to cheat on another.' And he meant it, too, as he stood there amiably nodding and smiling, looking from one astonished face to the other with utmost sincerity.

'Ay, well, I'll be getting along now,' he beamed, giving Steven's pocket an affectionate pat before ambling unhurriedly away leaving the young men looking after him and wondering if he was as devious as they imagined, or as he himself had said, 'just an honest hard-workin' lad earning his bread and butter like everyone else.'

The very next morning the *Mermaid* left the sheltered anchorage of Portcull Harbour and headed out into the Sound, cheered and waved on by Ranald and his mates and a small crowd who had gathered to watch proceedings, not interested so much in the actual departure as because Megan was accompanying the men south for a long holiday. She had left Lachlan to take care of things till she got back, 'Though I don't know when that will be, Lachlan,' she had told him. 'I – I might never come back. I feel as if I've never really been accepted here and have to get away to see it all in perspective. At the moment I can't do that, I'm too close and too jaded to be able to think clearly. I'll let you know one way or the other and make arrangements accordingly. I want you to feel free to use my car while I'm gone – at least it starts without any trouble,' she made an attempt at humour, 'Angus fixed it so well I've a feeling it will still be around long after I'm gone.'

He had taken her hands to squeeze them and study her face with concern. She *did* look tired. There were purple smudges under her eyes and a weary droop about her mouth. 'You're no' running away, are you, Megan?'

Her head jerked up. 'No – of course not – och to hell!

Maybe I am – maybe I have to for a while.'

'Just so long as it's no' a case of out of the frying pan. Don't do anything foolish, lass, I trust you and I know you won't let me down. When I nominated you to fill my place I didn't single you out for your looks you know, bonny as you may be, I chose you because I thought you were the best person for the job and still believe it.'

She had smiled at him uncertainly and kissed him on the cheek before saying her farewells to Phebie and Babbie, who had been in the kitchen partaking of a strupak.

'No doubt you'll be glad to get rid of me,' Megan had teased, smiling at Babbie with real affection, 'you and Lachlan will be able to work together like in the old days.'

'Ay, I will enjoy working wi' Lachlan again,' Babbie admitted frankly, 'but odd as it may seem I'll miss you around the place – after all,' she giggled, 'I canny very well have the cosy wee discussions wi' him that I had wi' you – like my preference for cotton knickers or how my bra size has gone up an inch since the start o' summer...'

'Ach, Lachy wouldny bat an eye if you said these things to him,' interposed Phebie mischievously, 'he's used to knicker talk for when Fiona and me get together it's all about clothes and underwear and – when she was younger – about pubic hair and breast development.'

They had all laughed at that, and had sat down cosily together to drink tea and be as lighthearted as possible. But it had been a different story when she had gone along to Mo Dhachaid to say her farewells to Shona, who had said she would take Muff for as long as need be. It hurt Megan badly to have to part with the little dog she had grown to love, and quite a tearful parting ensued before Shona led Muff out of the room to play with Sporran and the children in the garden.

'Megan,' Shona, coming back to the kitchen, looked at the doctor in her direct way, 'you're making a terrible mistake going off wi' Steven and I hope to heaven you see sense before it's too late for everyone concerned...'

'Who said anything about going off with Steven?' Megan interrupted sharply.

'Och, stop that, Megan,' Shona returned with equal asperity, 'of course you're going off wi' him! The whole island knows even if you don't. I'm disappointed in you, I really thought you had more guts – that you would stay and sort things out between you and the man you really love.'

'You really do take too much on yourself, Shona,' Megan was unable to stop her temper rising, 'what I do with my life is my business and it's high time you, and a few others, got that into your thick heads. How the hell can you possibly know who I love and who I don't? You're as bad as all the other gossips and I'll be glad to shake the dust of this place off my heels, if only to be rid of small minds.'

'Ach, go ahead and drown yourself for all I care!' Shona lost her own volatile temper at that point. 'You'll never grow up, will you? Aye the eternal schoolgirl, blushing and hiding and waiting for your white knight to come along. It's no' you I'm thinking of anyway, it's Mark. He's made such a fool o' himself over you, he's only half the man he once was and is ill because o' you and your foolish carrying on right in front o' his nose, where he can see you and be sick at the sight o' you and your precious sailor boy!'

'That's it! You've gone too far, Shona McLachlan! The way you go on about Mark anyone would think you were in love with him yourself!'

Shona's anger subsided, her beautiful blue eyes caught and held the other woman's blazing stare. 'I was – once – just a little bit,' she admitted softly, 'he saved my sanity when no one else could do anything for me. He's a very special person to me, Megan, and some small part o' me will always cherish him. Don't get me wrong, Niall is my life, and has been from the start, but Mark will never cease to be dear to me and I just canny stand by and watch him pining away without feeling that something inside o' me is withering away also.'

'Oh, Shona,' tears shone in Megan's hazel eyes, 'I'm sorry I was so angry just now, it's just – I'm so confused I don't really know what to do, where I'm going, all I know is I have to get away to think it all out. Mark has been hurt very badly by all this and I feel it's all my fault. He fought Steve to protect me but it hasn't made things any better for any of us, Steve feels very bitter towards Mark so the sooner we go away the better.'

'You'll write and let me know how you are?' Shona said softly.

'Yes, of course I will, take good care of Muff, won't you?' Turning on her heel she walked away, a mist of tears in her eyes and an odd, unexplained lump in her throat.

Now she was aboard the *Mermaid*, standing at the rails watching Rhanna slip away, alone as she wanted to be in those poignant moments – then Steven came up to stand beside her and the moment was over – too soon, far too soon for a young woman who had all at once realized how dear and sweet one small island had become to her. She took one last, lingering look back. Rhanna was far away now, a dazzling opal in a blue velvet sea – she saw the pale column of the lighthouse, and – was it a trick of the light or just pure fancy? Or was that really a spiral of smoke rising into the sky, beckoning, beckoning from the tall chimneys of the Manse atop the Hillock...?

Two people, who hadn't been down at the harbour to watch the 'Mermaid' sailing away, saw her nevertheless. On the lower slopes of Sgurr nan Ruadh a fair-haired girl sat amongst the wild flowers, hugging her knees and shading her eyes as she gazed out to sea, watching the yacht till she was just a speck in the distance.

'God go wi' you, Dan,' she whispered. Her head sank

onto her knees, her wash of fine, silken hair cascaded over her face.

'He'll love you and leave you, lassie, don't waste your tears on him.' How right her mother had been. He had loved her and left her, apologetically, his dark eyes serious, his farewell kisses warm but brief, telling her he wouldn't be back even while he promised he would – some day. She wanted to believe it, to bolster herself up with false hopes that would allow her better to thole the empty days ahead. But she was far too sensible for that. Her father might have been easy-going but he had been level-headed too, and his daughter had inherited that trait in double measure.

Eve sighed and stood up, her vision now trained on her mother's house sitting snug in the green fields below. She was a good mother, one who had always trusted her children to do what was right – but grief had taken its toll and she was a bit more edgy these days. Eve wondered how she would react when she discovered that one of her children had broken the trust she had always taken for granted – before, before a young man had come to the island out of a storm to wreak havoc in the heart of a girl who had never known what love was about till he had come into her life – and out of it just as swiftly.

On the silver white sands of Burg Bay a lone figure stood staring out to sea, his hand up to his eyes to shade them against the glare. The *Mermaid* was a good way off now, her white sails dazzling in a sun that shone and sparkled and turned the Sound of Rhanna into a vast silver lake. Megan hadn't said goodbye and he knew she hadn't forgiven him for that dreadful incident in Glen Fallan, the thought of which still made him cringe in shame and embarrassment.

No wonder she despised him, he had made such a fool of himself it had taken every ounce of courage he possessed to go out among people again, and – hardest of all – to climb into the pulpit and face his congregation. He had thought that people might stay away, that the kirk would be empty of all those staunch kirkgoers whose faces he looked down upon, week after week. But he had been wrong, it was more crowded than it had ever been before – panic seized him at that point. Had they come to ogle a minister so lacking in self-control he had lifted his hand to another man on the Sabbath? Or worse. Had they come to point the finger of scorn? To condemn and whisper and wonder among themselves, how long he could go on preaching about good and evil?

All his conjectures soon proved to be wrong. Everyone had been kind to him. There hadn't been as much as a single disapproving glance from Elspeth or a murmur of reproval from anybody else. They came to the Manse to visit him, and not one referred to his fight with Steven Saunders. Even old Behag had come sprachling along, bearing gifts of homemade tablet and a pair of hand-knitted socks to keep his 'feets' from getting cold in church. Yet nothing served to make him feel any less guilty and he decided that it might, after all, have been better if the affair had been brought into the open. The airing of it might have helped to reduce its enormity in his mind; as it was, it grew and grew out of all proportion till he felt he would go mad with his whirling thoughts.

The *Mermaid* was now just a speck on the horizon but still he stared at her till his eyes ached and he could see her no more. Mutt came bounding towards him, smiling, his tongue flying wetly from his mouth, his great hairy feet churning up the sands, leaving a trial that zigzagged all over the bay. His was a simple, wholesome joy that never failed to find an echo in Mark's heart. Bending down, he hugged the dog to him. 'You know, Mutt, I think I might take John Grey up on his offer to look after things. There's nothing here to keep me any longer. You and I could go to Perthshire in the autumn. It's beautiful there then with the woods and hills ablaze with colour and lots of rabbits for you to chase.'

Mutt barked, as if in full approval of the idea, and they set off to climb the cliff path together. At the top Mark kept his eyes averted from Tigh na Cladach, lonely looking already, drawn and shuttered to the world. His steps quickened as he passed by, but Mutt had other ideas. He bounded to the gate, looking hopefully back over his shoulder to see if his master followed.

'Come away, boy,' Mark didn't turn round, 'Muff isn't there, they've all gone, all gone away.'

Mutt's tail drooped, he gave a mournful little whimper. Mark stopped in his tracks and looked at his dog standing so dejectedly beside the gate. 'Well, I'll be...' He called the dog to him. He came, slinking, unwilling, hardly able to muster a twitch of his tail when Mark caught his ruff and knelt down to look into his sad brown eyes. 'You've lost your lady love too, haven't you, boy? I never realized – I should have known but I was too wrapped up in myself. We're in the same boat, you and I, and we'll have to comfort one another as best we can.'

He stood up. 'Come on, lad, let's go home, it's dinner time and there's a nice big juicy bone waiting for you.'

The dog stayed close to his master's heels, for once not running on ahead to check that the cats hadn't somehow found his bone.

The summer visitors were going, gradually thinning out, leaving on every steamer till only a handful remained. Mrs Dolly Hosheit was one of the last to go, having enjoyed her stay on Rhanna so much she had abandoned former plans to tour other islands.

Kate, in a burst of conscience, had invited the pleasant little lady to stay with her when Tigh na Cladach closed its doors. Dolly had accepted with alacrity, proving herself to be such an agreeable companion that even Tam looked sorry when she at last decided to leave.

'I must go, Tam, I really must. Emmit and I have some very dear friends living in Edinburgh and they have been pressing me to stay with them over the autumn. After that I simply must go back to England and visit all my old haunts. Who knows, I may decide to stay there, and if I do I will most certainly come back to Rhanna and see all my wonderful friends.'

She left soon after, loaded down with 'wee gifts' of all descriptions, one bag given over completely to the mounds of mealy puddings, bannocks, rock cakes and tattie scones made specially for her by Kate, not to mention a bottle of best malt whisky Tam hastened to acquire for her at the last minute. The majority of the islanders were like that, taking with one hand, giving back double with the other, and Kate was no exception, her generosity proving so overwhelming in these final moments that Dolly rushed away, tears in her eyes and fond memories in her heart that would remain with her wherever she travelled.

Chapter Eighteen

The dentist mannie had arrived on Rhanna, a brisk, bald, bespectacled little man with shiny pink skin and a huge smile which Kate likened to 'a row o' grinning piano keys.'

'Ach, maybe he got them made special to advertise his profession,' suggested Molly. 'It's a good way o' savin' money for these newspaper adverts can be gey dear.'

And she might have been right at that, for wherever Mr Niven McQuarry went, folk said his grin arrived first and incited so much comment the subject of teeth was never far from the limelight.

'Of course, mine are my own and will only need a bittie polish on them,' claimed Elspeth, puffing out her bony ribcage with pride.

'A likely story,' snorted Kate to her daughter-in-law, Mairi, 'she lost the whole jing bang o' them way back at the Battle o' Culloden.'

'But Kate,' protested Mairi with utmost seriousness, 'it was only men fought in battles like these.'

'Ay, then Elspeth was there right enough,' Kate said in exasperation.

'But her teeths *are* her own,' insisted Mairi, in her gently infuriating way.

'Ach, Mairi!' scolded Kate. 'Will you never see a joke when it's staring you in the face? Of course the cailleach's teeths are her own, no one else in their right mind would covet such great, brown molars. I've seen better wallies in a horse and 'tis little wonder Hector used to call her a nag!'

Elspeth wasn't the only one to cling on to her 'natural' teeth, no matter how ancient they might be. Several of the older Gaels attached disgrace to anything inside or outside of their bodies that 'wasny God's creation.'

But they were in the minority. No one else in the least minded anything that aided and abetted nature, and there was much jubilation when it became known that the long-awaited dentist mannie had arrived. The older members of the population hastened to locate dentures that were so painful to wear, they only saw the light of day for funerals, weddings, and the Sabbath. Those elderly souls who never deemed to wear them at all, gazed furtively at mouldering 'teeths' lying half forgotten in some little-used drawer, and wondered daringly if perhaps the dentist mannie might this time be able to perform some miracle and make them dentures that actually fitted.

'Of course, it's the way these old people wriggle and grimace when one is trying to get an impression,' Niven McQuarry confided to Lachlan in his 'very propa'' Edinburgh drawl. 'I do my best but the best is never good enough for some people.'

'Ach, you have to make allowances for the old folk,' Babbie said as she bustled about, setting out the dentist's tools of trade in the room Lachlan had hastily set up as a surgery until Megan either came back or a locum took over.

'Queet, queet,' Niven McQuarry swallowed his annoyance and flashed his big grin at Babbie, 'and with you to help me, my deah, I'm sure we'll manage just grand, ay, just grand.'

Phebie and Babbie between them had tried to organize some appointment system that would spread the dentist's work over a five-day period, but it was a useless task. So many people, it seemed, found the dentist's attentions imperative that double the amount of patients arrived on the first morning, filling Slochmhor's hall where a variety of seating had been quickly assembled.

Babbie, Lachlan, and Niven McQuarry spent an exhausting and busy day of it. Extractions, fillings, and polishings came and went in brisk succession. Those who had to have gas had perforce to recover in Phebie's parlour, from there to the kitchen to partake of luke-warm tea and much patient sympathy before reeling outside, to expose pocked gums proudly to those souls who were still trying to pluck up the courage to remain firmly in their seats till their turn came.

One or two of the old folks had arrived in huge wickerwork wheelchairs that looked as if they might have been tacked together by inexpert hands, but come they did, oozing a confidence they didn't possess, barking their nervousness at anyone who got in their way and, in a few cases, wangling their way to the front of the queue by quite simply battering their way forward, no matter the cost to human flesh.

The young folk hung back, giggling and gulping and voicing their fears, but remaining stolidly put while they bolstered one another up with visions of gleaming white teeth that were sure to be appreciated by the opposite sex.

For five solid days the road to Slochmhor had never been busier while in the surgery, teeth, blood, and hair flew, the last literally for old Sorcha screeched so much during the extraction of one ancient wisdom tooth, she quite unnerved Mr McQuarry who staggered and fell against her, his clutching hands grabbing her hair. When it came away in his hands his fright was such that he sent the hair piece whizzing across the room to land amongst the debris of teeth, cotton wool, gauze, and similar discarded accoutrements.

'My wig,' whispered Sorcha, forgetting her pain in the enormity of the moment, 'my bonny wig. It's covered in dirt and all manner o' dreadful things.'

Despite her girth she flew out of the high chair with alacrity, knocking Mr McQuarry aside in her hurry to get at her wig which, when retrieved and held up, looked like some abandoned ginger moggy, matted as it was with cotton wool and a fair number of bloody teeth clinging to the hairs.

'Look! Would you look!' Sorcha shrieked with pure rage. "T'will never be the same again! 'Tis ruined, ruined, I tell you! I will be putting in a claim for compensation, that I will. I'm goin' to *sue* you, Mr McQuarry!'

In those traumatic moments, no one thought to remind her that the wig had been acquired through the National Health and she was in no position to sue anyone. The dentist's own teeth had almost fallen out his head at this unexpected intrusion into his working day, so thoroughly agape was his heavy jaw.

Both Lachlan and Babbie could only stare at the enraged old lady, then with one accord they clutched each other and collapsed together onto a nearby chair, there to roar with uninhibited mirth.

Those waiting outside the surgery heard first of all Sorcha's terrible yelps and screams and they eyed one another in utter terror, Tam even going so far as to rise to his feet and seek out the door, while wondering how fast he could get to it for all the jumble of feet, legs, walking sticks, and shepherd's crooks propped about everywhere.

While his thoughts were thus engaged, Sorcha's enraged yells, her threats, filtered quite plainly through the surgery door. The waiting throng was aghast.

'Here, what do you think they have removed?' Todd the Shod breathed in round-eyed horror. 'It sounds serious.'

'Ay, as if they've maybe taken away something they shouldny have. She's sayin' something will never be the same again.' Fingal's face was deathly pale.

'Maybe it's her tonsils,' pondered Isabel hopefully. 'The old besom talks far too much and at her age is in no need o' her tonsils for she's aye sniffin' and snufflin' wi' the cold. A good sore throat will maybe keep her quiet for a week or two.'

'Ay, but Isabel,' Jim Jim wriggled uncomfortably, his weak bladder growing weaker suddenly with fright, 'they just canny go about takin' things out o' folk that is no' rightly theirs. I have had enough wee bitties taken out o' me to last a lifetime and I have no wish to lose my tonsils as well, they've been wi' me too long now.'

'Ach, it was only your appendix you lost,' his wife told him unsympathetically, 'and they only fiddled around wi' your prostrate thon time you was in hospital wi' your bladder.'

'It would be his prostate,' Molly put in knowledgeably, 'it happens to a lot o' men at a certain age though I'm glad to say my Todd has never been bothered that way.'

'Well, whatever it was I'm no' for losin' anything else.' Jim Jim rose to his feet to trip and stumble his way to the kitchen, there to ask Phebie if he might have the use 'o' the wee water hole.' Behind him he left a trail of crushed bunions and toes, whose owners were not shy about voicing opinions regarding his 'clumsy great feets.'

'Listen!' Imperatively, Tam held up his hand. Gales of merriment now issued from behind the closed surgery door. 'They're laughin', they're peein' themselves laughin'. It canny be all that bad...'

The door was suddenly wrenched open and Sorcha rushed out, whirling her soiled wig around her shorn head as if it was some battle-torn banner. With a warlike screech she went charging her way outside, leaving a trail of scattered chairs and shepherd's crooks in her wake.

'Here, it was her wig,' grinned Todd. 'I've never seen Sorcha without her wig before. She looks like one o' they scalped cratur's I saw in a cowboy picture thon time I was over visiting my cousin on the mainland.'

'Ay, that was the time I went with you,' Ranald enthused. 'It was a fair treat to watch they Red Injuns whoopin' about sawin' folks heads off – '

'Ach no, you're thinkin' o' head hunters,' corrected

Todd firmly, 'Red Injuns only take the scalps to hang on these totem poles they have round their tents.'

'Have you no decency?' berated Molly, glowering at Ranald as if she would like to deprive him of *his* head. 'That poor sowel was in a terrible state just now and if you were men at all you would have gone after her to see her safely home...'

'Next please,' Babbie put a glowing face round the surgery door. 'And please leave wigs and other sundries on the hall table. The medical profession can't accept responsibility otherwise.'

'Babbie, you're a rogue,' Lachlan laughed at her back, while Niven McQuarry strove to compose his face into the welcoming smile he always endeavoured to display to his patients, no matter how flustered he might be feeling.

Niven McQuarry knocked rather tentatively on the open door of Croft Beag, arranging his features into a pleasant smile on hearing footsteps in the hall. Dodie appeared, stuffing something into his pocket as he approached the door. Mr McQuarry introduced himself, but before he could explain the reason for his visit a beaming Dodie pulled him inside, insisting as he did so that the visitor must 'hae a wee look round Croft Beag.' The old eccentric was so pleased with himself these days that no caller was allowed to rest without first seeing round the place, and so Niven McQuarry was given a grand tour of the house, the garden, and the outbuildings.

Outside the byre Dodie stopped, his big hands folded across his chest, his gaze resting lovingly on the Swastika sign adorning the roof.

'Is she no' beautiful just?' Dodie asked proudly. 'I have looked after her for years for the weather has a habit o' peeling the paint away.'

'Ay, yes, queet, queet, very unusual.' Mr McQuarry said in some bemusement.

He was about to turn back to the house, but Dodie was having none of that. Cupping his hands to his mouth he emitted an oddly sweet calling note, and over the clover-strewn field trotted Ealasaid with her calf.

'My bonny Ealasaid,' Dodie introduced his cow as another might introduce a very grand personage. 'Every day at this time I come out to give her her potach, but seeing you're here I ken fine you would like to do it.'

From his pocket he withdrew a paper bag containing some pieces of oatcake. These he emptied into Mr McQuarry's unwillingly extended palm. He had had very few dealings with bovines of any description and expected to lose his hand at any moment, but the cow drooled gently over it, relishing every tasty scrap, and when every crumb was finished she slobbered her big green tongue around his fingers just in case she might have missed anything.

'She likes you, Mr Dentist,' Dodie said with conviction. 'It's no' everybody she'll take to.'

'Ay, ay, a fine beast,' Mr McQuarry was edging away as he spoke, but Dodie spent a few more minutes talking in the Gaelic to both Ealasaid and her calf before he would deign to make a move.

When finally they were back in the house, Mr McQuarry requested that he be allowed to wash his hands and was amazed at the alacrity with which the old eccentric responded. Gleefully he led the visitor to the sink, there to splash water into it with such enthusiasm that the dentist became alarmed lest he should flood the place.

'It's just like my own wee burn brought into the house,' Dodie explained with enthusiasm, 'I run it a lot so that betimes I can just close my eyes and think it's birlin' and splashin' over the stones on its way to the sea.'

By this time Niven McQuarry's head was in quite a spin but Dodie wasn't finished with him yet. The cuckoo clock was next on the agenda, and not until it had whirled out from its little door cheerily to proclaim the hour was the visitor allowed to seat himself and explain the content of his mission.

'Now then, Mr Dodie, if you will just listen to me for a moment.' Mr McQuarry cleared his throat, and was about to launch forth when he was stopped in mid-breath by a wheezing screech issuing from Dodie's widely stretched mouth.

The dentist, thinking that the old man was in some sudden and dreadful pain, jumped to his feet and taking hold of Dodie made *him* sit down, saying as he did so, 'Just you relax, Mr Dodie, and let me look at your teeth. I have my bag here and can rid you of that pain in no time at all.'

Dodie paused for breath, looked at the dentist with huge enjoyment, and muttered, 'Mr Dodie,' then he was off again, wheezing, screeching, clutching his stomach. He had never had dealings with the dentist mannie and was therefore not familiar with his precise and proper ways. He had been called many things in his time but 'Mr Dodie' was not one of them, and the novelty of it made him just about split his sides laughing.

When the dentist realized that Dodie was producing sounds of mirth and not of pain he settled himself rather dourly into another chair, took a deep breath and said carefully, 'Mr – er – perhaps it might be better not to be too formal so I shall just call you Dodie. Some of the villagers were saying that you had been having a very miserable time of it with your teeth so I thought I had better come along and take a look at them.'

'It wasny me, it was my cow.'

'Your cow was suffering from bad teeth?'

'Ach no, Mr Dentist,' Dodie spoke with gentle admonishment, 'my Ealasaid fell over the cliff last summer and died on me. I was that sore wi' grief I near died myself and would have done if it hadny been for the minister and the laird.'

Niven McQuarry was breathing somewhat heavily, so

that his glasses were fogging up and had to be removed and rubbed briskly.

Very neatly he placed them back on his nose, took another deep breath and said very patiently, 'Dodie, unless my eyes are deceiving me I saw your Ealasaid a short time back and fed her oatcake out of my very own hand. She appeared very hale and hearty and not in the least bit dead.'

Dodie was unable to understand this lack of comprehension on the visitor's part. Pityingly he shook his head and said very slowly and with great emphasis, 'Ach no, no, Mr Dentist, you are makin' a big mistake.'

'You mean,' the dentist mannie made a supreme effort to treat the matter lightheartedly, 'that was Ealasaid's ghost we saw out there? With clover sticking out her mouth and chlorophyll coating her tongue?'

The two men looked at each other in complete bafflement. Privately, Dodie decided that the dentist mannie wasn't quite all there and with great dignity he arose to put on the kettle to make a strupak.

When tea and buttered oatcakes had been drunk and eaten in almost total silence, Mr McQuarry arose carefully from his seat and tried very hard not to look as if he was hurrying to get outside.

At the door he paused. 'May I – if you don't mind that is – just have a quick peep at your teeth?'

Willingly Dodie exposed his ancient, tobacco-stained molars, thinking that he had better humour the most unusual visitor he had ever had. 'They are perfect teeths, Mr Dentist,' he said gently. 'They have never given me any bother in the whole o' me life even though I have never used that awful paste on them.'

'Queet, queet,' Niven McQuarry signalled his defeat succinctly, and was about to make good his escape when Dodie bade him stay where he was and went galloping away outside.

In minutes he was back, arms full of juicy red rhubarb sticks which he thrust at the dentist mannie. 'This is the best, the best you'll ever taste,' he explained earnestly. 'It might no' be very good for your teeths but it is a fine tonic for the bowels and will keep you busy for quite a whilie if you eat too much o' it.'

The dentist was lost for words. Making a strange half bow he went quickly away, clutching his bag and his rhubarb sticks and a bunch of yellow pansies that Dodie had thoughtfully placed in his hands at the very last moment.

Old Joe was next on the agenda. Mr McQuarry had saved him to the end as he always enjoyed a lengthy chat with the old man. He had already taken an impression of the old man's mouth and now it was just a case of getting the final bite in the dental wax he heated over the little Bunsen burner he had brought with him.

'I see you've been to visit Dodie,' commented Old Joe, grimacing at the taste of the hot wax in his mouth while he eyed the rhubarb and the flowers that Mr McQuarry had deposited on a table by the door.

'Indeed I have,' the dentist breathed heavily at the memory, 'a very strange creature he is too, he seems to think his cow is some sort of ghost returned from the dead and looked queet bewildered when I told him she was alive and well.'

Old Joe's eyes twinkled. 'You have to know Dodie to understand him, his cow *did* die on him last summer but the laird gave him another one recently together wi' a crofthouse. He's near beside himself wi' the excitement o' it all and canny explain things too well the now.'

'I see, I see,' the dentist was greatly relieved at the revelation, 'I really thought he was – er – queet round the bend but now I see it was all just a misunderstanding – though of course, he *is* what you might call a very eccentric type of person.'

'We have a few o' them on Rhanna,' Old Joe observed mischievously.

'I quite agree with you there, Joe.' The dentist spoke with feeling, still smarting as he was with humiliation over Sorcha and her wig.

'Ay, you'll have come across one or two in the last few days.' Old Joe chuckled, then growing serious he said urgently, 'I will have my new teeths in time, eh, Niven?'

'Of course you will, Joe, I'll get my secretary to send them by first-class post the minute they are ready. It may take queet some time but we have a very good dental mechanic at our disposal and he doesn't waste time footering around.'

'And they'll be as happy lookin' as your own, Niven? I aye liked the way your teeths went smilin' themselves about, cheerin' everybody up.'

'Ay, Joe, as happy as mine,' nodded the dentist, and left the house with a tear in his eye for he knew he would never see the old man again.

Shortly after that he sailed away from Rhanna, leaving in his wake an array of filled, polished and shining teeth plus many assurances to the older Gaels that their dentures would be posted as soon as was humanly possible.

In due course a large parcel arrived at the Post Office which, when opened, revealed a number of small boxes nestling snugly in their wrappings, each one beautifully wrapped and labelled in a tiny old-fashioned script that was very nearly indecipherable.

'I canny make head nor tail o' this writing,' cried Totie, aghast. 'Look, Doug, see if you can make out the names on these boxes.'

Doug applied his specs to his nose and studied the writing. 'As far as I can see there's a lot o' McKinnons here, on the other hand they might be McKnights or McLeans or any Mac you care to mention but as there's such a lot o' McKinnons on the island it must be that. As for the rest – well, I'll have to study them a whole lot harder before I can even begin to guess.'

Totie gave an exasperated sigh. 'McKinnons, ay, but what McKinnons? I canny make out the initials – och, to hell wi' this! I'm going to phone that mannie McQuarry and ask him what he expects us to do about this.'

But Niven McQuarry was not available, his secretary answered the 'phone in a pale, small fluttery voice that identified itself as belonging to a Miss Victoria Bird.

Miss Bird sounded rather hurt when Totie expressed her strong opinions regarding the handwriting on the boxes. 'Really? Oh dear, I've never had any complaints before – '

'Miss Bird' (how appropriate, Totie thought), 'have you ever had cause to send a parcel of dentures to the islands before?'

'Well, no, you see I haven't been here very long, though of course I have been doing secretarial work to doctors and dentists all my life and have considerable experience to my credit – '

'But you've never sent dentures by post before?'

'Well, no,' Miss Bird pulled up her chin and straightened the revers of her neat grey suit. Totie could hear the rustlings and could almost see the tightening of the severe lips. 'You see, Mrs – what did you say? – Donaldson, I have never had cause to post dentures anywhere, far less the islands. All my patients, you see, come to the surgery to have their teeth fitted and this is a completely new departure for me. Mr McQuarry,' here she fluttered badly and cleared her throat, 'Mr McQuarry has had several secretaries before me and now I can quite see why. A most unusual man, you would think it was enough for him to carry on his business here in the capital but no – off he jaunts every few months, trading his wares in the Highlands and islands, and for the life of me I cannot see why. It can't be for the money, he is a well-to-do man from all accounts, but there you are – peculiar traits will out and of course...'

'Miss Bird, can you help me at all with this matter?'

'Oh, well, dear me, I don't really see what *I* can do and it's no use asking Mr McQuarry because he would just jump down my throat and tell me it's my job – though mind you, I never realized when I took it on just how much would be involved and I simply cannot take on the responsibility of dispensing dentures to all and sundry if this is going to be the result – '

'Miss Bird, could you no' have typed the labels?' suggested Totie patiently.

'What? Typed? Yes well, that's all and fine but I have always used a manual machine and I'm a wee bit wary of Mr McQuarry's new-fangled electric thing – some strange golf ball affair which in my opinion is utter nonsense. Golf balls belong in golf courses, not dentists' offices. The thing is utterly erratic. It whizzes about and makes all sorts of errors if one dares to tap a key by mistake and besides, I seem to have jammed the awful thing and don't like to tell Mr McQuarry about it. He can be quite off-putting, you know, if one dares put a foot out of place and I have always been the sort of woman who likes to keep the peace. That was the reason I handwrote the labels, Mrs...'

'Donaldson – and, Miss Bird, you could have saved us both a lot o' time if you had mentioned all that in the first place.'

'Well, you didn't ask, just went on and on in such an excitable way. Oh dear, I feel quite faint. I am not used to this sort of thing, you see. I was brought up in a respectable home where I was taught never to engage in argument of any kind with people who will argue just for the sake of it. My father was a wonderful man, God rest him, a brilliant scholar you know and a professor of languages at Edinburgh University. He taught all three of his daughters at home though the boys of course were sent away to school when they were old enough. Mother too was an academician, owing to the fact that her father was a vicar who believed that girls as well as boys should have their chance in life. She too was taught at home and...'

Miss Bird rambled off into a world of her own. Totie made several valiant attempts to get her back onto the pertinent track but it was a hopeless task.

'Miss Bird – goodbye,' she said eventually, and putting down the 'phone she collapsed with a fervent 'phew' onto the little stool that was so beloved by Behag, the indentation of her bottom was imprinted into the tapestry seat for all time. 'That was a waste of time, Doug, we'll just have to try and sort out these names ourselves and pray to heaven we get them right.'

They were up half the night, painstakingly trying to decipher Miss Bird's script with the aid of a huge magnifying glass and endless cuppies. In the end, still uncertain about their eventual conclusions, they arose, stretched, and repaired wearily to bed, telling each other they would just have to trust to providence and a whole lot of luck.

Next morning a notice appeared in the Post Office window for the benefit of the residents of Portcull and District, while several of the packages were conveyed to various other parts of the island via Erchy and his post van.

By the end of the day all those concerned had received a set of new dentures, and it was as well that the first fitting of these took placc in the privacy of bedroom, bathroom, or water closet, for the apparitions that looked back from respective mirrors were grotesque enough to frighten the most level-headed Rhanna-ite ever to be born.

Yet hardly a murmur of derision against the perpetrator of such an almighty blunder was heard anywhere. Some sighed, blamed age for its inflexibility in all things, and shoved the new dentures in beside ancient sets that had never fitted either; the more stoic persevered grimly, suffering much torture in the process, while some spirited members of the population gritted toothless gums and vowed to 'get that dentist mannie' next time he dared to show his face on Rhanna.

Lachlan first suspected something was amiss when he tried one morning to engage Behag in a few pleasantries. Clapping her hand to her mouth she emitted a series of unintelligible sounds before scuttling away, red-faced with embarrassment. A similar experience overtook Babbie when she had cause to visit old Annack Gow of Nigg. The old lady, normally so garrulous that it took Babbie all her time to keep up, muttered and mumbled under the scarf she had tied round the lower part of her face. When Babbie asked if she was suffering from a sore throat, she seized gladly on the excuse and showed the nurse the door without even a mention of a strupak, the quality and quantity of which Annack was renowned for. Babbie had told Anton whom she was going to see that morning and had boasted that she would bring back the usual bag of seed cakes, a delicacy they both loved, and she was childishly disappointed to find herself empty-handed on the doorstep, gazing in bewilderment at the firmly shut door.

'I don't understand it,' she confided in Lachlan, 'old Annack has never done that before, in fact I can never get away from her house without taking half the larder with me, and though she agreed she had a sore throat she wouldny let me look at it, far less give her something to help it.'

'Annack has her own cures,' laughed Lachlan. He looked thoughtful. 'You know, I experienced much the same thing the other day with Behag. She muttered something under her hand and went haring away like a scalded cat. I just hope we're no' in for a crop o' sore throats or 'flu though it seems a bit early in the year for either.'

The same thing was happening all over the island, with normally gregarious old folk keeping conspicuously out of the way, even on the finest days. The situation remained so for several days until Lachlan overheard a strangely distorted conversation between Todd the Shod and Jim Jim down by the harbour.

'I've lost three pounds in body weight,' Todd was confiding mournfully, patting his rounded belly as if hoping to find all the loss from that quarter. 'I canny eat, I canny sleep for hunger, and when Molly isny lookin' I just take the damt things out and carry them in my pouch.'

'Ach well, Isabel is in the same boat as myself so we both just take them out to eat and put them back in again for show – though what's showy about teeths that hang down like thon stiff frills my granny used to put up at her windows, is beyond me!' He was about to hurl a gobbet of spit to the cobbles but hastily refrained from doing so. 'Damt things! I canny even spit in case they go fleein' out and smash themselves to pieces though that might be no bad thing...' He studied Todd's face reflectively. 'Here, how would it be if we was to try one another's for size? Anything is better than this buggering agony.'

So saying, he removed his dentures and swilled them round in Ranald's rain barrel while Todd did likewise. Tentatively the respective teeth were inserted and clattered together experimentally.

'Here! These fit!' Jim Jim exclaimed with joy.

'These too – like a glove! Well, is that no' strange, Jim Jim? Very strange indeed. I'm thinkin' maybe somebody has had our teeths mixed up – I didny like the look o' the label on that boxie I got, it could have been anybody's name.'

Lachlan, realizing at once what had happened, vacated the scene with alacrity and hurried home to tell Phebie about it, Babbie too, the minute she put in an appearance.

'No wonder the proud old rascals hid away in their houses,' she giggled. 'To some it wouldny matter one way or another since they've never worn teeth for years.

Others wouldny be seen dead without dentures in their heads and would persevere even supposing their mouths were filled with lumps o' cement.'

'But, what's to be done?' Phebie wanted to know. 'We can't very well go around chapping the doors on a teeth sorting mission.'

Lachlan's eyes gleamed. 'I have an idea. It will take some organizing but with a bittie luck it might work.'

Within a short time, notices were posted in every shop window that the villages of Portvoynachan and Portcull boasted. When Totie and Dugald received theirs, they were utterly dismayed at the contents. 'We never got them right after all,' Dugald gulped guiltily.

'Ach, it's no' our fault, Doug,' comforted Totie, 'if I could get a hold o' that Miss Bird I would personally thraw her neck for her, but wishful thinking will get us nowhere. We'll just have to put these notices up and hope to God Lachlan's idea works.'

It did, beautifully. As soon as it was clear that everyone had got the message, so to speak, Lachlan set up a denture sorting station in the Portcull village hall. From all the airts the old folk came, arriving in every kind of transport imaginable, furtively bearing little packages which were received by Phebie in an egg basket at the door. When all the teeth had been collected ('all the wallies in one basket,' Phebie couldn't resist chuckling), everyone was directed to wait in a screened-off section of the hall while she bore the basket to Shona, who carefully unwrapped each packet. So well tied were some that they might have contained gold rather than dentures, but eventually the job was done. Shona went off to make tea for the waiting throng while Babbie, Lachlan, and Phebie laid out the teeth on a well-scrubbed table, taking care to keep the different sets together. Nobody could quite keep a straight face and it was amidst much banter that everything was arranged satisfactorily.

One by one the islanders were bade enter, the

comparative youngsters in their ranks squirming with embarrassment and the 'shame o' it all.'

One after another the various sets were tried for size, and when eventually a pair were found to fit, the recipient went off, grinning mightily with triumphant relief, leaving 'the teeth committee', as they had mischievously christened themselves, to wash the remaining sets in bowls of fresh water which had been treated with antiseptic.

Gradually the pile of dentures diminished so that before long the last 'customer' made good his escape, leaving the hall empty but for the four committee members sitting back to enjoy a well-earned cuppy. Only one set remained, and these Lachlan had wrapped carefully to deliver personally to Old Joe who had been 'champing at the bit' since the start of all the bother.

'Do you know what I thought was the funniest thing of all?' Shona choked into her tea at the recollection. 'Old Annack Gow demanding to know who had been wearing which dentures in case she might be taking a set that had been used by one of her least liked cronies.'

'I know, I know,' Phebie chuckled. 'And Behag wanting to be first in for the first try in case she got germs from the rest.'

'And Fingal popping his into his peg leg where he says he aye keeps them to bite the ferrets who bite him.'

'Ay,' grinned Lachlan, 'and old Jock of Rumhor saying he didn't want the set that looked like a horse's – '

'And finding they were his in the end!' shrieked Babbie, laughing so hard she toppled off her stool to land plunk in the egg basket Phebie had used to collect the teeth.

Over the next few days Holy Smoke's shop had never been busier, with rump steak and pork chops tops for favourites. Dinner tables all over Rhanna sizzled with savoury meats and kitchens rang with the sound of much diligent chomping, made by those who had only partaken of soups and saps ever since Miss Bird's packages had fallen into the wrong hands, or to be more accurate, into the long-suffering jaws of proud old Gaels who would never forget the summer of 1966, when the arrival of 'the dentist mannie' had set off a chain of events that was to be the talk of the place for many a long day to come.

PART FOUR

Autumn/Winter 1966

Chapter Nineteen

There was a smell of autumn in the air as Shona and Tina walked along to the Manse, their feet stirring up the first yellow leaves to fall from the elms that lined the driveway. It was a calm, damp evening, the smoke from the Manse chimneys spiralled up into an overcast, wet looking sky, pockets of pearly mist lay in the corries of the hills and swirled in ghostly wraiths over the great wide stretches of the Muir of Rhanna.

Shona gave a little skip as she went along, breathing deeply of the rich scents around her, playfully kicking the tiny, gnarled windfall apples that were lying half-hidden among the leaves. She savoured the few hours of freedom away from Mo Dhachaidh for, much as she loved her home, her babies and her animals, they could all be a handful at times, and she blessed Niall for insisting that she go over to visit Tina who had promised to show her how to make rum fudge.

But Tina had left the recipe at the Manse along with some others and now they made their way there, Tina talking in her calm, unruffled way. As time passed, she had grown more like the Tina everyone knew. When she spoke of Matthew now it was not of how he had died but to recall some pleasant happening they had shared together. Only when Eve came into the conversation did the old worried frown crease her smooth brow as, since Daniel's departure, her daughter had grown morose and moody and tended more and more to want her own company. She didn't even have the stimulation of 'seeing to Doctor Megan', and often went alone to the house by the sea to unlock it and go inside to clean and polish and wander through the empty rooms.

It was of Eve that Tina spoke on the way up the Manse drive. 'I'm worried about her, Shona,' she confided. 'She's no' the lass she was and is so pale and off her food I'm thinkin' she might just pine away altogether for that lad.'

'Give her time, Tina,' Shona advised, trying to sound convincing though she too had noticed the drastic changes in Eve. 'It's a terrible thing to try and forget someone you have loved and I don't suppose she wants to yet...' She gave a little groan, 'Och, there I go again, putting my foot in it, as if you didn't know what it's like to have loved and lost.'

'Ach, it's alright, lass, I know what you mean, and Eve's is a different kind of loss from mine altogether. I wish Doctor Megan would come back, Eve would have something to keep her mind occupied every day, she enjoyed working at Tigh na Cladach and got on fine wi' the doctor.'

'I had a letter from Megan, only this morning.'

'Oh, and how is she?'

'Well, she didn't say too much about herself but was asking for everybody and missing us – she was also concerned about Mark, I think she's missing him too, more than she's letting on.'

They paused at the steps. 'Are you coming in?' asked Tina. 'Mr James will likely be in his study so I'll just creep in the kitchen, get my things, and then creep back out again. He'll never hear me.'

Shona smiled affectionately at Tina's earnest words, for when she attempted stealth of any sort she usually only succeeded in bumping into everything, both in and out of sight.

'Ach no, you go ahead, Tina, I'll wait out here. Mark might be busy with his sermons and won't want to be disturbed.'

But the minister wasn't in his study. Tina was greatly

surprised to find him in the kitchen, slumped into his chair, black stubble darkening a face that was a sickly-grey colour, a half-empty bottle of whisky sitting on a small table at his side. Mutt was lying at his feet and whimpered dejectedly at Tina's entry.

'Mercy on us.' Tina took one startled glance at the scene before going out to the porch to call down to Shona, 'Come away in at once.'

'Oh no!' Shona couldn't stop the horrified exclamation at sight of Mark. He was comatose and completely without muscle control, failing even to stir in protest when she spoke his name in his ear and shook him. He fell to the side of his chair, head lolling, mouth falling slackly agape. He smelled and looked terrible, and Shona's heart went strange and heavy within her while a tearful Tina came to take his head to her soft, motherly bosom where she held him as if he was a small boy.

'I had a mind I was smelling the drink off him this whilie back but thought it couldny be,' she shook her head sadly. 'Never a drop has passed his lips in all the time I've worked to him. Many's the time I've had a wee drop myself, at Ne'erday and the like, but he was aye content wi' his tea or a glass o' fruit wine – it was as if he despised the very sight o' spirits though never in a nasty way, just that nice crooked wee smile he has and a mannerly refusal.'

'Now we know why, Tina,' Shona said huskily. Her mind was whirling, taking her back to the occasions she had been in Mark's company. Tina was right, somehow he had always managed to evade touching strong liquor by making excuses that had sounded so right at the time – now this, this earth-shattering discovery – it explained everything, his strangeness of late, the look he had on him of a man who didn't know which direction to take in life. Sadness overwhelmed her, no wonder he had been keeping to himself lately, how lonely he must have felt, how alone he had been. She bit her lip and gripped Tina's arm with some urgency, 'You must never breathe a word o' this to another living soul – not until we have had time to decide what is the best thing to do for him.'

'As if I would,' tears filled Tina's eyes, 'I love the man as I would love a brother. He's been a dear, good friend to me and mine and I'll do anything I can to help him.'

'Ay, he's going to need all the support we can give him but first things first. We'll never manage to get him into bed in his state so we'll leave him here. Do you know where he keeps blankets and the like?'

'That I do, 'tis myself who washes his laundry and puts it away in the cupboard.'

She went off to return in minutes, arms piled high with blankets and pillows. Between them they made Mark as comfortable as possible, watched anxiously by Mutt and the cats who were padding back and forth, mewing and rubbing themselves against the women's legs, till an exasperated Tina went to pour milk into saucers which they lapped hungrily, while Mutt received an appetising bone straight out of the stock pot Tina had prepared that morning. But he refused to eat, turning back instead to the chair to coorie himself against the inert figure in it and tentatively kiss his nose.

'Ach, is he no' a wise doggie?' Tina patted the noble head affectionately. 'He loves Mr James and will no' let him out o' his sight if he can help it.'

Shona straightened and tucked an errant strand of hair behind her ear. 'He minds me o' my dear wee Tot – much bigger of course but the same faithful eyes and curly golden fur.' She glanced around. 'We had better go and leave them in peace – I'll just light the lamp and put it on the table in case Mark wakes in the night and wonders where he is.'

'Will we leave the window open?' wondered Tina.

'Ay, just enough for the cats to come and go. It's a mild enough evening and if we put some more peats on the fire it should last a good whilie yet.'

Tina dumped the remaining pillows and blankets on the refectory table, turned round and nearly tripped over

Tub sniffing around Mutt's bone. 'Damt cats!' Picking up the plate containing the bone, and the milk saucers, she clattered them onto the table. 'One o' these days I'll land on the floor wi' everything broken – that's if I don't thraw every one o' their damt necks first!' she ended darkly.

They checked everything thoroughly before going quietly away, leaving Mark in a snug cocoon of pillows and blankets with Mutt up on the armchair beside him, watchful, alert, and worried.

Tina and Shona spent a cosy, friendly evening together, stirring rum fudge in a big pan while they talked and laughed and tried not to mention Mark James, because if they did they were apt to grow quiet and awkward and forget to stir the fudge or just simply forget everything but that pale face of a man so dear to them both. In the end they gave up all pretence of enjoying themselves. When the fudge was put to cool in trays in the larder they sat at the fire, drinking tea and discussing how they could go about doing something to help the minister.

During a lull in the conversation, Tina glanced at the window. It was growing dark outside. Grey clouds were rolling up over the sea, piling one on top of the other, changing to a purplish-black colour as gloaming deepened into night.

'Donald will no' be in for hours yet,' Tina said casually, 'I have a fancy he's seeing a lass over at Portvoynachan and Eve is staying wi' her Granny Ann the night. She often does that now. I think she finds the old folks easier to thole than she can me. I ask too many questions though I should know better for she just doesny speak when she's in one o' they secretive moods o' hers – ' she glanced at Shona and added softly 'we'll wait just a whilie – then we'll go along to the Manse and see if he's alright.'

Shona nodded. 'I was hoping you would say that.'

Tina smiled gently and got up to refill the cups from the ever brewing pot at the edge of the fire.

'I see I'm just in time for a strupak.' Mairi put her head round the door, and came in to draw a chair in to the fire and plunge straight into an account of some of her family's latest exploits. Over her head Shona and Tina looked at one another. It would be a whilie before the visitor took her leave, and with good grace Tina went to get another cup from the dresser.

Mutt stirred a little to ease his cramped limbs. He gazed towards the window, his nose twitching longingly. The air was tangy with delicious smells, that of damp earth being the most prevalent, and the temptation to be out and about was sore on a young dog such as he. His inner clock told him that the time was nigh for that special hour he always shared with his master. Except for the cats ganging up on him to steal his food and commandeer his cushion, he revelled in his life in the big, old house and knew that the cats could never usurp him when it came to certain privileges he and he alone shared with the man of the house. The first of these was the bedtime joy of stretching himself at his master's feet or lying cosily on the bedside rug, knowing that odd, sweet joy of regular deep breathing that wasn't his own but might have been, so familiar was the rhythm of it.

The second highlight came with his dinner bone, a daily ritual which preceded that glorious after-dinner walk along the cliffs, where all the world smelt of rabbits and earth and great tree trunks that had been specially created for him to sniff and water at will.

But the best time of all was the hour of the cocoa dregs, of clocks quietly ticking and peat turfs sparking in the hearth, of himself and his master stretching and pretending a weariness that fled like magic the minute they were out the door and sniffing together blood-tingling scents that were magnified a thousandfold with the coming of gloaming over the land.

Now that hour was to hand, but tonight there were no cocoa dregs or crumbs of biscuit, just a strange, sickly raw odour that he was well enough used to by now, though he didn't like it any more than he liked the changes that were taking place in his once happy routine.

His flanks heaved in a long, drawn-out sigh which came out through his nose and stirred a wisp of his master's hair. But there was no response, even though he whimpered pitifully at the back of his throat and pawed the pillow beneath that dark, silent, unresponsive head that was just inches from his own.

All evening long the cats had come and gone from the window; now two of them arrived back from some nocturnal prowl, Tib carrying a mouse in her jaws which Tub, the boss cat, plainly coveted if her flashing paws and threatening growls were anything to go by.

But for once Tib was having none of it. Fighting for her rights in no mean manner she spat vitriol at the other cat, her flattened ears plainly displaying her displeasure.

In the end Tub retreated, green eyes flashing, tail swishing angrily. For a few minutes she roamed aimlessly about the room, before coming back to stand beside the table and raise her twitching pink nostrils upwards to savour fully the smell of Mutt's bone lying on its plate on the table.

After a few more minutes of padding round the chairs she leapt up on one, from there to the table. Mutt was instantly alert. Sitting up straight, he watched the cat stalking over the table top towards his bone. Reaching it she sniffed, licked, her purrs reverberating in the silence.

A warning growl rose in Mutt's throat. The cat glanced up, showed her fangs in a fierce hiss, one paw uplifted, spread claws ready to flash out if the dog's nose so much as came near the table. But before Mutt could make a move, Tab arrived on the scene, knocking over a vase on the sill on her upward leap. It clattered and rolled, startling Tub who sprang back, straight into the oil lamp sitting on the table. Over it went, spilling paraffin onto the pillows which quickly absorbed it. There was a loud whoosh as the bedding ignited. Within minutes clouds of dense, foul-smelling smoke filled the kitchen. The cats scattered, Mutt leapt to the window and with his nose to the opening began to bark frantically, his paws scrabbling against the paintwork as if he was trying to escape. But he could have done that easily enough if he had wanted to. It was a loose sash. He just had to wriggle his head through the gap and push upwards with his shoulders as he had done several times that summer in the pursuit of certain secret missions that not even his master knew about. But that was in happier days. Now he didn't want to escape, he had to stay, stay close to that inert figure who was groaning a little in his sleep as if sensing danger.

For fully two minutes Mutt barked, before withdrawing his head from the sash and padding back to the armchair at the fire where he grabbed the blankets in his teeth and began pulling. But it was no use. The smoke was filling his lungs, making him dizzy. Creeping back up on the chair he pressed his body close to his master's, placed his paws round the beloved neck and cooried in close, all the while whimpering and whining.

Mark stirred, came awake for a few, short, terrifying seconds. He opened his mouth to cry out. The black smoke billowed, seared his throat, flooded his lungs – he cried out once more – and then there was silence.

Dodie hurried along the cliff road from Nigg, anxious to be home in order to give his adored cow her potach of oats. He had been visiting Jack the Light, and the old man had kept him later than usual showing him some pieces of natural sculpture that he had picked up on the beach. In the old days Dodie would have lingered to the last, unwilling to abandon warmth and comforts that were so sorely lacking in his own cottage. But things were different now. With the exception of Ealasaid, he had never been so proud of anything as he was of his new house. He had even grown quite domesticated, instructing visitors to wipe their feet on the mat at the door and, 'no' to be laying anything on the furniture that might mark it.'

Mairi kept the place spick and span and he made sure it stayed that way, for the first time in his life actually going to the drastic lengths of exchanging his Wellingtons in the porch for a pair of cosy slippers that had 'grown too wee for Wullie' but fitted Dodie's feet perfectly as, outside of his clumsy boots, they were smaller than anybody might have supposed and weren't smelling nearly so bad these days either.

Now Dodie was pleased to get home to his slippers and his fire and the tasty supper Mairi always had waiting for him on top of the range. With all these undoubted comforts in his life he had taken once again to painting his stones, with Barra popping in now and then to encourage him and, lately, to demonstrate patiently the use of watercolours. So keen was he to learn that he often sat for an hour or so before bed, painstakingly trying to copy all the things Barra had shown him, and tonight he was anxious to get out his paints as soon as he possibly could.

Much like the Dodie he had been before sadness and illness had overtaken him, his loping stride carrying him swiftly along the treacherous cliff road, with never a glance to the right or the left of him since, at this time of night, with gloaming shrouding the landscape and the hill peaks glowering under the darkening sky, less fanciful minds than his were alert to the possibilities of spooks and bogles hiding among the heather knolls, not to mention water witches and warty green hags that might likely rise shrieking from the depths of the ocean to carry off unwary humans in their slimy clutches.

A growl of thunder sounded amongst the hills, making Dodie jump and hurry along faster. He had travelled the island all his life, in all weathers and at all hours, yet never had he become immune to the fears wrought by darkness, and he always carried with him a tiny silver cross left to him by his mother. It was his good luck charm and he fingered it now in his big, roomy pocket, and bent his head against the first drops of rain falling from the leaden sky.

Thunder clapped above him, lightning seared the heavens, in minutes the burns were foaming down through the heather to go gushing into the sea far below.

The first of the village houses hove into view, the doctor's house, dark, lifeless, sodden hydrangea bushes nodding big, pale heads in the gloom – automatically he turned his head, instinctively seeking out the warm, welcoming lights of the Manse up there on the Hillock – but it too was in darkness. He was terrified suddenly to hear the frantic barking of a dog drifting down, a ghost bark rising above the teeming rain, the thunder, the swollen burns.

He hurried on faster, anxious to shake off the deep feeling of doom that seemed to linger in that quiet spot with the black-eyed houses on either side of him and the thundering wail of the Well o' Weeping surging up from the hidden depths of lonely Burg Bay...

The dog had stopped barking. Pausing abruptly, Dodie forced himself to glance up at the Manse. It was darker there than anywhere else, a strange grey moving darkness that billowed and drifted as if from the hellish wastes of some witch's fire – fire and smoke – the two connected in the dim regions of his slow-thinking mind. He could smell the smoke now, awful, acrid fumes that rose in clouds to merge with the lowering sky.

'Mr James,' he whispered. He fingered his cross again. Just to know that it was there, in his pocket, gave him courage. His feet took flight, slithering, slipping on the wet ground but carrying him upwards just the same. He took the sheep track to the gate set in the walled garden and was at the house in minutes. Without hesitation he plunged inside and although there was no sound from the dog now, instinct led Dodie to the kitchen, the room in which he had often sat with the minister, enjoying a strupak and sharing a 'fill o' baccy' from the roomy leather pouch that was always kept handy on the mantlepiece.

He threw open the door to be met immediately by belching black smoke that rushed out to envelop him so that it both blinded and choked him.

'Mr James!' he cried out in terror. Falling onto his knees he crawled into the room, unwittingly following the most sensible course in a smoke-filled atmosphere. Gasping and retching, he reached the fireplace and began hauling at the senseless figure in the chair. With all the might of his wiry frame he dragged the minister to the door, crawling backwards all the time, slowly, painfully, his heart pounding in his chest.

Shona and Tina arrived as he reached the kitchen door and between them they got both Dodie and Mark outside, away from the smoke now gushing through the front door. Dodie tottered and fell onto his knees on the sodden grass but he waved the women away from him and gasped, 'The minister, see to him.'

Shona at once applied her attention to Mark. He was unconscious but still breathing, and for a few shocked moments she could only stare in horrified fascination at his rain-pocked face, at the rivers of soot washing down from his thick black hair. Then her nurse's training came flooding back, forcing the sensible, level-headed side of her to take charge and do for him everything she could.

'Dodie's gone back in!' Tina said in horror, her head jerking round as voices came from below, heralding the arrival of a dozen or so village men who, having been alerted by Todd the Shod, had come armed with buckets and bags of sand and anything else that might come in useful for fighting a fire.

Dodie came staggering back outside, holding in his arms the lifeless body of Mutt, his golden fur blackened by smoke, his big floppy paws dangling uselessly down, his head lolling, one long curly ear covering his eyes, his pink tongue hanging from the side of his muzzle. The men rushed past Dodie, carrying brimming pails which they had filled from the stream that wound its way through the Manse garden.

Dodie collapsed to the ground, tears marking a grimy course down his face. Laying the dog down, he tenderly arranged the paws so that Mutt looked as if he lay in a composed and peaceful sleep, still of the earth and ready to awake to its joys when the hour of rest was done. The rain washed his fur, cleansing away the smoke so that the bright colour shone through and even his muzzle showed the little patch of white that had made Mark James pick him out of the litter in the first place.

Dodie put his hands to his face and cried sorely. 'I'm sorry I didny save him too,' he sobbed, 'he was aye such a good doggie and would meet me at the door wi' a big happy smile whenever I came to the Manse to see Mr James.'

Shona, who had covered the minister with her own coat, got to her feet to go to Dodie and put a comforting arm round him. 'Dodie,' she murmured soothingly, 'you did a wonderful thing tonight – you saved a human life and are a very brave man.'

'I didny save him,' he choked miserably, 'the doggie did. I heard him barking and went running up the brae – but it was too late for him, he was cooried into the minister's arms when I found them but I couldny take two at the same time, I just hadny the strength – so I had to leave that bonny beast behind and I feel terrible just.'

'Ach, come on, Dodie,' said Tina kindly, 'you mustny feel like that. Mutt was likely already dead when you got here, his lungs would be too wee to take much o' they awful fumes so just you stop blaming yourself and be thankful to God you saved the life o' our very own Mr James.'

It took the men just half an hour to rid the kitchen of

fire. Most of it had been confined to the bedding on the table and had given off more smoke than flame, so that the damage to property was minimal. By the time the men were finished, Lachlan and Babbie had arrived and Mark James was taken to Slochmhor where he received the best possible attention. A few days later he left Rhanna for a mainland hospital, accompanied by Shona and Tina, the only people he trusted enough to be near him for, on hearing that his beloved dog had died in the fire, he blamed himself and suffered a collapse.

Mutt alone perished in the fire. The cats had escaped through the open window, leaving behind the smoke and the flames and a little dog who had stayed faithfully by his master's side, and who had died so bravely in the arms that had held him so often in the good days of dreaming and peace and sweet happy contentment.

Chapter Twenty

Megan returned to Rhanna at the end of September without telling anyone she was coming, not even Shona with whom she had corresponded once or twice during her absence. She wasn't quite sure herself why she did this but, deep down, something in her had to know that she had been missed, that the surprise displayed at her unannounced arrival would be of pleasure rather than mere acceptance that she was back.

The golden leaves of autumn swirled about her feet as she walked along to Tigh na Cladach. She saw with fresh eyes the harbour and the bay, the white houses of Portcull whose chimneys were puffing peat smoke into the tangy air.

In a surge of ecstasy she raised her head to sniff in the remembered scent of it and to gaze with appreciation at the bulk of Sgurr nan Ruadh, as red as its name suggested, furred with bracken that glowed like fire in the sunset. The slopes were scattered with rowans, so heavily-laden with berries that their branches dipped down to amber grasses that were mottled with purple scabious and delicate blue harebells.

And all around was the heather, miles and miles of it, spreading its purple haze over great tracts of moorland and all along the verges.

Everything was muted in tones of blue, with the hill peaks receding back, back, growing paler as they went, their outlines further softened by pearly mists that rose up from the corries to wander wherever the gentle breezes took them.

Megan wanted to hold out her arms as if to embrace it all to a heart that had pined for such glories, for so many things about this island she had grown to love almost against her will, and it was with a strange, breathless catch in her throat that her eyes travelled up the slopes of the Hillock to the kirk and the Manse chimneys silhouetted against the sky.

But all was quiet and empty-looking up there, with not even a wisp of smoke to tell her that the man who had never left her thoughts these last long weeks was so near to her now that all she had to do was to climb the brae, knock on his door and he would be there.

But of course it wouldn't be that easy. There was so much to say, so much to explain. She would start by telling him that she and Steven had gone their separate ways as soon as the *Mermaid* had reached the mainland, and that she was now free in mind, heart and spirit to love him in the way he deserved to be loved – if he still wanted her. She could hardly bear to think otherwise, yet she was aware of how badly his heart had been bruised, of how much she had hurt him. She would have to try and make him understand her confusion at Steven's return to her life, and that the only way she could sort things out had been to go away in order to get everything into its proper perspective.

She sighed. She would have to prepare herself for that first meeting – and before she was ready to face Mark she needed time to settle in and familiarize herself again with her surroundings.

Turning in at the gate of Tigh na Cladach, a pang of dismay went through her when she saw the garden. The flower beds were sodden, the grass awash with puddles of sea water. Great dollops of seaweed were draped about the walls or lay rotting on the tiny lawn; dahlias and chrysanthemums hung their heads for lack of support; her vegetable plot was choked with weeds. She had only been gone a matter of weeks yet already a sorry air of neglect pervaded the little garden that had been her pride. Her spirits lifted when she turned the key in the door and went inside. She was struck by the fresh smell of polish that met her. All the rooms were clean and bright, with not a single speck of dust or a spider's web in sight and on the windowsills were fresh posies of wild flowers straight from the hills.

With a little yelp of joy, she bounced down into one of the chintzy armchairs in the sitting room to gaze around her and absorb it all anew.

It was lovely, so lovely to be home, for this *was* her home now, all it had needed to help her realize the fact were these long weeks spent away from it.

Rhanna and all it meant was her reality, the place she wanted to be above all others and she could hardly wait to get started again, to begin afresh. Pushing back her hair with a carefree hand, she jumped to her feet and got busy lighting fires, something inside of her rejoicing in the jubilant thought that soon her smoking chimneys would proclaim to the island that Doctor Megan was back to 'cure its wee ails' once again. Her peat smoke would soon merge with all the other blue banners in the vicinity, marrying with them, blending and mixing and, 'no' a soul able to do anything about it'.

Giggling at her own frivolous train of thought, she said aloud, 'See my smoke, Mark, know I'm home, and be glad – oh please be glad.'

Her step was light as she went from room to room, checking on her fires, renewing her acquaintance with her rose-sprigged bedroom, her bright little bathroom, the views from her windows. She danced up and downstairs on feet that seemed to walk on air, behaving in fact as the schoolgirl Megan had behaved on her holidays in Wales, when her mother couldn't do anything with her until she had explored every last part of the old house in the valley as if to reassure herself that nothing had changed during her months away at school.

And now she was that child again, a rosy bloom in her cheeks, her hazel eyes sparkling, singing as she went about the house, smiling as she lit the oil lamps, glad that for this one night she could live as she had lived before she had acquired a generator so cantankerous, it often cut out just when she most needed it and required the expertise of Todd the Shod to get it going again.

But tonight she revelled in lamplight and firelight and found it quite a novelty to go into the kitchen and prepare her supper on the range, working by the flickering glow of candles and one paraffin lamp.

And that was how Eve found her, sitting at the fire with her plate balanced on her knee, the teapot singing on the hob, the kitchen warm and welcoming with its soft lights and fire shadows dancing on the walls.

'I saw the smoke and came as soon as I could,' Eve explained a bit breathlessly, a smile of real pleasure lighting her face for she had missed the young doctor and was truly glad to see her home again.

'Eve,' Megan set aside her plate and, jumping up, hugged the girl warmly, 'I expected dust and neglect on my return but instead found only one tiny wee cobweb cowering away in a corner.'

'Oh, where?' Eve cried in consternation, then relaxed and laughed along with the doctor who was holding her at arm's length and studying her quizzically. 'You look lovely, Eve, you've put on weight and are so happy-looking.'

Eve's colour deepened. 'Pregnancy isny an illness, as no doubt you have told a few o' your patients in your time.'

'Pregnancy! Eve! You're not!'

'Ay, 'tis Dan's bairn right enough. At first I wanted to die, especially when he went away and I kent fine I would never see him again. He was only playing himself, you see, my mother was right all along but I was foolish enough to think he was serious about me – ' she smiled her gentle smile. 'It's over now, Doctor Megan. I will cry no more tears for him for I know well enough now that he wasny worth a single one.'

'And – Tina, your mother, does she know?'

Eve's head sank a little. 'Ay, she does now. I was so moody and strange she sat me down at the fire one night and demanded to know what ailed me. It was very strange that, hearing my mother so firm and determined. She has aye been so calm and soft-spoken but since Father died there's been a wee change in her. It doesny often show but it's there, below the surface, and I suppose it will aye be there now. I hated myself for bringing more trouble on her but she was so understanding...'

A tear misted Eve's eyes at the recollection of how her mother had reacted to the news, without surprise, as if she had known all along and was prepared for it. For a good few minutes she hadn't made comment then she had smiled, that oddly radiant smile of hers, a little catch in her throat when she had said, 'Well, Eve, I canny say I'm pleased at you but I know well enough that rare is the lass who can go through life keeping her hand on her halfpenny all the time. You have done well in that respect for I was just a slip o' a girl when I let go o' mine, though of course I had your father's wedding ring on my finger at the time and it would have been a bittie awkward, no' to say painful, if I hadny got it out the way quick.'

At that they had both collapsed on the sofa and laughed till they were sore, and though Tina had later talked seriously to her daughter there had been no tears or recriminations.

Megan sighed. 'I'm sorry you were treated so badly by Daniel, I know how much you loved him.'

'How much I *thought* I loved him,' Eve said quickly, taking the cup of tea Megan poured for her and sitting down to drink it. 'I was never in love wi' him, it was just a flame that burned for a wee whilie and if I saw him again I really believe we would have nothing at all else in common.'

'I know exactly what you mean, Eve, only I wasn't as

clear-sighted as you. I hung on to memories and believed in my heart they were real and true until...'

'Steve came back and you knew you had been clinging to dreams.'

Megan smiled. 'You're also wiser than I am, Eve, I wish I had talked to you like this before.'

'Ach, I'm like my mother. I read a lot o' these romantic novels and get carried away by them. I was in love wi' the idea o' romance and Dan just happened to be in the right place at the right time.' She gazed into her cup. 'I hope one day I'll meet someone who will want me – for what I am and no' just for a bit of fun.'

'Oh, you will, Eve, you will,' Megan assured softly, real affection in her heart for the young woman who had always been there at Tigh na Cladach but to whom she had never really spoken till now. In just a short time a bond had sprung up between them, born of hurtful experiences for which they had both suffered in their own, individual ways.

'You're luckier than me,' Eve went on, 'you had someone who really loved you and would have died to have you for his own – ' she stopped abruptly, thinking she had said too much, but Megan was not offended.

'You mean Mark of course and you're right. He's worth a million of Steve and I only hope I can make him understand that. I've hurt him so much and pray that it isn't too late to let him know...' She broke off, the look on Eve's face filling her with sudden dread, 'Eve, what is it? You seem – '

'Doctor Megan!' Eve burst out. 'I thought maybe you had heard – och, but how could you? The minister has left Rhanna. There was a fire at the Manse, his dog died in it and the minister would have done too but for old Dodie and Shona and my mother.'

The colour drained from Megan's face. She stared at Eve as if unable to believe the evidence of her own ears. 'Oh God no,' she whispered, 'not that, please not that! Oh, my darling, my dearest Mark. If only I could have spoken to him before I left but I couldn't go to him, he was so strange, so changed from the man I knew. He shut me out – he shut me out, Eve...'

It was a cry from the heart. Gently, Eve put a comforting arm round the other woman's shoulders and said tearfully, 'He shut everyone out, he just seemed to sink inside himself and grow more and more lonely. It wasny your fault, Doctor Megan.'

'It was my fault, I should have gone to him, I ought to have been stronger but I couldn't bear the way he looked at me, as if I was a stranger he had never known or cared about. Oh, please don't tell me any more, Eve, I can't stand it!'

'I'll stay with you tonight if you like,' Eve offered unhappily, dismayed at herself for bringing the doctor such sad news on the first night of her return, yet knowing that if she hadn't someone else would have and with no bones about it either.

But Megan shook her head. 'No, Eve, I'll be fine, really. I need to be alone, you go along home, it's getting late. The fire should have heated the water by now, I'll have a bath and go right to bed, it's been a long day.'

That night she lay in bed, cold and afraid, all her exuberance extinguished as if it had never been. Lying on her back, she stared unseeingly into the dark shadows of her quiet room. Outside her window, the sea sighed and curled sleepily to the shore. It was a soothing sound but she felt that nothing could ever calm her again. Turning her face into her lonely pillow, she wept – and knew an echo of the pain Mark must have known in the long night watches when sleep had no dreaming that wasn't of sorrow and loneliness.

She rose at dawn, as unrested as she had been before going to bed. The things that had held such enchantment on her arrival home had lost their spell over her, and she gave only a cursory glance at the peaceful morning scene outside her window before going downstairs to make tea and sit at the empty grate, the cup warming her cold hands but nothing at all warming her heart. Her thoughts were too bleak for that. She had lost Mark, as surely as if she had personally driven him from the island – and in many ways she had done just that. She had twisted the knife in that sensitive heart of his until he hadn't been able to take any more.

In the cold grey light of morning she cried for him, for all the things that might have been theirs if only she had paid more attention to what was happening to him instead of dwelling so much on her own problems.

Eve had said she didn't know where he was, that nobody knew, but Lachlan might and it was to Slochmhor she went when she knew morning surgery to be safely over.

'Megan,' he greeted her with pleasure, his warm smile lighting a face that had grown slightly thinner from coping with full surgeries, for it seemed that all the 'wee ails' had been saving themselves for him and he had never had one free weekend to call his own. 'How truly good it is to see you, lass, and you've come back just in time too as I doubt if I could have carried on much longer –' he shrugged and laughed – 'I've become soft since my retiral and wonder now how I possibly ever managed it all.'

They repaired to the kitchen where Phebie had the cuppies all ready and steaming on the table, but Megan had barely taken a sip of hers before asking the question that had been on her lips all morning.

A frown furrowed Lachlan's brow when she had finished speaking. 'Mark? I'm sorry, lass, I don't know. He just seems to have disappeared off the face of the earth. John Grey has taken over from him and might know something but if so he's keeping it close to his chest...'

'Shona knows,' Phebie intervened at this point, 'but wild horses won't drag it from her. She and Tina went with Mark to the mainland and saw him into hospital but since then he's been moved and that's the last I heard.'

Megan stood up. 'I'll go over to Mo Dhachaidh right away, I have to collect Muff anyway – and I simply must find out where Mark is.'

She rushed out of the room leaving Lachlan and Phebie to look at one another.

'She's found out at last where her heart lies,' said Lachlan pensively.

'Ay, too late I'm thinking,' nodded Phebie and sighed.

A scant welcome awaited Megan at Mo Dhachaidh. Niall was out, Ellie, Muff and Sporran away with him, the babies were asleep in their big pram in the garden, one at the top, the other at the bottom, nine-month-old bundles of mischief who looked as if they had fallen asleep in mid-play, Joy with her frilly bottom upturned to the sky, Joseph on his knees, sucking his thumb and smiling.

No such pleasant expression was on his mother's face at sight of the visitor.

'It's yourself!' was her curt greeting. 'What happened? Did you get tired playing yourself? Or did you and your playboy friend have another row?'

'As a matter of fact I spent my entire holiday with my parents and brother in Wales,' returned Megan quietly, appalled at the coldness of her reception. 'When I left here, Steve and I parted company and I haven't seen him since.'

Shona tossed her fiery head. 'Och well, I wouldny worry too much. He might just pop up again in the next storm. The first should be approaching any day now and I'm sure the Rhanna lifeboat team are standing by ready. We might be lucky this time and not lose a single man which is just as well as good men are gey thin on the ground. Ministers are maybe different, they're perhaps more expendable, I'm sure we'll find another to take Mark's place...'

'Shona, stop that!' cried Megan, almost in tears. 'Just

who do you think you are to talk to me that way?'

Shona seated herself in her favourite chair and took her time answering, nonchalantly rocking herself back and forth, deliberately dispensing with courtesy and omitting to invite the visitor to take a seat also. With a studied air of indifference, she put her hand up to her mouth and yawned before saying with maddening calm, 'I'm the woman who thought you were worth having for a friend but I'm sorry to say my judgement on that score was sadly wanting.'

Megan threw herself down on a chair opposite Shona's simply because her legs were shaking so much beneath her that she couldn't trust her weight on them a minute longer.

'Listen, Shona,' she said softly, pleadingly, 'I have to know where Mark is, I must see him – oh, dear God,' she bit her lip, 'I can hardly bear to think of the fire – of the torture he must have suffered losing his dog, I feel it's all my fault, that I'm to blame for everything. At least if I could speak to him I could tell him how sorry I am, how much I hate myself for everything that ever happened this summer. I know you can tell me where he is, if not I'll go to Tina and get it from her.'

'Tina won't tell you anything,' Shona spoke quietly but with absolute conviction. 'She's devoted to Mark and would die for him. Neither she nor I will breathe a word to anyone...' Her brilliant blue eyes regarded the other woman consideringly. 'If I thought it would help him I believe I might break the promise I made no' to let anyone find him – far less you. But telling you won't help, you've hurt him enough already and just now he canny take any more heartache.'

'Shona, you must believe me when I tell you I love Mark, I really love him. These weeks away from him made me see how much.'

'It's too late for that,' Shona cried passionately. 'You think you can come creeping back here when it suits you, to find him waiting with open arms, ready to forgive and forget all, but life isn't that simple, Megan. Mark is very much a flesh and blood man and he had to stand by, watching you and Steve playing around all summer long...'

Megan stood up, agitated and near to tears. 'Playing around, was that how it looked? I spent the whole summer fending Steve off once I realized the kind of man he really was. At first I was still living in a fool's paradise but that didn't last. He was so shallow and vain, so much in love with himself he could never love any woman. He was jealous of Mark, I saw his jealousy and his selfishness that day we went to see old Dodie. Mark was so kind and gentle while all Steve could do was behave like a spoilt child. He took to drinking and nagging on about Mark till I thought I would go mad. That day in Glen Fallan, the day of the fight, I had told Steve it was over between him and me, later he followed me, saw me with Mark and goaded Mark into hitting him. I knew then I had to get him away from Rhanna before he could cause more trouble.'

'But surely you didn't have to leave aboard the yacht! Everyone thought you were going away with him, Mark more than anyone.'

'Steve had to save his face. He told me if I didn't leave with him he would see to it that Mark never preached again. Believe me, he was quite capable of carrying out his threats. He wanted to punish me as well as Mark – and he succeeded so well this is the result – besides...' she sounded exhausted suddenly, 'I needed to get away and would have gone anyway. I felt as if I was being torn in two, Mark pulling one way, Steve the other, everyone talking behind my back and pointing – for God's sake, Shona,' she beseeched wearily, 'haven't you ever made mistakes in your own life? Love is such a betraying emotion it can blind you and paralyse you with its power so that often you don't know what's real and what isn't – that's how it was with me and Steve. I thought I loved him till Mark came into my life and opened my eyes to what real love is all about.'

In the face of such heart-rending sincerity, Shona couldn't maintain her cool front any longer. 'Oh, Megan,' she sighed, 'you're a devious besom and know just how to get round people. Of course I've made mistakes, I think nearly everyone has when it comes to human relationships. You've managed to sneak round me but that doesny mean I'm going to tell you where Mark is – no' just yet. The Church has been very good to him. John Grey naturally had to report what was going on and came to me to find out how he could get in touch with Mark. With the exception of Tina, he is the only other person on the island who knows what's happened. He, and all of Mark's clergy friends from Glasgow and elsewhere have been to see Mark and have given him all the support they can. The Church has been very understanding and certainly is not prepared to let him go because he has proved that he's as human as the next man, so Steven Saunders could have cliped all he liked and it wouldn't have made any difference.

'But these are the only people Mark wants to see just now. The fire at the Manse and the loss o' his darling dog were the last straws for him. I go to see him whenever I can, and when I think he's ready for you I'll talk about you – but no' before.'

Megan gave a watery smile. 'I suppose that's better than nothing.'

'Indeed it is, where there's life there's hope and now sit yourself down and I'll get us a cuppy, all this talk has made me drouthy and besides – ' the dimples returned to her cheeks – 'you and I have a lot o' catching up to do. People may fade and falter a little but gossip never dies. Wait till you hear about the dentist mannie and Miss Bird – no' to mention the teeth sorting station – oh, and something else you'll never guess...'

She skipped over to the sink to fill the kettle. Megan sat back, a small hope burning in her breast, feeble as a candle flame to be sure but there just the same – and far,

far better than the icy lump that had lain in her heart since learning that Mark James was no longer of the island.

Chapter Twenty-One

Old Joe was dying, a beautiful old man, his hair a silvery halo round his head and his long, flowing beard brushed and smoothed over the counterpane. He was very frail in his hundred-and-sixth year, but there was a wonderful strength of character in his face and a light in his sea-green eyes that made him seem eternally young.

'The time has come, lass,' he told Grace, taking her dainty hand in his square palm and giving it a tender squeeze.

'That it has, Joe my man.' She tried to sound strong, but now that his hour was at hand she couldn't keep a tremor from her voice.

'I want the man o' God, Grace,' Old Joe spoke urgently, 'there is no one else I would trust to see me safely over to the other side. You see, Grace,' he held her hand tighter, 'now that my hour is nigh I have to confess to feelin' a wee bittie feart and Mr James is such a good, strong lad I just know I will be safe wi' him in my last breath.'

Grace said nothing. She couldn't tell her darling old man that it might not be possible to get the minister to come back to Rhanna, if indeed she had even known where he was, but keeping her doubts to herself she went from the room to seek out Captain Mac and speak to him of her husband's last wishes.

'I'll get a hold o' Shona McLachlan,' Captain Mac said at once, 'she knows where Mr James is.'

Shona listened to what he had to say, a soft little smile curving her mouth. Promising to do what she could, she waited till Mac was safely outside before going to pick up the 'phone and dial a number. A voice spoke at the other end, a deep, calm untroubled voice belonging to a man who loved a certain old sailor and who had vowed a long time ago to have the honour of seeing that same old man safely across the great divide to his eternal rest.

Old Joe was very weak. He wanted nothing more than to close his eyes and allow himself the wonderful luxury of just slipping away, without fuss or bother. But he and Grace had made too many plans for him to disappoint her by simply passing away without a word – and besides, he hadn't lived this long through faintness of heart, he was made of the stuff that had always ridden out the roughest of life's storms and he was buggered if he would allow himself just to slip quietly beneath the waves without first making a final bloody great splash of it, so when Tam came in to see him, cap in hand and a 'carpet slipper' expression on his face as the old man put it to himself, he seized a hold of Tam's cuff and asked if the whisky had been brought into the parlour for the funeral repast.

'That it has, Joe,' Tam said in a breathy whisper.

'And a damty lot o' good it will do me! Lyin' here dead and never a drop to wet my thrapple. Bring it in here – I want to share in my own funeral feast while all my faculties are in good workin' order.'

The word went round the island like wildfire, and that same evening the steamer slipped into harbour with hardly a soul to witness her arrival except for Niall and Shona, who were there to shake warmly the hand of a tall, dark man and take him back to Laigmhor where he was to stay for as long as he wanted.

The funeral repast was in full swing. All through that long, strange night the islanders came to drink a toast to

Joe and to wish him God speed on his last journey. It was the most unusual event the island had ever seen and it was also the most memorable. Old Joe had even insisted that Bob play his fiddle and Torquill his pipes and he lay in bed, surrounded by his friends, his rheumy fingers tapping out the well-loved tunes, his whisky glass held on his chest, his eyes as brilliantly alive as they had been in his younger days when he had held his fireside audiences enthralled with his wondrous tales.

'Do my teeths look alright, Grace?' he asked at one point.

'Ay, they look just grand, Joe,' she assured huskily. ''Tis just a pity the dentist mannie is no' here to see them, though on the other hand 'tis maybe just as well for he would be mad wi' envy to see that your smile is much, much brighter than his own.'

At various intervals, when Torquill or Todd ran out of breath and Bob out of steam, the womenfolk gathered to sing sea shanties in Gaelic and as the pure sound of their united voices rose up, the ocean seemed to beat upon the shore as if calling, calling, to an old sailor who had once ridden free on its breast.

Into this almost festive atmosphere came Mark James, thinner than anyone remembered, a sprinkling of white in his blue-black hair, his cheekbones honed to distinguished prominence, his jacket sitting too loose about his shoulders – but the warm smile of him was still the same as were the depths of eager, laughing life in those wonderful eyes when he looked around at all the familiar faces he had yearned to see again yet had rebelled against – in case they wouldn't smile the smiles of welcome he so badly needed to make him feel he had at last come home.

A short, stunned silence accompanied his entry, then, ''Tis the man o' God!' Old Joe whispered from his bed, his voice husky with all the emotions he had been bottling up all night long.

'Mr James! Och, 'tis a bonny sight you are just.' Kate

stepped forward, and without reserve of any sort she drew him to her and hugged him soundly.

After that he was surrounded by such genuine warmth that there were tears in his eyes when he finally went over to the bed to wrap Old Joe to his breast and murmur a few quiet words into his ear.

Night passed away but it didn't take the old man with it. When the pearly ghost of dawn spread above the horizon he was sitting up in bed drinking tea, rosy of cheek and sparkling of eye and never a hint to show that his heartbeat faltered within him and would have stopped long ago had it not been for the iron will that kept him nodding and smiling to all who came and went.

The procession seemed endless, children came to throw their arms about him and kiss him, along with all the 'bairnies' of yesterday into whose ears the grand old man had poured his timeless fables.

'This is what Grace meant,' Kate sniffed tearfully to Molly, 'she said her man would be the first on the island to smile a farewell to his friends and she was right – just look at the bodach, lookin' as if he was goin' away on a world cruise instead o' his grave. Betimes I could have wrung his thrawn auld neck but now – och, I'll miss him sore.'

She rushed away to weep in private and soon after that, just a few close friends and Mark James were left sitting at the parlour window watching the incredible peace of a Hebridean morning unfolding before their vision.

For a short while Old Joe and Aunt Grace were alone in the bedroom, holding hands, crying a little. 'These last months wi' you were the best o'my life, lass,' he told her in a whisper.

'As mine were wi' you, my bonny dear Old Joe,' she murmured tearfully.

After that they didn't speak. She held him to her bosom, happed him round with her love, stroked his silvery hair till he shuddered a bit and said weakly, 'Send for the man o' God, the time has come, Grace.'

Grace signalled to Tam who was standing just outside the door. He scurried quickly ben the parlour and Mark rose from the window. It was light and bright outside, a perfect day for old men to sit on the harbour wall and watch the world gliding serenely by.

A short while later Old Joe died in Mark's arms, Grace's head on his breast, her hand held tight over his as his life ebbed gently away. To the very last his hand remained strong in hers, then it slackened, slid away, and she knew her dear Old Joe was gone from her.

'I'll just see to him, Mr James, if you don't mind,' she said with great dignity.

'Ay, Grace, I understand.'

Left alone she arranged her man, combed his beard over the quilt top, crossed his hands, one over the other, put his pipe and his baccy neatly by the bedside as she had done every morning since he had taken to rising later and later in the day. He had died with a slight smile tilting the corners of his generous mouth, as it had done in life when all his awakenings had been blithe and busy. Bending down, she kissed that smile and just for a moment she seemed to hear the sea rushing and hurrying, then receding to a quieter tempo as if it was now lapping the distant shore of a far island unoccupied by mortal man – but perhaps, fancifully, inhabited by beautiful mermaids.

A golden sun lit the eastern sky as Old Joe's coffin was lowered into the earth. It flooded the kirkyard, bathed the old church in a mellow hue, shone on the countless mourners who filled the cemetery and spilled out onto the Hillock. The voice of Mark James rose up, resonant, sincere, the deep, dark timbre of it reaching every corner, filling every space in and around the time-worn stones, sending an old sailor sailing away and beyond life's seas with words that plucked the heartstrings.

'None of us will ever forget how he lived, his humour, his wit, his infectious joy which he spread around him with a generosity that was boundless,' Mark paused and smiled at Aunt Grace who was standing nearby, 'but more, will any of us here ever forget that joyous day of his wedding, to a lady whose heart was as big as his own, she gave him happiness beyond compare and a strength that made his last hours on earth ones that none of us will ever forget. We all shared in his happy life but thanks to both him and her we were also allowed the unique experience of sharing in his death. Will any of us here cease to remember his funeral repast? How he sat up in bed and joined in it with us? Can you ever begin to imagine the strength of will that kept him going through that long night and into the next day? A man half his age might never have made it but our Joe was inimitable among mortals and we who had the honour of sharing his life and his death with him couldn't fail to be the richer for that experience.

'He is gone, yet he is with us, he will live on in the hearts and minds of every man, woman, and child on this island. He was a story-teller, a seanachaidh, one of the best of a grand old order that knew its origins in the dim mists of a past he never allowed us to forget. He breathed life into his mermaids, his fairies and his witches, he made them live for us and enriched our lives by keeping them alive in our minds. We need fairy-tales in our lives, God knows,' his keen gaze swept the throng, 'for without them we smother and die in the dull fog of reality. God will bless him and keep him, nothing could be surer than that. Men like Joe earn their place in heaven by giving us a little bit of it while we are still here on this earth.'

No one would ever forget that day or Mark James standing so tall and commanding against the gold-tinted sky, not clad in his robes but in a dark suit, yet every inch a minister for all that; no one would forget the October leaves skirling over the dark earth, the glow in the heavens, the strange sad feeling born of life and of death, the powerful sensation that an old man still moved among them, grinning his roguish grin and wondering aloud if that was a seal out there on the rocks or maybe, 'a maid o' the sea wi' naught but her long, golden tresses to cover her birthday suit.'

Kate was voluble in her grief, Aunt Grace serene and dignified. On the way out of the kirkyard she took Bob's arm and held it tight.

'Look at that, just look,' hissed Kate to Tam, 'she canny be up to her old tricks already.'

'Ach, she's just needin' a bittie support,' returned Tam, his mind still on the service. 'She has lost her man after all and 'tis natural she'll need help to get over it.'

'Oh, she'll no' be long in doing that,' muttered Kate darkly and hurried Tam away down the brae, uttering a distinct 'Hmph' on passing Bob and Aunt Grace.

But they didn't notice. 'We'll wait a month or two,' Aunt Grace was telling Bob, 'it wouldny be decent to do it right away and I need a wee whilie to get myself used to another man.'

'Grace, you *are* a wee bittie upset at Joe's passing?' hazarded Bob, doubtfully.

'Of course I am,' said Grace, surprised. 'Never, never will anyone take his place. I loved that old rascal wi' all my heart but he told me himself, "after I'm gone you mustny allow the dust to settle under your bed, Grace, for if you do you'll allow only a chanty to disturb it and no chanty on earth is a match for a man's slippers, as you have discovered yourself."'

'Ay, Grace, I see what you mean,' nodded Bob, who didn't, and he was still puzzling over her words as he got ready for bed that night with his chanty tucked under the bed and his slippers safely anchored on his own two feet.

Everyone wanted to talk to Mark, to shake his hand and tell him what a fine job he had made of seeing Old Joe to his last rest, but more than that they wanted to ask when he would be coming back to Rhanna to preach for them again.

'I can't tell you that,' he replied in answer to all the queries, 'I don't know what my plans are for the future, and I would be lying if I said I was sure I was coming back at all.'

It hurt him to say that, but what hurt him even more was the genuine sorrow displayed by all those wonderful people he had come to know and love so well. He stood in the kirkyard, watching them walking dejectedly away and so lost was he in his reverie that he didn't hear a soft footfall behind him and started with fright when a voice said quietly at his elbow, 'It *was* a wonderful service, Mark, Old Joe would have loved every minute of it.'

'Megan,' he swung round to face her, 'I didn't see you in the crowd.'

'No, I stayed at the back, beside Shona and Niall and the others. I knew you were here of course – on Rhanna I mean. Grace called me out the morning Joe died – he had gone by then and so had you. I heard how you had come over especially for him, it was a fine thing to do.'

'It was an honour,' he spoke rather abruptly, 'I had always hoped to have the privilege of sharing his last hours and I'm glad he sent for me. It's an experience I'll never forget.'

A silence sprang up, thick, heavy, widening the distance between them although they stood so close to one another. The autumn leaves whirled about their feet, yellow; red; amber; emphasizing the poignancy of things that were done with, reminders that summer was past and the wild days of winter stretched ahead. He moved away from her suddenly. 'Please excuse me, I have to go, I promised Kirsteen I would be back in time for dinner and then I must pack. I'm leaving on tomorrow's steamer.'

He was away, walking quickly, reaching the gate almost before she had time to realize his intentions.

'Mark, please, wait, oh please.' Her breath caught, she ran to catch up with him and take hold of his hand. It was warm despite the chill of the day. Her fingers curled round his and she said pleadingly, 'Mark, we have to talk. I – I know how much you've been hurt and I hate myself for being the cause of any pain you have suffered...'

Roughly, he pulled his hand away from hers, his eyes dark with all the emotions he had locked away in his heart for so long. 'It's too late for recriminations, Megan,' he said harshly, 'if we could turn the clock back it might have worked but not now, definitely not now! I'm a changed man and nothing can ever be the same again.' He spread his hands in appeal. 'Don't you see, I've lost everything that was ever precious to me in my life? First my wife and daughter, after that my dog, my home, my self-respect – and worst of all, I've lost my faith! I can't go back to preaching now – ' he gave a short, bitter laugh. 'What could I talk about? Strength? Willpower? Me that has none of either left? I'm not a fit person to teach anybody anything.'

'Mark, please don't talk like that,' she begged, 'we all have our weaknesses and you couldn't help being ill...'

'Ill? Ay, that's as good a way of putting it as any. I have been ill – ' he broke off to stare at her for a long, timeless moment. 'Do you know where I've been all this time, Megan? Have you any idea at all?'

'Shona said something about a collapse – '

'I've been drying out, Megan. You, as a doctor, should know only too well what that means! I wasn't man enough to fight the situation I found myself in so I cracked up, gave in – call it what you like, it all amounts to the same thing in the end, and if I can't successfully run my own life without turning to the bottle how the hell can I pretend to help other people run theirs?'

'Because you have the strength to face up to your own shortcomings and are humble enough to admit you have them. And you are strong, Mark, you've come through this virtually on your own but it needn't be like that ever again. What I felt for Steve was infatuation pure and simple. When I saw him again I soon realized there was no depth to him, that it was you I loved and had done right from the start. He knew it too and was never done arguing about you. He was drunk that day in Glen Fallan because I told him I was staying here to be near you.'

Mark's jaw tightened. 'And yet you went off with him, in front of everyone, leaving me to think the worst and to hell with the consequences!'

She recoiled from his anger, and yet there was about her an aura of strength that he recognized and admired despite his bitterness. 'I went, Mark, because he threatened to make your life hell after what you did to him in front of half the island. He was going to ruin you and I – I just couldn't stand by and let that happen.'

'But it happened anyway, didn't it, Megan?' His voice was cold and distant. 'It was too late for all of us and what's done is done, there's no turning back now. I'm leaving the ministry, and – ' his gaze swept over the purpled hills and his voice broke – 'I'm leaving here. I won't bother you again with my clumsy attempts to win your affections. All that's over with, I promise you. I'll never allow myself to fall into the position of losing my self-respect for any woman ever again, it hasn't been worth all the sacrifice.'

'Very well, Mark,' she stepped back a pace, and already it seemed that a yawning chasm separated them, 'have it your way. But first – I want you to see something, to discover for yourself what the power of love and respect can do. If you come with me to the Manse I'll show you...'

His head jerked up. She saw a gleam of fear in the smokey-blue eyes that had once been so calm and fearless. 'No!' he spoke the word vehemently. 'I'll never go back there! I hate that house now!'

'Mark, give yourself one more chance. Come back

with me. I'm not trying to hurt you again, Mark, I only want to help.'

He hesitated, seemed about to walk away from her, then he said in a strange, stilted voice. 'Alright, but I can only spare a few minutes, I never wanted to go back there...'

Before he could change his mind she began walking ahead of him, glancing frequently over her shoulder to make certain he followed. He went along slowly, unwillingly, his dragging feet rustling the dry leaves that littered the driveway leading up to the door of the big, proud house. He kept his head lowered, never once looking up as he traced her footsteps up the stairs and into the hall, but when he saw that she was making for the kitchen he stopped dead and cried, 'No, Megan, not there! Please, not there!'

For answer she held out her hand, saying, 'If you don't face up to this now, Mark, it will haunt you for the rest of your days.'

Very slowly he went forward, like a man in some dread and terrible dream, till finally he stood on the threshold of the room that had haunted him for so long.

But all traces of the tragedy had been erased. The walls were bright with new paint and paper; half a dozen of Barra's little watercolours were arranged tastefully around the room; several of Dodie's painted stones decorated the gleaming windowsills together with huge vases of yellow chrysanthemums; the dining chairs and the refectory table had been completely restored to their original condition; the Welsh dresser and the big oak sideboard shone with fresh polish; the range had been black-leaded till its surface was like satin; a cheery fire leapt up the lum; Tib, Tab, and Tub were preening themselves on a big, fat cushion on the hearthrug – and on Mark's own special chair a small, golden bundle sat looking at him with meltingly anxious brown eyes, its fat, floppy, puppy paws hanging over the edge of the seat in perfect repose though tensing a little now, as if their owner had been caught doing something it shouldn't.

'Mutt!' The name was torn from Mark on a sob. For one tremulous moment he imagined that his beloved dog hadn't died in the fire after all, that somehow he had escaped and was here this morning to welcome him back. 'Mutt,' he said again, hopelessly now as he realized his mistake and didn't quite know what to do next.

Megan slipped quietly into the room to take the little dog in her arms. 'This is one of Mutt's pups, the other three were black and white, only he had his father's markings.'

'Mutt's pups.' Mark shook his head, remembering how a big, floppy, golden dog had looked at him beseechingly from Tigh na Cladach's gate...

'I know, it was a surprise to me too,' Megan kissed the pup's ears. 'They were here when I came home. Shona couldn't wait to show them off and Muff was very pleased with herself – Shona thought you might like to see this one, he's too young yet to be away from his mother, but – take him, he wants to go to you.'

Mark took the fragile little body in his arms. The puppy trembled, gazed at him in mute appeal, its small pink tongue coming out to lick his face and plant wet kisses in his ear.

'Oh God, you planned this, you and Shona between you – I can't have it, I won't – ' He sat down suddenly, hugging the animal to him, burying his face into the silky warmth of its droopy ears, the quiet tears spilling from him while the little dog whimpered its moist sympathies into his neck as its father had done before it, instinctively and without restraint.

'Who did all this?' Mark asked eventually, not looking up but making a sweeping gesture with his hand that expressed all.

'Everybody had a hand in it, John and Hannah Grey, the laird, who personally saw to it that the table and chairs were properly restored. The islanders painted and papered, Tina cleaned and polished, Dodie spent nights on end painting his stones and even then thinking they weren't good enough for someone like you. Barra did the paintings, local views of all the places you love best...'

Hesitantly she went over to kneel down beside him and take his hand. 'They all love you, Mark, and want you back very, very badly – as I do.'

He raised his head then and she saw in his eyes a return of the Mark she had known and loved before fate had intervened in their lives. 'Megan – Meggie,' he murmured, reaching out to touch her face, her hair. It was like silk. He ran his hand over it, through it, heard the soft, whispering swish of it gliding through his fingers. Their lips met, lingering, gentle, then he gave a little cry and crushed her to him, his mouth now hard and bruising over hers. Over and over they kissed till the puppy whimpered a protest beneath their pressing bodies. They laughed and drew apart to gaze at one another in a daze of longing.

'Mark, I love you so much,' she traced the outline of his mouth with her finger, 'I think I always knew it but that day up at Dodie's cottage, when you held him in your arms and were so patient and gentle with him, I didn't just love you for the passionate, warm man that you are, I loved you for everything you portrayed. You're such a good man, Mark. Watching you with Dodie I wondered if I could ever match up to what you stood for in this community. Later, when I thought about it, I decided I could never, never be as unselfish as you...'

'Oh, for heaven's sake, Meggie!' He sounded angry again. 'Don't make me out to be something I'm not nor want to be. I'm as human as the next man and certainly can't and won't live up to the image you describe. I think I've already proved what I am so don't try and make me out to be a martyr. I just couldn't live with it.'

She laughed a little uneasily. 'You're right of course. I think Shona must be right about me. She told me to grow up and stop behaving like a silly schoolgirl. It's just – when I came back here and discovered you had gone, I really thought I might never see you again. I can't believe you're back and that I'm sitting here with you now, loving you so much I can see nothing of reality for the pink glow in front of my eyes. But you're right, you aren't perfect and neither am I, both physically and morally...'

She reddened and turned her face away from him, but he put his thumb under her chin and made her look at him. 'Meggie, darling Meggie, none of us are morally pefect but physically you're beautiful – in every way that I can see.'

'That you can see!' It was her turn now to be angry. 'Do you know why Steve rejected me that first time? Because of my physical imperfection – oh hell! What's the use of trying to hide it? Look, Mark, look and see for yourself what he hated!' With an almost defiant gesture, she tore back the collars of her blouse to reveal a large birthmark staining the creamy skin over one breast. 'It's ugly, isn't it?' she demanded tearfully. 'Because of it, I've always felt ugly and unattractive and never thought any man would want me – Steve certainly didn't. He only followed me here because it bruised his ego to have any woman, no matter how flawed, run away from him.'

To her surprise he laughed, his eyes crinkling, his head shaking in disbelief. 'Ugly? Saunders wasn't just thick, he was blind as well. You're lovely, Meggie, never think anything else.' Tenderly he touched the discoloured skin, a smile hovering at the corners of his mouth. 'If you think that's bad, wait till you see mine – though on second thoughts I don't think I'd better show it to you, not yet anyway – and certainly never in front of the animals.'

They collapsed laughing into one another's arms. 'You'll stay?' she murmured into the tiny white hairs at his ears.

'Ay, I'll stay, Meggie, but – don't try to stop me calling

a meeting. I think the people have a right to decide if they want me back as their minister – or not.'

'Oh, Mark,' she pulled away to look at him, 'must you? No one need ever know – except for the few who do and who will never say anything anyway.'

'I know, Meggie,' he said softly, 'and so does God.'

Chapter Twenty-Two

There were so many people gathered in the Portcull village hall that latecomers were forced to stand at the back when it became clear there wasn't a single spare seat available.

Outside the wind was rising, squalls of rain blattered against the window panes, but such was the murmur of voices inside that no one heard anything other than what their immediate neighbours were saying. They were all wondering to one another why Mark James had called them here tonight, as in fact they had wondered why he was still on the island after Old Joe's funeral.

Speculation was high, fabrication was rife, imagination ran riot, and when Mark appeared and climbed onto the platform a great ripple of interest rose to a crescendo before it abruptly ceased so that everyone became aware of the rain on the panes, the wind soughing mournfully round the building.

All eyes were pinned on Mark, so alone up there, so tall and proud and dignified with the light catching in his hair, glinting on the silver pin he always wore in his lapel, a simple little pin depicting Saint Andrew, the Patron Saint of Scotland. Looking down on the sea of upturned faces he knew panic. Megan had been right after all. He needn't have called this meeting, no one would have been any the wiser if he had stayed quiet, kept his secrets to himself – he saw the bright gleam of Shona's hair, Tina's honest face, the Reverend John Grey's silvery thatch – *they* knew, they knew everything but their loyalty to him was such that they hadn't breathed a word to another living soul... He drew a deep breath and saw Megan smiling at him from the front row. She had tied her hair back. Her face was shining and looked newly washed. She looked like a small girl sitting in a school assembly hall. His heart lurched. He loved her, God, how he loved her. She had gotten over her horror at his proposal to lay his future publicly before the islanders. She was proud of him now, had given him every encouragement to face up to this evening.

And he had needed her support, God how he had needed it... McKenzie of the Glen got up suddenly from his place beside Kirsteen and began stamping at the floor with his feet in an effort to extinguish the contents of his pipe, which had spilled out in a careless moment.

The attention was switched to Fergus and from him to a red-faced Kirsteen who had hurried to her husband's aid.

It was all the diversion Mark needed. 'Thank you, Fergus McKenzie,' he said silently and cleared his throat. He began by thanking everyone for coming out on such a night. His voice, hesitant at first, steadied, grew calmer, deeper, so that very soon the resonant tones that everyone knew so well, reverberated round the hall, even reaching those at the back who had been worrying in case they would miss anything.

Pausing suddenly he looked around, including every last person in that one, penetrating sweep, 'You are all, no doubt, wondering why you are here tonight. The answer to that isn't so simple. I have been ill, I'm alright now but the question of my remaining here on Rhanna, or leaving for good, will all depend on what you think of me after I tell you – the things I must. I don't feel very brave standing here facing you all but it has to be done – you see,' he looked down at his hands, 'I keep remembering what a very good friend of mine once told me, that I was a human being, not just some elusive creature shouting thunder from the pulpit, but a man who appeared to be open and honest about his weaknesses and failings.'

At this point, Captain Mac grew somewhat red in the face and ran one big, horny finger round the rim of his collar, but no one noticed. A pin could have been heard to drop as Mark continued, 'Well, as it happens, I *have* been committing my wee sins in private. To some degree we all do that or we wouldn't be human, but my greatest offence was not only that of betraying my parishioners, it was of betraying my God – because you see, I had lost my faith in Him, myself, everything that was ever of any value in my life...'

He went on to tell them everything, not sparing himself in any way, quite brutally denouncing himself before them all, never once blaming anyone or condoning himself for his sufferings of mind and spirit. No audience had ever been held more captive, or been more spellbound, and when his voice finally ceased to ring round the hall there was a total, stunned silence, during which Lachlan seized the opportunity to leap to his feet and go quickly to join Mark on the platform.

Impatiently pushing an unruly lock from his forehead, he cried out, 'This isn't just a man o' God we have heard speaking tonight, this is a man of great personal courage and character and I for one feel that he has privileged each and every one o' us by being our minister and more, by showing himself to be the sort o' human being we can all turn to in time o' trouble and need. I am proud to say I know him and will never forget the lessons of humility and honesty I have learned here tonight through listening to him and knowing that his devotion to us, his parishioners, has gone far beyond the call o' duty.'

'By God, you're right there, son, ay indeed,' Captain Mac murmured while surreptitiously wiping his moist cheeks. From all around there were like reactions. To a man the islanders agreed with every word Lachlan spoke. If they had admired Mark James before, it paled to insignificance beside what they felt for him now. The hankies were out, furtively held to wet eyes, hastily applied to sniffing noses.

'Hear, hear!' Holy Smoke, completely carried away with the emotion of the moment, added his voice to the general murmur of approval, all the while vowing that never, never again would he pretend to the world that he was something he wasn't and, as if to prove his new found sincerity, he withdrew a crushed Woodbine from some inner pocket, proceeding to light it and draw on it so heartily that Behag poked him in the ribs and told him, 'no' to display his filthy habits in public!'

Much nodding and quiet conferring had followed Lachlan's speech, now chairs were scraped back as everyone stood up. After a rather haphazard start the notes of 'Amazing Grace' rose up, powerfully, poignantly, laying to rest Mark's fears, bring such surging hope to his breast that he felt dizzy with the strength of it.

'I once was lost but now I'm found, was blind but now I see.' He joined in the old Gaelic psalm and when it was finished he found Megan at his side, reaching up to whisper something in his ear.

He held up his hand, arresting those in the action of resuming their seats. 'This evening,' he cried, 'which began for me in uncertainty, has, thanks to all of you, ended with such happiness I feel my heart bursting with it. I want to thank my very good friend, Reverend John Grey, for looking after you all so well during my absence – and, just to complete the night, I must tell you that Megan has just asked me to marry her.'

'Mark!' she laughed, holding onto his arm and hugging him. 'You know that's not true. I said...'

Whatever she had to say was drowned out in a great cheer that raised the rafters and made Sorcha hurriedly turn down her deaf aid.

'Och my, 'tis what I aye wanted to hear, bless him, bless them both.' Tina's hanky was to the fore again while everyone else raised theirs like triumphant banners to wave them back and forth when the minister shouted above the noise that they were all invited to the wedding.

and not to forget to be at kirk on Sunday or he would have something to say about it.

It was Christmas Eve. Lights twinkled all over the island, the star-studded sky was like a diamond-strewn velvet cloak that happed the world in an embrace of peace. Snatches of carols drifted into the frosty air, from wireless sets, from children trying to sing themselves to sleep and from the lips of those out and about their crofts for one reason or another.

A strange, expectant hush hung over the island, the beasts in their stalls plucked strands of hay from their mangers but kept their ears pinned back, dogs scratched at imprisoning shed doors and whimpered restlessly, even the very sheep in the fields took longer to settle themselves that night yet all around the land dreamed peacefully; the sea lapped the shores; the gulls mewed tranquilly from the beaches; owls hooted from the barn slates and seemed in no hurry to begin their nocturnal prowls.

Not a soul was to be seen walking roads that twisted and snaked their way by shore and land... It happened quite gradually, first the opening of one door, then another, and yet another till little black dots were to be seen everywhere, moving without hurry, meeting up, eventually converging on the track leading to the Hillock and the kirk whose warm, soft lights spilled gently outside along with the subdued notes of 'Away in a Manger' which Totie was playing quietly on the organ.

Everyone greeted everyone else as if they hadn't seen one another for years, even though it might only have been an hour or so since the last exchange of words. But this was more than just another gathering arriving for the Watchnight service. Sunday best was still in evidence to be sure but it faded into near oblivion amongst a colourful array of frocks and suits, cheerily bedecked hats, flower-emblazoned lapels, and in a few daring cases, long, dangling earrings and – terrible just – high, spiky shoes that caught in grass and sheep sharn and proved such a nuisance altogether that their youthful owners vowed silently to send them back to the mail order catalogue from whence they had come.

The interior of the kirk was dim and mysterious with just a few oil lamps and candles set in the windows, and the coloured lights of the Christmas tree giving off an enchanting aura that seemed magnified a thousandfold now that the eve of Christ's birth was here.

They were the only lights in kirk that night to use as their source of energy the small generator that Mark kept in reserve to heat the building. In the Manse itself he preferred his peat fires and his oil lamps and had to be hard pressed indeed before permitting himself the luxury of electric lights, as the generator was an old one and used more fuel than it gave off power.

Therefore the old kirk was suffused in a romantic glow that washed over the mellow stonework and bathed the congregation in a rosy hue which softened weather-beaten skin and further enhanced the lovely pink and white complexions of every Hebridean woman present, whatever her age might be.

The usual coughings, rustlings, whisperings and nose blowings accompanied the settling-in phase but just when it seemed that everyone had sunk into that respectful, watchful hush preceding a church service, the door opened once more and Dodie catapulted in, as if he had been pushed by a giant hand, which might not have been very far off the mark at that for Captain Mac, brushed, combed, and polished, and doing his door duty, had intercepted the old eccentric as he hung about outside, displaying his customary unwillingness to intrude himself into any sizeable gathering.

'Go you away in, Dodie,' Mac had coaxed pleasantly, but when Dodie had hummed and hawed and run through just about every excuse in his book, Mac had finally lost his patience, and taking Dodie literally by the hand he had led him in through the porch and from there into kirk, giving him a well meaning but none too gentle push to aid him on his way, so that he found himself quarter-way up the aisle, his new shoes, chosen from Mairi's mail order catalogue after much deliberation, scuffing the polished wood of the floor, squeaking and squelching with every move and causing more heads to turn than any fashion model on a catwalk.

Dodie gulped and froze, his dreamy grey-green eyes raking the pews for a space and never finding even a chink in the tightly packed gathering. He wasn't just clean that night, he sparkled. Earlier in the evening, Mairi and Wullie had arrived at Croft Beag, the former loaded down with towels and other essential accoutrements, the latter's arms piled high with the new clothes Dodie had sent for and which had arrived at Mairi's house that morning.

Between them they had bathed, powdered, and dressed the old man, Mairi supervising the filling of the tub, Wullie attending to the business side of washing Dodie which meant soaping him from head to foot so that even the very hairs in his ears received a generous dollop of soap bubbles. He had wailed, moaned, protested with all the might of his new-found strength, but to no avail. His two attendants were merciless in their administrations and now the result of their labours stood transfixed in the aisle, as smart and warm as any gentleman in the land in a well-pressed grey flannel suit and a heavy winter coat of charcoal grey tweed. On his head sat a new cap of blue and grey tweed, tilted jauntily over one eye, an angle which allowed one large shiny pink lug to stick saucily out in all its newly scrubbed glory.

His face was plump and exceedingly healthy-looking, an impression that was doubly enhanced by the stain of red diffusing his cheekbones and flooding his ears.

'My, my, does he no' look a gentleman just?' commented Ranald.

'Ay,' nodded Todd the Shod, himself looking very

dapper in a neatly pressed suit with a red carnation in the buttonhole, 'if it wasny for his lugs I would never have kent it was our Dodie. I can smell the soap on him from here.'

'Dodie – Dodie,' hissed Mairi, 'in here beside Wullie and me.'

Standing up and reaching out, she hauled the old man into her pew and glad he was too of her timely intervention. So much in a hurry was he to capture anonymity that he stamped on Merry Mary's bunion, trod on Kate's hammer toes, tripped over Bob the Shepherd's crook, and landed without the least intention in Nancy's lap. All but the last tongue-clicked and cursed. Nancy merely helped him to his feet in her good-natured way and saw him settled, or more accurately, squashed, in between her brother Wullie and her sister-in-law Mairi.

Soon after that Captain Mac, his door duties done, slipped into his own seat kept warm by Elspeth, and the service began.

It was beautiful, as were all the Watchnight services in the little kirk on the Hillock, but this one was special, Mark James told the time-honoured story of Christ's birth; carols were sung; a passage was read from the bible by Lachlan in his pleasantly soothing voice. The stars winked in the windows, the lights glowed on the tree, time moved on towards midnight. Out to the front stepped ten-year-old Kyle Angus McKinnon, youngest son of Ethel and Angus McKinnon and grandson of Kate, a holy terror in the normal way of things but now resembling a golden-haired cherub minus the wings. With confidence oozing from every scrubbed pore, he waited for Totie to give him his cue. When it came, he opened his mouth wide and 'Still the Night' poured forth, rising, rising, pure liquid sound that blended with the ringing of the bells as they tolled forth, proclaiming that the day of Christ's birth had arrived.

All of Kyle's many relatives melted with pride and

forgot how often they had chased his unruly presence from their homes with the business end of a broom, everyone else stared and wondered that such a little monster could produce such sounds from a throat more given to mischievous chatter and uncherub-like oaths. Undeterred Kyle sang on, the bells kept ringing, far and wide the chimes travelled. Those that couldn't attend the service for one reason or another but who had gathered at some communual point, listened moist-eyed and told each other, 'Hear that, just hear that, och, it's come, it's here,' whereupon they hastened to charge their glasses in order to drink a toast to the 'Dawn of Christ' and then 'just a wee tate more' to be ready when the hands of the clock reached a certain point.

The bells stopped, their echoes died away, no one showed any inclination to leave their pews, instead a breathless hush descended over all.

A short interval ensued during which Mark James slipped through to the vestry, reappearing a few minutes later minus his robes and now clad in a dark suit, with a red rose in the lapel. A few steps took him to the altar where he was joined by a dark-haired young man who smiled at him nervously before composing his features into their former, serious expression. The Rev. John Grey, looking very dignified in his clergy robes, arranged himself in front of the two men; Totie flexed her fingers and set them upon the keys of the harmonium, her feet went into action, pedalling energetically at the bellows; the instrument wheezed, stuttered, burst into sudden, vibrant life. Totie sent up a silent prayer of thanks, her strong fingers were sure and firm as they moved along the keyboard – the notes of the Wedding March soared up, spilled outwards.

The door opened and in a cloud of white satin and lace Megan came in on the arm of a tall, distinguished-looking man; behind them walked a young woman dressed in blue silk. She was carrying flowers and blushing shyly.

Megan too carried flowers. She neither blushed nor seemed unduly nervous, her radiance of face and form sprung from an inner font of pure happiness that beamed its light on the man whose arm she held: Ivor David Jenkins, her father, a Welsh surgeon with a string of letters after his name and no side at all to his nature. He smiled back at her, guided her graciously along the aisle, both of them tilting their heads in acknowledgement of friends and relatives, reserving a special smile for a vibrantly attractive woman sitting at the front, Bronwyn Alice Jenkins, Megan's mother, who wore a white suit and matching hat with a flimsy little veil that failed completely to hide her wide, generous mouth, her lively dark eyes.

In no time at all they were at the front, Megan's younger sister, Morgan, relaxing a little now that the nerve-shattering experience of walking behind her sister down the aisle of a strange little church was over.

The eyes of Mark James and Megan Margaret Jenkins met, held, their hearts beat faster than before. Love was in the kirk on the Hillock that magical Christmas morning. It breathed and lived and became one enormous heartbeat, pulsing, growing, reaching every corner. The candle flames flickered, the oil lamps glowed, the fairy lights splashed enchantment over the green needles of the tree, the spirit of Christmas shone over all.

There was hush, expectancy, excitement, and hope, all mingling together and uniting everyone in a common bond of friendship and love. The young were silent, lost in wonder, the old were serene, safe in the knowledge that for them the storms of life were mainly over and they had come through, calm of mind and spirit. One and all recalled their own special moments, and misty-eyed they waited for the Rev. John Grey to unite their minister and their doctor in holy matrimony.

The silence lengthened. Gareth Thomas Jenkins, Megan's young brother, fidgeted a little and prayed the age-old prayer that he wouldn't drop the ring when the moment of that duty befell him. Mark's relatives by his first marriage, his clergy friends, his adopted aunts and uncles from childhood associations in Glasgow, thought about a young woman and a little girl who had died too soon and they cried inside themselves for things past but were glad that the time of sorrow was over for Mark James.

He thought about Margaret and about Sharon and he too cried silently, but knew that if he was to live a life of meaning he had to have love in it or he might as well be dead also.

The Rev. John Grey cleared his throat. Everyone looked at him, an old man now, with a mop of silvery hair and an aura of contentment about him that had never been there in the days of preaching his hell, fire, and thunder to a people he had only grown to like and admire, and who had drawn closer to him the day he stepped off his pedestal and became a human being 'who went to the wee hoosie to pee' like everyone else.

His voice had lost none of its command, but the content of his rhetoric was different these days and never more so than now when he spoke the words that joined Mark and Megan together as man and wife.

'Do you, Megan, take this man – ?'

'Do you, Mark, take this woman – ?'

They did of course, joyfully, wonderingly. Gareth didn't drop the ring. Very soon it was reposing on Megan's finger, a plain gold band which she wanted to hold up and show the world but instead, decorously, she bowed her head and kept very still – and then willingly, naturally, she was in Mark's arms, feeling the warm, firm promise of his lips against hers.

And then it was over, Totie pounded the keyboard, played the newly married couple out of kirk, her fingers never faltering till every last person had left, and then she collapsed in a heap against her music sheets and smiled a smile of complete relief that she hadn't struck one wrong note.

The congregation poured out into the frosty air. The bagpipes struck up. Torquill Andrew and Todd the Shod played the newly weds down to the village hall where the reception was to be held, since the tiny church hall could never have contained so many people in its rigid confines.

The hall was warm and welcoming. Christmas decorations jostled with wedding banners and balloons, a line of joined tables set at one side of the building held the wedding buffet, those on the other side contained the numerous gifts that had been showered on Mark and Megan from children and adults alike. In pride of place was a painting done by Dodie of Mutt sitting on his cushion in front of the Manse kitchen fire. Mark had been very touched by the gift. He had looked at it for a long time without saying anything, then he had gathered Dodie to his bosom and spoken in a husky voice which had so alarmed the old man that he imagined his gift had brought more pain than pleasure, till he saw the gratitude in Mark's moist eyes and the tender smile that lurked at his mouth whenever he looked at the painting.

Old Annack Gow, for the umpteenth time since the wedding plans became common knowledge, shook her head at sight of the groaning tables and commented on how strange it was to be celebrating a wedding on Christmas morning. In the beginning everyone else had thought as Annack did, that it 'was just no' natural to get married on Christmas morning.' The island had never known the like before, it was outwith all tradition and, to quote Sorcha, 'Doctor Megan is just like they flowery people on the mainland, doing all sorts o' strange things just to get noticed. I wouldny be surprised if she turned up in kirk wi' a shaved head and naught to cover her modesty but garlands o' flowers.'

But Megan had wanted her wedding to coincide with the Lord's birthday and of course she had got her way. In every respect, except its timing, the wedding was as traditional as every other on the island had been, and once the reception got into full swing even conventional beings like Annack forgot their doubts and threw themselves into the spirit of the event, literally, for Annack's father had passed on to her the secrets of his illicit whisky still, and in the two months leading up to the wedding Tam and his cronies had dared to make use of the 'wee secret room' in Annack's blackhouse with the result that a full barrel of best malt brew was ready and waiting for *the* night.

The whisky flowed, golden, tempting. Glasses chinked, laughter arose, the rest of the night passed in eating, drinking, singing and dancing.

Gareth Jenkins gently danced Eve round the hall. 'When is the baby due?' he asked at one point.

'It will come in March wi' the daffodils.'

'And the mad March hares.'

She studied him. He was slim but well-built with curly dark hair and brown eyes that had been serious to begin with but now glowed with life.

'You're no' as shy as I first thought,' she observed frankly.

'No,' he agreed and whirled her off again, not in the least put out by her 'condition', which had been the pivot of much talk ever since it became known she was expecting Daniel's baby.

'What is it you do?' Eve asked when she had to call a halt to catch her breath.

'I'm a teacher.'

'Of what?'

'Infants.'

'You don't look as if you've got the patience.'

'I haven't.'

They both giggled. Elspeth raised her eyebrows, so did Behag, not because of the young folk but because Captain Mac came up at that moment to lift Elspeth to her feet and birl her away round the floor at a very unsober pace.

It was the turn of Captain Mac's sister, Nellie, to raise her brows. She had come over from the island of Hanaay for the wedding and decided providence had sent for her in order to prevent a tragedy.

'He canny be serious about that wifie,' she confided into Behag's long and willing ears.

'If he isny, he's makin' a damty good job o' pretendin',' nodded Behag with vigour. ''Tis bad enough watchin' young folks creepin' into haysheds on no good business but at *their* age 'tis an affront to decency.'

'Never!' Nellie was suitably shocked. 'He's a stupid auld goat, that he is, but I tell you this, he will no' insult the good family name by giving it to that sour cailleach, no' while I'm around.'

Old Bob, who was sitting within earshot, his pipe in one hand and a dram in the other, leaned forward and said confidentially, 'You will have your work cut out trying to unhook Elspeth's claws from your brother, Nellie lass. She might look an auld prune but passion smoulders sore in the breast o' her, fine I know it too for she went full tilt at myself a whilie back and if Mac hadny come along when he did I doubt I wouldny hae escaped her clutches.'

With a wild 'hooch' he was up and away, seizing hold of Aunt Grace as he went and placing a shameless smacker square on her mouth.

'This island gets worse!' fumed an outraged Nellie. 'It's the talk o' the Hebrides from Hanaay to Skye! The whole place is just jumpin' wi' lust and sin and 'tis little wonder my very own brother has come under the influence...'

'Will you be havin' this dance wi' me, Nellie?' Old Colin of Rumhor, a widower with six children to his credit, beamed a beguiling smile all over Nellie's bristling girth. She fluttered and grumbled for a second while all around the fiddles played and everyone danced. 'Well, just this once, Colin,' she conceded coyly, and fleered away to hooch and yooch with the rest, leaving

Behag to wonder if there was one, single, upright soul left in the whole of the island.

In the course of the evening, Mark made sure he had at least one dance each with Shona and Tina, both of whom needed no words to tell them how grateful he was for the loyalty they had shown him during his illness. It was there in his eyes, in 'that nice wee crooked smile o' his' which came readily to his face these days so that one was apt to forget it had ever been missing.

Sometime during the festivities Megan had changed into a blue wool suit and at last she and Mark slipped away. It was three o'clock in the morning. The island lay calm and peaceful under the stars. Hand in hand they walked to the Manse where they would be spending Christmas with Megan's relations and Mark's friends. Both the Manse and Tigh na Cladach would be full to bursting for the next two days, afterwards the newly weds were travelling to London before going on to Greece to spend their honeymoon, from there to Wales to be with Megan's folks for a while – and then it was back to Rhanna and the Manse where they would live and work together.

The big, old house was dark and silent when they went in. But Muff and Flops, the latter named for obvious reasons, were waiting for them. With the dogs at their heels they wandered wordlessly down to the wide, white stretches of lonely Burg Bay, there to stand at the water's edge and look out over the vast, moon-silvered expanse before them. The music from the hall drifted down to them. The islanders would sing and dance for hours yet and still be up, bright-eyed, for the Christmas Day celebrations.

Mark slid his arm round Megan's waist and murmured into her ear, 'Don't laugh, but one of my secret ambitions has always been to dance with a beautiful woman on a moonlit beach in the early hours of the morning.'

'Nothing is impossible if you want it enough,' she

whispered back.

She went into his arms, their heads touched, his abrasive cheek rubbed against her smooth one. They glided together along the bay, silently lost in one another, holding passion at bay, savouring these shared moments of dreamlike movement, anticipating the minutes, the hours, the days yet to come.

Muff and Flops ran together, delighting in the novelty of the unexpected romp, dark shadows that quested the night as had another who had roamed these shores in the good days of freedom and sweet, happy contentment.

'We're an odd sort of couple,' Megan spoke a trifle shakily, hardly able to believe that she was dancing here, by the water's edge, in the early hours of Christmas morning, in the arms of this man who was now her husband. 'You a minister, me a doctor, how different we are.'

'I think we'll make a wonderful team,' his lips moved against her ear, making her shiver with delight, 'you healing bodies, me comforting souls whose bodies can't be healed...'

After that nothing more was said between them for a long time. He drew her in towards him. The scent of her made his senses whirl. Their mouths were close, tremulously tantalizingly close, then with a helpless little groan he crushed her to him, their lips met, blended together and all the pent-up emotions of the past were released as passions found expression in stirring limbs, awakening flesh...

Music drifted above them, around them, the dogs gambolled and played together, the sheep lay silent in the sylvan fields, Burg Bay shimmered under the stars, the sea chuckled, rattled the pebbles in the rock pools, and above all the moon sailed in its heaven and cast its ethereal beam over the tranquil, untroubled reaches of the Sound of Rhanna.